The Fruits of Winter

By the same author

NIGHT LABORER

HE WHO CONQUERS (GOD'S THUNDER)

THE SPANIARD

MALTAVERNE

THE FATHER'S VOYAGE

THERE STANDS HERCULES

INEXHAUSTIBLE PATIENCE (*a tetralogy*)

THE OTHERS' HOUSE

HE WHO WANTED TO SEE THE SEA

THE HEARTS OF THE LIVING

THE FRUITS
OF WINTER

Bernard Clavel

TRANSLATED BY PATSY SOUTHGATE

Coward-McCann, Inc.
New York

FIRST AMERICAN EDITION 1969

Copyright © 1968 by Robert Laffont
English translation copyright © 1969
by Coward-McCann, Inc.

All rights reserved. This book, or parts thereof, may not be reproduced in any form without permission in writing from the publisher. Published on the same day in the Dominion of Canada by Longmans Canada Limited, Toronto.

Library of Congress Catalog
Card Number: 72-81013

PRINTED IN THE UNITED STATES OF AMERICA

84
C576
XFr

To the memory of the mothers and fathers quietly killed by work, love, or war, whom history does not mention

B. C.

9 6 5 4 6

... it is the words they did not say that make the dead so heavy in their coffins.

H. DE MONTHERLANT

Part One
THE CART

--◀{ 1 }▶--

O N the morning of October 1, 1943, Père Dubois woke up
well before dawn. He had slept badly. A dull pain gripped his
head as though an iron band around it were tightening moment
by moment. He lay for several minutes with his ears straining,
listening to the night. No sound came from outside, and the
west wind, after having blown for three days, seemed to have
stopped without bringing rain. Père Dubois sat up slowly in
his bed, turned to the side, and put his feet down on the cold
floor in search of his slippers.

"Are you getting up already?" asked his wife.

"I thought you were asleep."

"No, I've been awake for some time. Why are you getting
up so early? It's still dark."

"I've got a headache."

"Stay there. I'll go downstairs and get you an aspirin."

"No. I have to get up anyway."

She sighed. The old man had started to put on his clothes in
the dark. The woman asked, "Is it that problem about the
wood that's got you worried?"

"It hasn't got me worried, but even so, I have to get the space
ready. I should have done it yesterday, but I was afraid it was
going to rain, and I wanted to finish up what had to be done in
the garden."

He heard the bedspring creak and realized that his wife was getting up, too.

"You don't have to come down right away."

She didn't answer, and the old man groped his way to the door of the room. In the hallway a feeble glow marked the location of the skylight opening onto the roof, but its contours remained dim. The old man hadn't covered it with black paper like the windows. It gave onto the dark stairs, where there was no other light and which they used only for going up to bed. The glow from a candle for a few seconds wasn't likely to attract any planes. Furthermore, the skylight wasn't visible from the street, and nobody seemed to care much about a house isolated at the bottom of a large garden. Anyhow, Père Dubois didn't put much stock in those stories about passive defense. What could the planes possibly find to bomb in Lons-le-Saunier? The Germans who occupied the Michel barracks and the École Normale? But the Germans were everywhere. In the smallest villages. How could the Americans bomb everywhere?

Having reached the kitchen, Père Dubois lighted a candle. In a half hour, daylight would come, and it wasn't worth the trouble to light the oil lamp. When his wife came in, he asked, "Shall we make a fire in the stove?"

"I know it's a lot of trouble, just to heat two bowls of coffee, but I have hardly any alcohol left, and they didn't give us any this month."

"Miserable, they're going to let us starve."

"For coffee, you just have to burn a few beanstalks."

"I know, but that doesn't do the chimney any good."

"You and your chimney, it'll outlast the both of us."

"That's all you ever say."

"But it's the truth."

The old woman was busy preparing the firebox. She poked the grid to make the ashes fall through and salvaged two half-charred pieces of log. She then placed a half page of crumpled

12

newspaper on the front of the firebox, and with her hands broke the dry beanstalks to which a few leaves still clung.

While dissolving his aspirin in a half glass of water, Père Dubois followed each of her gestures. To think they had come to that! Saving an old piece of newspaper and heating themselves with what they used to throw onto the compost heap. Of course, the chimney and everything in the house would last much longer than they would. Especially at the rate things were going. At seventy, you can't work from dawn to dusk on an empty stomach.

The fire had started to crackle under the little iron pot, where soon the coffee began to hiss softly.

"Don't let it boil," said the old man.

"But I haven't taken my eyes off it. I'm right in front of it. It's not going to run away, you know!"

"No one can ever tell you anything."

Mère Dubois stood before the range, her shoulders slightly hunched and her back rounded. She was wearing a large black wool shawl over her white nightgown, which hung down to her heels. When the coffee was hot enough, she removed the pot and put the stove lid back on the hole over the glowing embers of the burned-up beanstalks. The old man sat down in his place, his back to the window, while she placed two bowls, two spoons, a knife, and a piece of coarse gray bread on the table. Before sitting down, she asked, "Don't you think we could open the shutters? There must be enough daylight to eat by; it would save the candle."

"That's true. And we don't have to worry about not being able to see to butter our bread, do we?"

He got up and opened the shutters while his wife blew out the candle. An opaque dawn silhouetted the roofs and the trees of the École Normale. On the right, Montaigu hill could just be seen. The sky was a single piece of gray cotton stretched out fairly low from one edge of the earth to the other. The paler gray in the east revealed no streak of real light nor even any discernible shape.

The old man closed the window, saying, "The west wind has blown itself out, but it might still rain. It's not far away."

"I know, I can feel it in my kidneys and in my back."

Père Dubois started to eat. He, too, had his aches and pains. Especially in his wrists, his shoulders, and his ankles. Sometimes the pain was barely tolerable. Long stabs, as though iron spikes were piercing the marrow of his bones. He didn't talk about it. He felt too worn-out. What was the use of always mentioning it? His wife was worn-out, too. She was fourteen years younger than he, but work and privation had taken their toll. She often reproached him for being egotistical. It was perhaps true, after all, but if he complained, if he raged against their difficult life, it was as much for her sake as his. She still was only fifty-six. At that age, he'd been considerably stronger. Did she pamper herself too much? Women were always complaining, and from talking so much about their ills, they ended up believing in them. Of course, in her case, rheumatism could be seen in the deformation of her joints, in the twisted fingers she sometimes had trouble bending, but still, at fifty-six, did you have the right to feel old?

"Do you want a little more?" Mère Dubois asked.

"No. It tastes disgusting. You only used chickory?"

"Obviously, I still haven't gotten the October coffee ration."

"They're going to let us starve, I tell you."

With his hand, he pushed what remained of the bread toward the center of the table.

"When I think of the bread I used to make!"

"You say that every day, and it doesn't—"

He interrupted her. "Yes. I say it, and I'll say it as much as I like. Having made bread for more than forty years that people came from more than ten miles away to buy, and having reached my age only to be forced to eat this cement, I don't—"

A fit of coughing interrupted him. He stayed bent over for a moment, one hand on his chest; then having got up to spit into the stove, he said, his voice still choked, "A whole life of working yourself to death for this."

"You're not the only one. And people who don't have a garden have more to complain about than we do."

"The garden doesn't grow all by itself."

He emptied his bowl; the old woman stacked the dishes and spoons. They both got up.

While they were eating, daylight had flowed into the room and was now like muddy water bathing everything, painfully washing night from the black iron stove with its brass rail, the wooden staircase leading to the floor above, and the little square dresser with its tier of four big drawers.

"Do you need me to get that wood space ready?" asked Mère Dubois.

"No. I'll do it. I only hope that that Picaud doesn't disappoint us."

"But he promised you."

The old man made a weary gesture. "Promises, these days. If it was still old man Picaud, of course, he'd remember that I'd been one of his best customers while we had the bakery, but his son doesn't give a damn about that. He'd rather deliver wood to people who have tobacco or wine to give him."

"Speaking about tobacco, I'll go this morning and get your first ration."

The old man went out grumbling that he hadn't had anything to smoke for the last three days.

As soon as he'd opened the door of the big shed that stood at the very end of the garden, Père Dubois turned around to make sure that his wife hadn't followed him. Then, going around the workbench, he pushed open the shutter of a little window he'd built high up over his workbench for light on dark rainy days. Going back to the door, he looked once again toward the house; he placed a garden chair between the workbench and the window, got up on the chair, and took down a biscuit box that was on a shelf under the window. A whole series of boxes was lined up there, where he stored the bolts, hooks, screws, and nails that he didn't need very often. He got back down, brushed away a spider web stuck to the box, and opened it by pressing it against his chest. The box contained four packages of black tobacco, several packs of cigarette papers, lighter wicks, along with three little tubes of flints, and another smaller blue cardboard box. The old man opened this box and tipped it toward the light to examine its contents. He had about fifty cigarette butts left inside it. He took out three, which he rested on the corner of the workbench, and put everything back in place. When he'd taken the chair back, he planted himself facing the doorway, near a post supporting the beams. From there, hidden in the shadows, he could survey the path and the house. He unwrapped his butts, taking great care not to lose one shred of tobacco, rolled a slim but nice, straight cigarette, which he began to smoke slowly, savoring each puff. Almost at once, it seemed to him that his headache was getting better.

He let his cigarette go out twice for the pleasure of waiting a little before relighting it. He thought about the tobacco he'd been able to save up. It was a good little reserve. If his wife discovered it, she would certainly tell him he should agree to cut down on his tobacco ration in exchange for some eggs or butter. But he felt safe; she wouldn't find his hiding place. She had never rummaged through this little nook, where she had no business being. It was his private domain. When Julien had been there, he had come sometimes to repair his bicycle, but at present Julien was far away, and the bicycle hanging in the hayloft was no longer used by anyone. The tires were still good, and the old man knew people who would give several rations of tobacco for just a single inner tube. He had thought about that often, but he didn't feel he had the right to touch his boy's bicycle.

To avoid arguments, he and his wife tried to talk as little as possible about Julien. This morning he was thinking about him because of the possible exchange of tobacco for the tires of that useless bicycle. He was thinking about him, but it went no further than that. Anyway, he had other preoccupations. And to start with, this problem about the wood. To be in October and still waiting for your winter wood, that was really a situation that went beyond everything that a sensible man could imagine. Before the war, he used to start off every winter with a year's supply in reserve. This provision had allowed them to hold out until then without skimping too much on fuel, but now there were hardly enough logs left to last a month, perhaps two if winter didn't settle in too early.

The old man was looking to his left at the logs cut to stove length and piled against the boards on the open side of the shed. Two piles. Two partly used piles that didn't even reach as high as a man. Formerly, when the piles got down to that level, there would be, beside them, other piles six logs deep and more than two yards high.

That woodcutter who'd guaranteed delivery in August! Two months late. And the wood, he'd have to saw it into lengths and split it. And it might be this year's wood, all pissing with sap. Enough to ruin the chimney.

Since the month of August this question had been the old man's great worry. He didn't talk about it, but it was there, stirring around inside him, rising into his throat as soon as he took a moment to relax a little.

To think that he had built this shed in 1912. He remembered it very well. He had got four men to give him a hand. Tough guys like himself. Two months they had taken. And he'd only worked on it in the afternoons, once he'd finished his work as a baker, which he started at eleven o'clock at night. Still and all, that had meant putting in an eighteen-hour day. Four hours of sleep, two for meals, and that was all. Worn-out? He had every reason to be worn-out. Having led a life like that, having already lived through four years of another war, and finding himself now hoping for a cord of wood and counting up his butts.

Good Lord, people had no awareness, no memory of anything but trouble. It had been solely for wood that he'd built this shed. Wood for the bakery obviously, since at that time they burned nothing but wood. And for the woodcutter, that had meant several loads each month. He was an honest woodcutter, just as Père Dubois was an honest baker. There had never been the slightest misunderstanding between them. With almost forty years like that, they had become friends, inevitably. The son—he'd known him when he was no higher than the wheel of his father's first truck. But did he remember all that? Not at all. Profit. There was nothing now but making a profit. Deals. The black market. Finally, like it or not, corruption ate into everything. The endless egotism that pitted men against each other for a crust of that trash they dared to call bread.

Père Dubois sighed every now and then. He grumbled, began gestures that he restrained, shrugs of his shoulders and grimaces. Each time that he thought about the old days and looked at what he'd endured since the outbreak of this war, it was too much for him: A rage always ended by overwhelming him. And it was an evil rage that nothing could ever free him from. It lived inside him. He had to choke it back and keep it bottled up; it was always ready to rise again, to grab him in the pit of the stomach like a cramp whose effects no remedy can assuage.

From having lived through one already, he had dreaded this war. He had dreaded it like everyone else, but he had never imagined it would be like this. It was present everywhere without really being there. It didn't kill as the First World War had killed: It crushed out existence; it enclosed you in a sort of night that grew endlessly darker. Each week, each day brought its share of news which wasn't really too comprehensible, but which was never good news.

Things went on that you didn't even dare talk about anymore, and Père Dubois kept to himself several events which had touched him painfully, but which he avoided mentioning. Often his wife reproached him. She was astonished to see him concerned chiefly with what she still dared to call his comforts: food, tobacco, wine, heat, relatively peaceful nights, and a well-tended garden. He didn't answer. He let her talk, but the hurt was in him.

Julien's sudden disappearance had left its indelible mark on them; only he saw it differently from the boy's indulgent mother. And then, it was true, after all, that he thought about the garden, about the rabbits, and all the rest of it. But what of it? That was life. You couldn't let yourself starve just because—

He suddenly broke off his thought. A black shape had just passed behind the boxwood planted at the corner of the house. The old man had finished his cigarette a long time ago, but his fingers still clutched the damp crumpled butt that had gone out by itself. He knocked the ash off; then, twisting the paper to lock in the tobacco it still contained, he pulled a little white metal box, polished by use, out of his overalls pocket and put this butt inside it. Mère Dubois was coming down the path, right in front of the wide-open door. He headed for the left corner of the building and started gathering the onions he'd spread out on the ground on an old piece of canvas. When the old woman came in, he turned around and asked, "You leaving already?"

"Yes. If I don't want to stand in line too long, I have to get there before they open."

He had come forward as far as the threshold and found himself two steps away from his wife. She moved closer, hesitated a moment, frowned, and observed, "I thought you didn't have any more tobacco."

"No, I don't have any more."

"Just the same, you've been smoking."

"Oh, well, yes, I smoked an old butt I found on the work-bench. Here, see if I have any tobacco left."

He'd lost his temper. And as he took the little metal box out of his pocket, his hands were trembling. He opened it and held it out to his wife. "Here, see for yourself, since you have to con-trol everyhing."

Mère Dubois shook her head and sighed. "My poor Gaston. How you do fly off the handle for nothing. I'm not saying any-thing bad. I can smell that you've been smoking. Period, that's all. If you still have some tobacco, all the better for you."

"No, I don't have any. Are you satisfied?"

She had already turned back and was walking away, very tiny, as though huddling up inside her dark clothes and under that black hat, whose floppy brim completely covered the back of her neck.

Père Dubois remained alone with the anger that left a bitter-ness in his mouth, spoiling the taste of the tobacco.

--◁{ 3 }▷--

ALONE in the shed, Père Dubois returned to work. He finished gathering the onions and put them into three large baskets, which he took up to the loft one at a time. It wasn't easy. After the first climb, he stopped to catch his breath, glancing over the garden all rusty under the gray sky. He rested briefly again after the second basket. On the third trip, he had to stop halfway up the ladder, his knees against a rung. Clinging with one hand to the wooden upright, he shifted the weight of the basket from his shoulder to the ladder. The load had almost pulled him over

backward. He felt a spell of coughing coming on and with great
effort suppressed it.

"Good Lord," he groaned. "This weighs barely twenty kilos.
When I think that I used to carry sacks of flour up to the
storage room . . . Thirty and forty sacks in a row . . . What
can't happen to a person!"

He waited, listening to his pounding heart and watching
the luminous dots that flitted like fireflies before his eyes. After
a long moment, he became aware of a cramp in his raised right
arm and in his hand clenched hard on the basket he was afraid
of dropping. Slowly, husbanding his strength, he resumed his
ascent. At the top, he had trouble setting the basket down gently on the shaky floor. Once that was done, he slumped onto
a large black trunk and took off his cap. The air chilled his
sweating bald head, and he mopped it quickly with his handkerchief, which he then used to wipe the sweatband of his
cap. His back, too, was drenched, and his hands trembled.
He realized that this sudden sweat was caused by his fear of
falling from the ladder, not by the effort of climbing it. A bitter smile twisted his face, thinning his pressed lips tight over
his toothless gums. His white mustache, yellowed by nicotine,
drooped for an instant onto the prominent, gray-stubbled chin.
Less than six feet from the ground, he had been afraid of falling. And to think that in the old days, when he got out of
Joinville, he used to fling himself from one trapeze to the
other in a gymnasiun whose floor was covered with only a thin
layer of sawdust. His vision clouded again, but this time not
from fatigue or fear. More like the times when he would dive
from a bridge into the freezing waters of the D'Ain River. He
took a deep breath of air and stood up almost savagely. His
knee crackled like a breaking twig.

By God, you master your bloody carcass!

It's like a stubborn animal—you have to know how to use
the whip. Make it forget the harness by keeping it on the alert.
He leaned down to one of the baskets and grasped a big

onion. His rough thumb peeled away the reddish half-dried skins. He counted four of them. The winter would be hard; it might come sooner than expected. This divination awakened an image of the wood he was waiting for. He would have to saw and split it fast enough to give it time, if not to dry, at least to spit out a little of its water.

Before the war, he used to rent a power saw, but now only people with access to gasoline could use it. So he would have to do it all by hand. Nor could he neglect the garden and the sowing, which had to be finished before winter came.

Père Dubois laid the onion back in the basket and climbed down. He still had to clear away a pile of crates—they would make good kindling—and some bundles of bean poles, still useful for one or two more seasons. He had always ordered his stakes for peas and beans from Picaud, but could Picaud's boy be counted on?

Several times he interrupted his work to go to the top of the path that led to the road between his black iron garden fence and the wall enclosing the École Normale park. From there he would stare at the road and strain his ears. No, it wouldn't be the woodcutter's truck, but some German vehicles maneuvering in the courtyard of the school. Naturally, Picaud's boy was late. Two months late, despite his promise to come this morning . . .

On his last trip, Père Dubois hurried back to the shed as soon as he'd reached the top of the path. His wife was returning. She'd scarcely had time to get to town and back. Could she have been first in line? Or else, then, there wasn't any tobacco.

It seemed to him that she walked faster than usual. Had she forgotten the ration cards? The old man wanted to get back to his work, but his wife must have seen him. He let her get closer, then went to meet her.

As they drew near each other, Père Dubois could see her face more clearly under the brim of her hat. Her expression seemed hard, strained, as on the days when news was bad.

When she reached the house, instead of continuing toward him, she turned right and started down the little path that led to the kitchen. The old man quickened his pace, took the little path, too, and reached the first stone step just as his wife was entering.

"Well," he asked, "what's the matter?"

She turned around on the threshold and snapped, "You can come up this far, can't you?"

From the tone of this question, Père Dubois understood that something was wrong and that he was implicated in it. He climbed the steps without hurrying, left his galoshes on the landing, and went in.

Mère Dubois was sitting on the second step of the inside staircase, elbows on her knees, her body bent forward and her head down. She hadn't even taken off her hat. From the heaving of her shoulders, he saw that she was out of breath, and he stood there without saying a word for several minutes. He could hear nothing but his own wheezing breath. He looked at his wife and didn't dare speak. It was only when she sat back slightly to bring her hand up flat against her chest that he asked, "What's the matter? Don't you feel good?"

She slowly raised her head toward him. Her composure was shattered. Her chin was trembling. Her eyes were more gray than blue, with a look that was laden with reproaches. He had the feeling that only her anger kept her from bursting into tears. His arms dangling, awkward and embarrassed, he took a step forward and said in a shaky voice, "Well, what is it? Tell me. I think I have the right to know."

A painful smile creased Mère Dubois' face on either side of her mouth. Her lips moved several times before she could bring herself to say, "Let me recover . . . And then, with you, I never know how you're going to react."

Père Dubois raised his arms and let them fall back, hands flat against his overalls. "That's it, start taking it out on me . . . There you go—"

23

She interrupted him, "You see, you're getting worked up already without even knowing what it is."

Forcing himself not to shout, he said, "I'm not getting worked up. But you must admit you're provoking, all the same. You come home, I don't know what's the matter with you, and here you are attacking me for no reason."

"For no reason . . ."

She appeared crushed, incapable of going on. Her body seemed to slump down again; then, as if she'd suddenly got her strength back, she stood up and took off her hat with an annoyed gesture, one hand yanking at the elastic caught in a hairpin in her chignon.

"Your tobacco," she flung at him, "you can go get it yourself if you like."

She placed her hat on the wooden pommel of the bannister and started to unbutton her woolen jacket. The old man was about to question her when she went on, "Ah, you were ashamed to show your face in town because they claim that Julien has gone to join De Gaulle. Well, now you can show it —the shame has been removed."

She had emphasized the last words, looking straight into Père Dubois' eyes. He felt his throat tighten.

"What will you dream up next!" he stammered.

It wasn't really a question, but as soon as he'd finished, he realized that he'd gone too far just the same.

"Dream up . . . Dream up." she cried. "Ah, I dream things up! Well, just go to the tobacco bureau. And you can ask the people standing in line if I'm dreaming. And if you have the nerve to stand there with them and wait for your tobacco, it's because your need to smoke is greater than your self-respect."

This outburst triggered Père Dubois' own fury. As his wife moved closer to the window, he advanced, too, and slapped the table with the flat of his hard hand.

"It would have astonished me," he shouted, "if you *hadn't*

24

started right in blaming me for the one pleasure I still have.
It would have—"

"Oh, be quiet. That's not what I'm talking about."

As happened each time he got carried away, Père Dubois
started to cough. Half-choked by mucus, his eyes full of tears,
he took a long time catching his breath. Mère Dubois went
into the laundry to get him a glass of water, which he drank
slowly, sitting on his chair, one elbow on the table. He hadn't
induced this attack, but it had come on just in time to save him.
When he was able to speak again, he said, "There. I lose my
temper instead of talking calmly, and I only hurt myself."

Looking from beneath the gray visor of his cap, he watched
his wife, who stood between the table and the stove.

"Do you want some more to drink?" she asked.

"No. That's fine."

He realized that this interruption had not ended his wife's
anger. One way or another, she would say what was on her
mind. However, the time gained, this moment of calm recap-
tured . . . He pricked up his ears. No, it wasn't the sound of
a truck. If only young Picaud could arrive right then.

He forced himself to breathe more evenly. "These things
kill me," he murmured.

His wife pulled up a chair and sat down also.

"Me, too—these outbursts are bad for me. But the slap in
the face I just got in front of more than twenty people, I swear
to you, that was much worse for me."

In a voice he wished were more assured, but with great
trouble getting the words out at all. Père Dubois asked, "Well,
what is it? Say what you've got to say, and let's get it over with."

"Over with? It's not quite that simple. These troubles will
only end with the war—or with us."

She had paused before the last words, and the old man had
been struck by them. There was in her voice, as well as in the
meaning of her phrase, something that worried him in spite

of himself. She did not speak about death lightly. On the contrary. Whenever the old man happened to say, for example,
"Better to be dead and buried than living in a world like this,"
it was she who would scold him.

"It's maybe not so far off at that," he said. "I've never felt
so exhausted."

Now it seemed that his wife hesitated. That she was backing away from reproaching him, as though the prospect of her
own anger returning had frightened her. He was curious to
find out what had happened to her, and yet he had an instant
of hope that she might resign herself to silence.

"When I think," she finally said, "when I think of the
scene you made the day the police came."

He tried to interrupt, but she raised her voice and continued, "And how you start up again every time they come back."

"And does it amuse you, having them at the house every
month? With the neighbors asking questions?"

She gave a laugh and said, "As of now, they may be asking
questions you'd like even less. When they ask you if you're a
member of the militia, for example, I wonder what you'll find
to say."

"I've never gotten mixed up in politics. And people who
know me know that very well."

He had spoken loudly, not shouting, but with a firm voice.

"That doesn't stop your son Paul. Not even from selling
photographs of Darnand right out in the middle of the street."

"What do you mean by that?"

Already his voice was less assured. He searched vainly for
something else to say. The old woman beat him to it.

"Just what I said. He was with two members of the militia in
uniform. And he was selling the photographs. He was offering them to everyone standing in the line. And when he got to
me, he had the nerve to say: 'And you, old lady, wouldn't you
like one to send to your Communist?' That's what he had the
nerve to say to me. And I— And I felt like spitting in his face."

She had begun to tremble. Her face had drained of blood, and when she finished, two big tears were rolling down her hollow cheeks. Père Dubois' forehead burned. He had trouble swallowing. Only after a long pause was he able to say, "Do we really know what it is, this militia?"

"If you don't know, you must be the only one who doesn't. You do everything you can to ignore the war. You try to live outside the world."

"I do not hibernate like a bear, despite what you say every day. But I don't aim to get mixed up in politics. All that I can see is that this militia is a—has something to do with the government and that I have lived seventy years without ever once doing anything against the law."

Now it was she who tried to interrupt him, but he raised his voice to finish his thought.

"Whatever my boy Paul does is none of my business. He is more than forty years old, and a free man. As for you, you can just say that he's not your son."

"I've never been as happy about that as I was today."

She had shot out that sentence like an arrow and it took the old man by surprise. After a stunned but very brief silence, they both began to shout at the same time:

"You'd do better to worry about what's become of Julien since the police started looking for him."

"I'd rather die of grief wondering if Julien is still alive than die of shame."

Père Dubois had finished before her. But it was she who had shouted the loudest, standing up all at once, leaning over him, her breath short and her hands trembling. She stopped, however, in the middle of her sentence. The door had remained partly open, and someone had just called from the bottom of the steps. Père Dubois got up as his wife headed for the doorway. Just as she was going out, he recognized young Picaud's voice asking, "Well, do you want this wood, or shall I go on up to the clearing?"

27

The scene with his wife had exhausted the old man. He watched his wife disappear down the steps and, before following her, had to rest for a moment, leaning against the door-jamb, feeling as giddy as he had felt earlier on the ladder to the loft.

YOUNG Picaud was a strapping fellow with a reddish face and sparse gray hair clipped short. He smelled strongly of wine, his pipe, sweat, and that odor that always clings to men who spend the great part of their lives in forest clearings and saw-mills. Père Dubois shook the large rough hand held out to him.

"Old folks, they're just like lovers, squabbling every chance they get," said the woodcutter.

Père Dubois forced himself to smile. "Where did you leave your truck?" he asked.

"On the road."

"You should have driven right in. You know the way."

"This year, that's not possible. I've got the big truck. It would be a tight squeeze, and I might get stuck."

Père Dubois looked confused. He was still stunned by the scene with his wife. When he didn't respond, the woodcutter explained in his gravelly voice, "I don't have any more gasoline. I have to use the big truck, which runs on a gas generator."

Père Dubois took off his cap and passed his hand over his forehead.

"Good Lord—I'm going to have to lug two cords of wood all the way over there in my cart!"

Picaud hesitated between a laugh and something undefinable that pulled a little at the corners of his mouth. But no doubt because he was an easygoing fellow, he placed his huge paw on the shoulder of the old man, who was two heads shorter than he, and Dubois, my good old friend, explained, "Well then, it's a lucky thing I didn't bring you all of it. Makes it easier for you."

It was Mère Dubois who intervened. "Not all of it? What are you saying?"

"My poor lady, wood, it's like everything else, we do what we can. I've brought you half of it, and that's just because you're friends."

"You don't give a damn about me," the old man shouted.

"Come on," said the woodcutter, "we have to unload. I've got other deliveries to make."

He went striding off down the path. Père Dubois and his wife followed. The old man fussed and fumed. But Picaud calmly persisted in repeating, "It's not possible. I can't give you any more. But with your coal ration, it ought to be enough."

"Coal! We can't burn coal," Père Dubois explained. "Our stove isn't made for it, and it's too old to be converted. Good Lord, have mercy. If we don't have heat, it's the end of everything."

By the time they'd reached the road, Père Dubois, who wasn't in the habit of walking that fast, was too out of breath to say another word. He leaned his back against the garden gate and wiped his brow while contemplating the enormous truck loaded with wood. The woodcutter and his helper were already throwing logs onto the sidewalk. The old man watched each log fall. He no longer knew what to think. He hurt. That was all.

When the unloading was finished, Père Dubois pointed toward the wood remaining on the truck and asked, "Really, couldn't you let me have a bit more?"

Picaud took a pigskin pouch out of his pocket and, filling a short fat pipe, said, "No. It's not possible."

Further insistence was useless. Père Dubois lowered his eyes and watched Picaud's hands closing up his tobacco pouch. The other noticed his look. He held out the tobacco to him. "Maybe you'd like to roll one."

Père Dubois took the pouch, got the little box out of his pocket, and opened it to get his cigarette papers. "Well, I won't say no to that. I'm really at the end of my ration."

"Take enough to get you through the day."

The old man hesitated.

"Go ahead, take it. I've got a buddy in customs who brings it to me from Switzerland."

They went back to the house, where Mère Dubois counted out money for the wood while the three men drank a glass of wine.

Père Dubois couldn't ask again for more wood from Picaud, who had been so generous with his tobacco. However, without really complaining, but in a quavering voice, he began to talk about the old days, when woodcutters used to come crying to bakers to try and get their trade. "I never bought a log from anyone except your father," he concluded. "Never!"

"Listen," said Picaud, "I'm going to make you a proposition. I have two clearings above Pannessières where everything's left but the firewood. And the trimmings aren't just twigs, you know. They're good-sized branches. If you want to go up there, you can help yourself."

Père Dubois turned toward his wife who was leaning against the brass rail on the stove. They looked at each other a moment; then it was she who asked, "Where is it exactly?"

Picaud gave them directions, drawing on the oilcloth with the end of his big, scarred-up finger, whose nail resembled a misshapen horn tool. With shortcuts, it wasn't too far. Three or four miles at the most, but of course, the hill was fairly steep.

The Cart

"And you'll be able to bring what we cut down for us?" Mère
Dubois asked.

"Ah, that, that's not possible. I always come down with my
truck full. But you've got your son Paul. With all his wholesale grocery deliveries, one of his trucks must go near there, at
one time or another."

Père Dubois lowered his head. The silence deepened. The
man emptied his glass and got up. "It's up to you," he concluded.

His helper headed for the door, and Picaud started to
follow when Mère Dubois asked, "Could we get up there with
a four-wheeled handcart?"

The huge man enveloped the two old people with a look
that seemed to appraise their strength. "You might make it,
but if you have nobody to help you, it's quite a climb—" He
interrupted himself and started over in a more positive tone.
"When I go up there, I go up empty. If you won't be using
your cart tonight, we can put it in the truck, and I'll leave it
up there for you on my way."

They discussed the exact location again and debated whether
the cart might get stolen.

Père Dubois was a little frightened by the prospect of that
much of a walk and that long a haul, but he dreaded even more
the departure of the two men. They had brought life with
them; it had filled this whole part of the morning, and the old
man knew it would go with them, leaving an immense emptiness. He cast a hasty glance at his wife and tried to prolong the
conversation. The woodcutter, however, had the rest of his
wood to deliver. He repeated this several times as he made for
the door.

"And you," he said finally, "you have your wood to get in.
If you want me to pick up your cart this evening, you'd better
get started with it."

He told them again that he would leave their cart near the
woodcutters' cabin and that it would be in absolutely no

31

danger. He also explained where the key to the cabin was and added, "If you want to sleep there, it doesn't exactly have all the modern conveniences, but it might be useful."

As he walked away, Père Dubois followed him with his eyes. He sensed his wife beside him. Without turning his head, he could see her out of the corner of his eye, standing on his right, also watching the woodcutters, who had reached the end of the long path bordered with fruit trees.

Now the old couple stood there side by side, as though rooted in the morning silence. Soon the dull rumble of the truck could be heard. They stood there unmoving; something kept them separated, but something else joined them together.

When the sound of the truck died away, Père Dubois turned to his wife and said, "I don't think it's going to be so easy."

"No. But what can we do? It's that or else taking a chance on freezing without a fire if winter drags on a little."

"Well, I'd better take care of that wood."

"I'll help you."

"It's no work for you. With your hernias, you shouldn't carry such heavy logs."

"They aren't all that big. Besides, with two of us, we can take more each trip."

Père Dubois knew that. He also knew that she would help him as she did with everything. All the same, he got a sort of ill-defined pleasure from constantly protesting, from pretending he could do a job himself, when he knew that it might be too much for him. He always carried on like that, but this morning much more than usual. As he headed for the shed where the cart was kept, he felt the need to repeat, "My poor woman, this is no job for you. You'd kill yourself . . . That's all that you'd do."

His wife said nothing. She walked beside him to the shed, and when he lowered the tongue of the four-wheeled cart, she was there beside it, her hands on the crossbar, ready to help him pull it with all the strength she had.

The Cart

─◄ 5 ►─

THEY worked until noon. It was hard work, and the path was just barely wide enough to let the cart through. Protruding stones jolted the wheels, throwing the cart tongue sharply to the right or left. Père Dubois was sometimes taken by surprise; the lashing tongue almost tore his arms from their sockets. The worst times were when a wheel caught against one of the paving stones bordering the garden. That would really shake him. He would stop, curse, start off again, biting his lips between his toothless gums.

They had tried, at first, to use the path that paralleled the garden. It was wider, but the ground was more uneven. In places, there was mud and their feet slipped; the iron rims of the wheels sank in. They gave it up.

On each trip, they hauled about ten logs. Taking more wasn't possible because the slope between the house and the shed was too steep. When you walked up the little hill, you scarcely noticed its angle, but with the loaded cart, it was another matter. At the start of each trip, Père Dubois would shout, "Let's go!"

He would lunge against the crossbar of the cart tongue; they would then make a big effort, straining and digging into the ground like two whipped beasts. If the wheel hit a bad bump, they might find their hard-earned headway suddenly lost. Père Dubois would moan, close his lids over eyes burning with sweat, groan again, and throw the entire weight of his body forward.

That little hill was more exhausting all by itself than the

whole rest of the journey, although it measured only a hundred yards.

Before noon, the baker's apprentice, who had gone out onto the doorstep to take the air, came and offered to lend them a hand. He was a big fellow from Bresse. Père Dubois liked him because he knew how to listen when the old man talked about his younger days.

"If you could just help us with one or two trips, we'd appreciate it."

The boy gave a hearty smile. "We won't need your woman anymore," he said. "Let her go make the soup."

Mère Dubois thanked him, and the old man watched her leave as he said to the apprentice, "This is no work for her. I'm well aware of that, but what can I do? She's stubborner than I am."

The rest of the wood was transported in two trips. The boy had taken over the head of the cart, and he went so fast the old man had to give up trying to follow him. Outdistanced by the cart, whose frame squeaked under the load, the old man followed, muttering, "If he hits a stone, he'll break my cart for me."

On the little hill the boy leaned farther forward, his head and his broad back disappeared behind the load, and the cart seemed to climb by itself, without slowing down. When Père Dubois reached the shed, the boy had already started to throw the logs onto the pile.

"Let me do it," he shouted in mid-throw, "won't take long."

"It's good to be only twenty-five," said Père Dubois.

The work seemed play for this short-legged boy, whose arms were encased in a fat that hid the muscles, but took nothing away from their strength.

If this boy could go up to the forest with them, if he had a few free afternoons to come help him cut the wood . . . Père Dubois considered asking him this favor. He would pay him. Perhaps not as much as the bakery, but for something to do in his spare time, it would be a way for the kid to make a few extra pennies. The old man didn't dare. But if the boy took it into his head to speak to him about Julien, to ask what had happened to him, wouldn't he be willing to help him, too?

When the cart was unloaded, the old man simply said, "Now I'll have to saw that all up. And by hand, too. I'm not through sweating over it."

"It's true that wood always warms us twice."

The boy began to laugh. The old man persisted. "If I could find a strong fellow like you who wanted to make a few cents—"

"If I had the time, I'd be glad to come. But it's not possible."

"I know. Everyone has his own things to do."

Père Dubois had spoken without sadness. He had let himself go for a few minutes, imagining the boy sawing logs while he split them and Mère Dubois stacked them in piles. In his head, he had seen the work finished in a few days and space cleared for a big load of good bundles brought down from the forest. He felt a vague pain in his chest when he told himself that nothing had been done yet. He would be left alone with the job which he would have to complete before the first frost.

"Well"—he sighed—"come, so we can settle what we owe you."

"You're joking."

"No, I never make people work without paying them."

He was about to speak about the days when he himself employed apprentices, but the boy interrupted him. "I've got to go," he said. "The boss will be wondering where I am."

"At least come have a glass of wine."

The boy had already lifted his long white apron to one side and tucked the corner into his belt. Without turning around, he shouted, "Some other time!" And he started to run toward the road.

Left alone, Père Dubois sat down on an empty case, got out the box he had filled with the woodcutter's tobacco, and slowly rolled a cigarette. He had worked the whole morning, refusing to pay attention to his body. He had turned a deaf ear to complaints from his back and legs. But now that he was sitting still, long pains forced their way through him. They started from each joint and ran like acid between the bones and the muscles, piercing them every now and then when they found an opening. It was like a multiple inexhaustible spring. And this spring fed itself from the thousand impalpable elements that time had accumulated throughout his being. The slightest movement goaded them, gave them a new vigor which allowed them to press their advance and widen the path already taken.

His elbows on his knees, his head bent, and his gaze lost at the limits of the grass outside and the gray dust covering the ground of the shed, the old man thought about himself. He drew little puffs on his cigarette, which he held for a long time inside his lungs. The woodcutter's tobacco was strong, with a pleasant taste and aroma, far superior to that which the state doled out so stingily.

Père Dubois thought about himself, about what he had been before, and about what he had become after so many accumulated troubles and endured privations.

— 6 —

A LONG time went by. Without lessening, Père Dubois' fatigue went numb. It was like water that ice immobilizes. Here and there, an eddy still rippled it, but the main currents no longer had the same force. At present, there was something else on his mind. In a moment his wife would come down to the foot of the steps and call him in for lunch. They would sit down at the table, they would certainly eat their soup without mentioning anything other than the struggle they'd had and the help the baker's boy had given them, but fatally, they would end up returning to the conversation interrupted by Picaud's arrival. Mère Dubois wouldn't let things stand as they were. That was certain. And he would have to go through it all again, go through that exhausting rage or the no less exhausting battle to suppress it. What was the point of all these arguments when it was already hard just staying alive, just keeping well enough to carry on a life of nothing but work that barely allowed you to eat without having to sell the few things under the sun that you owned? This war had destroyed money. At least the money of small savings. The few bonds Mère Dubois went to cash the coupons from periodically were no longer worth anything. They had, however, bought those bonds with gold francs. Francs saved up by dint of nights spent before the kneading trough and the open oven. Each centime perhaps represented a whole batch of good white bread. Today, when the old man mentioned this to well-informed people, they would smile. The labor of an entire lifetime was nothing more now than a few pieces of paper that no one would take in exchange for a stick of butter or a cord of wood. But the officials responsible for this disaster didn't give a damn. They must have their gold in Switzerland or an interest in the munitions factories. Nothing ever touched them. They lived off the fat of the land on the backs of the working classes.

The old man let his thoughts wander down this tortuous path, riddled with ruts where the water was bitter. From time to time, he would clench his fists. They were robbing him of everything he had. They snatched away his hard-earned right to finish his days in peace, and there was nothing he could do about it.

Not only did he have to struggle and toil for a piece of bad bread, but also the war had come and sown its seeds of discord right in his own house. The other war had brought plenty of misfortunes. Two years of fighting—the duration in a military compound making bread for the soldiers. In 1915 his first wife had died, and he had had to close the bakery. In 1919 he had remarried; he had reopened his business and got back into the harness. More years of hard work to put aside enough to retire on and live off his garden and rents from the house where the bakery was. It wasn't paradise, but it was a semi-tranquillity, with outdoor work that was better for his lungs than the dust from the oven. He wouldn't have known how to live without keeping busy anyhow. He had never refused to go to the limits of his endurance. But since the outbreak of this new war, the limits were no longer visible. The more you wore yourself out, the more there was to do, and the less you had to show for it.

That's what it always came down to. He felt totally preoccupied with this worry and with his fear of the moment his wife would summon him to the dinner table. He didn't have too much trouble imagining what she would say to him. He prepared his answers, but he knew perfectly well that at the last minute those wouldn't be the words that came to mind.

He had just put the butt away in his tobacco box when a footstep crunched on the ground in front of the shed. Père Dubois raised his head. It was M. Robin, one of the tenants in the house behind the shed.

"I was on my way to see you, and I heard you cough," said M. Robin.

Père Dubois got up. M. Robin was a man of about thirty, with curly blond hair and a baby face that was a little too pale.

"We wanted to get the wood in," said the old man, "so we're late eating."

"I brought you the newspaper, but you know, it doesn't say

much. However, I got Switzerland on the radio, and the Allies are in Naples."

In the beginning of September, when the Americans had landed in Italy, M. Robin had come saying, "This time the Germans are done for." Père Dubois had had great hopes, but since then, he had come to think that the war might last forever. They wouldn't beat the Germans that easily. And what he dreaded the most was someday seeing the front move closer. The debacle of 1940 had spared his house, but nothing led one to believe that the war would end having left the Jura untouched. For the moment, however, Père Dubois was more concerned with the danger that threatened him directly, and he saw in his neighbor's arrival a new means of putting it off.

"Come up to the house," he said.

"If you haven't eaten yet, I don't want to disturb you."

The old man insisted, and M. Robin followed him.

Mère Dubois had already set the table and served the soup. "I was just about to call you," she said after returning M. Robin's greeting.

Père Dubois took his place, saying, "Sit down a minute—you have time."

The neighbor sat down, and while the old couple began their meal, he explained what he'd heard on the radio. "The Russians have advanced again," he said. "And it seems that the Maquis in the Haut-Jura have received arms."

"I thought as much," said Mère Dubois. "I heard planes, two nights ago."

"I didn't hear a thing," said Père Dubois. "But if trouble's brewing up there, there'll be more firing squads, like at Besançon last month."

"Now," said M. Robin, "we know how many they shot. There were sixteen of them. They were executed on September twenty-sixth. There was one young boy, twenty-one years old, who came from my wife's part of the country. We saw his mother. I don't know why that poor woman didn't die of grief."

There was a long silence. Only Père Dubois kept on eating. His wife stared at M. Robin, whose slightly twisted face expressed grief and anger at the same time.

"How old were they?" the old woman finally asked.

"I think that the youngest was seventeen and the oldest twenty-nine."

M. Robin fell silent once more. There was a sort of uneasiness between them, and Père Dubois wondered if M. Robin might not have seen his son with the militia, too. He searched for a moment for something to say to break the silence. But M. Robin was the first to speak. "One day we'll really have to make them pay for all that."

"In '14"—Père Dubois sighed—"we were saying the same thing, and they never paid for anything at all."

"Don't always talk about the past," said Mère Dubois. "We've got enough problems with what's going on right now."

She had spoken in a firm voice, almost hard, and the old man feared that she might start blaming him for his son's attitude. For an instant he regretted having brought M. Robin there, but he quickly got over that. No. That wasn't possible. His wife wouldn't speak about these things in front of a stranger. He couldn't imagine her capable of such a thing. And yet, he felt almost relieved when M. Robin stood up. Mère Dubois got up, too, to accompany M. Robin to the door, and said, "I won't be coming to listen to London tonight. We have to get up very early tomorrow to"—she hesitated—"to do some work we have to finish."

"If there's any important news, I'll keep you informed," M. Robin promised.

Mère Dubois closed the door, picked up a plate of cheese as dry and gray as an old piece of plaster, and put it on the table. Père Dubois helped himself, saying, as he did at every meal, "To think that they call this cheese!"

The old woman let several seconds go by before answering, "Yes, and *your* grocer probably has plenty of good Gruyère to eat."

The old man hadn't foreseen that she would open up the discussion from this angle. He reacted more violently than he might have wished. "What!" he shouted. "You're not going to start that all over again. What goes on at Paul's house is none of our business. And furthermore, you *say* that, but you don't *know*."

He shut up. He was on the wrong track. He sensed it, but his wife's reply hurt him more than a pistol shot.

"Up until today there was reason to doubt it. But now that he has the militia wrapped around his finger, he'll be able to trade on the black market in perfect confidence. No one's going to go and ask to see his accounts. He'll have plenty of gas for his trucks. And he doesn't give a damn if his father has to break his back hauling wood around on a cart."

She had talked louder and louder, and her last sentence had broken off bluntly. Père Dubois felt himself go white. A desire to vomit turned his stomach, and he had to make an effort not to walk out and slam the door. He thought that would be a stupid reaction. She would undoubtedly follow him, and if they quarreled in the garden, the neighbors would hear them. He was hurt. And it wasn't just because of her shouting, but more because it seemed unfair to him to accuse his son like that. After all, he wasn't the only one who'd gone over to the Vichy government. Could they be sure that people who did this were wrong? The old man himself had suffered too much from the war not to hate the Germans, but what could be said for the English who were bombing French cities? For a long time now, he'd given up taking sides. He didn't understand the complex situation well enough, and besides, he had other fish to fry.

"I've already told you I don't want to hear another word of this," he said in a firm tone.

"Oh, let's not exaggerate, please. I think I've had to listen enough to you repeating over and over that Julien deserted. You're in no position to ask me to be quiet."

Père Dubois sighed. "In every household where there are children of two marriages, there is always war. And we expect nations to get along together!"

"Don't try to change the subject."

He suddenly felt his anger diminish. It gave way to an immense lassitude that was not linked to the pains brought on by the morning's efforts.

"I'm not trying to do anything," he muttered. "I know that you always end up having the last word."

His voice was weak. Mère Dubois must have taken pity on him, for she seemed to hold back a sentence that had been on the tip of her tongue. She coughed, hesitated a moment, then, resting her elbows on the table, shook her head, and said with a pained expression, "You're right, it's not worth it, stirring up all that rubbish. Only, at least realize that what happened this morning wasn't very pleasant for me."

He could only raise his hands and let them fall back onto the oilcloth. "My poor woman. What do you want me to do?"

"Nothing. There is nothing to do but accept our shame and hope that it doesn't go too far."

"Where do you expect it to go?"

The anger seemed to flare up again in her eyes as she looked at him, and he regretted his question. However, without raising her voice, his wife explained, "Just now, when Monsieur Robin was here, when he was talking to us about the executions in Besançon, didn't you notice there seemed to be something he was not telling us?"

"I don't understand," admitted Père Dubois.

"Do you know who it was who arrested those poor people?"

"How do you expect me to know?"

"Well, it wasn't the Germans who caught them. It was Frenchmen—the militia—"

From the movement of her lips, the old man saw that she had stopped in mid-sentence. She had probably kept herself from adding, "Like the ones who were with Paul this morning." He was grateful to her for having been able to contain herself. It was true that she had never hurt him just for the fun of it. If she had got carried away, it was undoubtedly because that scene at the tobacco bureau had upset her. But also, why did Paul have to get himself mixed up in these things? Politics wasn't something you got involved in when you were in business. And why take it out on the old lady? Was it really true that he had spoken to her like that? Père Dubois felt like asking his wife what Paul had said when she left without buying a photograph, but he was afraid of provoking another outburst. He said simply, "He shouldn't have done that. But you shouldn't take it out on me."

"It gave me such a shock."

Père Dubois thought she was going to start to cry, and he dreaded her tears as much as he feared her anger.

"You're overtired from hauling that wood," he said. "And me, too, I'm worn-out. If we want to go to the clearing tomorrow, we'd better get a little rest."

"Go on upstairs. You know that I can't sleep in the afternoon."

Père Dubois had looked forward to the moment when he could finally retire without seeming to flee, but now that that moment had come, he could no longer find the strength to get up from his chair. He looked at his wife. She was there, close to him, just as tired as he and no doubt just as miserable. What was she thinking about? Usually, as soon as they'd finished their meal, she got up to clear the table and wash the dishes. But today she sat motionless, as though crushed by the silence that thickened around them, filling the room and passing through the walls to envelop the house and spill over onto the town. Were they to remain like this, paralyzed by the burden of their pain, which was harder to bear than the load of work awaiting them?

The old man sighed deeply, pushing back his chair as he slowly got to his feet.

"If by any chance I don't wake up, call me around four. I have to grease the cart before they come for it. And then, I'll get the ties ready for the bundles and sharpen my billhook."

"My poor Gaston, I wonder if we were right to accept. You shouldn't be doing that kind of work anymore."

Père Dubois suddenly felt relieved. Work was taking its place again in the center of the stage. It would always be less painful than the rest.

"Bah," he said, "whatever we can get done will still be something."

He headed for the stairs. As he was about to put his hand on the wooden bannister, he saw his wife's hat still hanging from the pommel.

"Do you want me to take your hat up to the room?" he asked.

"No," she said. "Leave it there. Around six I'll go back and get your tobacco. The first in line will have been served. There'll be less of a crowd than this morning."

7

Père Dubois, from his years as a baker, still had the habit of taking a nap after the noonday meal. He did it as long as the good weather lasted, preferring to get up at dawn and keep going until nightfall. That afternoon he was not able to get to sleep. Several times he dozed off for a few seconds, only to wake up immediately with the disagreeable sensation of rising up suddenly from the bottom of a dark and narrow well. The shutters were partly closed, and the still-cloudy day entered the room, casting a long green reflection onto the brass footrail. His eyes half-closed, his head buried in his two pillows, the old man stared at this reflection, which blurred as his eyelids came closer together. His fatigue was no more than a quiet water, but he knew that the mere act of getting up would roil it down to the sludge.

His wife must be in the garden. She was probably finishing clearing out the patches he'd promised himself to spade and sow before winter. She must be thinking about Paul and that stupid incident this morning. She had never liked the boy much, and Paul didn't like her either. That was true. But he'd never been really mean to her. He lived his own life! Of course, he probably ate a little better than his father did. But after all, that was normal. His business had been a success. He'd known how to get ahead. Why should anyone hold that against him? He didn't help his father. But did Julien ever think of them? Had he ever made a move to come to their aid? At twenty, you're a man, after all. His mother defended him. She loved him in the wrong way. She'd always spoiled him too much. It was true that she was too good to him. Perhaps too good to everybody, but her love for that boy sometimes blinded her and made her unfair. Whenever she got in a bad mood, she always took it out on her husband. What had he done, actually, after all? Nothing! He'd worked without asking anything from anybody. He used his life in the service of work as he used his spade in the service of the seasons, always turning the same earth over. Since the age of twelve, he had been a beast of burden. Nothing more than an animal that works for its keep. He had started out with his father, and since then, he had never left the harness. In his whole life, the only easy time

he'd had was his two years of military service. Class Ninety-three
—he'd also had the luck to draw lots and get a good number.
Only two years. Forty-fourth Infantry Regiment—but because he was the best athlete in the regiment, he'd been sent
to Joinville. He could have reenlisted. Had a career as a coach.
Enjoyable work that doesn't ruin your health and leads peacefully to a guaranteed pension. He'd thought of it, but his father's death had left him no choice. His mother was alone. As
soon as he was released, he'd taken over the bakery and the
whole business. Slavery it was. From then on, he'd never had
any free time. He had never planned his life; work had always
arranged it for him. One after the other, and each with its
task cut out, the years had passed without ever bringing anything but nasty surprises. And yet he had got pleasure from
his work. If he missed anything from his younger days, it was
really most of all those long nights at the oven, shaping and
baking the bread that people came from so far away to buy.
And the brioches on Sunday. It suddenly seemed to him that
the room was filling with the hot luxurious odor that burst
from the mouth of the oven at the moment you took out those
golden crowns, baked in the heavy paper women burned their
fingers on when they peeled it off. His mouth was watering.
He had never been a big eater, but the mere thought of that
bread and those brioches in the old days got him all stirred up.
Who would have dared to tell him then that one day, in his
oven, they'd be baking bread made out of bran and sawdust?
He was glad he wasn't a baker today. In his garden, at least,
he grew real vegetables and picked wholesome fruit. But
kneading that gray cement and daring to sell it as bread, he
would have died of shame.

Shame. The word revived in him the memory of what his
wife had said about Paul.

Did he really attach more importance to his work than to
what his son was doing? He wondered if the rage that haunted
him might not be mostly against Paul. Well, yes, why not?

46

What harm was there in liking your profession? He had always given his own his very best. No one had ever made the slightest complaint to him. How many bakers could say that?

He had had apprentices who came from other shops and laughed in his face for not taking the usual shortcuts. Their kind didn't last long. There are no two ways about being honest.

Of course, other bakers had got rich by skimping on everything, by cheating everybody. Today they were rolling in gold, not worried by the war or by the winter. Honesty can't take the place of food or fuel, but it is important just the same to know that you've got to the age of seventy without owing a cent to anyone. On the contrary, if all the people who still owed him for a loaf of bread suddenly came to pay him, there'd be a damned big crowd in his garden. He still sometimes ran into these people in the street. He knew that some of them spent even more time in church than they did in cafés and that people liked to hold them up as models of virtue. As for himself, he'd never needed religion to keep him on the straight and narrow, without once going astray. He'd done it quite naturally because it had never occurred to him to act otherwise.

And today there he was, worn-out by fatigue and filled with pain. There he was, searching vainly for the sleep in which his exhausted body could find the strength it would need to carry his one-track life on a little farther, carry it on alone, as he had always done, and without expecting from anyone the help he'd never really hoped for.

-⊰ 8 ⊱-

IT WAS six o'clock in the evening when the woodcutter's truck came back and stopped in front of the garden. As soon as it left, carrying the cart off to the clearing where it would spend the night unattended, Père Dubois felt invaded by anxiety. He said to his wife, "We didn't think, but I could have ridden up with them, since there's a cabin you can sleep in."

"No," she said, "you would have caught cold. It must be badly built and drafty."

"Just the same, leaving a cart like that in the middle of the woods."

"My poor Gaston, you're not going to get in a stew about a cart. Who do you think would want to take on that antique?"

She'd already put on her hat and picked up her shopping basket.

"I'm going to get your tobacco," she said, "and I have one or two other errands to do."

"Good. I'll go see about the rabbits."

He watched her walk away. She was a funny one, all right. Always worrying about trifles, but when it came to something serious, she wasn't in the least concerned. He was perfectly aware that his cart wasn't new. It was almost as old as he was. But it was still rolling. It was sturdy, not too heavy, and when you put up the rails, you could still move a good load of hay or wood with it. The old lady was surely wrong to think a cart like that was safe overnight in a clearing more than three miles out of town. It could look just as tempting to a farmer as to a woodsman. And then there was the brake cord. A good twenty-foot length of rope. Flexible and strong. The kind of rope they didn't even sell anymore. No, decidedly, he had been wrong to let that cart go. He should have at least removed the cord. One never thought enough. Père Dubois sensed that he wouldn't sleep well. He already hadn't slept that afternoon because of that business about the militia, and tonight, just when he had to get up early the next morning, he'd be tossing and turning, trying to get to sleep. It seemed there would always be something to ruin his life.

He picked up a sack folded on top of the rabbit cages, lined up under the little porch attached to the house, and headed for the shed to get a load of hay. In the shed he looked at the empty space left by the cart. It was the first time this space had ever seemed so empty to him. He wasn't used to seeing it like that. Since he was the only person who ever used the cart, when it wasn't there, he wasn't there either. For years it had been that way. One pulling the other, they'd gone a damned long distance. The vegetables he took to market, the green grass or hay they went to get halfway up the hill at Montciel. The trips with kindling, with potatoes, not counting the daily loads of wood from the shed to the bakery when he was still in business. Never, up until this evening, had he thought about that cart so much. It really played a big role in his life. When you got right down to it, it had done almost as much work as he had. And like him, without ever complaining. He had spent a half century dragging it about, greasing it, painting it to prevent wear and tear, and today, without thinking, he had let it leave on a truck to spend the night unprotected in the forest. That was really behaving like a child.

The more he thought about it, the more the idea took hold of him that he would never see that cart again. Tomorrow morning they would go up to the clearing. They would find it gone; they would look for it everywhere, and there would be nothing left to do but come back down again. No point in trimming the branches since there would be no way of transporting the bundles. And the old lady would certainly say, "You see, if your son had taken them on his truck, this wouldn't have happened. You would still have your cart." It would be her great triumph, the old lady's. And in truth, she would be right. He knew that perfectly well. But could you ask a wholesale grocer to waste a driver's time and risk damaging a truck in a clearing for the sake of a few sticks? If he'd gone and asked him a thing like that, Paul would probably have answered, "My drivers have better things to do. You'll just have to do like everyone else and burn coal." Was he capable of understanding what their life was like? Could he see that they shrank from the expense of converting the stove?

Père Dubois had gotten down the hay and tended his rabbits. Now, in the evening that rose slowly from the earth, he was standing at the corner of the house totally absorbed in the thought of his cart. The truck must have got to the clearing by now. Awhile back, they'd called over the baker's boy to help hoist the cart onto the truck platform. The four of them, each taking a wheel, had had a hard time because the truck was quite high off the ground. A good cart is light when it's rolling, but when you have to lift it up, it's a different story. To unload it, Picaud would be alone with his helper. They'd promised to use the cord to brake it and to be very careful, but they both were young. To people like them, a cart didn't mean much. It was sturdy, even though the old lady thought of it as an antique, but if it fell and landed on one wheel, it would break for sure. Of course, with a broken wheel, no one was likely to steal it, but then what would he do tomorrow morning with a broken cart? Not to mention the fact that seeing a broken cart in the middle of the forest, people might think it was abandoned and carry off a wheel or the axles or rails or even that good twenty-foot rope.

To think that he'd had all day to plan it and only now was taking these dangers into account. When it was too late. The cart was no doubt already alone in the forest, perhaps with a wheel broken or the tongue in pieces. That tongue wasn't very strong. The bolts that attached it had eaten into the wood a little. There was some play, and the pins he had driven in were barely holding. If that tongue let go when they had a load of wood, they'd really be in trouble.

Decidedly, this adventure was too much for their age and strength. They hadn't thought about it enough before launching into it. And now it was in danger of costing them more than converting the stove and buying coal.

Père Dubois walked slowly to the angle of the two paths and took out the little box where he'd put the tobacco young Picaud had left him. He rolled a cigarette, which he held between his lips for a moment before lighting it.

The evening advanced. Darkness flowed over the black earth of the bare patches in the garden, avoiding in its progress the piles of russet leaves the wind of the last few days had blown across the flagstones. They remained like islands of light forgotten on the ground. The still-yellow peach trees also held more brightness than the heavy sky. Père Dubois turned toward the west.

Behind the hill at Montciel, the clearer sky was tinged with pink. There was still not the slightest breath of wind, but perhaps a hint that a little breeze might pick up from the north to clear the sky during the night.

IT was almost dark by the time Mère Dubois got back.

"We'll have to light the lamp to eat," the old man said.

"I can't help it—I couldn't get back any sooner. I wanted to get something to take along to eat up there tomorrow."

"And you found something?"

"Yes, I was able to get some pâté and some head cheese. We'll bring some hard-boiled eggs and some fruit."

"For tonight, you'd better just heat up some leftover soup. I don't want to load my stomach, and I'd really like to get to bed early."

"If you like. But then you'll have to eat a little more tomorrow morning before we leave."

They had gone into the kitchen, and while Mère Dubois was letting down the cord to light the oil lamp, the old man pulled the shutters to and then closed the window. When the wick was trimmed and the lamp back up again, Mère Dubois lighted the fire and put on the soup.

"Were you able to get the tobacco?" Père Dubois asked.

"Yes, I got two packages from your ration and two from mine. If we can put one aside, I'll try to get some butter."

The old man didn't answer. He had nothing to say. His wife had every right to dispose of her tobacco ration as she saw fit. She had never smoked, but he knew other women who smoked as much as a man. Last month M. Robin had given him a pack of cigarettes; perhaps he'd give him another one this month. With what he had in reserve . . .

The soup started to hiss on the fire, and Mère Dubois put two plates and two spoons on the table, along with the gray bread that made you sick just looking at it.

"Did you remember bread for tomorrow?" Père Dubois asked.

"Yes, it's in my basket. I'll get all that ready tonight."

"We'll have to take the big musette bag. I'll put my bill-hook in it, too."

"That might make it too heavy."

"No, you can carry the roll of wire."

Père Dubois was still thinking about his cart and this adventure that seemed madder and madder to him. However, he didn't say anything about it for fear his wife would start in again about Paul and his trucks.

She served the soup, and they began to eat in silence. Between two spoonfuls, the old man stopped at times to listen to the night. If the north wind came up, the threat of rain would be over.

They had almost emptied their plates when Mère Dubois put down her spoon and sat back in her chair.

"What's the matter?" asked the old man.

"You didn't hear anything?"

"No. It's the wind coming up. That means we'll have—"

She interrupted him. "No, it's not the wind; someone's coming."

"But I already locked the gate."

"It must be a neighbor coming through the back."

"We'll never have a moment's peace." Père Dubois groaned.

He could hear the footsteps the moment the visitor turned the corner of the house to get to the steps.

"It's not Monsieur Robin," said Mère Dubois, " or Monsieur Durelet."

She got up and went to the door. The footsteps came up the stoop.

"Still, it's someone who knows the way," the old man said.

He was suddenly anxious. A visit at this hour could mean nothing good. He thought very quickly that the woodcutter's truck had fallen into a deep ravine, and they were hurrying to tell him that his cart was in pieces.

Mère Dubois opened the door the moment the visitor reached the landing. Père Dubois, watching her, understood from her face that this visit didn't please her. Without saying a word, frowning and hard-eyed, she drew back to let in Paul, who said, "Good evening. I'm not disturbing you?"

"Ah, it's you," said the old man. "You came through the back?"

"Had to, since you lock up so early."

From the tone of his voice and his too-brilliant eyes, Père Dubois saw that his son had been drinking. He knew that this happened more and more frequently, and it pained him. Several friends had said to him, "Your boy can really put it away, you know." They said it jokingly, but not once in his life had Père Dubois drunk more than was good for him or admitted drinkers into his circle of friends. However, he'd tried not to pay attention to the gossip.

As soon as his son had crossed the threshold, he'd felt his heart tighten at the realization that the battle with his wife would start again; until that moment he'd stopped thinking about it. He stared at the boy, repeating to himself, "He's been drinking. That's true for sure. My boy, taking to drink. Good Lord Almighty."

Paul had pulled up a chair and sat down, saying, "Finish your soup. It'll get cold."

The old man swallowed a spoonful of broth. Mère Dubois was going back to her place when Paul asked, "Wait a minute, Mother, before you sit down, would you mind getting me a glass of wine?"

She stopped and was about to go around the table when Père Dubois shouted, "No! You've already had enough to drink!"

Paul looked taken aback. His thin face tightened into a grimace that accentuated the red patches on his prominent cheekbones. His father looked at him more closely and noted that the whites of his eyes were bloodshot. So he really drank in earnest.

Mère Dubois, still on her feet, seemed to be waiting, wondering what to do. Père Dubois looked at her. He had spoken loud and fast, in a fit of rage. Now he wondered if he hadn't been too hasty. If he hadn't, in advance, given his wife a new case against this boy whom she already detested. Paul had pushed back his little brown hat with the turned-up brim, revealing part of his already bald head.

"Good Lord"—he sighed—"when my own father refuses me a glass of wine, I've seen everything."

"I'm not refusing you anything," said his father, "but you've already had too much to drink, and it shows."

"If I've had a few, it's because all day long we've run into people who offered us a glass." He looked at Mère Dubois. "People who aren't quite of your political opinion. Who aren't in favor of selling France to the English."

He had spoken in a progressively rising voice. The old lady, who was still standing, turned toward her husband. In her eyes, the anger had vanished to give way to a flicker of distress that shattered Père Dubois.

"Shut up, Paul," he cried. "If you came here to talk politics to us, you'd do better to go home and go to bed."

His voice was trembling, and he knew it. He was struggling against the turbulence inside him. He looked back and forth between his wife and Paul; then he shouted at them, "Aren't you ever going to leave me alone? I spend my days breaking my back working, and you have to come and spoil the few hours of rest I ever get."

Reassured to see that his father was no longer angry just at him, Paul seemed to relax. He settled into his chair. He pushed his hat back a little farther, making a sort of dark halo around his head, and took a pack of cigarettes and a lighter out of his pocket. He took out a cigarette, tapped it on the edge of the table, lighted it; then sliding the pack across the oilcloth in his father's direction, he said, "If my intention was to bother you, I wouldn't be here. I came to do you a favor, and you welcome me as if I were a fox in your rabbit hutch."

Père Dubois was looking at the pack of cigarettes. He struggled against his hand, which wanted to move forward and take it. His look flew in a triangle from this blue pack to his son's face, then to his wife's. Paul asked, "You don't smoke any-more?"

"Yes, but at night, you know."

"Take one anyhow."

Père Dubois helped himself as though regretfully. He took out his package of papers, broke the cigarette in two, and opened one half, saying, "I roll them. The paper's better."

Mère Dubois, who hadn't sat down yet, removed the plates without having finished her soup. When she returned, she placed a half-full bottle of wine and two glasses on the table. The old man watched her. Might she be more indulgent than he was? Was she acting like this because Paul had just said he wanted to do them a favor? And what had Paul meant by that? Had he heard about this business of the bundles, and was he going to offer to go get them in a truck? If that were the case, the old lady could no longer say they were a pair of ego-tists, Paul and Micheline.

He finished rolling his cigarette and lighted it. He took a puff. Today he'd practically used nothing from his ration.

Mère Dubois poured the wine. She half filled Paul's glass, and the old man said, "Just a drop for me. You know I never drink without eating, especially at night."

"You're making a mistake," said Paul. "On certain days, if we didn't have wine to sustain us—"

"You know that it pains me to hear you talk like that," said his father. "What is it you came to tell us?"

The old woman had brought to the table a little brass ash-tray that Père Dubois had made, in 1916, out of a shell case. She went back to her place but appeared to be sitting on the edge of her chair, as if it might break beneath her weight. Paul drank half his wine; then, blowing a big cloud of smoke over the table, he said, "I came about what happened this morn-ing—"

"Listen—" Mère Dubois tried to interrupt, but the old man interrupted: "Let him speak."

He saw that his wife was making an effort to keep quiet and stay in her chair.

"Yes," Paul went on. "I told Micheline about it at noon. She bawled me out. She said, 'I know your stepmother well enough to know that she must be really upset. Just because Julien has behaved like a fool is no reason to take it out on her.'"

At that, Mère Dubois sat up even straighter in her chair. She drew herself up to her full height, and Père Dubois realized that he couldn't stop her from speaking.

"Julien has not done anything foolish," she snapped. "He joined the Armistice Army because he thought it was the right thing to do. The day the Germans invaded the free zone, when he saw that they would probably get arrested or put into service with the Germans, he left. And that's all, period."

The minute she stopped, Paul burst out laughing. "Left," he said. "You have quite a way with words. He deserted—that's something else again. And deserted to sneak off to England probably, like a lot of idiots who don't know what's in store for them."

"If you know where he is," Mère Dubois shouted, "you're pretty lucky. I, his own mother, I'd give anything to know."

Her voice broke. She wasn't crying, but her throat must have been choked up, and her eyes were wet with tears. There was a very brief silence. Since Paul seemed to be groping for words in the alcohol fumes, his father took advantage of the opportunity to say, "I thought you'd come here to do us a favor."

"Exactly. It's about him. If he's still in France, it would be better if he gave himself up rather than wait for the police to get their hands on him. It would be preferable, for him, as well as for you."

Mère Dubois stood up. Her whole body had started to shake, and her hands, resting on the table, were like two animals ready to spring. The old man was frightened. He didn't have a chance to get a word in edgewise.

"If you've come to ask me to turn my son over to the militia," she cried, "you can have me arrested, you can have me shot, but you'll never get a word out of me." By this time she had choked back her tears. Only a great anger showed in her face. She turned to her husband before continuing. "And you let him say things like that under your own roof. You let him threaten us without doing anything to stop him!"

Père Dubois felt little. Lost. Sick and helpless. He would have liked to be far away at the ends of the earth or even under the earth, where you finally find peace. What should he do? What should he say?

Mère Dubois fell back into her chair. She seemed exhausted, but her hands, resting on her knees, still trembled, and her look was suddenly drained of all expression.

"You didn't understand me," Paul said in a calm, almost gentle voice. "You know very well that they're looking for Julien and that we're all mixed up in this. You're perfectly free to believe that I hate him. You're too stubborn for me to even try to convince you otherwise, but do you think it would give me pleasure to see him arrested? Do you believe that that would be helpful, to you or me?"

"In other words"—Mère Dubois sighed—"you're still thinking of yourself."

"You're not being fair," Père Dubois said gently.

Paul stopped him with a gesture.

"Even admitting that I'm thinking only of my father and myself, if it's still possible to keep Julien out of prison, we mustn't wait until he gets arrested. It's up to him to come forward and say, 'I made a mistake. I admit it. I was forced into it . . .' Or something, I don't know, but we'll find a way to get him out of this mess."

The old man looked at his wife, who had turned toward him. She looked as if she no longer knew what to think. Paul took note of his advantage. He went on, "Without getting into politics, don't you believe that it's better to stay within the law?"

The old couple were still looking at each other. Paul let several seconds go by before concluding, "Believe me, it would be better to tell him to come back while there's still time."

"But what's the use," said Mère Dubois, "since I assure you that we don't know where he is?"

"You're not going to tell me you've never heard a word from him!"

Père Dubois had it on the tip of his tongue to explain that in August they had simply received a postcard that came from Toulon, without any address, saying only: "All goes well." Since then, there had been silence. An interminable silence that ate away at both of them. He kept his mouth closed. The look his wife had given him would not let him utter another word.

"Well"—Paul sighed—"you are the best judges."

"But we tell you we haven't had any news," said his father. "Do you think it's fun for us, not even knowing where he is?"

Paul gave an incredulous smile. Raising his hand to impose silence, he said, with a superior air that annoyed the old man, "At least, I've done my duty. I've given you fair warning. Because I don't want to be blamed for having been disinterested in Julien. He is only my half brother, but that's no reason to let him fall by the wayside."

He stood up, picked up his pack of cigarettes and his lighter from the table, readjusted his hat, and added, "There, that's all I had to say to you."

He had already started for the door when Père Dubois got up, saying, "Wait, I'll take the key to the garden and see you out. It will be easier than going through the back."

Mère Dubois had already opened the door. Their eyes met, and Père Dubois saw that she was uneasy. Since Paul was already out on the steps, he said, loud enough for Paul to hear it, "You see, everyone figures that we've heard from him. But nothing, not one word. If only we knew where he was!"

--◀ 10 ▶--

THE night was black as pitch. Once the door was closed, Père Dubois groped for the iron railing with his hand. He heard Paul hesitate on the steps.

"Watch out," he said. "You can't see a thing."

"I don't come here often, but I can still remember the way."

At the foot of the steps the old man bumped into his son's shoulder. He could smell the reek of alcohol on his breath. They took several steps without saying a word; then after a great deal of hesitation, Père Dubois asked, "Why do you drink as much as you do? You're going to ruin your health."

"It doesn't happen often, but today we were going all over town selling those photographs."

"As a matter of fact, I wanted to talk to you about that. Do you really think that's any of your business?"

He sensed that his son was stopping. He stopped, too. Now that his eyes had grown accustomed to the night, he could make out the white spot of Paul's face under his dark hat.

"What do you mean?" asked Paul. "You're not going to tell me that you're for De Gaulle and the revolution?"

"I'm not for anything. I'm for trying to live and being left in peace."

They spoke harshly, but without raising their voices.

"Exactly. Living in peace—that means living with the ones who are the strongest."

"And do you think they're always going to be the strongest? Look at what's happening in Italy."

"In Italy? But that doesn't mean a thing. Remember, in 1917, how the Italians cleared out of Caporetto. Hitler was wrong to trust them. They folded up at the first sign of real fighting, but the SS will make short work of pushing the Americans back to the sea."

"In 1917," the old man observed, "some people didn't want to believe in American aid either. And yet—"

Paul interrupted him. "You don't really think in spite of everything that Stalin can get along with Roosevelt and Churchill? Sooner or later, they'll be at each other's throats, and Hitler will move in and restore order. And it's a lucky thing; it wouldn't be long before we had the Communists on our backs. And then you'd see what would happen to your buildings and the few cents you've put aside."

Père Dubois had always been susceptible to the threat of Communism. At the time of the *Front Populaire* he had trembled for his few belongings, and what his son had just said awoke this old fear in him.

"You know," he ventured, "I'm not exactly a big capitalist."

Paul gave a snicker that grated on the old man and made him uneasy.

"Big or little, you'd have to hand it all over and move to the old men's home."

"There are some days when I wonder if they aren't happier in there than I am living out here. At least they get enough to eat, and they don't have to kill themselves, working and going without things the way I do."

Paul got out his pack of cigarettes. Père Dubois guessed what he was doing.

"For example," he said, "just to get a little tobacco—"

"Take it," Paul said, offering him the pack. "It's all right. Keep the whole thing."

His father thanked him. Paul wasn't as egotistical as the old lady claimed. He felt like speaking to him about the stovewood, but he didn't dare. He contented himself with saying, as he pulled a cigarette from the pack, "You know, for old people like

THE FRUITS OF WINTER

us, it's not so easy all the time. Money's not worth anything anymore."

He leaned toward the lighter Paul had just lighted. For a moment, their faces were very close, framed beneath the hat-brim and the visor of the cap, which were almost touching, and separated from the night by their hands raised on either side of the flame. When the lighter had gone out, there was once again the empty darkness and, for a few seconds, the memory of that blinding brightness.

"If you need money," said Paul, "sell one of the houses."

"Sell what?"

"For the little rent you get, go ahead and sell, and you'll have enough to eat for the rest of your life."

Père Dubois was floored. He felt as though his son had landed a violent blow in the pit of his stomach.

"To think that my own son would ever be giving me a piece of advice like that! So then, if I understand you rightly, you don't care if strangers get hold of everything?"

"Not at all. But if you have nothing left to live on . . ."

Père Dubois coughed, caught his breath, and slowly, emphasizing each word carefully, he finally said, "I don't have much. But I still have two hands. They've provided for me for the past sixty years. And they'll provide for me to the end."

They started walking again, and when they'd taken about ten steps in silence, his son said in a detached tone, "You know very well that if you start running short, nobody's going to let you starve to death. But if someday you did want to sell a house, perhaps it might be arranged so that it didn't leave the family."

Père Dubois did not answer. He'd understood very well what Paul meant, but the proposition had caught him too much off guard. You don't decide that easily to sell what you've spent your whole life building or consolidating, even to a son. And besides, there was his wife, and there was Julien.

They had reached the gate, and the old man felt around for

the lock. He opened it and stepped aside to let Paul through. Paul went out, saying, "In any case, I mean what I said about Julien. If you can reach him, get him to come back as quickly as possible."

"Of course, if we hear from him—"

Paul interrupted. "I have no reason to doubt your word, but you must admit that it seems a little odd to everyone, this disappearance. And you know, if the police take it into their heads to find him—"

He didn't finish. Père Dubois sensed that he was moving off. Indeed, he took two steps onto the sidewalk; then turning back, he added, "Anyway, if you do hear from him, the police will know about it. Your mail is certainly being watched."

⚜ 11 ⚜

WHEN Père Dubois got back to the kitchen, after putting out his half-smoked cigarette with his fingers and dropping it into his box, his wife had already packed the musette bag for the next day.

"I just have to put in the hard-boiled eggs," she said. "And the fruit. You'll have to remind me, but it's better to leave them in the cellar for the night."

"My billhook," asked the old man, "did you wrap it in a piece of newspaper?"

"Of course. What are you going to wear on your feet?"

"My boots."

"You haven't worn them for a long time. Are you sure they won't hurt you?"

"No, no, I used to wear them with two pairs of socks."

"Yes, but that was in winter. When the weather's warmer, your feet swell."

"And you? What are you going to wear, with your corns?"

"I have no choice, besides my wooden shoes and my best shoes, I have only one pair that's good enough."

"They won't hurt your feet?"

"I hope not."

Père Dubois tried to think of something to say. He was enjoying this conversation centered on their expedition the next day, keeping them off other subjects. When he could think of nothing further to add, he hastened to say, "We ought to go up to bed fairly soon."

"Go ahead, I'll get undressed and follow you."

He was surprised that she hadn't ventured even one word about Paul's behavior. He hurried to get his chamber pot out of the laundry under the stairs; then he started up, saying, "We'll probably be awake early enough, but you'd better set the alarm clock all the same. You never know."

His wife agreed, and he continued up the winding stairs, which plunged him into darkness. Once inside the bedroom, he slid the pot under the bed, always in the same place near the left foot, and, after closing the shutters, got undressed in the dark. If his wife had had nothing to say downstairs, perhaps it was because she meant to speak to him once they were in bed. He dreaded that. He would have liked to get to sleep very fast, but he knew that wasn't possible. Too many things had happened during the course of the day. They all lay inside him like a sea tossed by an interminable storm. He thought about the wood he'd got in, which certainly wouldn't last them through the winter; he thought about his cart which had been taken away on the truck; about the visit from his son; about his other, absent son, about whom he would have at least liked to know if he were alive or dead. It all got mixed up, adding to the fatigue of his overburdened day, to make his head heavy. He felt exhausted, and yet nothing in him announced the prompt arrival of the sleep that would deliver him.

Mère Dubois came upstairs and got into bed without saying a word. There was a long silence, broken only by the sound of their breathing and the creaking of the bedsprings when one of them moved, trying to find a more comfortable position for his aching body.

Père Dubois forced himself to lie motionless. If he didn't move, perhaps sleep would come more quickly; perhaps at least his wife would think he was asleep. Above all, he had to avoid getting into a conversation. He knew that it would drag on forever or turn into a fight. He wanted to sleep. To rest, to escape from everything that wasn't his own life, from everything that didn't have to do with his work. For a long time, he turned that sentence of Paul's over in his mind: "Just sell a house, and you'll have enough to eat for the rest of your life." Good Lord. At seventy, selling your property in order to live. And it was his own son who spoke to him like that! Did Paul really think he might buy one of his houses? And what for? As an investment? Well, then it was true that he was making piles of money. His wife was right. Well, if he was getting rich, so much the better for him. That was nothing to be ashamed of, especially if he was running his store honestly. If he'd been lucky enough to live in times that were good for business, could he be blamed for that? Of course not. At present, times were harder, he was trying to hang on to what he had, and he was right.

He was accused of dealing on the black market. But who could boast of never having done as much? Who could cast the first stone in these times when everyone was struggling to survive? Some vicious gossip had it that he was selling to the Germans. But so what? Could you refuse to let them have merchandise that they were willing to pay for? Last year, when there had been all those deaths among the wounded being cared for at the École Normale, some Germans had come right here to order flowers. His wife had had to make funeral sprays for one whole day. Had it been possible to refuse? And this militia—M. Robin said lots of bad things about it, but M. Robin said bad things about everything having to do with the government. After all, it was nothing but a new police force. Perhaps they attributed a lot more sins to it than it could have committed. Of course, in Lons, it hadn't exactly attracted the cream of the crop. But was M. Robin equally aware of some of the disreputable types that were in the Resistance? If you listened only to one side, you got only half the story. Anyhow, Paul wasn't a member of the militia. If some of them had asked him to go with them to sell photographs of this Darnand, perhaps he hadn't been able to refuse any more than the old lady had been able to refuse flowers to the Germans. No, all that wasn't really very serious. Paul wasn't a bad person. And not as egotistical as his wife claimed. A proof—the nearly full pack of cigarettes he'd given him. And it wasn't done to impress the old lady, since he didn't do it in front of her.

The more Père Dubois thought about it, the more he regretted not having mentioned the stovewood to his son. He would have offered a truck for sure. But if he hadn't asked for help, in the last analysis, it was because of his wife. She always jumped to conclusions without knowing the facts. It was a terrible habit of hers. And at this very moment, because of her, perhaps his cart had already been stolen. Or broken or abandoned in the woods. Besides, they said that young escapees from the forced-labor service hid out in those woods, and they might be just the ones to make off with the cart. And surely not to use it, but more to sell it to some farmers for money to buy liquor.

Mère Dubois raised herself up in bed to change position. The old man, from forcing himself to remain motionless, felt his right leg going to sleep. He moved, too, and his wife asked, "You're not asleep?"

"Not yet, no."

"Try to sleep," she said. "Otherwise you'll be too tired to go up there tomorrow."

Père Dubois sighed. She wasn't trying to start a conversation anymore. He moved again to settle his head comfortable on his pillows and, more relaxed, finally let himself drift into sleep.

—◄{ 12 }►—

THE minute he had waked, Père Dubois had felt around for his lighter which he always left on a chair beside the bed. Scarcely had he lighted it than Mère Dubois was saying, "Do you realize what time it is? The clock just struck four."

She was lucky, being able to hear the clock downstairs, in the dining room, all the way from the bed.

They got up at the same time, and the old man hurried outside to have a look at the weather. The sky was clear and spangled with stars. A good breeze was rustling the leaves.

He went back into the kitchen, which was already filling with the aroma of coffee.

"I had a little real coffee left," said his wife, "I made it. Whatever we don't drink, I'll take along in a thermos bottle."

Père Dubois rubbed his rough hands, grown stiff with the immobility of night, one against the other.

"You did well. We'll enjoy drinking it after a cold meal."

This morning, he felt less strained, almost happy with the day, which promised to be fine and would take them to a forest where he hadn't been for many years. Before this war, sometimes he used to go for mushrooms up to the first plateau, and seeing the musette bag on the table and his cane hanging over

67

the bannister of the stairs, for an instant he had the impression of being younger and about to relive a time that had marked his life in a pleasurable way. He had never had a vacation or much free time, but only a few simple joys, like taking a Sunday afternoon walk to Montciel. A school holiday. Or even picking mushrooms with a group of friends. Their great luxury then had been to stop for an hour or two in a village inn and eat an omelet that would be prepared for them while they played ninepins in the square. It hadn't been much, but when those memories came back to him all of a sudden like that, because of a musette bag, a cane, and a pair of boots, a little bit of warmth and strength would spread throughout his being.

As soon as they'd eaten and drunk their coffee, given the rabbits a good supply of hay, and made sure that the doors of the cellar and the shed and the shutters of the house were locked, the Dubois' were on their way. As he turned the key in the lock on the garden gate, the old man remarked, "It's been quite a few years since we left the house alone for a whole day."

"What do you think could possibly happen to the house?"

"Nothing, but after all . . ."

"I told Mademoiselle Marthe that we'd be gone for the day. She said she'd check on things from time to time."

Père Dubois looked at the still-closed shutters on the second floor of the house opposite the garden. Every day Mlle. Marthe spent long hours behind that window, looking at the street and the garden. The old man had never liked her because of this immobility. He couldn't understand how a woman, even though old, could stay so idle. For him, a life without work was deprived of meaning. He didn't like her eyes, which sometimes followed him in his comings and goings and seemed to say, "All that work you do fatigues me, Monsieur Dubois." However, that morning he felt reassured by the idea that no one could come onto his place without Mlle. Marthe knowing about it.

Walking in step, the old couple went up the Ruè des Écoles.

Père Dubois' iron-tipped cane and his hobnailed boots rang out on the pavement. Dawn was just breaking. The street was empty, and they passed, without turning their heads, before the gates of the École Normale, where a German soldier was standing guard inside a sentry box.

The old man could feel the musette bag hit his buttocks at every step. His cane was light in his hand, and once they'd crossed the town and the Parc des Bains, he was surprised to find that he wasn't winded. They'd been walking at a steady pace, without talking and without leaving the middle of the road. It wasn't unpleasant at all, this walk before sunrise. The brisk air was good to breathe, and as they turned onto the road to Pannessières, Père Dubois heard the old refrain of the Sambre-et-Meuse Regiment sing out inside his head. Without even realizing it, he lengthened his stride, throwing his cane a little higher at each step.

"You're going too fast," said his wife.

"You tired already?"

"No, but at this rate, you'll get out of breath, and we'll have to stop."

He slowed down and looked at her. Her face was already strained. Her left hand was clutching the roll of wire ties she'd hung over her shoulder. Her right hand moved from time to time to her stomach to pull up her hernia bandage with a quick motion.

"You ought to rest a moment," he suggested. "You know the way. As long as you get there around noon, why don't you come along slowly and take your time?"

She shook her head no.

"Give me the ties," he said.

"No, they're not heavy."

They began to climb, following the road whose first turns uncoiled slowly. Père Dubois observed the perfectly clear sky lightening in front of them, outlining the wooded crest where the lacy leaves stirred in the wind. Soon they were looking down on the town behind them. On their left, villages appeared below. The old man tried not to talk. It now seemed to him that his breath was coming less easily. He kept up the pace, however, but more and more frequently, he turned toward his wife to look for signs of fatigue on her face.

When they'd passed the village of Pannessières and reached the big bend where you could look down on the plain, the light hit them smack in the face. The sun had just emerged from the forest. Père Dubois lowered the visor of his cap down over his forehead, thereby uncovering the back of his head. It felt as though a damp, icy towel had landed on his neck. He hadn't even realized that he'd been sweating.

"If you'd like us to stop a moment," he said.

His wife looked at him. She hesitated a little before saying, "If you like."

"At any rate, I have to take a piss."

He really didn't have to, but it was a way of not admitting that he needed a rest. While he was turned toward the woods, his wife sat down on a rock on the edge of the road. When he rejoined her, he explained. "In the Forty-fourth, when we went out on maneuvers on the plateau, we always made our first halt here. Then we would climb up to Vevy. And then next, we sometimes—"

She interrupted him. "Don't talk so much. Catch your breath. And dry yourself off a little; you're soaking wet."

He took off his cap and mopped his bald head with his handkerchief.

"I really should have brought you along an undershirt," she said. "You could have changed when we got there."

"Don't worry. Up in the woods there's no danger of catching cold."

As soon as they'd abandoned the highway for the rough forest path, the air was less brisk. As they crossed a recent clearing, the sun already burned their skin as though it were a day in the middle of summer. The ground was uneven. Now it was rough

70

rock worn by carting, now deeply rutted earth, now big loose pebbles that rolled underfoot. The path climbed, went down again, leveled off in a flat place or in a hollow to descend and climb up once more. Walking became difficult, and Père Dubois had to stop on several occasions to cough and spit.

"You see," observed his wife, "we were walking too fast; you're worn-out."

"No, no. It's the difference in the air."

"We would have done better to stay on the highway. It's longer, but the going's easier."

"No. This way, we cut off almost a mile and a half. But going back down, we'll take the main road. I'm afraid the cart might break down along here."

They resumed their walk, going more slowly, with frequent stops. Because the path narrowed in places, Père Dubois went first. He'd shifted the musette bag to his other shoulder but refused to give it to his wife, who was still carrying the roll of ties. In the bushes along the path, a whole population of often invisible lizards fled beneath the dead leaves. During a halt, Mère Dubois asked, "Are there many snakes around here?"

"I'll say—no shortage of them!"

"You'll have to be careful, working up there—they often hide under the branches."

"Don't worry. I may be deaf, but I'm not blind."

The wind was still blowing, but it seemed to skirt the interior of the forest, contenting itself with skimming the tree-tops and plucking up big armfuls of russet leaves that sparkled in the sunlight as they fell to earth.

When they came to a fork in the path, Père Dubois stopped.

"Well, well, this isn't the way it used to be," he said.

"Have we gotten lost?"

"Of course not. But that path on the left sure looks to me as if it heads back down again after that first bend we can see from here."

He fell silent. He tried to assemble his memories. But he

suddenly no longer felt sure of anything. Mère Dubois looked at him anxiously, her face all lined with wrinkles under the old braided straw hat she wore for gardening. Her forehead, flecked with minuscule spots of sunlight, was glistening. She passed the back of her hand across the beads of sweat clinging to her eyebrows.

"You're hot," her husband said. "I knew this was no kind of work for you."

"Don't worry about me. Instead, try to figure out which path we ought to take."

When she repeated that they would have been better off staying on the highway, Père Dubois shrugged his shoulders and started down the right-hand path without being really certain of not making a mistake.

"You're sure this is the right way?" she asked.

"Yes, don't worry. I'm not about to get lost in a forest I've known for fifty years."

Nevertheless, without slowing down, he tried to see between the tree trunks what direction the path to the left they hadn't taken was going, but the woods were thick, and it was soon lost from view. He tried to calculate how much time had elapsed since they had left the highway, but it wasn't easy. They hadn't been walking steadily; they'd made numerous stops, and so he couldn't really tell. From the woodcutter's directions, he'd understood very well where the clearing was located in relation to the highway, but from here it wasn't so obvious. The way he'd remembered things, it had all seemed much simpler, but the forest began to look increasingly unfamiliar to him. He'd remembered it as being much flatter. Hours went by, and the sun got higher, beating down more and more.

Père Dubois waited a long time before stopping to take off his jacket, which he refused to give to his wife. He hung it over the musette bag, which he shifted to his other shoulder because the strap was hurting a little.

At each halt, Mère Dubois would ask, "Are you sure you didn't make a mistake?"

Père Dubois wasn't sure of anything, but he persisted. They'd gone too far to turn back, and he hoped that the path would eventually cross a cleared rise from which he could at least see a stretch of the highway and orient himself. He was beginning to wonder if they weren't actually heading in the direction of Briod. Judging from the position of the sun, that's what they were doing. This idea gradually took hold in him, but he still hoped to be able to spot the road and get his bearings. Too often he'd assured his wife that he couldn't get lost up here to retrace their steps deliberately, just like that, simply saying, "I made a mistake."

As time went by, fatigue climbed up his legs and gripped his chest. His hand clenched the hard wood of his heavy cane, the musette bag weighed him down, and the air got denser, almost unbreathable.

Near a rock, he stopped, sat down, and said, "We'll have a drop of wine; it'll put the strength back in our legs."

He was starting to open the musette bag when his wife raised her hand, saying, "Don't you hear something?"

"No. The wind, that's all."

Mostly he heard the beating of his heart and the wheezing in his bronchial tubes.

"There are some woodcutters on our right, not very far from here."

Père Dubois strained his ears, but he heard only the moaning of the wind and the crackling of the branches.

"I'm sure," said his wife. "I'm going to see."

The old man got up. "No, you'd just get lost away from the path. I'll go."

That's what he said, but the hill ahead, with its bad footing, frightened him.

"I couldn't get lost," his wife observed. "It's uphill. On the way back, I just have to go downhill. I can't possibly miss the path."

He made one more feeble attempt to stop her, but his fatigue completely undermined his will. Sitting on his rock, he watched her move off uncertainly, leaning against the trunks, lifting her feet to step over the underbrush. When she disappeared, Père Dubois felt alone, really alone in this wood, and regretted not having had the strength to restrain her.

Since they left, he hadn't once lapsed back into his depression of the night before. He had walked with pleasure, then with pain, but always with just the idea of walking. But now he was starting to feel a little lost again. Not at all because of the forest—he did know it well enough, after all, not to have any fears on that score—but because of what was stirring up again inside him.

He would never reach the end of this business with the stovewood. It was starting off too badly for there not to be more nasty surprises in store for him. When they got there, he would probably find that his cart had been broken or that it had disappeared. And then, making bundles takes a lot of work. If the wood had been down for several months, it would be partly dried and not easy to cut. He was no longer twenty years old, and neither was his wife. How much could they get done in a day? Ten, fifteen bundles, at most. It was a lot of trouble for not much of anything. It wouldn't do to get started back too late, to find themselves on the highway at night. And what was the path like, between the clearing and the highway? Picaud had said that it was passable, but he had his oxen to haul out his wood.

Père Dubois left his rock to go sit on another one that was in the sun. There wasn't really any wind in this hollow, but every now and then, long cold gusts would chill his back. The few steps he took proved that his fatigue was more serious than he'd thought when they first stopped. It burned the insides of his knees, and a few shooting pains, starting at the back of his neck, hit him in the forehead. He forced himself to breathe more slowly. This was no time to feel sick. His wife would panic. It would be a real mess.

But what was she doing? She'd thought she heard some wood-cutters; she'd gone off half-cocked and undoubtedly would get lost, wind up someplace where she'd go around in circles, and finally start back down the wrong hill.

Père Dubois forgot about his fatigue. Now it was anguish that gripped him. It seemed to him that an eternity had passed since his wife's departure. In going off like this, she was making them lose precious time. She was always wanting to do things her way and making a fool of herself. For more than twenty years, it had been like this. With Julien, as with everything, she did only as she pleased. He had been wrong to let her go off the path by herself and chase after that sound of axes she was probably just imagining. Because she didn't know these woods. You can get lost in any woods when you aren't used to them. She could have fallen into a hole, stepped on a snake. Good Lord, how stupid it was, this stubborn streak of hers.

Père Dubois struggled against his anguish for a long time. He pulled the bottle of wine and water out of the musette bag and took a swallow. Then he rolled a cigarette, which he lighted and began to smoke, savoring each puff, forcing himself to concentrate on the sense of well-being the tobacco brought him. It was really his only pleasure. A pleasure that dwindled from day to day with the rationing and the necessity of saving up a little of the ration to exchange for other luxuries.

As he felt numbness creeping over him, he got up and took a few steps in the shade, in the direction his wife had taken. The wind-filled shadows were in constant motion. Spots of light raced across the ground or climbed the tree trunks. The old man listened as hard as he could, but all he heard was the interminable song of the wind.

"This wind is making me drunk," he grumbled. "She might call, and I wouldn't even hear her."

He thought for a moment about going to look for her but told himself that in the thickest parts of the woods they could pass within ten yards of each other without even knowing it. If she came back and found only the musette bag and his jacket abandoned on the rock, she might get scared, go back up into the woods again, and they could lose hours that way.

He stood for a while with his back against a thick trunk, his eyes tired from searching for her in that flickering light and shadow. Then, almost in spite of himself, he cupped his hands around his mouth and began to shout, "Fernande . . . Fernande . . ."

He called like this in several directions but had the feeling that his voice didn't carry any farther than he could see. Then he fell silent and came back and sat down on his rock.

He felt weak. Those repeated shouts had left him light-headed, they had only aroused the pain that lay dormant in the depths of his chest, and he had to stand up to cough, hands on his chest, bending double, his throat choked with mucus and his eyes clouded with tears.

—◄ 13 ►—

"Good night, how long you took," said Père Dubois, sighing when his wife emerged from the trees.

"It was farther away than I thought," she said, sitting down beside him. "Sounds are very deceiving in the forest."

There was a long stretch of silence. Scarcely over his fit of coughing, the old man was having trouble recovering, but he nevertheless observed that his wife looked exhausted. Sweat was pouring off her face, her chest was heaving, and her back was bent as though the whole weight of the forest were resting on her meager shoulders.

"Well, did you see anyone?"

"Yes," she said. "We took the wrong path."

Père Dubois had thought as much, but his fatigue was such that this piece of news could add nothing to it. He let several more long moments go by before asking, "Is it far?"

"We have to go back to the fork, take the other path, and walk for quite a ways."

He felt like saying, "It's too far. Let's go home." But there was the cart. This thought was the only thing left to give him the strength to start off again.

"You can't go any farther," he said.

"Yes, I can. Come on."

He got up and started walking behind her. He went along, his eyes fixed on her skinny legs and the hem of her gray cloth skirt. So they had to go all the way back down this path again and then up another one.

They'd been walking since daybreak. They'd walked for nothing, because he'd stuck stubbornly to this path even after he'd sensed it was the wrong one. His wife had followed him. She'd also walked a long way farther, much farther, far away from any path, while he rested; then when she got back, she'd said, "We took the wrong path." She hadn't said, "You were wrong." She had given him no look or word of reproach, and now here she was, going first, not complaining, not even breathing a word about her own fatigue. She was younger than he, of course, she didn't suffer from the chest trouble that kept him from breathing freely, but she had her hernias, which must have pulled her stomach downward at every step she took.

Père Dubois walked, drunk with fatigue, gradually overcome by a drowsiness which only inhabited his head and let the rest of his body function like a slightly used piece of machinery that still worked from force of habit. From time to time, he roused himself enough to say to himself, "You should lead the

way. It's your duty. She's already done more than you have."
But aloud he said nothing. It seemed to him that the walking
was easier and that if he changed anything, if he came out of
his silence and broke stride for an instant, he would never get
going again.

When they reached the fork, Mère Dubois stopped, and the
old man almost ran into her back.

"I'll go first now," he said in a barely audible voice. She
turned around, looked at him, and appeared alarmed.

"You can hardly stand up," she said. "We have to rest."

"If we stop again, we're done for."

He'd spoken in a cracked voice, and a bit of coughing followed that happened because he'd made a considerable effort to choke back a sort of sob. Good Lord, he wasn't about to
break down and cry—no! Or else he'd really become a nothing.
Not even a shadow of what he used to be.

His wife made him sit down on a stump, a few feet off the
path.

"We're going to eat," she said. "I'm sure it's after ten o'clock.
It will do us good. My head is starting to spin a little."

He guessed that she was lying. She was acting this way for
his sake. He sensed this but said nothing. He had no resilience,
no strength to argue. The thought of time passing, of the wood
to cut, of the cart all alone in the woods still haunted him, but
it was very remote, motionless, heavy as a stone at the bottom
of a hole—a stone sinking imperceptibly into the mud. Soon it
would be covered over; there would be nothing left but the
compact dirt of fatigue.

Mère Dubois opened the musette bag and took out their
meal. At first, the old man had trouble eating. His tongue was
half-paralyzed in his mouth, where the saliva had dried up. He
had to force himself to swallow and repress a nausea he had sel-
dom known before. Then when he had got the first mouthfuls
down and drunk a half-glassful, he admitted that his wife had
been right. She had guessed that his fatigue came primarily

from the fact that he'd eaten very little before leaving. Unquestionably, he wasn't as feeble or worn-out as he'd thought a little while ago. When you've been the best athlete in your regiment and spent half your life wrestling with two-hundred-pound sacks, you aren't done in by going a few miles a little too fast, carrying a measly musette bag. Of course, at seventy, you aren't what you were at twenty, but you don't start folding up like a woman; there is still quite a difference.

He undoubtedly couldn't knock out as much work as he had in his youth, but he could still cut wood. He would prove it as soon as they got to the clearing. He looked at his billhook. It was there at his feet, its blade worn from trimming branches and being sharpened on the whetstone. He had made its handle himself, and his hand had worn it so well that it seemed to him when he took hold of it that his fingers and palm found places molded just to fit them. This old billhook would serve him again. He liked it because it was well balanced, not too heavy, but heavy enough to lend its weight to the strength of the man using it. It was an old billhook for cutting branches. And they would cut more branches, the two of them. Good, clean, uniform pieces as few of the younger fellows could turn out. They'd lost more than an hour, no doubt, taking the wrong path, but judging from the time it must be now, they'd easily make it up.

The still-hot coffee crowned the return of his enthusiasm. Now they just had to find that clearing and hope that the cart was still there, with all four wheels intact, as ready to carry the load as he felt ready to cut his share of branches.

As soon as his wife had packed everything again, he shouldered the musette bag, grasped his cane, and started off down the path. He went with a firm step. A step that was no longer the step of a worn-out old man.

—✠{ 14 }✠—

No doubt because he was sure of walking in the right direction, Père Dubois didn't find the path to the clearing long at all. The minute he saw, between the ash and oak trunks, the black roof of the cabin, he quickened his pace.

"You're going too fast." His wife panted.

"But we're here."

He could feel his heart pound. He could almost have broken into a run. He saw the tar-paper roof, the log cabin walls, the piles of big wood, the tree trunks lying on the ground among the branches, but still no cart. His heart was pounding hard, and it wasn't just because of the long walk.

"The cart. Dear God of dear gods, the cart!"

"What are you saying?"

Père Dubois had just spoken aloud without even realizing it.

"Nothing, nothing," he said, lengthening his stride even more.

Now his fatigue was completely forgotten. The long way they'd come no longer weighed on his legs. A single idea possessed him: the cart. He left the path as soon as they reached the clearing and turned sharp right toward the cabin. He stepped over stumps, stumbled, got caught in branches, swore at the woodcutters who had cleaned up the clearing so badly. He'd have liked to bound over the piles of logs as he used to. He went around them. His fear both spurred him on and held him back. The closer he got, the more convinced he became that his cart had been stolen. He gripped his big cane harder, his other hand clenched around the strap of the musette bag. Good Lord, he'd catch the ones who did it. Ah, the dirty rats. Did he dare look all the way? All the way around this shack built in the forest?

"You're mad!" cried his wife, whose voice was already far behind. "Don't go so fast!"

He didn't listen to her. Instead, he went even faster. And now there was nothing left between him and the cabin but one last pile of logs, which he passed. Nothing. In front of the cabin the ground was cleaner than in the rest of the clearing. Here it had been trampled a lot. Père Dubois paused a moment, but immediately his rage whipped him on. He went the length of the cabin, turned the corner. And then it seemed to him that all the air on the plateau and on the mountain rushed into him in a single gust.

He stopped.

It was there. It was there in front of him, a few steps away. He didn't dare move. His eyes flew from one end of it to the other, from one wheel to the other, nimbly climbed the length of the tongue which stood like a cross of light against the dark of the undergrowth.

It was there, and they hadn't broken it.

He just had time to give it this quick once-over before his eyes filled with tears.

Père Dubois took out his large checked handkerchief and wiped his eyes. His wife was behind him. He could sense her more than he could hear her.

"You were running like a fool," she said after a moment. "What's the matter?

The old man thought she was talking about his eyes, which he was wiping.

"It's the sweat," he said. "It's burning my eyes."

He took three steps, laid down the musette bag, picked up his cap, which he'd knocked off in passing the strap over his head, and slowly circled around his cart. He didn't take his right hand off the edge of the platform. He bent down before each wheel as though this were a thousand-year-old ritual. He studied the hubs where the rose-colored grease shone in the sun. He didn't mind at all that his wife was watching him. He had found his old cart again, after trembling so for it. He wanted to ask it if it had had a good trip, if the woodcutters had been too rough with it, if it hadn't been too cold during the night.

His head felt split in two. One half kept saying, "Gaston Dubois, you are a fool. You are seventy years old and you're talking to a cart exactly as a four-year-old would talk to his toy wagon." But the other half wouldn't listen. It cared only about the cart.

After this detailed examination, the old man stepped back to take it in again in one glance. Then he turned to his wife. She had sat down on a tree trunk; she wasn't even looking at the cart. She had her back to it. She wasn't any more worried about it than if they'd brought it with them. And Père Dubois found this indifference absolutely monstrous. Decidedly, this woman would never understand anything. For her, a cart was just a boring antique. If she had slept badly that night, it certainly wasn't because of the cart being alone in the forest.

Mère Dubois got up. At first her legs straightened and raised her body, but then it seemed to want to stay in a sitting position, exactly as though her back had jammed. Her stomach must have been pulling her forward, for she brought both hands to it. Slowly, she straightened and turned. On her face, a grimace of pain gradually gave way to a smile that had trouble forming among her wrinkles.

"Well," she said, "here we are. You see, they put your cart out back so it couldn't be seen from the path."

Père Dubois assumed a casual air of answer, "You know, these days people are too lazy to come this far to steal a cart."

The old woman's smile broadened. Was she making fun of him by any chance?

He shrugged his shoulders; then taking his billhook from the musette bag hanging on the tongue, he went toward the clearing, saying, "And that's not all, but now, we have to get to work."

His wife unhooked the musette bag and carried it over to the shade of the cabin, took off her woolen jacket, and picked up the roll of wire. Père Dubois had already stopped before a pile of branches. He spit on his hands, rubbed them together a little, and taking his billhook out of his belt, he went to work on the first branch.

–◄ 15 ►–

THEY worked a long time without speaking. Père Dubois felt in his element. Steady on his legs, he pulled the branches one by one from the main branch and cut them off clean with his billhook in one or two strokes, right at the joint, always with the grain, always close to the bark, neatly. What they needed was more small logs rather than twigs. They had enough kindling with what they pruned from the fruit trees in the garden. So he tried to make good-size bundles where the pieces as big around as his arm were more numerous than the rest. He kept the width of his cart in mind, and that was the length he cut to. He stripped, cut, and tossed the wood to the side. His wife would pick them up and tie them into bundles.

"Not too big," he would say. "So we don't have too much trouble loading them."

When a bundle was finished, she would tie it loosely with the wire.

"I'll tighten them later," her husband would say. "You wouldn't have the strength."

When she'd assembled a half dozen, Père Dubois hung his billhook on his belt, took the pliers, and tightened the ties. He would put his boot on the bundle, the toe next to the wire knot where the rest of the tie hung loose. Then he would pull with all his might, shaking the bundle when one branch refused to fit in among the others. Before getting back to his cutting, he took out his tobacco box and peacefully rolled a cigarette.

"At this rate," he said, "we'll soon have our load."

"Would you like a little to drink?"

"No, I'm just fine. We'll take a drink later on."

He lighted his cigarette; then he said, "What you should do, when you take a walk, is see what condition the path to the highway is in."

She smiled halfheartedly and remarked, "Take a walk—you know, I've already done quite a bit of walking this morning."

"You don't have to run. There's plenty of time. But I'd rather know, so we don't start off with a load and get stuck in a pothole."

His wife laid the ties down on a finished bundle, picked up a branch the length of a cane, and moved off. Père Dubois sat down for a moment to finish his cigarette and watched her progress. She seemed to be struggling as though walking through quicksand, though the ground in the clearing was quite firm. Decidedly, she might be younger, but she wasn't as strong as he was. He noted this with a sort of pride which kept him from considering the effort his wife must be making. He put out his cigarette and stashed the butt; then he went back to work.

Mère Dubois was gone for quite a while before returning to report, "You know, it must be a good mile from here to the highway. And the path is worse than the one we took coming. The oxen must have been over it with big loads of tree trunks. There are ruts fifteen inches deep, and in one hollow, there's still some mud."

"We'll have to get through somehow."

"I wonder if we wouldn't do better going back the way we came."

"With the loaded cart? But you don't realize!"

She made a gesture of helplessness. Père Dubois told himself that she must be exaggerating. Fatigue was clouding her judgment.

"That mudhole," he asked, "can't we go around it?"

"Oh, no. The only part that's been cut down is this clearing; the rest is the forest. You can't go off the path. And in that spot, it's very leafy, so the ground holds the moisture."

"If it's just one spot," he concluded, "we'll put down some branches and roll right over it."

"Well, I think you ought to go see for yourself."

Père Dubois felt so fine working—there was so much pleasurable vigor in his arm as it wielded the billhook—that he didn't even answer. He hadn't come there to take a walk, but to cut stovewood, and he was cutting stovewood. He and his cart had been through this before. The main thing was to have a good, well-packed load, and not to have come all this way for nothing. He was already mad enough at himself for having wasted time getting there. He had to keep his mind on making it back. He also blamed himself for that moment of weakness he had experienced, and he'd got it into his head to work hard enough to forget about it. Women always worry about things before they happen. If you listened to them, you'd never undertake anything important. Besides, his woman didn't know a thing about the forest. She didn't know how to evaluate anything. Neither the worth of a good cart nor the capacity of her man, whom she took for a worn-out old fuddy-duddy. One look at the wood he'd cut during her absence, however, and she ought to be able to get an idea of how much work he could really knock out.

"Let's go," he snapped. "Start making the bundles. I'll tie them up."

He'd got into a good working rhythm. He went along steadily, gauging each stroke, judging at a glance what ought to be cut away and what saved. He imagined what each finished branch would mean in terms of heat. Good small logs give off a lively heat and leave a nice bed of coals in the firebox, where you can lay a big log to burn slowly, with the draft closed. That would stretch out the wood young Picaud had delivered, and no two ways about it. He'd had a great idea, that fellow, with his bundles!

The sun beat down hard on the clearing, sheltered from the wind that continued its autumn song and dance up among the treetops. It was certainly perfect weather for work like this. Luck was with them; they must take advantage of it.

Père Dubois turned around. A good dozen bundles were already lined up.

"You see," he said. "It doesn't take so long."

"Perhaps we should start loading them now," suggested his wife, "and see what it looks like."

He started to laugh. "Don't you worry about the cart. It can carry twice that much."

"It can, maybe, but what about us?"

"You don't really think we're going to take off with the cart half full?"

"Whatever you say."

Mère Dubois wasn't smiling. She was always accusing him of being too gloomy, and yet today she was the one who was making a long face, while he felt more cheerful, more alive than he had in a long time.

He got back to work. It went a little slower because of a pain that had just flared up in his wrist. It wasn't serious, but it was enough to put a damper on his spirits. He had to give two or three strokes with his billhook to a branch he would have cut with one blow a quarter of an hour ago. Perhaps the wood was a little drier? He stopped a moment and turned in place to examine the other branches. Over there they seemed leafier. They must come from a more recent cutting.

"You're moving over?" his wife asked.

"Yes, the wood looks better to me over there."

"But we'll have to carry the bundles a longer distance."

"We're not even twenty yards from there . . . Go get us something to drink, and while you're at it, bring the whetstone out of the musette bag; I want to sharpen my billhook."

While waiting for his wife to return, he sat down on a stump, put his tool at his feet, and, gripping his right wrist very hard with his left hand, started clenching and unclenching his fingers. He could feel the ligaments tighten inside their girdle. The pain let up a little, diffusing into his whole forearm finally to lose itself.

"Does your wrist hurt?"

He hadn't heard his wife come back.

"No, no, I'm just limbering up my fingers a little."

"You scraped your left hand," she remarked.

"Bah, it's nothing." He rubbed it against his pants.

"You'll get it infected."

"No danger of that. In a forest everything is clean."

They each drank a glass of their wine mixed with water, which had got rather warm.

"The sun has moved," Mère Dubois said. "The bag wasn't in the shade anymore."

The old man looked at the sky. His wife must have read his thoughts, for she said, "You really should have brought your watch. We can't tell exactly—"

"It's surely not much later than three. I'll finish what's left to be done, and we can load up."

When he stood up, he had to press his lips together to stifle a groan. A knife had just cut through his back. He stiffened, and its blade sliced all the way up his spine, meeting up with two others that started in his hands and went up the marrow of his bones to the back of his neck. There the three shooting pains joined, knotting together like thongs pulled by a terrible force that could break his back.

"Good Lord"—he groaned—"I've dislocated something."

He scarcely dared breathe. That pause had cooled his body off. In wanting to get it moving again, he had reawakened all his fatigue. He made an effort of will, gripped his wrist again hard in his hand, and spit on the stone to sharpen his billhook.

"I should never stop—never."

He put the stone down and set to work on a branch. At each movement, he felt as if he were being stabbed with knives, whipped with nettles. It made a turmoil of pains inside him which battled with each other, fighting over each of his muscles. While he wrestled with the wood, he also had to struggle against this continual inner harassment.

He soon realized that the wood was no easier to cut here than elsewhere and that the fact of having sharpened his tool hadn't given him back any great facility. He stiffened his resolve, however, clinging to the idea that he hadn't taken all the trouble to come up this far just to go back with a half load of wood. He had told his wife that they would carry back two dozen bundles. It had been said, and he refused to go back on it. All the same, he turned around more and more frequently to count the bundles that she was lining up behind him. He had just counted eighteen when she asked, "Don't you think that's just about enough?"

"I said two dozen," he muttered, hardly opening his lips.

His face and body were drenched with sweat. He put down his billhook and took off his cap and his shirt.

"Don't get undressed," his wife snapped. "You'll catch cold."

"No, on the contrary. I'll take off my undershirt to let it dry, and I'll put it back on for the trip home."

His wife took the soaking undershirt and spread it in the sun on a pile of wood, saying, "My poor man, you really should stop."

He put his shirt back on and went back to work. When he turned around again, he noticed that his wife was making much smaller bundles. He felt like yelling at her that that meant wasting wire, but he said nothing. He decided to make two extra bundles, just to show her that he wasn't fooled, and yet when she came to stop him, saying that they had their limit, he heaved a long sigh and sank his tool into a log beside his undershirt.

"Shouldn't we make two or three more?"

He said that, but the question didn't really call for an answer. He knew what his wife would say, and she said it exactly. "Let's load what we have first. Then we can see."

Père Dubois fastened the ties. And that was another painful job because it reactivated muscles that had grown numb for a while, muscles that had lain dormant, wrapped in dimly remembered pains. But these pains revived like great hungry flames. They returned, sharper at each movement. The old man could feel them coming. He sensed their progress, waiting for the culminating moment. There was a kind of game between them and him, but the sides weren't evenly matched. All the rules were unfair. There was no point in his saying, "This time you won't get me," when, one after the other, they bit into his stubborn flesh. He had, however, never stopped working. He wasn't one to be surprised by fatigue because his body wasn't used to exercise. But the chores that he did in his garden every day were different from woodcutters' work. There had been the endless walk this morning, and then this job he'd tackled too hastily. He had hoped to find his old rhythm again. But before, he'd been a lot younger, and when he'd come to the forest, it had just been to cut bundles of stakes or pickets for his fence. He had thrown himself into this work like a wild animal to prove that he was still young, and the mechanism of his body had betrayed him. Warmed up, it had functioned while building up fatigue that didn't show at first. But once the limit had been reached, it all spilled out at once and now to his fatigue was added his fear of the return trip. What his wife had said about the path separating them from the highway came back to him. Had she really exaggerated? Would they, just the two of them, be able to get a fully loaded cart out of this clearing?

89

When the bundles were finished, they dragged them to the edge of the path and went to get the cart.

At first, the loading was almost restful. It was comforting to lift those nice firm bundles nestling in their ties. Père Dubois enjoyed counting them and finding that not one of them stuck out beyond the cart. It was a handsome load. The old folks who saw it going through town would certainly say to themselves, "That Père Dubois can still cut fine bundles of wood. He has an eye for it. And his cart is damn well loaded."

As the pile grew higher, the effort he had to make intensified, pulling the muscles in his arms and back. When he'd just hefted up the fifteenth bundle, he started to cough and had to stop. His wife hastened to get him a drink, but he took a long time catching his breath.

"We overestimated," she said. "We've got much too much."

He realized that she was right, but wouldn't hear of it.

"We'll move the cart over beside this woodpile," he said. "I'll climb up on it, and you'll just have to lean the bundles against the pile—I'll load them from up there."

"You'll break a leg."

"Don't worry."

It was as painful for him to talk as to work, and he dreaded a new coughing fit. His wife had to help him move the cart, which was already heavy. He put one foot up on the wheel hub and climbed onto the woodpile. The logs were thick, and the old man kept his balance easily. He was happy to see that the bundles reached all the way up to the rails. He would have a real load. He'd calculated just right. He got down, threw the rope with a precise gesture, and tightened it until the wood on the cart squeaked.

"We'll tighten it a little more when we get to the road. It will have settled into place."

His wife looked at the sky and said, "We'd better hurry. It's going to get dark soon."

It was true. The sun had begun to go down, and shadows invaded the clearing.

"I'll put my undershirt back on once we get to the road."

They hung the musette bag over a rail. Père Dubois stood near the tongue, and his wife at the back.

"All right," he shouted, "let's go!"

He leaned forward, pulling with all his might and prodding awake the pains which started up again along his arms and back. Once in motion, the cart began to bump along down the dry dirt of the path. There was a slight decline, and they just had to avoid the ruts and biggest roots to keep it rolling without too much trouble.

When they got in under the trees, darkness was already sliding over the ground. The air was less clear, and Père Dubois had trouble breathing. He felt like stopping a moment to catch his breath, but he noticed that the slope of the ground had changed direction. They were nearing a little rise, and it was better to keep up the momentum of their load to help them get to the top. It wasn't a very steep hill, but their pace slackened all the same and the old man shouted, "Ho."

Perhaps his wife was pushing less hard than at the beginning. This was no time to stop, to go see. He pulled harder, but the path was narrow, and it became difficult to avoid obstacles. When they got to a big root, half-eaten by the passage of the oxcarts, their front wheels jolted so hard that Père Dubois felt for an instant that his arms were being wrenched from their sockets. The front of the cart got over the root, but their pace was slowed so much that the back wheels didn't make it. The cart paused, Père Dubois threw his body and all his will into one last effort, but the inert weight of the bundles won out. They rolled back slightly, and he yelled, "Hold tight."

They let the cart roll backward until the front wheels were blocked against the root; then Père Dubois cried, "Put on the brake. I'm holding it."

Mère Dubois turned the little handle, and when the iron rims were locked, Père Dubois let go of the tongue.

"Goddamn root," he grumbled.

His wife was supporting herself with one hand on the handle, the other on her belly, which she seemed to be trying to knead and flatten. Her face was red and running with sweat under the shade from her hat. There was a long silence filled, for each of them, only by the turmoil of their bodies.

"We'll never make it," she gasped.

Père Dubois, a little frightened by the oncoming night, insisted, "We've got to, by God."

He looked around and went off a few steps to pick up a branch. He broke off the weakest end and slid the branch down between the rear rail and the bundles.

"If we stop again on an upgrade," he said, "wedge the wheels with this. It's faster than the hand brake. Come on, let's get going."

He gripped the tongue while his wife released the brake; then, as soon as she called out that she was ready, he shouted, "Let's go, ho!"

With a great, well-coordinated effort, they got over the root and reached the top of the hill without stopping. Through the shadows, Père Dubois could discern another hill, but the rise beyond didn't seem too steep. They would just have to get up a little speed, and they would make it. Pushed downhill by the load, he started to run. The cart bumped, the tongue jolted his arms, but he knew that everything was holding fast—the cart, as well as his own body.

When they'd got to within a few yards of the bottom, Père Dubois saw that this must be the place where his wife had noticed the soft ground, but he was going too fast to stop. He would have to use their momentum to try and get through.

"Ho!" he cried again.

It seemed to him that his wife wasn't pushing at all. As soon as they reached the flat stretch, the cart felt as if it were full of lead. It slowed, slowed and came to a stop despite the old man's best efforts, even though the ground felt fairly firm under his boots.

"By God," he roared, "it's not possible!"

He dropped the tongue and turned to find that all four wheels had sunk into the sides of the road where the ground was much muddier than in the middle.

A wave of rage swept over Père Dubois, and he began to shout, "That does it! You couldn't even warn me that this was the spot where we might get stuck! I would have gone ahead and looked, and I would have put branches over this crap."

His cough seized him, and he had to stop. When he was able to hear again, his wife explained, "This isn't the worst place; it's much farther on."

Père Dubois raised his arms.

"Well, then, it must be a swamp. You might have said so—"

"But I did say so."

"You didn't tell me anything at all. You wanted me to come and see. As though I had the time to spare. And if I'd wanted to come, there was no point in both of us wasting our time— and you weren't exactly eager to cut the branches. So now, my poor woman, you've gotten us into a fine mess—and you're not about to get us out of it either."

The more he talked, the more he realized that he was being unfair. He'd been wrong not to listen to her, but that made twice in one day that she'd been right, and it was too much. Especially in a field that he knew better than she did. He was aware of the injustice he was doing in getting angry at his wife, but his anger dominated him. He had no more energy left, except enough to feed that anger. It would be the ruin of him, but to stop it, some force superior to this flood of words would be required.

Mère Dubois said nothing. As always, she waited, her eyes fastened on her husband. And this look expressed nothing but a total submission. She accepted everything. She seemed only to be saying, "Well, then, be quiet. If that's the way you want things to be, then that's the way they'll be—I'm the one who got us into this mess. But don't wear yourself out shouting; you'll start coughing again." Père Dubois also knew that was the way his anger would end, but without really admitting it, he counted on that cough to save him from an unkind answer.

This time the fit lasted so long that he had to sit down by the side of the path to recover.

When he finally raised his head, darkness had flooded the path. The sky still looked light between the branches, but a few stars were already shining. The old man murmured, "What are we going to do?"

His wife walked around the cart several times. "Do you think that if we got branches—"

"Branches—we should have gotten them before this. Now that we're stuck in the mud, we're in it for good. We can't go forward, and even less backward."

"So?"

"Well, by God . . ."

He fell silent. Everything was crushing him. His exhaustion, this void the anger had left behind it, the swiftly advancing night, and now the cold that gripped his shoulders and plastered his soaking shirt to his skin.

"We could go home," suggested his wife, "and come back tomorrow morning."

Père Dubois rebelled at the very thought of going that long distance two more times. He started to shout again, but this time the fear of tearing his chest apart once more stopped him.

"Good Lord, good Lord"—he sighed—"I'd rather die here —lie down right here and die like an animal. At our age, to have to lead a life like this, it shouldn't be allowed. What can we have done to the good Lord to deserve this!"

He held back a sob, but his body was shaken by a chill, and

he stood up. Besides the cold of evening, the cold of the ground where he'd been sitting penetrated him. He was too afraid of pain to let himself go like that and lose control.

The thought of the nearby cabin and its key, which young Picaud had told him where to find, had just slid into his head. He didn't dare express it, but he said, "I don't think I have the strength to go back down again. And you're almost dead on your feet yourself."

"Well," his wife suggested, "while it's still light, we should go and see if we could really sleep back there."

Père Dubois was visited by the thought of his house, which would stand empty overnight, of his rabbits which might get stolen, but he had reached such a degree of exhaustion that he rejected these thoughts.

"To get out of here," he said, "we'll have to unload the bundles. It's the only way."

Mère Dubois unhooked the musette bag, picked up their clothes, and started walking.

"Give me my jacket," said Père Dubois, "I'm cold."

She turned around and put his jacket over his shoulders. Then, painfully, they made their way back to the clearing, where a little daylight still awaited them.

⊸⊸❨ 16 ❩⊷⊷

THE woodcutters' cabin consisted of one room, fairly large, where there was a long table made from an assortment of rough boards resting on six stakes stuck into the earth, two crooked benches, and a sort of alcove covered with straw. Holding his lighter at arm's length, Père Dubois embarked on a tour of the room, pulling down spider webs here and there with his free hand. An odor of rotten wood rose from the ground.

"It's very damp," said Mère Dubois, "and we don't even have a blanket."

At the moment the old man was thinking about his house and his bed, where he would have loved to lay down his aching bones.

"Do you want to try to get back home?" he asked.

"No," said his wife. "It's too late. We'd never get there."

Père Dubois discovered an old iron stove in a corner of the room. The stovepipe rose up straight to the roof, where a hole twice its size had been cut, letting the daylight in.

"We'll have to make a fire."

They started by burning a handful of straw to make sure the stove worked. A good draft was established almost instantly. The light from the flaming straw revealed a pile of wood chips and pieces the men had left there.

"A little fire will do us good," said Père Dubois.

"My poor Gaston, we're acting like children. We're staying here, and we don't have any blankets and nothing left to eat except this hunk of bread."

"I'm not hungry."

"Eat anyway."

She held out three-quarters of the bread to him.

"What about you?" he muttered.

"I have enough."

They didn't say much. They looked at the fire, held out their work-worn hands to it, their stiff limbs and their faces, where sweat had left furrows in the caked dust.

"We're not much to look at," said Père Dubois.

For a long time, they stayed like that, gradually growing numb from the heat. The old man was sitting on a wooden block he had dragged up close to the stove, his wife on a rickety crate. Père Dubois wasn't thinking about anything. His fatigue inhabited him; it was the only life inside his body and in his brain. He finally brought up to his mouth the bread that he'd been holding in his hand, a hand so tired there was no feeling left in it at all. He began to chew slowly, and as if she'd been waiting for this signal, his wife began to eat, too. They had no more coffee, but a little wine and water was left in the bottom of their bottle. Mère Dubois poured it into a cup which she held out to her husband.

"What about you?" he asked.

"I'm not thirsty."

She was certainly lying, but Père Dubois didn't have the strength to argue. He drank slowly. Handing back the cup, he sighed. "Now we have nothing left."

The old woman shook her head. The fire crackled. Tall flames rose from the belly and leaped snapping up the pipe, which was pierced by a multitude of little holes.

"With that rotten old flue," said Mère Dubois, "we could get asphyxiated."

"As long as the fire's burning, there's no danger. It's only later, when there's nothing left but coals."

He made a vague gesture, and his hands fell back onto his knees. If they were to die there, the two of them, they'd be freed from everything. Someone would come find them in a few days. They'd probably say, "It was lack of money that caused this tragedy." They'd also say, "But they had property. And children. And there they were, like tramps, without even a drop of water."

Père Dubois pulled out his tobacco box.

"If you smoke," his wife observed, "you'll get thirsty."

"No, a cigarette would relax me."

She gave a bitter little laugh. "Then I should smoke a whole pack."

"My poor woman! When I think that we could be nice and comfortable at home, with a good soup and a good bed . . . Good Lord, good Lord. To have worked like slaves and end up like this. To have killed ourselves raising two kids and now to be left all alone."

"If you get yourself agitated," Mère Dubois observed calmly, "you'll start coughing. And you won't even have a drop of water to drink."

Père Dubois swallowed his anger. They sat facing each other, with the fire half lighting them and burning their faces. They sat there, and between them, there was something more burning, more vivid than this fire. They looked at each other. The old man knew that his wife was thinking about Paul and his trucks. And he was thinking about Julien, who was young and strong, Julien, who would be able to get the wagon out of the mud and pull it all the way to the road. It was true. They each were right in their way. Paul was hardhearted, selfish, and Julien didn't give much of a damn about what the old folks might be doing. He was never around, that boy. He came home only to bring his dirty laundry to be washed and mended. And Paul went off and got mixed up in politics.

Those children were more trouble than fatigue or poverty. Worse than all their other hardships. And this trouble stood between his wife and himself, as hot as the wood-chip fire they constantly fed. But he didn't even have the right to talk about it. If he talked about it, his anger would erupt, and a new trouble would be generated. So they would remain sitting face to face, without saying anything except what was expressed in their eyes. They would continue to brood over their fatigue and their distress, waiting for a dawn that would bring nothing but work that was beyond their strength.

Had they really come here to die without even being able to say what was in their hearts?

As the fire was getting low, Mère Dubois stood up and put two or three pieces of bark on the embers. For the moment, it was nice and warm in the room.

"You ought to lie down for a while," she said. "Even if you don't get to sleep, at least you'll be able to rest a little."

He looked at the alcove. Seventy years old and ending up on a handful of hay already all flattened by other sleepers. Worse than his time in the regiment, worse than their billets in 1914, when they at least were able to find water and fresh straw. Where they had blankets and a coat to roll up under their heads.

As though she had been reading his thoughts, his wife picked up the musette bag and emptied it onto the table. Then, going over to the alcove, she stuffed the bag with straw.

"Here," she said, "this will make a good pillow for you."

"And what about you?"

"I don't feel like lying down for the moment. I'll stay near the fire."

Père Dubois got up. He was assailed at once by his horde of pains. He headed for the door, opened it, and went outside.

The sky was still clear, and the stars were twinkling as though there were a heavy frost. It was cold. The old man went to relieve himself a few feet from the cabin and hurried back inside. The cold had enveloped him, and long chills shook him, taking his breath away. He thought that they would go to sleep, the two of them, the fire would go out, and the shack would cool off at once. He took off his shoes and lay down on the straw that his wife had gathered at the end of the alcove. When he was settled, she turned up the collar of his jacket and fastened it under his chin with a safety pin. Already bathed in his pains, now diluted and mingled with his immense fatigue, Père Dubois let himself go. All he said was, "When you want to lie down, wake me up, and I'll tend the fire."

"All right," she said, "don't worry."

With his head on the musette bag, Père Dubois stared into the fire. He stopped thinking, and soon he was asleep.

—❦ 17 ❧—

DURING the night, Père Dubois had waked several times from his sleep, and each time he had seen his wife either sitting near the fire or busy putting more wood in the stove. He had opened his eyes; he had sought in himself the strength to get up and say, "Go and lie down in my place, I'll watch the fire." But he hadn't moved. And each time his fatigue had nailed him to the spot, incapable of action, at the mercy of the sleep he fell helplessly into.

He got up, however, a good hour before dawn, after having fought a terrible need to urinate as long as possible. His wife, who was leaning back against the cabin wall, raised her head.

"Did you get any sleep?" the old man asked.

"Oh, yes, don't worry about me."

Her voice was hoarse and weak.

"Lie down in my place. I don't feel like sleeping anymore."

She got up and went over to the alcove, where she lay down without a word. Père Dubois went outside. There were no more stars, and the wind had dropped. The sky must have been cloudy, but it was still very cold. When he came back inside, he said, "If it starts to rain, we're done for."

Mère Dubois must have reached the limits of her endurance. She scarcely opened her eyes. Père Dubois was frightened. She had the face of a dead woman. He looked at her for a moment and then went over to throw a few more chips on the fire. There was hardly any more firewood left. He had slept while she tended the fire. He felt guilty, but he told himself that she was younger and hadn't worked as hard as he had. He

100

was thirsty. His tongue felt sticky. He hesitated a long time but finally rolled a cigarette. The first puffs tasted awful, but soon he felt the smoke wake him up completely. His pains hadn't disappeared altogether, but he felt much stronger. While continuing to feed the fire, he got up from time to time to open the door and look at the sky. As soon as he saw it begin to pale beyond the treetops, he went back and stood by the alcove. His wife opened her eyes.

"You weren't asleep?"

"I was just dozing a little."

"It's almost daylight."

She heaved a great sigh that raised up her hands crossed over her stomach, turned on her side, and sat up on the edge of the pallet. When she had put on her shoes, she stood up, murmuring, "Let's go."

She emptied the straw out of the musette bag and repacked it with the billhook, the whetstone, the thermos, and the empty wine bottle. Père Dubois made sure the fire was out, carefully closed the door of the stove, and went outside first.

"To think we haven't even got one drop of coffee," said Mère Dubois.

The old man blamed himself for having let her sit up all night. From then on, he would have to see to it that things went smoothly, so she wouldn't have to work too hard. When they got back to their stalled cart, it was still barely light in the dense forest. Père Dubois had already taken hold of the rope to untie the load when his wife suggested, "What if I went to Pannessières to see if I could get a man to come and pull us out with a horse?"

"If we had to pay wages for a man and a horse, these would be pretty expensive bundles. Let me do it. We have the whole day ahead of us. We just have to hope that it doesn't rain."

He felt strong. Not because his fatigue had vanished overnight, but simply because he'd stopped really thinking. One idea filled his head: to get out unaided. The whole world had abandoned him. Even his children wanted to see him dead. Well, he wasn't about to die! He'd get his stovewood out, and he'd get it out alone. His wife had lost her strength and her courage, so he'd show her what a seventy-year-old man was capable of doing. He had an idea. When you don't have the strength, you can get out of a bad spot with a good idea.

He untied the rope and climbed up on the rail. He had made good sturdy bundles; that was lucky. At least he could throw them onto the ground without fearing that they might come apart.

"Get out of the way!" he shouted.

Mère Dubois moved back. He had twenty-four bundles there; he counted out sixteen, which he threw onto the edge of the path. When there were only eight left on the platform, he climbed down off the cart, saying, "We'll be able to pull what's left, I think. Come on."

"And you're planning to leave the rest behind?"

"Don't worry. You'll see. We're going to pull, and you just warn me before we get to that swamp you told me about."

He picked up the tongue, braced his feet carefully, and yelled, "Come on, ho!"

His wife wasn't thinking clearly. He knew that. It was his brain that would have to plan everything. The old woman had nothing but a tiny bit of strength left to add to his.

He pulled, turned the tongue to the right, then to the left, but the cart only rocked imperceptibly. He straightened up, crying, "Hold it, don't kill yourself!"

"We'll have to unload some more."

"No. It moved. It'll get out. You come and take my place. You just take care of the steering and pull a little. I'll do more good on the back."

Mère Dubois obeyed. He realized that she was no more than an animal without a will and that he just had to urge her on and not listen to her. This weakness in his wife redoubled his own strength.

When she had taken her place at the tongue, he braced himself behind the cart, legs flexed, shoulder against the floor beam, as if he actually wanted to lift the load.

"Let's go!" he shouted.

Eyes closed, jaws clenched, he strained his body and started to push with his legs. He felt that the cart was slowly rising, that the wheels were pulling out of the muck in the path. From the depths of his chest, a cry burst forth that sounded like the roar of a wild beast.

"Ho!"

The cart broke loose all at once, went at least a half yard, then stopped as Mère Dubois cried, "Stop!"

The old man straightened up and ran to the front, shouting, "For God's sake, don't stop! We're out—"

His wife was on her knees, her hands on the ground. She had trouble getting up, and he had to help her.

"When it started moving," she panted, "I slipped."

He felt like hitting her, but the sight of her ravaged face stopped him.

"Did you hurt yourself?"

"No, I'll be all right. My poor man, I'm nothing but a burden to you."

That word did him good. He felt like taking her in his arms, but it had been so long that he had forgotten the gesture. He simply said, "Now that it's out, it'll go. But I'm going to take the tongue again. It's too dangerous for you. When a wheel bumps, those things can throw you right onto the ground."

Mère Dubois went back to the rear, and they started off again. The path wasn't easy, but they got to the mud hole without too much difficulty. Père Dubois stopped the cart before the little stretch that sloped down to it.

"I think we can get through," he said, "but it'll be easier if we put down some branches."

He took his billhook and started to cut low branches off

the nearby trees. His wife dragged them over to the mudhole and laid them across the path. When the mud had a good thick covering over it, they started off again and were able to get through without incident. The rest of the path to the road was better, and they got to the end with only two stops.

"And now," said Père Dubois, "we only have two more trips to make."

His wife had no doubt guessed his intention, for she showed not the slightest surprise. She merely looked at the sky, where thick clouds were scudding by, and then sighed, "Provided it doesn't rain."

"Come along now. Once we've got it all out of the woods, we'll be all right."

Père Dubois felt strong enough for both of them. Since they'd been able to get through on the first trip, they'd make it on the others. And indeed, they succeeded. It wasn't exactly easy, of course, but the cart went well, and the old man felt at ease. It seemed to him that if he'd had something to eat and drink, he would have gladly cut a few more bundles. But hunger and thirst were gnawing at his throat and stomach.

When he had repacked and secured his entire load, he asked, "Did you bring any money?"

"Of course not. With the danger of losing it in the woods, it wasn't worth it."

"That's stupid, we could have had a drink at Pannessières."

"I know, but I didn't think of it."

On the way back, the road went downhill all the way to town. All they had to do was steer the cart and work the brake according to the steepness of the slope. Père Dubois walked ahead, leaning on the crossbar of the tongue, which banged into the small of his back. His wife held onto the side of the cart, ready to tighten or loosen the brake. At Pannessières, they stopped to drink at the fountain. The water was cool, and they wet their faces.

"You're hot," said Mère Dubois. "Don't drink too much."

Père Dubois went back to his place; his wife released the brake, and they were off again. At first, the old man had turned around several times to check his load. Now he didn't even bother. All was going well. He knew it. He had behind him, nudging him in the back, his long lost cart and two dozen good bundles of stovewood he'd cut with his own hands and his old billhook.

And it was a beautiful piece of work. A job well done, by a man who had never done anything halfway. Bread, soil, wood —it all got worked in the same way: with his heart, as well as his hand. Nowadays people had almost forgotten that, but he saw no reason to stoop to laziness and shortcuts. He had to answer to his own conscience. Never had he even thought of cheating, and he wasn't about to begin after sixty years of labor. What the young did was no concern of his. They were alone, his wife and himself? Well, so be it; they'd be able to make it alone. They needed neither Julien's youth nor Paul's money. Asking favors wasn't in his nature. He had been right to hold out against his wife. If he'd gone and asked Paul for help, he would have risked getting an answer that hurt him. If Paul had agreed, the job would have been easier, and they undoubtedly would have brought down twice as much wood, but even so, it was better like this. He didn't know why, but he really thought so. He believed it, despite the immense fatigue that pushed him down the slope with an even greater force than his well-filled cart. He kept clinging to this idea, even when he got to the bottom of the hill and had to start hauling his load once more.

In town, there were a few upgrades, and no one was around to lend them a hand. That was because it was almost one in the afternoon, and people were still eating. Père Dubois took a kind of fierce satisfaction in this. All alone. They would see it through to the end alone.

They'd reached the top of the Rue des Écoles when he felt the first drops of rain tingle on his face. The sky seemed to hesitate a moment; then like an April shower, the downpour burst all at once. The street filled with a strong odor of wet dust. The swastika in front of the gates of the École Normale snapped in a gust of wind, and Père Dubois saw the guard, dressed and helmeted in green, take shelter in the black and white guardhouse. It even seemed to him that the soldier laughed at them as they went by, but he didn't give a damn about that laugh.

"The brake!" he shouted.

The iron blocks screeched against the wheel rims, and the load pushed more gently. Père Dubois stopped his cart outside the garden gate and set the brake.

"We'll bring it in when it stops raining," he said, taking the key to the gate out of his pocket.

They hurried as fast as they could up to the house, but before climbing the steps, Père Dubois went to count his rabbits and gave them a handful of hay.

When he got inside the kitchen, his wife had already opened the shutters. She brought two glasses and the water pitcher from the laundry. They drank slowly, savoring each swallow.

Now there still was the fire to start and the meal to cook, but the old couple sat on their chairs, motionless, nailed down by the exhaustion uniting them.

From time to time, they looked at each other. They felt no need to talk. They were sitting face to face, in their long-lost house, with the rain beating angrily on the windowpanes.

They looked at each other without speaking, but they both knew that this trial shared in common had brought them closer, no doubt closer than sharing a great joy could have done.

Part Two

A LONG WINTER NIGHT

THAT evening, shortly before nightfall, a blast of wind coming from the northeast made the fire growl. Père Dubois went over to the window and watched the dead leaves race across the black earth of the garden. Then, coming back to sit down, he rested his elbows on the edge of the table, put his feet in their heavy gray wool socks up on the stove door, and sighed. "Now winter's really here."

For a long time, he listened to the wind. His eyes went from the denuded tall pear tree whipping against the gray sky to the clear flame that danced behind the firebox grill.

Finally, when the wind had settled in, when it had fixed its rhythm and course and pushed the disorder of its first fury beyond the horizon of somber hills, Père Dubois stood up again to put two logs from the arbor on the fire and regulate the draft. When he'd hung the poker back on the brass rail, he returned to his seat and repeated, "Now winter's really here."

"Do you think it's going to snow?" his wife asked.

"As long as this wind holds, you can't tell. But if it slacks off, we might get quite a lot. The cold weather's setting in. I've felt it coming since this morning. My shoulder hurts . . . And the proof that I had a hunch about it is that, just now, in going to lock up the shed, I put some sacks in front of the rabbit hutches."

He got up again to stand in front of the window, his feet stuck into the toes of his slippers. He stood motionless a moment, one hand on the sill and the other plunged into the front pocket of his big blue smock. The visor of his cap touched the windowpane, which fogged up gradually from his rapid breathing.

"I think you can light the lamp," he said. "I'll close the shutters. What we'll lose in light, we'll save in heat."

When he'd closed the heavy wooden shutters he'd lined with black paper to block the cracks, he closed the window again, drew the flowered curtains, and went back to his seat. The effort just made and the blast of icy air he'd inhaled cut off his respiration. He sat without moving for several minutes, one hand flat on his chest, the other gripping the corner of the table. His wife finished trimming the lampwick, slowly raised it back up on its squeaky chain, then peered at her husband. "You seem very short of breath tonight."

"You know perfectly well that the first cold weather always does this to me. I'll have to start taking my syrup again."

"You can't get syrup anymore. You need a prescription. And even then, they'll give me that unsweetened stuff that makes you feel like vomiting."

"We might as well just drop dead. When I think that it's only the beginning of December . . . What will we do if the cold really sets in!"

He said this without anger. It was a simple statement. Everything seemed to be conspiring to hasten the end of old people like themselves who'd lost the means of fighting back. He repeated these same words endlessly, and they always got the same answers. Again, tonight, his wife said, "My poor Gaston, everybody's in the same boat. Everybody's suffering."

"Yes, and everybody's going to end up dead."

Mère Dubois did not show the slightest sign of anger either. They sat there, the two of them, with their troubles, but with no desire to revolt. In the long struggle that their life had been, their best resources had been exhausted, and all that was left was just enough strength to cling to the little bit of life that remained in them. The old man sensed it. He groused about the cold, and yet it sometimes seemed to him that winter was the easiest season to get through after all. The nights stretched out; the days were like a long twilight that forced him to stay quietly beside his fire. He would sit huddled up, like a lamp whose wick had been lowered to save oil. And then even the war would seem to go to sleep. It all happened very far away, in countries whose names meant nothing to him. Here, even the Germans seemed to quiet down, and if they ordered a six o'clock curfew, it wasn't as inconvenient as in summer. In short, living this way, there were long periods of the day when everything seemed normal. It was the past that occupied more time, and Père Dubois spent hours looking back over his life, selecting for himself some episode to relive with all its images intact in every detail.

Mère Dubois had put a little pot on the back of the stove. The steam from it smelled of good cooked vegetables. She lifted the lid, brought up another pot and her food mill, and started passing the soup through it. It was an old food mill. It stuck sometimes, and the effort she made wrenched her back.

"Don't force it," said Père Dubois. "Turn it back a little. If you force it, you might break the handle, and you'd never find one to replace it. These days—"

She turned around and cut him off with a gesture. He was about to raise his voice to say that he did have a perfect right to make an observation, but from his wife's expression, he saw that that wasn't why she had turned around. She was standing sideways, one hand in the air and the other holding the mill over the pot with the broth dripping into it. Her eyes were fixed on the door. Her face was strained.

Père Dubois tried to listen harder, but all he could hear was the crackling of the fire and the bubbling of the pot.

"It's the wind," he said.

"Be quiet. I'm sure someone rattled the cellar door."

"Well, then, I'll go have a look."

"No, you'll catch cold."

While she was putting down her mill and the old man was getting into his slippers, there was a sharp rap on the shutter.

"This time I'm not dreaming," said Mère Dubois.

Père Dubois had heard it, too. His heart had started beating very fast. It seemed to him that all the peaceful warmth of the kitchen was about to dissolve into the cold of the night enveloping the house. Nothing good could come of this. Was someone after his wine? His rabbits? His wood piled in the shed?

A minute ticked by, interminably. Finally, Mère Dubois took the flashlight, whose battery was almost dead, and, not making a sound, opened the door a crack. Aiming the orange beam onto the stoop, she stuck her head outside and cried in an uncertain voice, "Who's there?"

Père Dubois was standing behind her. He'd picked up the poker, which he held in his right hand.

There was a bang against the trash can, and the clang of metal seemed enormous in this night where they could no longer even hear the wind whistling.

"That you, Mama?"

Mère Dubois opened the door wide and took a step out. The old man wasn't sure he'd recognized Julien's voice. He went out anyhow. The flashlight beam revealed only the stone steps and the corner of the house, but the voice came again. "You all alone?"

"Of course, son. Come up. Come right up."

Père Dubois stepped back a little to let his son in. But his mother hadn't waited for him to get inside the kitchen before flinging her arms around his neck and hugging him. The icy wind cut like a knife in through the doorway. The flame inside the lamp wavered in spite of the glass. The old man contained himself for a few seconds, then said, "Come inside. You're chilling the house, and the light can be seen from outside."

He hadn't yet looked at his son's face, but once they got into the light, he could only stammer, "Oh, good Lord. Oh, good Lord."

Julien had grown a chestnut-colored beard, and his hair, formerly cut very short, was pulled back to just above his coat collar, where it curled up into a sort of ducktail.

"Oh, good Lord," his father repeated, "I can't believe it."

What could be seen of Julien's face was tanned, and his blue eyes seemed lighter.

Père Dubois turned to his wife, who was standing speechless, her hands outstretched, her mouth hanging open, and her eyes brimming with tears.

Julien kissed his father on both cheeks; then taking his mother back into his arms, he lifted her up a little and held her for a moment like this, pressed against him. Père Dubois took off his cap to scratch his scalp and, shaking his head, sat slowly back down. There was a long silence, during which Julien took off his overcoat and hung it on the bannister post.

"You—you don't have a suitcase?" his mother asked.

"Yes. It's in front of the cellar door. It's all right there for the moment."

His father couldn't take his eyes off that bearded face. At first, he had felt a blow to his heart, with a kind of contraction of his whole chest, and then, now, it was like a big void opening up inside him. Nothing. He found nothing to say. Nothing to ask. And his wife must feel the same way, standing there, rooted between the table and the stove, staring at their boy, who had sat down on the second step of the stairs and was taking off his shoes.

The winter night, disrupted for a moment, chased far beyond the limits of the garden, crept back gradually, with whispers of wind in the pear tree, the muttering of the fire, and the monotonous song of the water in the kettle with the copper lid.

Slowly, Père Dubois settled down again. His body sank into its slightly stooped position of waiting in his chair. Elbows on the table, he stretched out, flattening his hands on the oil-cloth while his feet slid out of his slippers to return to their place propped up on the stove door.

—⊷{ 19 }⊶—

AFTER a few interminable minutes, during which Mère Dubois wiped her eyes several times, there came a moment of frenzy. She started running around the kitchen, asking questions and answering them at once herself.

"Have you had anything to eat? Of course not. And you must be starving. What can I make? There is some soup. There must be a few eggs left. If it wasn't so late, we could have killed a rabbit. In any case, I'll peel some potatoes. Here, Gaston, would you mind finishing the soup?"

Père Dubois put on his slippers and got up. She was crazy! And it was the same story every time Julien came back after a long absence. Only tonight there was the fact that they'd been a million miles from expecting him.

From time to time, while working on the soup, the old man turned to glance at his boy, who was still sitting on the stairs. His mother kept running around, opening the cupboard, go-ing into the laundry, pulling on a drawer that was stuck, which she shook to loosen with a great rattling of silverware. Père Dubois felt irritation sweeping over him. He fought for a mo-ment against the desire to shout at his wife to calm down a lit-tle, but finally, he turned to Julien to ask, "Whatever got into you, to grow a head of hair like that?"

The boy started to laugh.

"It's a big joke," he said. "But still, if I don't want to get caught, I have to take a few precautions."

"You know that the police are looking for you," said his father.

"That doesn't surprise me!"

"But it doesn't seem to frighten you."

"Well, you know, I'm not the only one."

"Come, now," said his mother, "let him at least tell us where he's come from."

Père Dubois swallowed his anger. His son's almost ironic tone of voice had hurt him. All right, then, this boy was a deserter. The police were on his heels. They thought he was in England, and here he comes and shows up here, all smiles, with a ridiculous beard and hair like a girl's. That's the way it was, and his mother seemed to be saying that it was nothing to get upset about.

He fished the rest of the vegetables out of the bottom of the pot while Julien explained. "I've come from Marseilles. I was staying with a friend. A painter. A very nice guy. I didn't write you because I didn't want any trouble. The militia are everywhere, even in the post offices."

"But what were you doing in Marseilles?" his mother asked.

"Painting, with my buddy. I could have stayed there; only it's hard to get food down there. And I don't have a ration card."

He stopped. His father had turned around. His mother had stopped setting the table to listen to her son.

"You don't have a ration card?" she said.

"No. I was able to get a false identity card, but ration coupons are another story."

His father was thinking, *Now we're really in a fix. We can't even get enough for ourselves.* He said nothing, and it was his wife who asked, "My poor boy, but what did you do?"

"We managed. But you know, it wasn't always so easy."

She had gone over to Julien, who stood up.

"You're just skin and bones," she said. "With your beard, it's not noticeable at first, but now that I take a good look— My God, it's lucky you were able to get home."

"We still haven't had our dinner," said Père Dubois. "He can tell us all this just as well while we're eating."

He noticed that his wife shrugged her shoulders. However, she said nothing, threw her black wool shawl over her head, took the key to the cellar, lighted the flashlight, and went out. Père Dubois had sat down again, but he sat a little stiffly in his chair, not leaning back, looking at his son seated across from him at the other end of the table. He was trying to think of something to say, a question to ask, when he suddenly jumped. His wife had screamed.

"What's the matter?" he asked.

Julien got up, seemed to hesitate, then, heading for the door, said, laughing, "Damn, I'd forgotten all about him. She must have run into Séraphin."

"What did you say?" asked his father.

But Julien was already on his way out, adding, "Don't worry, I'll go. He's not a bad guy."

Père Dubois didn't dare get up or really sit down either. He stayed on the edge of his chair, straining his ears, trying to make out the voices of his wife and Julien. They were talking down there—that was certain—but with the wind, he could hear only a confused murmur. So Julien wasn't by himself. But what in the world could that mean? Good Lord, to be so peacefully at home, with all the doors closed, with a good fire going, and suddenly to find yourself in all this commotion, with the doors constantly being opened and the winter rushing in—perhaps with a stranger about to arrive. And who was it anyhow? What kind of person? An artist, a bohemian perhaps? A whole life of hard work to wind up with your few hours of peace interrupted. And with nothing to say about it. One wrong word, and your wife

116

would be on your back. He just knew it. She'd say he was being egotistical again.

There was a bump against the bars of the outside railing, then another against the door, which slowly opened. Mère Dubois appeared. She held three eggs in one hand and the flashlight in the other.

"Bring in your suitcase," she said, "but leave the rest on the doorstep."

She seemed paler than usual. Père Dubois got up and heard: "You're kidding. Then you should have let me leave him in the cellar."

Julien had just pushed the door wide open with his foot, and the old man stood with his mouth agape, one hand holding the visor of his cap, the other resting flat on the table. He stared; that was all he was capable of doing. Not one word came to him. Not even one thought.

Julien entered, holding clasped against him a human skeleton. A skull, arms, all made of bone, all held together by three large pieces of string that also secured a roll of white paper, which the skeleton appeared to be clutching to its ribs.

As the boy put down his suitcase and his mother prepared to close the door, in a voice that sounded very shaky, Père Dubois said, "You're not planning to— You'll kindly do me the favor of leaving that outdoors."

Julien looked surprised.

"What?" he said. "It's not dirty. It's Séraphin. It's been at least thirty years since he kicked the bucket."

"But you're not going to bring that thing into this house."

This time the old man had shouted very loud. His son seemed to hesitate.

"I could at least put him in my room. He's a tool of the trade."

"A tool of the trade," the old man stammered.

For several seconds, these words rang in his head. A tool of the trade! That beats everything. He looked at the skeleton, and at the same time, he saw a kneading board, a spade, his billhook, his wheelbarrow. A tool of the trade, that!

"Listen, Julien," said his mother. "Your father is right. We don't keep things like that in the house."

The boy appeared not to understand. He looked from one of them to the other, astonished, with a half-smile that made a light stroke above his beard.

"My goodness," he finally said. "If you insist, he can sleep out on the stoop. I guess he won't catch his death. But all the same, I'm going to keep my paper with me. The dampness would ruin it."

He laid the skeleton down on the floor and took a table knife to cut the strings. His father sprang forward.

"Not with that."

"What?"

"Come on, that's disgusting. Use the old scissors."

Julien sighed, and obeyed, saying, "I don't understand you. Here's a guy who was just like the rest of us. All right, he died. They cleaned him. And since then, he's been in my friend's studio."

He put his roll of paper on the sideboard and picked up the skeleton, whose dangling arms clattered against his ribs.

"If he were made of plaster," said the boy, "it would be exactly the same thing."

"Leave him on the stoop overnight," said his father, "but tomorrow morning, we'll have to get him out to the shed as soon as possible. If somebody came—"

Julien came back inside.

"You know," he said, laughing, "it's been a long time since he bit anyone. And in his lifetime maybe he was a good guy. We don't know; maybe he was a murderer. Condemned criminals often end up like that. But at least he didn't have his head chopped off, his cervicals are perfect. He's very well-preserved, you know—"

His mother interrupted him. "Go wash your hands. And

118

don't talk about that anymore. You're upsetting your father."

"Oh, yes," said his father. "He's upsetting me all right. To think how we worried about him, and to have him arrive like this. With—with that hair and with that dead man."

Julien was in the laundry. He'd left the door open to let some light in. The cold came into the kitchen almost as sharply as if it were coming directly from outdoors. That was a bad sign. Père Dubois thought about it, then returned to the idea of the skeleton.

"And you got on the train with that?"

"Well, yes. And you see, he doesn't even have to pay the fare."

"For someone who's wanted by the police and doesn't want to look conspicuous, you're off to a good start."

"Exactly. The cops would never suspect someone so outlandish. And then, on my identity card, I'm listed as a professor of drawing. As my friend says, you have to look the part."

His father couldn't get over it. His mother asked, "A professor of drawing? You? At your age?"

"But on my card, I'm twenty-nine."

Julien came back and sat down at the table. The old couple were still standing, not daring to look at each other, watching this bewildering boy, who had just come with the night and the first cold.

Père Dubois shook his head. His son was there. He had a beard and hair like those you see on Christ in religious pictures. He came from Marseilles. He called himself a professor. He was carrying an old dead man under his arm. And he was his son . . . He was named Dubois like himself . . . He had a beard . . . A dead man under his arm . . .

-⅏{ 20 }⅏-

THE boy arrived just like that, without any warning, with his
artist hairdo and that atrocious dead man. He arrived, and the
old lady went crazy. It was as if someone had set the house on
fire. She turned everything upside down. She served him two
huge plates of soup and, besides, told him to put bread into it.
As if bread weren't rationed. She made him three fried eggs.
As if eggs . . . And he didn't even have a ration card. Say something about it? The old man wasn't about to do that. He
knew the answer in advance: "He's your son! You act as though
you weren't glad to see him!" Glad? Of course, he was glad. But
just the same, seeing him in that condition gave him quite a
shock. Was his mother really blind? She was devouring him
with her eyes. She was drinking in his words. That boy could
show up someday and announce that he'd committed a crime,
and she'd give him the same welcome. And to think they'd
thought he was fighting with De Gaulle. But no. Not even that.
What had he been doing since his desertion? He was in the
process of telling them, all the while eating soup and eggs and
enormous pieces of bread. He'd been living with a friend, leading a bohemian life. And he said it without blushing. To him,
it was perfectly natural. He'd left Marseilles only because his
friend was going away, and he didn't feel up to getting along
by himself.

For a long time, Père Dubois remained silent, bent over his
empty plate, stealing looks now at his son who was talking,
now at his wife who was listening stupidly with an air of
breathless admiration that irritated him. Finally, unable to

stand it any longer, he broke down and asked, "And now— what are you planning to do now?"

Julien made an evasive gesture and a face that twisted his beard.

"I don't know exactly . . . Here I can probably hide out for a while."

There was a triangular exchange of questioning looks. The boy hesitated a moment before adding, "I have some work to finish. I could do it here."

"Work?" asked his father.

"Yes."

"But what kind of work?"

"Oh, I can't explain it to you. It's very complicated."

"Of course, and we're not intelligent enough to understand." Mère Dubois intervened.

"Come on," she said, "don't get mad, Gaston. But if it's a painting job, it's quite true that we don't know much about it."

"Painting?" asked the father. "But where can he do any painting around here? And that's not work at all."

"No," admitted Julien, "it's not painting. It's a . . . thing I have to write. Anyway—"

He stopped, looked at his mother, his father, then sighed, pushed his empty plate away, and took a pack of cigarettes and a box of matches out of his pocket.

"What!" said his mother. "Do you smoke now?"

"Well, yes, I do. I'm old enough."

Before helping himself, he held the pack out to his father, who hesitated.

"I don't smoke at night."

"Come on, just this once."

Père Dubois felt a crowd of contradictory thoughts jostling inside him. If he accepted this cigarette, he wouldn't be able to say a thing to Julien. And yet a cigarette, could he bring himself to refuse? In spite of himself, his hand advanced toward the pack.

"You'll be coughing all night long," observed his wife.

"What do you mean?" said Julien. "One cigarette's not going to hurt him. You know very well that if Papa coughs, it's because of his asthma."

"Exactly," she said.

But the old man was already bringing the cigarette up to his lips and pulling his lighter out of his pocket. Without conviction, his wife added, "You know, he smokes too much already."

Père Dubois savored the first puffs. It was pleasant, smoking like this, without hiding, without having to go out into the cold or down to the toilet. There was a comfortable silence, during which he thought it would be nice to live like this, with the good taste of tobacco. However, one question was burning his lips. He swallowed it back several times before letting it slip out between two puffs of smoke. "If you don't have any coupons, how do you manage to get tobacco?"

Julien started to laugh.

"In Marseilles, you know, it's easier to find tobacco on the black market than bread or potatoes. The waiters in all the cafés sell cigarettes. And I suppose it must be the same way here."

"I don't know," said his father. "I never go to a café. In any case, the price would be too high for my budget."

"Besides," his wife put in, "you get enough to make you cough from your ration."

Père Dubois felt like answering his wife harshly, but other words were stirring in him. When he'd mentioned cafés, an idea had come to him, but he'd wanted to talk about prices, and he hadn't expressed it. It was still there, however, and he might as well say it.

"No"—he sighed—"I've never been a man for cafés, but in the old days, I used to stop and have a glass with friends now and then, when we met in town. But now I go out as little as possible."

He thought that Julien would ask him why he didn't go out anymore, but the boy remained silent, staring at the cigarette burning between his fingers. Avoiding looking at his wife, Père Dubois went on. "I wouldn't want to criticize you—you just got here, you must be tired, but after all, we'd still like to know what happened. You were a soldier, you deserted, and here we are with the police on our backs!"

Julien was about to speak, but his mother broke in, "You can't say that they've given us much trouble."

"They haven't given us much trouble because they know me. But in any event, it's not a spot to be in, and now that he's here—"

He had raised his voice, but his wife interrupted by talking louder than he.

"They don't come every day, and they've never searched the house."

"Why," asked Julien, "have they come several times?"

"Several times," snapped his father. "Well, I should say they have come several times, do you think that—"

This time he was cut off by his cough. While he was getting up to spit into the fire, his wife poured him a little water.

"Your tea will be ready in a few minutes," she said.

"Which means that I'll go up to bed. And leave you two in peace."

"My poor man, one can't say anything without your getting angry. I mentioned your tea because you were coughing, and that's all."

Julien started to laugh, saying, "I see you haven't gotten over your habit of squabbling over everything."

Père Dubois could see that the conversation was about to take a turn that would keep him from getting to the point of his idea. He must avoid losing his temper, but things had to be clarified.

"Well," he said, "you must be aware of what's going on. And of the risks you're taking—and us, too."

"Risks, you know—right now there are millions of young guys going around with false papers who left the STO."

"But you are a deserter."

"Deserter from an army that was sold out to the Germans. That's nothing to be ashamed of."

Père Dubois looked at his wife. He realized that she wasn't on his side. That was natural. If he got angry, she would talk about Paul and the militia. And there would be his rage again, a fight that would leave him torn, a victim of his cough while the others kept on talking.

"The tea must be ready," he said.

His wife got out a bowl and the sugar. As she was about to pour, Julien got up and said, "Don't put any sugar in it. Wait a minute."

He opened his suitcase, took out some dirty laundry and some papers, then a pot of honey, which he put on the table.

"Good heavens, where did you find that?" asked his mother.

"In my suitcase."

"But where did you get it?"

"From one of my friend's uncles. He lives in Provence. He used to bring us some occasionally. My friend said, 'Here, take this to your folks.' He's a good guy, you know."

His father looked at the pot of honey. For more than a year it had been impossible to find any at a reasonable price.

"And it's lavender honey," said Julien. "Help yourself. It's good."

"You see," observed his mother, "you're lucky to have a son who thinks about you."

From her look and the movement of her lips, Père Dubois saw that she hadn't finished the sentence. And he could easily guess what she still had to say. If she hadn't stopped herself, she would have said that Julien, who had nothing, could still find something to give his father, while Paul, the big grocer who had everything, didn't make the least little effort to help them. That's what she thought. And Père Dubois resented her thinking this way, but at the same time, he was grateful to her for not having said it. Why had she kept quiet? Was it really to spare him? Wasn't it rather to avoid an argument that might drag on and force him into going upstairs to bed so that she could be alone with Julien and tell him everything? For she would certainly speak to him about Paul and that incident with the militia. As soon as they were alone, she would jump at the chance. And of course, Julien would be only too happy to insult the half brother he detested.

He just turned up, with his hair all queer-looking, a dead man under his arm, and now here he was handing out cigarettes, putting honey on the table. It was a way of thumbing his nose at his father. And again to show how generous he really was, here he was saying, "A pot that size, if you only use it in your tea, ought to last you quite awhile."

"And you," his father asked, "don't you like it?"

"Oh, me, I ate pretty well down there, you know. And I've always heard you say that it was good for your throat."

"That's true," said his father.

He served himself, slowly stirred his tea, inhaling the aroma of linden that rose from the bowl with the steam. The honey must be very good. It added to the perfume of the infusion. He took a swallow.

"This is very good honey," he said. "And besides, sugar is so scarce."

They all three sat there, looking at one another without saying a word. Slowly, the aroma of the tea filled the little room, replacing the odor of the vegetable soup and the fat the eggs were cooked in.

"You know," said Mère Dubois, "we were worried about you. We thought you'd left for Spain or England. I used to go over often, in the evening, to Monsieur Robin's to listen to London on the radio. I said to myself, if he's there, perhaps he'll send us a message."

"A message? But what message?"

"Oh, I don't know, something I would have understood."

"Well, I don't quite follow you on that. Besides, you know, you don't just go to London as you might go to Montmorot."

"But anyhow, when you—when you left the army, you must have had some sort of plan?"

"Naturally. I joined the Maquis in the Montagne Noire, but that didn't turn out so well. I had a buddy who got killed, and then I got picked up."

"Yes," his father broke in, "we heard about what happened. You were imprisoned in the barracks in Carcassonne, and you escaped after knocking an officer unconscious. I don't know if you realize—"

Julien interrupted. "He was a dirty bastard. A lousy Pétainist. But what they didn't tell you was that the reason I was able to get away was thanks to the captain. He was a good man. He stays where he is strictly because that's where he can be most useful to the Maquis, and he'll certainly be able to pass the English information."

Père Dubois was of two minds. Should he go up to bed or carry on this conversation which inevitably would lead to an argument? He took a few more gulps of tea; then trying to remain calm, he said, almost timidly, "A spy, of sorts."

"If you like. But they're needed."

"I don't know if they're needed or not, but I'd rather see you keeping other company. Those situations never lead to anything good. I remember the Dreyfus affair well enough—"

His wife interrupted. "But that's ancient history. You're always living in the past. You refuse to face up to the present, or else, when you do look at it, it's always from the wrong point of view."

"You're not going to start that again!"

This phrase came out before he'd had time to think about it, and Père Dubois immediately regretted it. His wife was already rising up in her chair, ready with her retort. However, she said nothing. They measured each other with their eyes for a moment. Was she going to bring up Paul? Did she understand that her husband regretted what he'd just said? There was a long silence; then sinking slowly back into her chair, without anger, she murmured, "This war dirties everything. It divides people. It does harm even where nobody's fighting."

"The only thing to do," said Julien, "is try to live through it without getting hurt."

His father felt like asking him if he regretted having deserted, but he didn't dare. It seemed to him, however, that he'd sensed it in what Julien had just said, and he decided to let that hope ride. So he merely said, "But you won't be able to hide indefinitely, will you?"

"I'll just have to lay low till the end of the war. Once the Germans have gone back home, I can come out."

"Then you really think that—"

Père Dubois wasn't able to finish, for his wife broke in. "Your father isn't up on anything. He never goes over to listen to the radio. We don't get the papers anymore, and at the moment, he's rereading old *Illustrations* from before the First War."

"I don't have to read the papers; you tell me what's going on. And you always know everything!"

"I try to keep up with the times."

It was more painful than a real fight, this conversation that toed the line between anger and the false peace they'd known for a few seconds when their son had brought out his cigarettes and that pot of honey. Père Dubois struggled against both the desire to go up to bed and the longing to shout that gripped his chest.

Peace—that was all he really wanted. And when he thought of peace, it was of the peace he could still find when he sat quietly at home or worked in his garden. He who had a genius for exasperating his wife! But when you got down to it, what harm could it do if he tried to live by participating as little as possible in outside events? If everyone had acted this way, wouldn't a lot of tragedy have been avoided? Except for the curfews and restrictions, could they really complain about the Germans? All you had to do was ignore them. Not step on their toes, and they would leave you alone. That was really fairly obvious. But his wife wasn't about to admit it. She always had to get mixed up in everything. She lived as much with what went on outside the house as with what was actually the heart of their existence. And now what were they going to do with this boy who was wanted by the police?

The old man suddenly felt overwhelmed by an immense lassitude. It wasn't comparable to the fatigue that beset him on evenings after the hardest days of work. Nor was it in the same family with the distress that filled him when he thought about the years gone by, about his vanished strength and youth. It was a feeling of emptiness. A little as if Julien's arrival had chased far from the house something which had no name, no face, but which nevertheless existed and helped him live, like this warm air rising from the stove all day long, giving the kitchen that good warmth in which to quietly doze and let winter go by.

21

PÈRE DUBOIS decided to go up to bed without waiting any longer. He finished his tea, took his chamber pot and his night-light, and retired to the bedroom, where he noticed that a little frost glistened on the wallpaper.

"If this weather sets in," he grumbled, "we'll have to light a fire up here before going to bed. That won't help the woodpile any."

He got undressed as quickly as possible and slid between the sheets, where his wife had put the bed warmer wrapped in an old stocking. After a while he brought it up along his body, moving it a little to his right, to the place his wife would occupy. But tonight she wouldn't be up early. Now that he'd left them alone, they'd probably talk for a long time, the two of them, and he knew exactly who they'd be talking about. In deciding to retire, he'd given in a little to his fear of getting into an argument. He told himself that he always went up to bed at around nine o'clock, but that had only been an excuse. And now he blamed himself for having beaten a retreat like that. In acting that way, he'd left Paul at their mercy, and the old lady would undoubtedly drag him through the mud. Hadn't he been a bit cowardly? Paul was his son after all. Should he let him be run down without saying one word to justify his position?

He'd been afraid of taking a beating if he got involved in a fight, and now he was tortured by remorse.

For an instant, he felt like getting up, tiptoeing down to the door at the bottom of the stairs and listening to what they were saying. He could even go into the kitchen, pretending to have a headache, and take an aspirin. His right hand pushed the bed warmer down along his hip. The bed had gotten cozy and warm. With his cotton nightcap pulled down on his forehead and the sheet pulled up to his chin, Père Dubois felt comfortable. The slightest movement would cool the bed off again. He thought of the icy floor, whose boards would squeak under his feet, of the lamp he would have to relight . . . And then, if he did hear them saying bad things about Paul, what would he do about it? How could he try to defend his son when he knew nothing about politics or the international situation? No, whatever his wife and Julien might say was unimportant. What mattered was peace. That's all. And he wasn't the only one to think this way, since

Julien had just said a little while ago that the main thing was to
live through this war without getting hurt. And his mother was
already talking about him as if he were a hero. What a fine hero,
with his artist's hairdo and his vacation in Marseilles! He was
just like all the soldiers in this war, trying to see who would be
the first one across the Spanish frontier. The men in the first
war were a different breed. They'd known how to fight.

Père Dubois gave a long sigh. He shifted the bed warmer a
little again, and it no longer burned his hand. He tried to keep
the icy air of the room out from under the covers. He lay flat on
his back, his head snuggled into the hollow of his two pillows.

Still and all, he had a curious son. Taking up painting and
traveling from Marseilles to Lons-le-Saunier with that dead man
under his arm—that was out of the ordinary. In both his and his
wife's families, however, there had been nothing but sensible
people, absolutely normal, who worked hard all their lives. But
that boy had never been quite normal. Where could he have got
such peculiar tendencies? Going around with a real dead man
under his arm. A dead man. As though it shouldn't be against
the law.

For some time, Père Dubois hadn't been able to get the
thought of that skeleton on the stoop out of his head. Had Julien
laid him down along the balustrade? Had he stood him up in the
corner? The idea bothered him. Who could the poor fellow
have been to have got skinned like that instead of put into a coffin? It was certainly the first time Père Dubois had seen a thing
like that up close. He knew that such things existed in museums
and medical schools, but to have one in your own home! No, it
was beyond his comprehension.

Was it wise to leave it out there on the stoop? What if the
police took it into their heads to pay them a visit very early tomorrow morning? What would they think finding themselves
face to face with that dead man?

Imperceptibly, a kind of uneasiness crept over Père Dubois.
Without his wanting to admit it, it was the idea of death that

was really bothering him. And not only of death in general, but of his own death. That dead man downstairs had probably been a man like himself, with a life of hard work and pain. Perhaps even a baker, who knows? Or else a farmer who had loved his land. Perhaps a man who had never left his part of the country during his lifetime. Had anyone asked him his opinion about being made into something to be lugged around as carelessly as an umbrella? Séraphin. Julien had called him Séraphin. Then he knew his identity. Yet he treated him without respect, without consideration. Of course, once dead, you can't feel anything. Lying out on the stoop or rotting in a hole in a cemetery, from a certain point of view, came down to the same thing, and yet, after a lifetime of work, wasn't it only natural to have a little peace? A stone on your chest with your name carved on it? Even if no one ever stopped in front of it, it was still something solid that endured. And then, there were always people who remembered. Père Dubois never visited the cemetery except on the eve of All Saints' Day and for burials. On All Saints' Day he would weed the graves of his parents and his first wife and set in pots of chrysanthemums he had grown especially. And each time he would repeat to himself that his place was there with them and that his wife would come there also. They would all be together again. There might not be anyone left to bring them flowers, but there would always be the stones with their names. And for years to come, on days when there were burials, people going by in twos and threes would read his name. And they would say, "That Gaston Dubois, there's a man who certainly earned the right to rest in peace. He used to work like a dog, moving his sacks of flour." The people his age or a little younger would remember the bread he used to make. They would say, "There aren't any bakers like that around anymore." And their mouths would water at the memory.

It wasn't much, that thought, but it was still enough to make him a little less sad at the prospect of being carried out feetfirst one of these days.

Père Dubois thought about this, yet he always came back to that dead man with no grave who lay so far from the other dead, all alone on the stoop, whipped by the north wind. He'd probably been hearing nothing but art students' bawdy jokes and songs since the day he died. And they were hardly suitable company for a serious dead man.

When Mère Dubois came up to bed, he still wasn't asleep. First he heard a commotion in the little room that Julien occupied next to theirs, then the door opened, and she came in without making a sound.

"You don't have a candle?" the old man asked.

"No, I gave it to Julien. But aren't you asleep?"

"No."

Mère Dubois got undressed, then slipped into bed, bringing the cold air from the room in with her.

In the long silence the only sound was the creaking of the bedsprings as she tried to get comfortable. Finally, before dozing off, Père Dubois murmured, "All the same, that dead man he brought with him, that's really crazy."

—◁ 22 ▷—

As soon as he woke up, Père Dubois realized that his life was going to be disrupted by Julien's return. He'd waked up several times during the night, and always with a vision of that skeleton on the front stoop. When he was half asleep, the feeling would come to him that death was at his door and that it was waiting to enter the house.

The minute he was up, he dressed in a flash and went out to remove the skeleton. Dawn was just breaking, gray streaks mingling with the remains of a stubborn night. Père Dubois lugged the skeleton out to the shed, climbed up to the loft, and hid it behind a pile of empty hutches he was saving for kindling. The whole thing made no sense to him at all. You'd really have to be crazy to go around with those old bones under your arm. This dead man, like everyone else, had a right to his plot of ground, and for him to lie there like that on the rickety floor of the loft just wasn't suitable.

He took the opportunity to bring a load of wood back to the house, and by the time he reached the kitchen, his wife had already lighted the fire and made the coffee. Père Dubois sat down in his place by the window without saying a word, drank his *café au lait,* then began to wait. It still wasn't light enough to read. And in any case, he didn't feel like it. He looked at the garden. He was waiting.

He was waiting for his son to get up by going over in his mind what he would say to him. The words came to him easily. And he congratulated himself for not having said anything the night before. It would be better to discuss things fully, find out what the boy really had in mind. Père Dubois told himself that Julien couldn't have come back without having some specific intention. Did he want to mend his ways? Try to get back on the right side of the law? What did they do to deserters? Did they always put them in prison? He repeated Paul's words to himself and decided that perhaps there might be a chance of a reconciliation there. If Paul helped Julien out of the mess he was in, his wife could say nothing further against this son of his who was not hers. She wouldn't even have a right to criticize his attitude toward the militia anymore, and perhaps peace would descend once more on the household.

This morning, everything was calm. In appearance, things were just as if Julien hadn't come. The first thing Mère Dubois had done was to unpack his suitcase, from which she had taken several books, two paint boxes, and quite a bit of dirty and wrinkled laundry. Only the books remained on the table, and after long hesitation, Père Dubois finally pulled the pile in front of him. He picked up one of the books and started to leaf through it. It was called *Les Fleurs du Mal,* and it was by someone named Baudelaire. The old man put on his glasses, but the book contained nothing but poems, which he didn't even try to read. He put it back down, leafed through the others, then pushed away the whole pile. There was nothing there but poems and, on certain pages, only a few lines, some of them very short. For Père Dubois, this wasn't serious work. A little like a baker cheating on the weight of his bread. He thought it was stupid to buy books that contained so much blank paper. The more he thought about it, the more his son seemed foreign to him, different from the kind of people his family had always known.

Mère Dubois didn't say a word. She did her work in silence, trying to open the door as little as possible so as not to let the heat out of the room. From time to time, the old man glanced at her. It seemed to him that there was something she wanted to say, but that she didn't dare say it. It was just an impression he had, with no real foundation.

When she'd finished putting away the dishes from the night before, she carried an iron pot full of vegetable peelings meant for the rabbits to the stove. Then she poured a little bag of lentils onto the oilcloth and started picking over them.

"Do you want me to help you?" asked Père Dubois.

"No, there aren't that many."

There was another silence; then Mère Dubois said, "Last night, I wasn't any too warm in bed."

"That's true. The cold has gotten into the house now. Tonight we'll have to make a fire to dry out the walls a little and make it healthier."

"It's so damp that to do the job right, we really ought to keep a fire going all day."

"All day? But that would be madness. It's more at night that we should have some heat, as we used to before the war during the cold spells. Only, with the wood we've got, there's no point in even thinking about it."

His wife fell silent, and Père Dubois thought the conversation had ended there. They'd already talked about this last winter, and the old woman knew full well that wood was too scarce to heat that room properly.

For a long moment, there was nothing but the sound of lentils being pulled one by one across the oilcloth and dropped into the bowl the old woman held on her knees. Then, after a sigh, she finally said, "Still, all those bundles we made—that's really quite a lot of wood."

"Those bundles aren't cut yet. And you know very well that I haven't even finished sawing the big logs."

"I know. But Julien can do that. If he's careful, he can get out to the shed without being seen."

Père Dubois didn't know what to say. Of course, if Julien could saw and split that wood, it would be a big help. But if his wife was talking like this, it meant that he'd expressed the desire to hide here, to live unobserved in this house that was only separated from the town by the garden. The old woman must think that he'd been seduced by the prospect of all the favors the boy could do for him, for she went on.

"You see, if he hides here for a while, he won't be able to work in the kitchen. The three of us in this little room. And besides, at any moment, someone might come to the door. Since there's no stove in his room, he'd have to set up a table in our room. Only—only, of course, he'd have to have some heat."

Père Dubois clenched his jaws. His hand gripped the corner of the table. A flood of words rose into his throat. Nothing came out. He opened his mouth several times, but he couldn't find a thing to say. What his wife had just told him was so far from everything he'd hoped and even everything he'd dreaded. None of the phrases he'd turned over so carefully in his mind could be of any use to him. Decidedly, he would never succeed

in understanding either his wife or Julien. When he was alone
with her, life was never absolutely easy, but still, the work they
shared in common always brought them together, and the struggle to survive smoothed out plenty of differences. However, as
soon as Julien appeared, their world was disrupted so much
that he hardly knew where he was.

So the boy had thought he would live with them, doing nothing, hiding beside a fire they would have to keep going just for
his sake when they were already short of wood. And his wife approved of this. She was willing to support this drifter who hadn't
even been able to stay in the army. Good God, if the army
couldn't even make a soldier out of him, chances were he'd never
be able to do anything with any hope of success.

This news took him so much by surprise that he felt incapable
of expressing his anger. He sat there speechless, looking at his
wife, wondering only whether she was giving all her attention to
her work or whether she was keeping her head down to avoid
looking him in the eye.

~◄⦃ 23 ⦄►~

It was after ten when Julien came downstairs. Forcing a smile,
his father remarked, "You must be tired; you almost slept
around the clock."

"He must have been glad to be back in his own bed," said his
mother. "My poor boy, did you have enough blankets?"

"I was just fine."

Julien sat down in front of his bowl, which his mother filled at
once, saying, "There's not much milk, and it's not really possible
to get more."

"It's like everything else," said his father. "We have nothing. nothing at all. It's quite simple."

There was a silence. Julien had started to eat, and his father was watching him. That skinny, bearded boy was really his son. He wondered if he hadn't doubted it a little, last night, seeing him come in. In any case, this morning he recognized him clearly. During the night and since he'd been up, he hadn't stopped pondering a lecture he meant to give the boy, urging him to live like everyone else, to take what he considered the right path, but at the moment, not one of his well-thought-out phrases came to mind. In looking at his son, he was reminded about all of the months they'd spent waiting for him, his mother and himself. A hundred times they'd believed he was dead, and each time they'd suffered. They'd never talked about it, but Père Dubois always could guess what was going on in his wife's heart when it came to Julien. A hundred times he'd felt like saying to her, "I'm suffering, too. The thought that he might be dead hurts me as much as it hurts you, but you always think that I don't love him, that I have no heart." He'd swallowed those words so often that he'd never be able to say them out loud. He knew that, but he also knew that he'd have a lot of trouble lecturing Julien. Why? He asked himself that. He had difficulty understanding what went on inside him every time he found himself confronting this boy. The anger that he felt as long as he was alone melted the moment Julien appeared. If he succeeded in finding it again, he had to make an effort to shout, and almost always, things turned out badly because his words never exactly expressed his feelings. It was so complicated to get along with a kid twenty years old, so different from himself.

As yet, he couldn't resign himself that quickly to just accepting everything. It didn't involve only him; it involved the tranquillity of them all. His wife must be absolutely blind not to see the danger of having a deserter wanted by the police in their house. They couldn't let him move in here without knowing what he intended to do.

For a long moment, as though to give himself the strength to speak, Père Dubois tried to picture what might happen. He saw the police at his house, the militia, even the Germans, trials, humiliation, the house searched, looted, burned. He worked himself up this way with the most pessimistic forecasts until, unable to stand it any longer, he asked in a voice that trembled slightly, "Well, what are you planning to do exactly?"

Julien, who had finished his breakfast, lighted a cigarette, leaned a little closer to his father, and offered him one, saying, "Well, I told you, I have some work to do."

"But really, staying here is like staying in the lion's mouth. You can't live like a prisoner, after all, never sticking your nose outside the door."

"You know, if I can get settled in your room and work, I won't be too badly off."

Père Dubois hesitated a moment. He knew that what he answered might provoke his wife. Up until now she hadn't said a thing. She was in the laundry with the door almost closed, but she was undoubtedly listening. He forced himself to laugh.

"You won't be too badly off," he said, "but what might be sort of badly off is our wood supply."

"Well, it's hard to believe you can't get enough wood from countryside like this."

His father was about to answer when his mother emerged from the laundry, saying, "Your father's right. If you knew what we had to go through to have enough wood for the winter. It's not easy, you know."

She paused; then, turning to her husband, she said simply, "All the same, we have enough for the winter. And you must realize that he can't spend the day in this kitchen hiding every time we hear someone coming. If he wants to work, he needs a place to do it in."

Père Dubois bowed his head. What all that really meant was: "He's your son. He's come to hide here. You're not going to let him freeze. You're not going to throw him out. Even if we have to die of cold and hunger because he doesn't have a ration card, we have to keep him with us as long as possible. He's my baby. He's here; I'm not going to let him go again. And as for you, you're nothing but an old egotist. I've already told you that a hundred times, and I'm telling you again."

Yes, Père Dubois could just feel it. It all was written clearly in his wife's eyes. And besides, in that look was the threat of bringing up Paul. Paul, and hauling the bundles, and the food he and his wife bought and sold on the black market, and his friends, and his relationships Julien, having quit the Vichy army, would no doubt disapprove of.

"What I'm asking you," said Julien, "is to keep me for a month, long enough to get this work done, and then I'll be able to shift for myself."

"My poor boy," his mother sighed. "That means you'll be leaving again—and God knows for where!"

"Don't worry," the boy said, "don't worry."

There seemed to be a complicity between them that Père Dubois detected at the very moment when perhaps he had been about to resign himself to silence. No doubt they'd made good use of their evening to arrange everything so that he'd be taken in. This was what triggered his fury.

"Very well," he snapped. "I'm perfectly willing, but you don't think the police are going to get tired of looking for him, do you?"

He had almost shouted, and his wife looked surprised. She seemed to have more sadness in her eyes than anger.

"If you think he'd be in less danger staying with strangers or out on the road, you should ask him to leave."

She had spoken calmly, but the old man could just imagine all the things she still might say. There was suddenly in him a sort of contest between the calm he'd been enjoying since the beginning of winter and the war which might break out between them, disrupting everything. If he chanced one wrong word, his wife would scream at him, "So what you want is his death. His

death so that your other son will be alone and get everything."
She had never spoken that way, but Père Dubois knew that to
defend Julien, she would go that far.

Alone.

Once again he was alone. Once again his peace of mind was
threatened. He looked at them both, one by one; then, lowering
his eyes, he turned his head aside, put his right elbow on the
table, and murmured, "My goodness, do as you please. Whatever I say about it is mostly for Julien's sake."

The end of his sentence was barely audible. He had already
put his feet up on the stove door, and slowly, his body sank
down, settling naturally into its position of repose.

--✠ 24 ✠--

TIME began to flow again, slowly, as though winter had found
its old interminable rhythm after a few days' interruption. Julien never got up before nine o'clock. He came downstairs to
wash and eat breakfast; then he went back up again and shut
himself in his parents' room, where he started the wood fire. At
noon, when there was too much danger of an unexpected visit,
Julien did not come downstairs. His mother took his meal up,
sometimes making two or three trips. In the evening, once the
garden gate had been locked, the boy came down into the
kitchen, but they all stayed on the alert.

What did he do, sitting all day long at that table he'd pushed
over in front of the window? His father would have loved to
know. Every night, when he went up to bed, he looked at the
table, but Julien left only his pad there, a pen, some pencils, a
dictionary, and an ashtray often full of cigarette butts. Père

Dubois would appropriate a few of them to store in his tobacco box, shake his head, and go to bed. The room smelled of cigarette smoke and the wood fire. Once the night-light was out, he would lie for a long time with his eyes open, looking at the reflections dancing on the ceiling. A log was still burning in the little stove with the blackened, chipped surface. There would be cracklings; there was also that sound so characteristic of wood still weeping its sap onto the embers. Listening, Père Dubois thought about the forest, about the trouble they'd had, he and his wife, getting this wood the boy burned all day long.

But he took great care not to say anything about that. He knew that his wife would take any mention of it very badly. On the second day, he simply asked, "But what on earth is he doing?"

Mère Dubois answered, "I don't know. He's working."

"But isn't he making drawings?"

"No. He's doing some writing work. And he's studying his books. You have to leave him alone. He's certainly not wasting his time. You have to remember he left school at fourteen to become an apprentice. He hasn't studied much. There are some boys who study till they're over twenty years old."

Père Dubois didn't answer. These words meant that a boy could stay in his parents' care much longer than Julien had done. There was nothing to say. He couldn't even ask his wife how she got enough to eat, was able to find bread without ration coupons, or by what miracle Julien was able to smoke so many cigarettes without even having a tobacco card. The old lady didn't spend any more time shopping, and nothing had changed in her daily life. It was best to wait, letting the hours go by, being careful to show neither ill humor nor astonishment. Times were strange. Nothing was done normally, so it was natural not to be astonished by anything.

The fourth day after Julien's arrival the weather warmed up suddenly, and the wind stopped to let a violent rain fall.

"I felt it coming," said Père Dubois. "My shoulder's been hurting me for the last two days."

"I'll take the opportunity to go saw some wood," said Julien. "In weather like this, no one's likely to go down to the end of the garden. I'll put on a hood to get to the shed, and even if a neighbor does see me, they won't be able to recognize me."

"I'll go with you," said his father.

"You'll catch cold," his wife observed.

"No. It's not cold out. I'll do the splitting and piling. If someone comes, tell them to wait here, and you come get me. In the shed, Julien can always hide in the loft."

They worked all morning, and the old man tried several times to ask his son questions about what his life in Marseilles had been like. But Julien would talk only about his friend the painter, whom he admired a lot.

So there was that morning, and then peace fell once more. From time to time, a neighbor dropped by, would stop a moment to talk, then leave after giving news about the war, the people who were being arrested, those who were shot, and those, too, who simply disappeared without leaving a trace. It was mainly M. Robin who kept them informed because he listened to the radio from London every night. But for Père Dubois, everything he told them was an echo of distant events. The names of the countries were for the most part unknown to him, and for example, when M. Robin announced the formation of the Tito government, Père Dubois wondered how in the world that could concern him. M. Robin had said to his wife, "You're not coming to listen to the radio anymore, Madame Dubois?"

"No, it's too cold to go out at night."

During every visit, M. Robin would ask, "Still no news from Julien?"

"No, still no news."

Occasionally M. Robin would bring a little butter or a piece of cheese or even a package of tobacco for the old man. Then Mère

Dubois would go out with him, saying, "We'll stop by the cellar. I want to give you a few onions and some apples for the little boy."

M. Robin also brought the newspapers, which Père Dubois tried to read, leafing through them to look at the pictures.

Life went along like this, with visits from a few neighbors and the winter, which fluctuated between cold, fog, and rain.

One afternoon, when the gray day was beginning to darken, Paul Dubois turned up.

"I was passing by," he said, "and I saw that the bedroom chimney was smoking. I got frightened; I thought perhaps my father was sick."

"No, no," Père Dubois stammered, "only you see—"

His wife intervened. "With the rain we've had these last few days, so much dampness has gotten into that room. The walls are so wet the wallpaper's starting to peel off. So we have to have a little fire. Anyhow, we make a little fire every winter."

"Of course," said Paul, "but usually, I know you only light it in the evening; that's why I thought my father might be in bed."

"I lighted it a little early this evening," said Mère Dubois, "to dry the walls out."

"That's just what I noticed. When I went up to the station at about two, it was already smoking. I didn't pay any attention at the time, but this afternoon it came back to me. I said to myself, 'For them to be making a fire during the day, there must be something unusual going on.'"

He had sat down; he had unbuttoned his raincoat and pushed a little hat made out of raincoat material onto the back of his head. He was wearing a half-smile and looking from his father to his stepmother. He got out a pack of cigarettes, took one, and slid the pack across the oilcloth toward his father.

"Here, have one."

Père Dubois hesitated. He felt uneasy. His son's gaze seemed to be searching him.

"You know, I'm smoking less and less," he said.

There was a slight creak from the ceiling. Mère Dubois coughed, but Paul had raised his head. He started to laugh, then said, "It seems that drying out the house makes the floor creak."

"It's time for me to go up and put on another log," said Mère Dubois, heading for the stairs.

"Wouldn't you like me to go?" Paul offered. "It'll save you a trip. If you have a fire going all day, you must have to go up and down quite a lot."

"I'm used to it," she replied dryly.

She went upstairs. The stairs creaked. Père Dubois' heart was in his throat. He looked at his son through the smoke from their two cigarettes. Had Paul guessed the truth? Would he talk? Would he do anything else? Just what was the militia anyhow? No. It wasn't possible. He wouldn't dare. He couldn't do it. And yet, if his wife had agreed, perhaps Paul was the one they should have asked for advice. But now it was too late. Too late? Perhaps not.

It all whirled inside the old man's head. He realized that his hands were trembling and his face was strained. Paul must have noticed it. He smiled. Was he amused? Was he aware of his father's discomfort? Still smiling, he said, "It's true, it must be hard on the old lady, keeping a fire going up there all day. If you had a coal stove, you could load it in the morning, and it would last all day. I've got one that I could lend you."

Mère Dubois was coming back down already. She must have warned Julien. But the old man, who'd been straining his ears, hadn't heard her close the bedroom door. Was that so Julien could listen to what they were saying?

She appeared calm. She offered Paul a glass of wine, and he accepted. She poured it, her hand absolutely steady, and Père Dubois wondered how she could do it. Paul drank half his wine and asked, "Don't you think that coal would be more practical? I have a little stove I could lend you. I'll send one of my drivers to install it."

"No," Mère Dubois answered, "burning coal in a bedroom is unhealthy. You could get asphyxiated."

"I only mentioned it to try to do you a favor."

"And we thank you," said Mère Dubois, "but we can get along very well as we are."

"The favor you could do us," said his father, "is to bring us a few sacks of wood if someday you have a truck going up the mountain. There must be some left where they did the sawing."

Père Dubois had spoken all in one breath. Not having planned what he wanted to say, he found himself taken aback at having said it.

"I'll keep it in mind," Paul promised. "The next time we have a delivery to make around Morez or St. Claude, I'll tell my driver."

He fell silent. He seemed to want to add something. His eyes flicked from one of them to the other. He was still smiling, but not in the same way. Finally, in a graver and lower voice, he said, "But I can't promise you anything. When a truck goes up there, we don't even know if it will come back. Some of them have been attacked by the terrorists. They not only steal the load, but keep the truck, too. One of the drivers almost got killed for putting up a fight. I personally don't want any of my employees taking that kind of risk. So I only make deliveries to the mountain if they give us some protection."

As he spoke, he grew increasingly irritated. The tone of his voice rose, and his words came jerkily. He paused a moment, but nobody said a word. He took two puffs from his cigarette and then went on.

"That's right, I ask for an escort. We work so that people won't starve to death. If we weren't there to make deliveries, they wouldn't even have what they're entitled to by their ration cards. So it's only right that we should have police protection. And when the police can't do it, well, the Germans can, and do. That's right! I know there are some people who don't like it at all. But I don't give a damn about them. I'm doing my duty. Whether they like it or not, it still costs them the same price."

His smile had vanished. His face was tense, his expression hard.

The afternoon got darker and darker, and soon they would have to light the lamp. But Mère Dubois didn't move. She sat very straight in her chair, her hands resting flat on her knees. Only the right side of her face was clearly visible. Père Dubois turned his back to the window. He was glad he had thought of that. Paul was facing the light, but his features were getting less distinct. Only his eyes kept shining. There was a long silence. Then, in a voice that was quieter but still vibrating like struck metal, he added, "I am a businessman. I run my store. And believe me, it's not so easy all the time. We live in a time when no one does anything about the criminal elements. You can ask anyone. You'll see that in Lons all the types who've joined the Maquis are the worst kind—young hoodlums just waiting for a chance to give free rein to their instincts for looting and murder. Those are the ones who make up your Resistance, as they call it. Oh, it's a fine group!"

His voice had risen again; then, suddenly stopping himself, he started to laugh.

"But I didn't come here to talk to you about that," he said. "I came to find out if everything was all right because I saw the bedroom chimney smoking. That has nothing to do with it."

"No," snapped his father. "As you say, that has nothing to do with it. And besides, all that has nothing to do with us."

Père Dubois had not shouted, but he had spoken in a firm, almost tough voice.

The words had come out because they had been inside him for some time. They had gushed forth, as the plug in a barrel of wine bursts when the fruit is fermenting. Now he sighed. Then he stood up and said, "It must be time to light the lamp and put the soup on to heat."

146

Paul rose. He buttoned his raincoat, then said before leaving, "I won't ask you if you've had news from Julien. I'm sure that if you had, you would have told me."

⁓◄ 25 ►⁓

As he left, Paul had given a little laugh. He'd taken his time going, and a rush of cold twilight had swept into the kitchen. After the door had closed behind him, the old couple listened to his footsteps going down the steps, then fading off on the courtyard paving stones before disappearing onto the path. It seemed to Père Dubois that the cold that had invaded the room had come from his son's laugh. It was a curious and painful impression, which he would have liked to rid himself of, but which persisted until the moment his wife pulled down the lamp and said, "If you'll close the shutters, I'll light the lamp."

When Père Dubois had closed the window and turned back, Mère Dubois was trimming the wick she had just lighted, and Julien was standing at the foot of the stairs. Leaning outside, completely absorbed in the task of unhooking the shutters, the old man hadn't heard him come down. Their eyes met. Julien's expression was at once severe and ironical.

"You shouldn't come down until I've gone and locked the gate," his mother said.

Julien began to laugh.

"There's no reason for me to hide anymore," he said. "In an hour, the whole town will know I'm here."

Père Dubois had been dreading this reaction, and yet the words came as a slap.

"Just what do you mean by that?" he shouted.

"The truth. If you didn't get it, you must really have a thick head."

"Julien!" cried his mother. "Please."

There was a silence. Mère Dubois had pulled the light back up, and the flame had steadied. They all stood there, in the light that fell from the shade onto the table that separated them.

Père Dubois was out of breath, but more from the anger oppressing him than the effort he'd made in the cold air outside.

"You have no right to say that," he said, taking hold of himself. "Your brother doesn't know that you're here. And even if he did know, what makes you think he'd go shout it from the rooftops?"

"He won't shout it from the rooftops, but he'll know exactly whose ear to let it fall into to be effective."

"But why do you think he'd do a stupid thing like that, idiot!"

Père Dubois could no longer contain himself. Something still told him that he was wrong to get carried away, but his rage was choking him. He didn't even quite know against whom it was directed, but a force beyond his control compelled him to free himself from it. Julien shouted louder than he. "Why? But he told you why. Because he's in with the Germans. Because he needs them. Because without them, he couldn't keep getting richer on the black market."

"Julien, you're going too far!"

Père Dubois was cut short by a fit of coughing that seized him just as his wife broke in. "Shut up, the both of you. If anyone was coming, they could hear you from the middle of the garden. Julien, you go back upstairs. I'm going to lock the gate."

Julien shrugged his shoulders. He stood undecided a moment; then, as his mother took a step toward him, he turned on his heels and went rapidly back up to the bedroom.

Père Dubois stood rooted between the window and the table, staring at his wife. Her stubborn back, motionless at first, began to shake slightly, and the old man understood at once that his wife had begun to cry. He sighed, lowered his head, and sank back into his chair.

His anger was still there, but he knew it wouldn't flare up again. He made no effort to control it; it was just like a part of his being that gradually detached itself from him. Like a snake coiling up, hardening into nothing more than a heavy, cold lump. A thing barely alive, but which nevertheless kept him from breathing freely.

Without looking at him, without a word, Mère Dubois threw her shawl over her shoulders, took the key to the gate, and hurried out.

As soon as she'd closed the door behind her, all was silence. A sort of bottomless pit into which Père Dubois had fallen in spite of himself. A sort of fog, heavy with soot, where his voice would die without the slightest echo if he tried to call out. Everything in it was hostile to him. The words spoken by Paul. The words spoken by Julien. And he was all alone in the midst of it, no longer knowing what to cling to. While he sat there alone, he could only say over and over, "It's the war. It rots everything. No good will come of it."

26

As soon as Mère Dubois got back, she put the soup on the stove. Père Dubois watched her stealthily, not daring to risk a question or a look that might meet hers. A moment passed, and then she went up to the bedroom. The old man strained his ears, but no sound reached him. He waited. The house felt like a huge weight on his shoulders. Up there, his wife and his son were talking. But he, alone in the kitchen, he was out of it all.

Without having followed the train of his thoughts, he suddenly found them stopped at the loft over the shed, behind the pile of hutches where the skeleton lay.

Was this dead man any lonelier than he? Had he had children, too? Who could have given or sold him to be carted around like this in the world of the living?

Upstairs a door closed, and his wife's footsteps creaked on the wooden staircase. When she appeared, the old man asked, "He's not coming down to eat?"

Her voice sounded natural. "No," she said, "he's gone to bed."

"And he doesn't want anything to eat?"

"No."

"He's being impossible."

"The best thing is to leave him alone."

"My Lord." Père Dubois sighed.

His wife waited awhile before saying, "Oh, I know perfectly well what you're thinking."

"Oh, yes? Well, tell me, what?"

"You're just thinking that you haven't had a moment's peace, since the boy got back."

Père Dubois struggled not to shout. He passed his hand over his chin twice before answering.

"It's true, that we haven't had a moment's peace. And you're also right to call him a boy. Because he's behaving exactly like a child who can't see beyond the end of his nose. And if we haven't had any peace, it's because we're worried about him. About what might happen to him."

His wife sat down slowly. She crossed her arms on the table and fixed her eyes on his in such a way that he knew at once she was about to have another go at him.

"Nothing will happen to him if nobody turns him in," she said slowly.

She showed no anger, and everything about her seemed astonishingly calm. This calm was even a little disquieting.

Lowering his eyelids, Père Dubois murmured, "Nobody will turn him in."

"I hope not," she said.

Then she got up to go get the plates, which she brought to the table. When the places were set, they began to eat in silence, and it was only after she'd finished her soup that Mère Dubois, still very calm, announced, "He wants to leave."

Père Dubois felt something like a great breath of fresh air enter into him. He tried not to let his relief show. He succeeded fairly well, for something bitter came to spoil this onset of well-being. A feeling which he couldn't quite pin down, but which added itself to his fear of betraying himself. He swallowed three spoonfuls of broth before asking, "Leave? But where does he want to go?"

"He won't tell me. And I even think he doesn't know himself. But I—"

She had to hunt for her words. She spoke slowly, hesitating at each sentence.

"I," she went on, "it worries me a great deal. I don't know if he'll be able to find a place to hide so easily. He could have stayed here at least until we could find him a safer place—in the country, for example."

"Nobody's forcing him to leave."

"No . . . of course . . . nobody . . ."

This word remained hanging in the warmth of the room. It was there like a ghost, and Père Dubois could still hear it.

Mère Dubois said nothing more. No doubt she thought her husband could guess what was going on inside her. When you've lived face to face with someone that long, there are occasions when silence is enough. You say one word like a clue, and all the rest falls into place.

When the plates were cleared, Mère Dubois brought to the table a bowl and the pot of honey from Provence. She put the tea to steep in a little pot of water; then, going back to her seat, she said very quietly, with a glance at the stairs, "He's very unhappy, you know."

"Nobody's very happy—with the times we're living in."

"I know. Those are the times, but for him, there are other things that he won't tell us."

She was still talking under her breath and hesitating. In spite of this, Père Dubois, who had to strain his ears to hear her, realized that she had a lot to say and that she was going to say it.

"You know," she went on, "when he went to join the Maquis, his friend who was with him got killed. I believe he thinks about that a lot. And then . . ."

This time she paused so long that Père Dubois thought she'd decided not to go on.

"Well?" he asked.

"I also think that he was in love with a girl and that it didn't work out. So you see—"

"Did he talk to you about it?"

"No. But I could tell that things were going badly. And the other morning, while you were sawing the wood, I read what he's writing at the moment."

Père Dubois shook his head. His fingers began to drum on the oilcloth. He murmured several times, "My goodness. My goodness."

What more could he say? Nothing. There was nothing to add. He too had seen his friends die. And by the dozens. He could remember their names and their faces. But still, that was very long ago. As for this girl that his son had loved . . . But first of all, loved . . . What did that mean exactly? That he'd hoped to marry her, and she'd refused him? A stroke of luck. What would he have done with a wife in his present circumstances? Père Dubois' youth hadn't been like Julien's; he couldn't understand what went on inside this boy who was so different from himself. In his day, he'd had to work so many hours that he'd had precious few left for anything else. He'd married once. He'd had a son. His wife had died, leaving him alone with the bakery on his hands. Of course, it hadn't been very easy, but he hadn't become a hermit just for that. He hadn't shut himself up alone in a room just to write that he was sad.

His wife seemed to be waiting for some other response from him. After a long moment of silence, she served him his tea and asked, "I feel we ought to go and see Vaintrenier. What do you think?"

Still pondering this sentimental despair of his son's, Père Dubois was taken aback.

"Vaintrenier," he said, "but what has he got to do with this?"

"He used to be deputy mayor. He resigned after Pétain came into power, which proves he's not on that side. If he's not on that side, he's sure to know where we could hide Julien."

Père Dubois raised his hands. All this frightened him.

"What crazy ideas you get," he said. "If you start telling everyone that Julien is here—"

He suddenly stopped. He regretted what he'd just said, but the reaction he feared didn't materialize. Mère Dubois didn't bring up Paul, and he concluded that she wanted at all costs to avoid any arguments that might complicate matters. He was about to go on when she said, still in a low voice, "Listen. Looking perfectly innocent, I asked Monsieur Robin a few questions. He said to me, 'If someday you happen to hear from Julien, go see Monsieur Vaintrenier. I'm sure he'd be able to do a lot for him.' "

Père Dubois looked at her for a long time. She didn't lower her eyes, but he nevertheless felt that she wasn't telling the truth. Probably she'd already told M. Robin about Julien's return. Père Dubois had no reason to doubt his neighbor, and yet fear suddenly gripped him. Even without intending to harm them, M. Robin might be indiscreet. He might confide the news to his wife, speak in front of their little boy. Inside Père Dubois' head, there was a vast upheaval from which a whole series of events poured forth. His fear allowed him to think very fast. He saw all at once his house being searched, burned; he saw himself dragged off by the SS and imprisoned while they shot Julien. And out of all that, what he was left with, what became insupportable to him, was the image of his son being executed. Could it be that in carrying that old dead man under his arm, the boy had brought his own undoing here?

Although he'd refused to admit that Paul might even make a slip, he felt it was to be feared from a stranger. He knew very well that Paul was friendly with the Germans while M. Robin made no bones about criticizing them, but the idea gripped him just the same. One thoughtless word and all would be lost. And people might even think that Paul was the only one responsible.

His head was ringing. Everything was boiling up inside him. He hurt from trying to put some order into his thoughts and master the fear that clenched his stomach. Little by little, that fear turned into anger. And inexplicably, it was against M. Vaintrenier that this anger was directed.

"Good Lord!" he shouted. "If Vaintrenier refuses to help us, he's a real son of a bitch. After what I did for him during the evacuation!"

"You made some bread because all the other bakers had left and the town was dying of hunger," Mère Dubois said calmly. "I know you didn't have to do it, but I don't see why you're getting angry."

Père Dubois realized that this outburst of rage was ridiculous.

"I'm not getting angry," he grumbled. "But I know people. They're very strong on asking for favors. But when it comes to doing a favor, you can't even find them."

"Before you say that, at least wait until you've asked him."

"Asked him? After all, we can't go and ask him tonight."

"But it would be the one time when I'd be sure of finding him at home."

154

Père Dubois felt partly relieved. His wife would take charge of going to speak to Vaintrenier.

She looked at the clock and said, "There's more than an hour left before the curfew. I have plenty of time to get there and back."

And without even waiting for an answer, she got up and started getting dressed.

--◀ 27 ▶--

MÈRE DUBOIS had dressed very quickly. Her husband had followed each of her gestures, each of her comings and goings, without really noticing them. She was leaving. She was going to try to convince M. Vaintrenier to help them. That was all.

And then, as soon as she'd left, Père Dubois muttered, "She's going over there. Good Lord, good Lord, I'm the one who should have gone. She won't know how to persuade him. But with all the trouble I have walking in weather like this, how could I have done it?"

He said that while another voice in him answered, "You didn't go because you didn't want to get mixed up in it. You don't want to take care of Julien. One more thing to feel guilty about. And this time it serves you right."

But why? Was he responsible for the boy's mistakes? Who brought him up? His mother. His mother, all by herself. She'd always been opposed to his taking a hand in his son's education, and she'd spoiled him rotten.

And now here was the result. Not only was Julien risking prison or even a firing squad because of a rash impulse, but also he was endangering them all by coming to hide out here. They all might be done for, and the house as well. But what actually counted the most? Was he just thinking about himself again, himself and his old worn-out carcass? The most important thing was for Julien to be able to hide. Escape the searches. The rest mattered very little.

He repeated that to himself, but another idea was gnawing at him. Paul. If Paul was able to get an escort for his trucks from the Germans, that meant that he was able to talk to them. Get along with them. Who knew but what some little gesture on his part might not fix everything! But his wife would never agree. And yet it would mean peace for all of them. What might the neighbors think? But the neighbors wouldn't know anything about it in the first place. And then what could they think?

Père Dubois turned this hope over in his mind, but the more he played with it, the more a sort of bitter stench arose from it. Everything got mixed up; everything acquired a sickening taste. He thought back over Paul's words. He could see his son again getting furious as Paul explained:

"What about the Germans? What have you all got against them? They beat us. And so? We shouldn't have declared war on them. What are you afraid of? That they're going to steal your belongings? They're not the ones who'll do that—that's the Bolsheviks. And the Germans are defending you against Bolshevism. Do they get in your way here? They buy things. They pay for them. They've created the *Commissions d'Achat* when they could perfectly well have just taken what they wanted since they're the strongest. As for me, I work with them because I'm a businessman. You were one all your life yourself. Did you ever refuse to sell to clients? I've never seen you set foot inside a church, but that didn't stop you from making bread for priests and their schools. If there weren't a lot of idiots around to shoot them in the back, the Germans wouldn't have to crack down on us the way they do. Obviously, when we kill their men, they take hostages. That's only normal. Pétain signed the armistice; we have to abide by it. You were in the First War, do you know who Pétain is? You'll tell me he's a coward. But that De Gaulle—do you know who he is? Have you heard of him? What is he? He's an adventurer. That's all. So he has some followers among the young people. Our duty is to enlighten them, to bring them back to reason."

Oh, yes, Paul talked like that, and others who also talked about reason saw in Pétain a traitor and in De Gaulle a savior. Whom could you believe? A whole life of making bread and working the ground didn't leave much time for politics. And Père Dubois had a lot of trouble seeing clearly inside himself.

Up until now the war had not touched him, except through all the complications and restrictions. They were enormous, but they were nothing compared to what he had seen in 1914 in the combat zones.

At certain moments he sometimes imagined that nobody could ever touch either his garden or his house. This little plot of land had been spared until then, and it seemed to him that it would stay that way until the end of the war. For the war would have to end someday. Only, if you wanted a little peace, you shouldn't bring a barrel of gunpowder into the place. And Julien was nothing but that for the moment, an explosive that could blow up everything.

Several times Père Dubois had to stop thinking because his head hurt him so much. From time to time, he would lift his eyes to the clock. Time was passing. The fire was dying. Should he put on another log? Did he have the right to go upstairs to bed before his wife got home? Wouldn't she accuse him of indifference if he didn't wait here?

He sat there, one elbow on the table and his feet up on the stove door. He tried to remain calm. To tell himself that everything would work out, and yet shivers ran up his back and neck, followed immediately by sweats worse than those that soaked his shirt when he was working his land under the blazing summer sun.

He'd got used to long and hard and sometimes disappointing work. Effort had always been a part of his life, but this ache that belabored his head was a thousand times more painful.

The night weighed on him. He sat there. Julien was sleeping just above the kitchen. His wife was walking through the darkness. Nothing seemed to be alive, and everything seemed to be leading up to a great tragedy for them.

--�}{ 28 }{--

When she returned, Mère Dubois explained that M. Vaintrenier had welcomed her very warmly. He had listened without appearing surprised; then he had said simply, "Very well, I'll come see you tomorrow, early in the morning."

That promise only partly reassured Père Dubois, who spent a bad night troubled by nightmares, which woke him up incessantly.

He was up well before daylight.

"Early in the morning," said his wife, "for Monsieur Vaintrenier, that probably means around nine o'clock. There's no cause to get all in an uproar."

"We've got to wake Julien . . . If he'd at least shave off his beard, he'd look more presentable."

"Listen, don't start in on that."

Julien got up. His mother told him about the impending visit from the former deputy mayor, and Julien said simply, "Ah, that's good."

And then they ate breakfast in silence. A heavy silence seemed to exude from the sky like the gray light of this dawn frozen along the ground.

Only the fire was alive, where an acacia log crackled cease-lessly.

"In the old days," said Père Dubois, "a serious woodcutter would never have put acacia in with the firewood. But today they don't give a damn about anything."

"We're still lucky to have enough to keep us warm," said his wife.

And that was all. Silence once more.

Père Dubois looked at Julien, who was smoking, having finished his breakfast. Forearms on the table, hands folded, head bowed, the boy seemed lost in thought.

A long moment passed; then Julien got up and went up-stairs to the bedroom. His father heard him moving around and realized that he was lighting the stove. He felt like telling his wife that perhaps it wasn't worth it but restrained himself. He sensed that it would have sounded ridiculous. Vaintrenier was coming, but he undoubtedly wasn't going to say to Julien, "Come with me. I'll take care of you."

Père Dubois listened to each noise. He imagined his son stuffing logs into the old stove, which must be roaring. You wouldn't believe how much wood that stove used up in the course of a day. A month like this, and the first pile would be gone.

The hours went by slowly. The morning stagnated in the grayness that drenched the hills like muddy water.

Vaintrenier arrived a little before nine. As soon as he was inside, he took off his hat, which he placed on the little dresser, and unbuttoned his black overcoat.

"I'll take it for you," said Mère Dubois.

She carried the garment into the dining room. Vaintrenier sat down at the table. He must have been walking fast, for his face was red. He passed his handkerchief over his forehead and his curly gray hair.

"Well," he said, "where is your phenomenon?"

Père Dubois gestured at the ceiling.

"I'll go up and get him," said his wife.

Alone with the former councilor, Père Dubois observed him a moment before saying, "Thank you for coming, Hubert. Its very kind of you."

"I'm not here out of kindness, but simply because it's natural for people to help each other. When I asked you to bake some bread during the debacle, you did it."

Père Dubois raised his hand.

"That," he said, "is ancient history. And you didn't ask it for yourself, but for others. And they didn't seem to appreciate it very much, by the way."

"Why do you say that? Because I'm no longer on the council? Let me set you straight. No one threw me out. I resigned because I didn't want to be taking orders from a government I don't approve of!"

His voice had hardened a little. And Père Dubois had the impression that there was, in those few words, a veiled reproach addressed to himself. He muttered, "Me, you know, politics, at my age."

"Of course," said Vaintrenier, "but it's not just politics—"

Then he fell silent. But Père Dubois felt that he had something more to say. Before the war, Vaintrenier had been elected by the people of the Popular Front. He was just a little older than Paul Dubois, and the old man knew they had never got along. No doubt it was about Paul that the former councilor wanted to speak. If he was determined to do it, it would be better to get it over with while they were alone. But if his wife's presence would constrain him to silence, then she'd better get back downstairs quickly. Very quickly.

Père Dubois strained his ears. His anguish mounted. Vaintrenier said, "We're living in atrocious times, Père Dubois. War is never funny. But I wonder if a real war isn't a little less unhealthy than this situation where the French are tearing themselves apart among themselves."

There was a noise in the stairwell, Vaintrenier stopped speaking, and the old man breathed more freely.

When Julien appeared, the councilor stood up to shake his hand, and he burst out laughing, saying, "Good heavens, your mother told me you'd taken up painting, but she didn't mention that you'd grown the hair to fit the part."

Julien shrugged his shouders. "It's mainly so I don't get recognized," he said.

"Personally, I think he should shave off that beard," said his father.

"Of course not," said Vaintrenier. "I'm not saying that it lets him get by unnoticed, but I assure you that if I'd run into him on the street, I wouldn't have known who he was. When you remember him with his crew cut and his sporty look, it's quite a change."

Père Dubois halfheartedly pressed his point, talking about bad impressions, but Vaintrenier interrupted him to observe, "Even if he wanted to shave it off, I'd advise him against it at the moment. He's very tanned, and if he took off his beard, it would show. And that's when he'd look like someone who was trying to alter his appearance."

Père Dubois made a weary gesture. Decidedly, nothing was normal these days.

Julien went to get a chair from the dining room, and they all sat down around the table. Mère Dubois served Vaintrenier a little glass of marc, and he took a sip before saying, "You don't get to drink this very much anymore."

"I have a few bottles left," said the old man, "but I'm afraid they won't last through the war."

"Who knows!" said the councilor. "The Fritzes aren't doing so well in Italy or in Russia."

He paused a moment. Then, straightening up a little, he looked at Julien and asked, "Well, what are your plans?"

"For the moment, I'm not doing too badly right here."

Vaintrenier shook his head no, slowly, two or three times, before saying in a very gentle voice, "No, my friend. It's not possible. You couldn't live like this, in such a small house, without being spotted sooner or later. You can hide anywhere else, but above all, not here."

"If nobody turns me in!" Julien snapped, almost aggressively.

Vaintrenier gave a sad smile and shook his head again. He sighed. "Of course . . . but that's something else. You seem to believe in miracles."

As Julien was about to speak, Vaintrenier raised his hand for silence and went on in a firmer voice.

"I'm not saying that someone might turn you in out of meanness, but out of carelessness. Or out of jealousy. You forget that there are thousands of young men your age leaving for Germany to do forced labor. You forget that others are drafted to serve as guards or to work here in factories. Perhaps their parents don't like seeing them go off, but if they knew that others were hiding, without meaning to harm them, they might say something unfortunate."

He hesitated, looked in turn at Père and Mère Dubois, and added, lower and more slowly, as if he regretted having to say the words, "And then there are the police and also the militia —their ears and eyes are everywhere."

Père Dubois bowed his head. They listened to the crackling of the fire. He felt like shouting at Vaintrenier, "You don't really think Paul would turn him in!" And yet he didn't dare. He simply murmured, "And what if he came forward—what if he went and told them—"

The former councilor interrupted him with a short laugh that wounded the old man.

"Ah, no, Père Dubois," he said. "It's all right to stay out of everything, but you can't totally ignore what's going on. I'm not saying that all the adherents of the Vichy regime are sons of bitches; there may be some of them who are genuinely misguided. But the ones in the militia—ah, no! Ah, no!"

He must have stopped short of some word for fear of hurting the old man. But Père Dubois had understood. He fought back his anger. He would have liked to say that all that was none of his business, that he no longer felt responsible for the actions of his sons. One of them was too old. The other had never belonged to him. And besides, he'd been a soldier. There was a war on. It was the governments; it was the world that was responsible for all this mess.

The words were inside him, rolling around and knocking into one another like walnuts in a basket. It was deafening, but they wouldn't come out. He knew he'd never have the last word with a man like Vaintrenier, who was used to politics and complicated discussions. He felt paralyzed. He hunched over. His eyes fastened on the blue and white squares of the oilcloth, chipped and peeling. The world was like that, all cracked, worn down to its bare threads, and none of it could be replaced.

Before Père Dubois' rage subsided completely, it roused him enough to make him snap, "Hell! The only thing left for us to do is just to drop dead!"

Vaintrenier did not appear moved, not even surprised. No doubt he understood what was going on inside the old man. Père Dubois realized this and felt a certain uneasiness. Vaintrenier's clear gaze probed into him. He lowered his eyes, sighed, and relieved by the simple cry of despair he'd given, he knew that, at least for the time being, his anger would leave him in peace. He realized that everything to be said and done from now on would be outside his experience. After all, since Vaintrenier had come, it must be because he could help Julien, and the best thing was to let him talk and act as he saw fit.

The councilor took another sip of marc, smacked his lips, and said, "All this is getting us nowhere. The important thing is that Julien can't stay here."

He fell silent. He frowned. His gaze lingered on Mère Dubois, then on Père Dubois before settling on Julien, whom he stared at for a moment in silence.

"Now," he said finally, "it's up to you to decide what you want to do."

Julien shrugged and stuck out his beard.

"You don't have too many alternatives," Vaintrenier continued. "You can either join the Maquis or else go and live in a big city where you aren't known."

"The Maquis," muttered his father.

Vaintrenier looked at him, but he didn't say anything further. However, the councilor had guessed his thoughts.

"It's not exactly what you imagine or what people may have told you about it," he explained. "It's an army . . . Clandestine, but still an army. You know my ideas. I've never been a militarist. But today there's only one thing that really matters: giving the Germans a good kick in the ass that will send them back home. Certain people are taking care of that. Others don't look forward to it at all, and—and still others would like to see it happen but don't want to have to get their hands dirty."

He'd hesitated a little over these last words and, when he finished, said nothing more. Since no one spoke, he emptied his glass, placed his large hands flat on the table, and leaned toward Julien. He seemed to have made a decision for him.

"Very well," he said. "I know what happened to you when you tried to join the Maquis in the Montagne Noire. It's a sad story, and I don't want to go back over it. I don't want to influence you. You think it over. When you've made up your mind, come see me."

He leaned his hands a little harder on the table, bent forward, and slowly stood up.

When he'd put on his coat, which Mère Dubois had gone to get, he seemed to think of something else and asked, "Show me what your identity card looks like."

Julien went upstairs to his room. As soon as he'd gone, his

mother asked, "The Maquis, Monsieur Vaintrenier, really and truly it frightens me a little, you know."

"That's an absolutely legitimate fear, Madame Dubois. But you see, in the cities there are raids all the time; they pick up anybody. They put people in prison, and if they need hostages, they just take them out of the crowd. So, you understand, the dangers—"

Since Julien was coming back down, his mother interrupted the councilor to ask him very quickly, "And on a farm?"

The man raised his hand.

"That," he said, "might be a solution. But I'm not the one to help you with that."

He examined the identity card Julien handed him closely. Then he finally asked, "Do you have any other photos?"

"Yes. I have one left."

"Give it to me."

Julien rummaged in his wallet and gave the photo to the councilor who slipped it in between the pages of a dog-eared little notebook.

"I'll be back this evening. In the meantime, try not to let yourself be seen."

Then, turning to the old couple, he added, "If anyone asks you what I was doing here, say that my wife owed you for some vegetables, and I came to pay you."

He shook their hands and was heading for the door when Mère Dubois said, "Monsieur Vaintrenier, he hasn't got a ration card for food."

He turned back. And in an almost cruel voice, he snapped, "I know that. You already told me twice last night."

He jammed his hat down onto his head and left hastily. Mère Dubois took a step out onto the threshold and waited until he'd reached the bottom of the steps before closing the door.

−◄{ 29 }►−

AFTER M. Vaintrenier's departure, no one spoke for a moment.
All three of them stood there, as though awaiting further orders.

Père Dubois looked at Julien, who was wearing an old pair
of pants covered with paint and a heavy brown turtleneck
sweater that came up to his blond beard. He was taking long
drags from his cigarette. He stooped a little, like an old man.
Père Dubois thought he was going to say something, but he
turned without a word and went upstairs.

His mother followed him with her eyes, seemed to hesitate,
then said wearily, almost inaudibly, "Dear God, what are we
going to do!"

It wasn't even a question. In any case, her husband wouldn't
have known what to answer. As he started back to his place, she
went upstairs and joined Julien.

Left alone, Père Dubois poked the fire, sat down slowly, and
looked at the garden. The earth, turned over for winter, was
black. Bare. Gorged with water.

But between Père Dubois and the earth he stared at without really seeing it, there was Julien. Scrawny. Bearded. His
hair too long. Looking sad and poor. Not with the poverty of
people who have neither food nor shelter nor money, but
with an indefinable poverty. That's what it was. To his father,
Julien was poor. And he saw him rich again. Rich with everything he used to have before. Strength. Health. The look of a
solid man. Molded by sports and manual labor. It seemed to
Père Dubois that his son had changed. Of course, they'd never

got along very well together; there had always been a kind of gulf between them, making it hard for them to talk to each other. And yet, when Julien had come back from his apprenticeship with a trade in hand and the muscular arms of a good workman, despite all his faults and quirks of character, his father had felt closer to him. Today he was another boy. A boy who was about to leave again without knowing where to go.

"Would you rather see him go off to join the Maquis or know that he was in some city leading that bohemian life he was leading in Marseilles?"

The question was there, as though it had been asked by the dead earth of the garden or the fire that wept softly behind the grill. It was there, and Père Dubois refused to answer it. It seemed to him that it called for some sort of verdict he didn't feel he had the right to give. The notions he had about the artist's life were such that he was sure, deep inside him, that nothing could be worse. He felt a little like a stream seeking a path across the earth and suddenly running into a rock. As soon as he'd rejected the prospect of city life for Julien, he came up against the idea of the Maquis. And he stopped. The Maquis was against the law. There was the danger of being captured, condemned, shot, or killed in combat in the mountains. The Germans were leaving, they shot those they could capture, and in reprisal, they burned farms whose owners were often only innocent peasants. Could a father advise his son to follow that path? Vaintrenier was a brave man, but his ideas were very far to the left. The Maquis were a bunch of Communists!

Then there remained the other solution: sending Julien off to a farm.

Gradually, from turning over all the pros and cons in his teeming brain, Père Dubois ended by seeing nothing except the land. The land was still the cleanest thing left. The war had dirtied even the bakers' trade by making the men knead that filthy stuff you couldn't call flour. It had forced the best workmen to cheat on everything, and the most honest tradesmen to sell the worst junk at the price of gold. Of course, in the cities they accused the farmers of getting rich by selling their produce on the black market, but if he left for a farm, Julien would only be an agricultural worker. He wouldn't be mixed up in selling produce. He would only have to work the land, and the land was always the land. In other words, the only thing that withstood the corruption of war.

Without even realizing that his brain was working exactly as if Julien had already decided to hide out on a farm, Père Dubois began to think back over all his old friends who lived in the country.

They were everywhere. In Courbouzon, in Gevingey, in Cousance, in St.-Maur, in Vernantois. A whole geography of friendship gradually took shape. Faces with indistinct features emerged slowly from the past; others, sharper, appeared suddenly, as close to him as if he'd left them only the night before. Comrades from his regiment or from the war, clients from the days he used to deliver his bread on horseback, winegrowers from whom he'd bought wine for years. Each one arrived, bringing with him the memory of their first meeting, the memories of their subsequent meetings, a whole series of thousands of insignificant facts whose details he still had stored in the depths of his mind. A life is made up of things like that. And his was full to the brim of these contacts that leave an impression on you. You forget them, and then one day, for one reason or another, they all come rushing back into your head at once. And this crowd invades your brain and heart the way it might jam into Place Lecourbe on the day of a big fair.

The morning, smudged with the ashes of winter, began to lighten. All around Père Dubois this crowd, which rose from the past like a stream swollen by melting snows, began to come alive. It caused quite a stir. It poured into him like a light wine. One of those wines that hold the sun prisoner in a dark cellar for a long time.

His face relaxed. He suddenly found himself sniffing the air in the room as he did on holidays when he'd just uncorked one of his best bottles.

⊸❦ 30 ❦⊷

THE room was filled with a comfortable warmth. Père Dubois sat there for a long time, huddled in his chair. He didn't move. He let his memories run free, dreading only the instant when the present would intrude itself once more.

And that instant occurred as soon as his wife came downstairs. Père Dubois tried to hold onto everyone who had come to life around him, but it was no longer possible. The presence of his wife was enough to frighten away those people who had come from so far away just to see him.

"Well?" he asked.

"He's going to leave."

"Where's he planning to go?"

"He claims he has enough friends in Lyons to be able to find a place to stay. And he's sure he'll be able to work there."

Père Dubois asked what kind of work he had in mind when Julien came down to get a suitcase he'd left in the dining room. He heard the question and said, "I have a trade. There's no reason why I can't get along as well as the next man."

His father felt a glow of warmth. So Julien was going to go back to work. Take up the trade of pastry cook again, that he'd learned and then abandoned. The old man had one worry though, and he asked, "But are you sure you'll be able to find a job? With all the rationing, pastry isn't doing very well."

The boy at first seemed completely taken aback; then his face suddenly relaxed, and he began to laugh.

"But who said anything about that! My trade is painting. Pastry, hell, if that's what you call a trade!"

He picked up his suitcase and climbed back up the stairs, still laughing.

His father hadn't had time to answer, and he perhaps would have found nothing to say, so hurt was he by that laugh. A simple word can wound you so deeply that you are left speechless. A trade! If that's what you call a trade! Julien had said that with such contempt, such disgust, that his father was stunned. His wife lowered her eyes and said, "I'll have to get his clothes ready."

She disappeared before Père Dubois could find a word to say. He was still shocked. His hands were trembling. His throat hurt. And then, gradually, something opened up inside him, letting loose a flood of words that rushed into his head.

His trade, good Lord, what next? Did he despise it to that extent? Then he despised all trades. Including the one his father had worked at so lovingly for the better part of his life. And he had been planning to talk to him about the land. About possibly leaving for a farm. What an idea! Were the times responsible for this, or was the boy quite simply a monster?

Would his mother finally understand that her son lacked common sense, logic, courage, everything that allows a man to lead an honest life? Paul? At least he had a trade. He was a success.

Painting, a trade? A trade that consisted of letting your hair grow and going around with an old dead man under your arm?

Père Dubois muttered on and on. In this way he freed himself of some of his anger, and as it gradually left him, he told himself that the best thing to do was to say nothing. Starting an argument before Julien's departure would be useless. Julien was leaving, and perhaps then peace would be restored in the house.

-◀{ 31 }▶-

JULIEN's departure was quicker and easier than Père Dubois had expected.

That same night M. Vaintrenier brought over his identity and ration cards. He did not mention the Maquis. No doubt he had understood that neither mother nor son really wanted that. In a solemn, almost mournful voice, he explained, "Your name and age are changed. Your card was issued here because you lived in town after the debacle, but you were born in Philippeville, which you left when you were very young because your parents moved here. So you remember nothing about it, which is only normal. We're doing it this way especially so that it will be impossible to verify."

"And what name have you given him on that card?" asked Mère Dubois.

"Forgive me, Madame Dubois, but I think it's better if nobody knows. I know you won't go out and tell everyone you meet, but it's a security measure."

Mère Dubois didn't object. Père Dubois was watching Vaintrenier, but the councilor's face expressed nothing in particular. He appeared to be performing a perfectly routine duty.

"You know," he said, "it's a security measure that even the wives are very willing to accept. You won't be able to write to your son, but he'll be able to send you his news from time to time, by writing you a postcard whenever he moves."

Vaintrenier paused a moment. Then he finally said more curtly, "Julien isn't wanted by the Gestapo and the militia, like people who are suspected of belonging to the Resistance. He's only out of line with the STO and wanted by the police because of his record of desertion. In these times they aren't going to mobilize a brigade of cops to put on his trail. If he behaves himself, he's in absolutely no danger . . . I even wonder if your mail is really being watched."

There was something mocking in his tone of voice. Père Dubois looked at Julien, but the boy didn't move a muscle. He was holding his cards in his hand and glancing at them from time to time, not daring to open them.

Vaintrenier didn't stay long. He declined a drink, shook hands with all three, and left, saying to Julien, "I wish you good luck all the same."

On the stoop, he turned around to add, "Of course, about those cards, I'm counting on you. You know what could happen to me."

It all had gone so quickly that Père Dubois didn't even have a chance to get a word in edgewise. His wife had barely been able to thank M. Vaintrenier. And now here they were, the three of them, left speechless. Julien, whose name was no longer Julien, was still holding the cards without daring to open them. He finally slipped them into his pocket and said, "That's good. I'll leave tomorrow morning on the six o'clock train. It will be dark, so no one will see me."

His mother sighed. "My Lord, what a lot there is to do."

Père Dubois coughed, got up to spit into the stove, and went back to his seat.

Then there was silence. A silence broken only by the sounds of Mère Dubois fixing their meal and setting the places. Julien smoked, his elbows on the table. Facing him, still turned at a three-quarter angle with his feet up on the stove, Père Dubois also smoked—a cigarette Julien had just given him.

There they were, with their last evening to spend together. Silence enveloped them. Night lay around the house. In the stove the wood burned quietly. There was no wind. Nothing.

Then, when the meal was over and the table cleared, there was a real emptiness.

Père Dubois drank his tea, got up, and said, "Good night."

Julien got up also and said, "I'll say good-bye to you now."

"No, I'll be up before you leave."

"Don't bother."

"Yes, I'll be up."

Père Dubois put his foot on the first step of the stairs, regulated the flame on the night-light he carried in his right hand, picked up his chamber pot in his left hand, and repeated, "Good night."

The others answered, and he slowly went up to bed.

PÈRE DUBOIS had barely dozed off two or three times during the entire night. He had heard his wife and his son come up to bed more than two hours after him. He had said nothing. And all night long, he had clearly sensed that his wife wasn't sleeping either. She couldn't have thought he was asleep, but she didn't speak.

They had lain side by side, forcing themselves not to move. Very close to each other and yet separated by the silence enclosing them.

In the morning Mère Dubois had gotten up very early, without making a sound, to go downstairs to light the fire and make her son's breakfast. Père Dubois had waited until the boy was up before going downstairs himself.

Now they were all three sitting in the kitchen. Mère Dubois

had lighted the lamp, and because of that, the morning seemed more like an evening.

Two suitcases were standing beside the door. A roll of newspaper which must have contained drawings was tied to the handle of the smallest one. Julien's coat was hanging on the bannister post. Père Dubois looked at it all. And then he looked at his son, who was slowly eating his bread and oatmeal, into which his mother had grated a square of chocolate. The kitchen was full of the odor of chocolate.

Père Dubois drank his bowl of bad coffee, then got out his tobacco box, and rolled a cigarette.

"It's too early to smoke," said his wife.

"I won't smoke any more because of that," he observed. "You know very well that I keep only a day's ration in my box."

They fell silent. Julien hadn't even raised his head.

"He should take the boulevard to the station," Père Dubois said. "It's longer, but he's less likely to run into anyone he knows."

"At this hour?" said Julien.

"Your father's right. No point in taking risks."

"Very well. I'll go whichever way you say."

There was something sad about Julien. A resignation that seemed to weigh on the whole house. Père Dubois would have liked to say a few words of comfort to his son, but they didn't come to him.

Several times Mère Dubois repeated, "My poor boy. My poor boy."

She also recommended several times that he be careful and sensible. Julien would say, "Yes, yes. Don't worry about me."

But the silences between these remarks seemed to drag on interminably.

When it was time to go, Père Dubois asked, "Have you got some money at least?"

"Yes, I have enough."

His father knew perfectly well that his mother wouldn't let him go off with nothing in his pockets, but that was all he'd been able to find to say. Embracing the boy, who leaned down over him, he added simply, "Let us hear from you before too long. And try not to do anything foolish."

That was all. Julien picked up his suitcases and went out behind his mother, who wanted to go with him as far as the garden gate.

Left alone, Père Dubois picked up the scallop shell that served as his ashtray, emptied the ashes into the stove, and put the butt Julien had left behind him into his tobacco box. Next, he opened the shutters and put out the lamp. It was still dark, and the light from the fire dancing behind the grill played over the linoleum. The old man sat down in his place, put his feet up on the stove door, and looked at the fire.

Julien had gone. He was going to the city. They were left alone. The war was everywhere. You didn't see it, but you could feel its presence even in the depths of this night that seemed to stay glued to the earth. Père Dubois tried to imagine the blacked-out streets, the station with a few bluish lights, but the images that came to him were those of another war, which he had known when he was still in the full vigor of his youth.

Now he was an old man whose strength was leaving him. Never had he felt it as fully as this morning, when he wondered if dawn would ever break behind the earth that he could barely see.

When Mère Dubois got back, she said simply, "Well, you put out the lamp already?"

"Yes, we won't be needing it."

"That's true—now."

And the word was left hanging, caught in time which was coming to a standstill.

Mère Dubois was sitting in her place between the stove and the table. They couldn't see each other. Père Dubois knew that like him, she was staring at the fire. Doubtless also trying to follow their boy in her thoughts.

Minutes flowed by that he could no longer count. A half hour, perhaps; then his wife murmured, "That's it. The train's left."

"You heard it?"

"Yes."

Père Dubois hadn't heard a thing.

"He had plenty of time to make it."

"Of course. The trains are always late," she said.

Daylight still hadn't come, and the silence settled again. The wood burned down without either of them saying a word. When there was nothing left but a few embers, Mère Dubois got up to put on a couple of logs.

"Still and all"—the old man sighed—"we're living in peculiar times."

"For us, it's nothing—but for the young."

Père Dubois didn't answer. His wife closed the stove door and sat back down, adding, "He could easily have stayed here if we'd been sure no one would turn him in."

These simple words stirred up a bitter residue in the old man's heart. He closed his lips against the acid response that came to him. His hand clenched the edge of the table. He gripped it so hard that his joints cracked. A shooting pain went up into his shoulder.

Nothing. He said nothing. And his wife didn't add another word.

Père Dubois' eyes left the stove grill to look through the window for some sign of this day that refused to break. He knew that from now on, he and his wife would stay like this, side by side, but farther apart than they had ever been.

They would live in expectation, but what good could they hope would come from this interminable night stretching out before them?

The sooty sky oppressing the frigid dawn would bring no real light.

It was winter.

There was silence.

There was a stale smell all over the earth, like the odor which penetrates and chills you when you enter a death chamber.

Part Three

THE FLOWERS OF SUMMER

WINTER had passed slowly, dark and wet. Then spring
had come, bringing no real joy, offering nothing more than a
vague hope. Would the war finally be over? Yet who could say
that he would live to see the end of it? For it was there, in a
form that grew more frightening every day.

People talked without knowing exactly what was going on,
but it was certain that they were killing people everywhere for
no reason, rather haphazardly. They were also arresting a lot
of people. One morning, men from the Gestapo or the militia
would come; they would take away some people who would
never be seen again. On certain days the curfew had been set
for six o'clock in the evening, and a retired old man in Village-
Neuf who had been out in his garden had been shot down by a
patrol. You had to close yourself in, lock your doors and windows, live in the shadows without ever going outside. There
had been the arrival of the Mongols from Vlassov, the burning
of several villages on the first plateau, and not a week went by
without hearing of the deaths of people you knew. In April
the Germans had assassinated Dr. Michel simply because he'd
taken care of some members of the Resistance.

Père Dubois never left his garden anymore except to go get
water at the fountain, and whenever his wife went out to buy

the few provisions their ration coupons gave them a right to, he was anxious.

The police had come three times looking for Julien, but they hadn't been difficult.

The sergeant would say, "You know, this is just a routine check. It has to be done, but by now the administration realizes that he won't be showing his face around here until the end of the war."

Père and Mère Dubois each time gave the same statement, which they both signed and which was limited to this: "Declare that they have not seen their son Julien since his disappearance and are ignorant of his whereabouts at the present time."

It was almost the truth. They didn't even have to lie since they never were asked if they'd had any news of him. Anyhow, could you really call news a few words hastily scribbled on a postcard, signed with an illegible name, mailed once from Lyons, another time from St.-Étienne, and again from Marseilles? It was almost no news at all. Barely enough to remind them from time to time that Julien wasn't dead.

Paul's last visit had been at the beginning of January. He had come to wish them a happy new year. He had drunk a cup of awful coffee with them, affirmed that he still believed in Germany's ultimate victory, left his father two packages of tobacco, then departed without making the slightest allusion to Julien's disappearance.

For Père Dubois, the war was a long silence and a solitude that nothing brightened.

The old couple had even stopped squabbling. They carried on their work in the garden, which kept them from starving to death.

The neighbors continued to buy a few vegetables and also brought them news of the war. But the war didn't really penetrate their solitude until the day when they were certain that the Allied landings in Normandy had succeeded.

A breath of hope passed over the countryside and came to stir the warm air of this early June, even in the depths of their garden. It was M. Robin who brought the news. He was wearing a big smile, and he said there soon would be an end to all this misery.

But after this breath of hope, a wind of anguish came up. The Germans got harsher and harsher, and it was feared that the war might sweep through the whole country.

"In 1918," said Père Dubois, "it was also the Americans who dealt the final blow, but it wasn't done without destroying the part of the country where the fighting was."

And the old man's anguish increased when it was learned, on August 16, that more troops had landed at Cavalaire. For the first time in years, Père Dubois pored over the map of France on the back of the post office calendar.

"If they come up from the south," he said, "we stand a good chance of being right in their path."

They'd been without news from Julien for four weeks, and his wife simply said, "If only I knew where he was."

Père Dubois did not answer. They had never talked much, but for months now, they'd learned to understand each other from half words. He knew that his wife's simple phrase had meant: "You'll always be the same old egotist. You think about your garden and your house, which might be destroyed. You think about your own life, but none of that really matters to me. What matters to me is my son. He'd certainly be in less danger here with us. But he's alone. He might be killed in an air raid, arrested, tortured, and we don't even know where he is."

Père Dubois read that in her eyes, in her way of shrugging her shoulders when he talked about their property. She had cut herself off completely from everything, even from him. She continued to look after him, to share that miserable black bread with him; she also shared the interminable nights they spent side by side pretending to be asleep—and all out of habit.

Because this was the way it would be until the end of their lives.

But there was nothing left of this life except the taste of bad food. It no longer even advanced in rhythm with the seasons, where the hardest is always followed by a gentler one. Summer had come; it had brought nothing good. They had hoped so long in vain that hope itself was exhausted.

"You're too pessimistic," M. Robin would say. "The Allies are advancing. We'll be liberated in a few weeks."

Père Dubois would shake his head. "In 1917," he would say, "they used to play the same tune. I know the Germans. They won't be beaten as easily as that."

What he feared the most was to see the war come into their area and stabilize itself in a line right near the Jura. That would be the end of everything. The house destroyed, the garden in ruins, the two of them fleeing with nothing into unknown and hostile countryside. They had been spared in 1940. For a long time, Père Dubois had clung to the idea that this plot of ground where he lived would be preserved, but now, without quite understanding why, he was filled with fear. He saw himself being dispossessed. He imagined his lifetime of work coming to a grievous end, with everything destroyed and plundered.

He went on with his labors, but he felt his strength ebbing away, and often he would look at his garden with disgust. Grass was growing along the paths. It was even creeping into certain beds, and he could only repeat to himself, "I break my back, but I can't do it anymore. I can't do it all."

Sometimes he had spurts of pride, and when someone came, he would gesture angrily at his garden, less well cared for than it used to be, and say, "I could do it. I still have the strength, but I don't have the time. When they set the curfews at six in the morning and six in the evening, the days just aren't long enough. Especially at my age, when I have to work in the hot noonday sun, I don't get anywhere, and I tire easily."

One afternoon in the second week of August, when he was

working not far from the street, Père Dubois heard the gate click. He straightened up and leaned on his tool. A young girl had come in and seemed to be looking around. She was scanning the garden, peering between the trees. When she spotted Père Dubois, she followed the path toward him and, from a little distance, asked, "Could I please speak to Madame Dubois?"

The old man didn't know her. She was slight, with long chestnut hair, and was wearing a simple, short-sleeved dress. She carried a small leather satchel.

"What's it about?" Père Dubois asked.

"I've come for some flowers."

Since the war, flowers hadn't sold very well, and Père Dubois had grown less of them, leaving more room for vegetables.

"Go way down to the end. She must be near the pump. But you know, we don't have very much in the way of flowers."

The young girl moved away. Père Dubois followed her with his eyes for a moment, then went back to his work. He worked for a few minutes, but the young stranger's presence worried him. Where could she have come from? He was sure he'd never seen her around there, and clients they didn't know were extremely rare. Leaning his hoe against a pear tree, he went along the fence, slowly, being careful to stay hidden behind the row of trees.

When he was about twenty yards away from the pump, he stopped. Between the peach tree branches, he could see the visitor, who was partly shielding his wife. He moved over to the left. Mère Dubois was reading. The young girl was standing motionless in front of her. After a while Mère Dubois raised her head. Her face was in the shadow of her canvas hat, and he couldn't see her expression. However, he could tell that something serious was going on, for his wife stuffed the piece of paper into her apron pocket and, suddenly lowering her head, hid her face in her hands.

Père Dubois struggled for a moment against the desire to join the two women, but he didn't move. The air was heavy, still and humming with the flight of a thousand insects. On the other side of the École Normale wall a German truck was maneuvering.

The truck stopped. Now Mère Dubois was talking, but he couldn't hear what she was saying. Unable to get any closer without being seen, he went back to where he'd left his hoe. Something had just happened. Something serious, no doubt, and his wife hadn't even called him. Was it about Julien? Probably. But why would his wife want to keep the news from him? Did she think he no longer had a right to know what was happening to the boy? What had he ever done to deserve this kind of treatment?

He'd started working again, and because of his anger, he worked at a pace that was too fast for him. His shirt was soon drenched with sweat. Drops beaded his forehead and ran down the end of his nose. When he straightened up, a fit of coughing seized him, and he had to drop his tool. His eyes filled with tears; he saw the young girl go by. She nodded to him, but he could barely nod back.

She was carrying a few peonies.

--❦{ 34 }❧--

PÈRE DUBOIS had scarcely caught his breath when his wife joined him.

"You're coughing," she said, "and you're dripping wet. You really should stop a moment."

He was thirsty. And above all, he wanted to know who the young girl was. However, he said, "No. I want to finish this bed today."

186

"You have to come anyway for a minute. There's news from Julien. And you could change your shirt at the same time."

He started off after her. His throat was burning, and he had to wipe his eyes again. His wife had spoken calmly, but he had noticed her furrowed chin, her red eyes and strained face.

Had something serious happened to the boy? She seemed to be walking so slowly, and yet he was afraid to find out.

In the kitchen, with the shutters closed and the shade down, it was almost cool. A group of flies buzzed around under the lamp.

Père Dubois drank a glass of water while his wife went upstairs to get him a clean shirt. When he had changed and sat down in his place, she settled herself at the table and took Julien's letter out of her pocket. She put it on the table and slowly smoothed the wrinkled paper with the flat of her hand.

Since she couldn't seem to bring herself either to speak or to read the letter, Père Dubois finally asked, "Well, what does he have to say?"

"Well, my heavens—"

She stopped. Her mouth was moving, trying to form the words she couldn't articulate.

"Come on," said the old man, "read me the letter. He seems to have written more than usual, from what I can see."

"Yes. That's because he has a lot to tell us. And also, because his letter didn't come through the mails, he could write more freely."

"Do you know that young girl?"

Mère Dubois shook her head. She let a few more seconds pass; then, slowly raising her tear-filled eyes, she murmured, "I don't know her . . . But—but she's his fiancée."

That was the one piece of news Père Dubois hadn't anticipated. He had imagined the best and the worst, but that really had been a million miles from his thoughts. He could only mutter, "His fiancée, you say?"

"Yes . . . they're going to get married."

"But who is she?"

As though this question had come as a relief, Mère Dubois answered very fast in a much more assured tone of voice, "She's a girl from St.-Claude. You don't know her. Naturally. Her name is Françoise—Françoise Jacquier . . . That's a very well-known name in those parts. Her father is a mason. She met Julien in St.-Claude at a sports meet. They hadn't seen each other since, and then they met again in Lyons. She works there."

Mère Dubois fell silent. She must have told everything she knew about the girl. She took a deep breath and bowed her head. Père Dubois sensed that she was hiding something else that wasn't so easy to talk about.

"And he sent her all the way here to tell us that? I don't suppose they'll be getting married right away, will they?"

When his wife didn't answer, he asked, "How did she get here? Only the Germans have been allowed to use the trains for at least ten days. Monsieur Robin told us that again this morning."

"She didn't come on the train. And anyhow, she's on her way to St.-Claude. That's why she wasn't able to stay longer. If she has time, she'll stop by to see us Monday on her way back."

"At least"—the old man sighed—"I hope he won't get married until he's found a job. The way things are these days!"

"From what he says in his letter and from what the child told me, it seems that so far he hasn't been making such a bad living."

"From his painting?"

"Yes. From his painting."

Père Dubois spotted a gleam of triumph in his wife's eyes. But she lowered her eyelids very fast to add, "Obviously, since the landings, people have had other things to do than buy paintings."

"In any case, that's not a job. And even if the war does

end, he'll have to wait until he's found work before he can think about getting married. I hope that girl understands that."

As he was talking, his wife turned the letter over twice on the table. He noticed that her hands were trembling. He was about to question her, but anticipating him, she said in a broken voice, "They can't wait—they—they've been foolish."

She clearly was having a hard time holding back her tears. Père Dubois felt a flood of anger rising up inside him, but his wife's anguished face gave him the strength to contain himself. He simply said, without raising his voice, "Good Lord! That's all we needed!"

She must have been expecting him to get angry, for she gave him a look of astonishment. And she must have noticed that he was still poised on the brink of his anger, for she quickly said, "Don't get angry, Gaston. I beg of you, don't get angry. I already have enough troubles."

"I'm not getting angry. It wouldn't do any good."

That she had admitted her vulnerability and her pain so spontaneously comforted the old man. If he started shouting, if he blamed her for everything by reminding her that she'd always spoiled Julien, supported and overprotected him, she would be defenseless. He hesitated a moment, but the weight of these last years endured together silenced him.

A new war between them was unthinkable. All around this house, their sole refuge from the madness outside, there was already too much trouble to bear, too many dangers, too much suffering. They must at least be able to look each other in the eye without hating each other and talk without hurting each other.

"My poor woman"—he sighed—"what can we do about it?"

Soundlessly, not sobbing, she started to cry.

Père Dubois waited a long time before asking, "He said this in his letter?"

His wife wiped her eyes and slowly read: "My dear Mama. Françoise will be bringing you this letter. She will explain to you that we have to get married as soon as possible. I know that you always wanted to have a girl. I hope that you will welcome Françoise as if she were your own daughter."

Her voice broke. After a long silence she added, "Next, he talks about his work. And he says that the war will be over before the end of the month."

Père Dubois snorted. "Over! But under what circumstances? And what will have become of us by then?"

"That little Françoise said just the same thing as Monsieur Robin. That it will be a complete defeat for the Germans as it was for us in 1940. That they'll just be trying to get out of here as fast as possible. It seems that a lot of them have already left Lyons."

It all was getting more complicated, taking on a different complexion. There was no longer just the concern about the war. They knew that Julien was alive, but now this girl from St.-Claude appeared, bringing them a new pack of troubles.

"And this girl actually told you that they had to get married?"

"Yes."

"She had the nerve to say that to you?"

"Julien wrote it in his letter. I asked her if it was true. She blushed, but she answered yes . . . and—and I don't know how to explain it, but I had the impression that she wasn't really too embarrassed to admit it."

"Good Lord, we really are living in peculiar times. I've told you that often enough. And I'm not wrong either."

More quietly, his wife answered, "Exactly. The times make these things happen. If Julien didn't have to live under a false name, they'd be married already."

"Still and all . . . still and all . . . coming to tell you a thing like that. That girl must really—she must not have any shame."

He'd almost said, "That girl must really not be worth much." But he'd restrained himself.

"I didn't have much of a chance to talk to her," said his wife, "but she didn't leave a bad impression on me."

"Did she—did—"

Père Dubois paused. Sensing what he hadn't been able to express, his wife explained, "Of course, I should have called you. But—but I wanted to talk to you first. And then she was in such a hurry . . . And already frightened enough at talking to me."

Père Dubois' anger had subsided, and he almost forced himself to raise his voice: "Julien must have made me sound like an old bear. But I've never eaten anybody, have I?"

His wife's eyes were still moist. She smiled anyhow, and leaning toward her husband a little, she murmured, "My Lord, when I think of the news we might have gotten instead . . . My Lord. Don't you really think we're sort of lucky?"

·◄ 35 ►·

THIS unexpected news had changed nothing in the course of events, and yet the anguish that had been oppressing Père Dubois for several weeks abated slightly. Inexplicably, it seemed to him that nothing further of any importance would happen. It was a little as if the war had reserved for each man his share of hardship. Père Dubois had received his share. With his load shouldered, he could expect to go his way more or less undisturbed until the end. All this was blurred in his mind, but he felt that the girl's visit had set time in motion again—time so long suspended on the edge of a precipice neither he nor his wife had dared to plumb.

Since he had only seemed mildly disgruntled, his wife

often mentioned Julien, Françoise, and what they should do for them. These references annoyed the old man, but he silenced his ill humor. His wife talked, and it stirred a little life into the backwater of their solitude.

And then this time the German rout was turning into a reality. The fever of it reached their neighborhood. Convoys rumbled by on the boulevard and down the Rue des Salines. At the École Normale, there was an almost constant coming and going that Père Dubois watched through a crack in his bedroom shutters. M. Robin came five or six times a day bringing news reports. At ten o'clock he announced that the Allies were at Lyons. At noon he came to say that they were as close as Valence. At four he stated that Paris would be liberated during the night. Then, a few minutes before the curfew, he came running to announce that there was a battle going on near Alençon that would put an end to the war.

"That man is crazy," Père Dubois said.

"We're the ones who are crazy," his wife claimed. "We've buried ourselves here. With no news. But everybody else is on pins and needles."

"And where does it get them?"

When he thought about the war, Père Dubois was always divided between the desire to have it over before a battle took place in their area and the wish that the Germans would finally know what it was like to have a war in their own country.

He knew that the Russians had already invaded Poland, but that was very far away. Too far for him to have a clear idea of it.

On several occasions M. Robin spoke about skirmishes with the Maquis in the Haut-Jura. After he left, Mère Dubois said, "Let's hope that little girl doesn't get caught in one of those messes!"

"She must have been mad, traveling at a time like this."

"She had to do it."

"I'd like to know why!"

"She didn't tell me, but I think it was important."

"In any case, it's a sure thing she won't be able to get back to Lyons for a while."

When Père Dubois said that, he saw his wife's face tense. She sighed several times; then under her breath, as if she didn't really want her husband to hear, she murmured, "I didn't see much of her, that little girl, and yet, I don't know—it seems to me that if I knew that she was with him, I'd rest easier."

And then in a whisper she added these few words Père Dubois almost had to guess by reading her lips: "She's so much more sensible than he is."

THE nights were endless because of the curfew that began at six in the evening, when the sun was still high in the sky. Père and Mère Dubois ate in the half-light of the kitchen, leaving the shutter open a crack. When they finished their bowls of soup, they would sit for a long time, listening to the noises, peering at the thin slat of light where the foliage, still drooping with heat, was alive with the zigzag flight of insects and the singing of birds. It sometimes happened that they sat for more than an hour like this, not moving, not speaking, only, from time to time, heaving a sigh that seemed to despair of expressing the weight of the evening. When a shot rang out somewhere in the town or the surrounding hills, they would prick up their ears, look at each other, then settle down to waiting again in a heavier silence.

One night they heard gunfire right near their house. The next day M. Robin told them that a man, living in a building

on the Boulevard Jules-Ferry, had been wounded as he was
opening a window onto his garden.

After this interminable wait, Père and Mère Dubois would
go upstairs to bed. It would still be light. The old man would
glue his eyes to a tiny knothole in the bedroom shutters.
Through it he could see a large part of the École Normale park
and garden, where the setting sun lengthened the grotesque
shadows of trees and bushes across the reddish sand of the
walks. Sentries, helmeted, booted, and dressed in green, stood
motionless at the corners of the buildings. Others walked the
length of the enclosure walls down by the cheese factory. That
meant that still others were walking less than thirty yards from
the house, along the wall that separated the Dubois' garden
from the school park. Each night, thinking about that, Père
Dubois would see images from the First War again. He had
been thirty years younger. The world had been different, his
life, too, and it was with stories of those times that he tried to
fall asleep. But often, he would only find sleep very late, after
exhausting his store of memories.

During the night of August 24, Père Dubois was awakened
simultaneously by his wife shaking him and by a crackling that
sounded like a big green wood fire.

He sat up in bed. They were shooting. Machine guns. Sharp
detonations. Other duller ones. Mortar-shell explosions.

His wife's clenched hands gripped his forearm.

"Gaston—they're shooting all over."

The gunfire grew louder, devouring the night.

"We've got to get up," he said.

"Don't talk so loud."

"Why the hell not?"

His first alarm over, Père Dubois felt very calm.

"Get dressed," he ordered, "and above all, don't light anything."

"I'm not insane."

He noticed that her voice was more assured than when she'd

wakened him. He pulled on his pants, adjusted his suspenders, and put on his slippers. Then he felt his way over to the shutters.

"Don't go near the window, Gaston. Stay here."

"Let me handle things. I'm not going to open them, silly!"

He found the hole with his hand and glued his eye to it. The explosions followed one another with increasing rapidity, and he could clearly see flashes near the station and at the foot of the Montaigu hill.

"They're near the station," he said. "It must be an attack on the railroad tracks."

"Or on the Gestapos' hotel."

"That's possible."

They were silent a moment. The shots came closer.

"It sounds as if they're firing over by Montciel, too," Mère Dubois remarked.

The old man listened. It could have been the effect of an echo against the flank of the hill, but it did seem to him that the firing was coming from all over. This side of the house was blind, but there was no thought of going outside to see what was happening.

"Let's go downstairs," said Père Dubois. "We'll be safer down there."

"Suppose they come into the house—"

He snorted. "If they come in, there won't be any point in hiding. But the real danger would be if a mortar shell landed on the roof and set fire to it or ripped it open. In case of fire, we'd be able to get out faster downstairs."

He went first, groping with his hands and feet.

"If only we didn't have to go outside to get down into the cellar," said his wife.

"Sure, but we'd better not try."

In the kitchen, Père Dubois lighted his lighter.

"No," said Mère Dubois, "leave it dark."

"What are you talking about? You know perfectly well that

absolutely nothing shows through the shutters— Come on, don't lose your head like this. I just want to see what time it is."

He raised his hand to bring the flame up to the clock. His hand was not trembling. He noticed at once that his wife was ashen. Her face looked ravaged. Fear deepened each of her wrinkles. She had thrown her shawl over her shoulders and was holding it to her chest with clenched fingers.

Père Dubois put out his lighter. It was quarter to three.

As soon as the flame was out, the darkness seemed thicker, except for the memory of that glow, which left a colorless hole in the night. The shooting kept up, like a sea whipped by waves. A sea swirling around them, advancing, retreating, returning faster and closer.

"I really think they're fighting just about everywhere," observed Père Dubois.

"Do you think they've attacked the town?"

"Probably."

"The Americans?"

"How do you expect me to know?"

There was a lull; then, suddenly, firing erupted much nearer the house.

"We can't stay here like this," said Mère Dubois.

"If they're really fighting in the streets, it will be the end of everything!"

Père Dubois had almost shouted. He did not feel fear, but a sort of rage that made him clench his fists.

"Don't shout," his wife implored. "Don't shout."

"But we're done for," he cried. "You don't understand—everything will be lost!"

"My God— My God."

They stood there like that a few more seconds, at the foot of the stairs, in the dark. Then, abruptly, Père Dubois reached for his wife's arm and grabbed it, saying, "Come on, you never know."

"But where are you going?"

"To the cellar."

"You're going outside?"

"No one will see us—it's too dark. And they've got other things to do."

"You're out of your head."

"No, believe me. I know where we'll be safest."

"My God—"

Père Dubois pulled his wife toward the door. He groped for the lock, turned the key, pulled the bolt; then, before opening the door, he paused. "Do you have any money here?"

"Yes—and the deeds."

"We've got to take everything."

They went into the dining room. Père Dubois lighted his lighter. His wife opened the left-hand drawer of the buffet and began feeling around inside. Her hands were still trembling. She took out papers, things she flung down anywhere on top of the buffet. The breeze she stirred up made the flame flicker, and it went out three times. Père Dubois swore. His lighter wouldn't light anymore.

"We'll have to find a candle."

"There's one in the kitchen, and there's a lighter too."

The old man hunted, groping, bumping into objects that he knocked over.

"Great God Almighty! We're wasting time."

There were three explosions, louder than the others, which shook the house, rattling the windowpanes. The sputtering of a machine gun had got closer. Père Dubois lighted the candle and went back to his wife, who had not moved.

She held the papers up to the flame, which wavered with their breathing.

"Don't go starting a fire," said the old man. "They'll take care of that without any help from you!"

"What shall I put them in?"

"Don't you have a bag?"

"A bag?"

"Yes, anything."

They both were getting jumpy. Père Dubois sensed that the battle was coming closer. If they didn't get out in a few minutes, it would be too late. Men might come into the garden to attack or defend the École Normale.

He went back into the kitchen, opened the door to the laundry, and took down a heavy canvas shopping bag that was hanging behind the door.

"Put it all in here," he said.

He also took down his watch, which was hanging near the window, and stuffed it into his pocket.

"We ought to take some clothes," said his wife.

She got out the coat she'd made from the overcoat of the soldier they'd taken in during the debacle and threw her cape over her shoulders. They went to the door, and Père Dubois blew out the candle, which he put in his pocket along with the two lighters.

The gunfire and grenades were getting closer and closer.

Père Dubois listened hard, slowly opened the door a crack, and turned around to ask, "Can you hear anything moving out there?"

His wife came forward.

"No."

"Then we'd better go. Keep as close to the ground as possible. And if any shooting starts nearby, lie down and don't move."

He opened the door wide enough to let them through. He crouched down into an old forgotten posture from the First War. He took a step onto the landing and felt his wife holding onto the edge of his cape.

Just as he was about to turn around to say, "Close the door, but don't slam it," a series of explosions ripped through the night as if they'd been fired at their feet. Between the branches, the old man saw flashes lighting up the façades of buildings on the Rue des Écoles. Shoving into his wife, he turned around and roared, "Good God, it's too late!"

They crashed into each other. Père Dubois felt his wife lose her balance and clutch at him. He tried to hold her up, but the momentum he'd gathered was too strong. They both fell into the kitchen, slamming the door wide open back against the doorframe.

Grenades were exploding even closer, and four red flashes lit up the room.

Père Dubois got to his knees, helped his wife move across the linoleum, and closed the door.

37

"Good night," Père Dubois muttered. "Good night. We're done for."

The door was closed again. They both were lying side by side on the cold linoleum floor of the kitchen. Mère Dubois didn't say a word.

"Are you hurt?" asked her husband.

"No—and you?"

"No. You didn't drop the bag outside?"

"No, I'm holding it."

"We can't . . . stay here."

The noise was so close that they had to shout and wait for moments when the shooting let up a little before speaking.

"But where can we go?"

"Not behind the door. I'm going to go upstairs and get a mattress. We ought to be in the dining room, in front of the buffet; then we'd be away from the window."

He felt his wife move. He followed her into the dining room. They moved on all fours, like children playing.

"Here. This is the best spot. Lie down against the buffet—I'm going upstairs."

"No. Stay here."

"But I won't be in any danger. I'm going up to get a mattress."

His voice was firm. Authoritarian. Nevertheless, his wife said, "I'm coming with you."

"No. Stay here!"

He moved off. He found his way easily, knowing every corner of the house as he did. He wouldn't have gone any faster if it had been day. He didn't feel tired or out of breath.

When he got up to the bedroom, he went to the window. On the way, he felt along the cool marble top of the nightstand where he put his tobacco box each night. He slid it into his pants pocket. He leaned toward the window and glued his eye to the hole. The night was still alive with flashes. They were shooting down near the station. They were shooting near the cheese factory and over toward Village-Neuf. Trees and houses were briefly silhouetted in the night.

Père Dubois turned back to the bed, and only then did he think that his cape would get in his way. He threw it back over his shoulders, pulled the covers off the bed, folded the mattress in three, and wrapped his arms around it. He felt his strength that he used to have at thirty coming back again. He lifted the mattress effortlessly, carried it without staggering. His arm bumped against the bannister post, but he felt no pain. He calmly went down the stairs.

"Do you want me to help you?" asked his wife.

"Get out of the way."

A pause.

"Here," she said.

He slid the mattress down and laid it on the floor beside the buffet.

"For the moment," he said, "we'll sit on top of it. If the shooting gets too close, we'll sit up against the buffet and put the mattress in front of us."

They sat down side by side, their legs straight out in front of them. There they weren't in front of the window. They had the width of the room between them and the very thick wall. Behind them, they had the buffet, then the partition wall, then the kitchen and another wall. And behind the partition there was the cast-iron stove. Père Dubois had heard only a few explosions that sounded like mortar fire. All the rest were just volleys of shots, machine-gun fire and grenades. The bullets could come through the shutters, but not the walls. Only the shells were to be feared, but for the moment, there was no artillery fire.

"You got overheated," his wife said, "bringing down that mattress. Wrap yourself up in your cape."

"Don't worry about me."

What he worried about most was fire. One bullet would be enough to catch the roof. Between the tiles and the ceiling, in the false attic where no one ever went, there probably was a lot of highly inflammable debris. And the shed, with the hay, the dry hutches. Good Lord, it would all go up like tinder!

Père Dubois was astonished by his calm. He knew that he must hold onto it. He got the candle, the lighter, and his tobacco box out of his pocket and placed them beside him. He lighted the lighter.

"You're lighting that? What are you going to do?"

"Roll a cigarette."

"My God."

He lighted the candle and held it out to his wife.

"Here, hold this."

Her hand was trembling.

"You know very well that you can't see a thing from outside. Come on now, hold it for me."

She moved closer to him. For the time it took to unwrap sev-

eral butts and roll a cigarette, their faces were very close together, illuminated by the flame that made the polished metal
of the tobacco box glow. Père Dubois closed the box and put it
on the mattress. It was almost as if they both were in the front
lines, in the trenches. He lighted his cigarette from the candle flame.

"I'm sure that they're fighting out front," said Mère Dubois.

Her husband listened a moment. It sounded as though they
must be on the boulevard, as well as in the Rue des Écoles—
that is, on both sides of the house.

"But what's going on? What on earth is going on?" The old
woman sobbed.

"There's no doubt about it anymore. It must be the Maquis.
If it were the Americans, there would be shelling. There must
be a lot of them—there's fighting on all the roads into town."

"But I told you they're already in our street."

"That could be the Germans, firing from here."

They spoke quickly. And then, for long moments, they would
stop to listen, to try to follow the battle in their minds.

"If we only knew what was happening in Lyons," said Mère
Dubois, "knew whether that little girl was able to get back."

Two mortar explosions rocked the house. Père Dubois got
up.

"Don't move," cried his wife.

"Let me go. I'm going to open a window. Otherwise, all the
panes will fall out."

He went and opened the kitchen window, and the din was
suddenly much louder. From the kitchen he called, "Have you
got any coffee made?"

"Yes, but it's cold."

He went back to get the candle. His wife was huddled in the
corner between the wall and the buffet.

"Don't move," he said. "I'll be back."

He brought the alcohol stove and a little pot into which he
had poured some coffee.

"You're crazy," said his wife.

"No. If we have to go, I'd like to drink my coffee first."

By now there must already be men in the garden. Everything would be ruined. During the other war, Père Dubois had seen too many villages where fighting had gone on to still think that his garden, his house, and his shed had a chance of being spared. But what could he do? Nothing. Go out and yell at them that they were mad? That they had no right to come and fight on his place? That he was out of it all, and there were plenty of other places where they could go fight?

Hadn't there been hundreds of men in every war who felt like acting like that?

As long as war circles around you like a menacing patrol that keeps its distance, there is always hope. But the day the patrol closes in, comes into your garden and tramples everything to lay siege to your house, what is the proper thing to do?

Père Dubois clenched his fists. He puffed nervously on his cigarette. By God, if he only had a gun. He'd stand at a window and at least kill a few of them before they got him!

He felt alternating waves of hatred and tenderness surge through him. There were a thousand things he'd have liked to tell his wife, who was clinging to his arm and sobbing.

"My poor woman—we've been through a lot in our day. Sometimes we shouted at each other; we shouldn't have. I've been to blame."

"Be quiet," she murmured. "I've been wrong, too."

"When we meet again in the next world, we won't fight anymore."

Shots rang out so close that it sounded as if a furious hailstorm were dashing against every part of the little house.

They were silent.

They pushed back the mattress, lay down on the cold floor, and pulled the mattress up over them as if it were a big quilt.

Then there was nothing to do but wait.

⊷⊰ 38 ⊱⊶

THEY lay there for a long time. The floor was hard, the cold gradually crept through Père Dubois' body, and he finally stood up. The shooting was more sporadic.

"I don't know where it is," he said, "but it seems to have moved off a little."

"We don't even know what time it is."

The old man pulled his watch out of his pocket and lighted his lighter. It was almost five o'clock.

The noise diminished even further; then soon there were only a few occasional shots.

"Stay here," said Père Dubois. "I'm going upstairs to see what's happening."

"Be careful."

He went up to the bedroom and looked out through the hole in the shutter. Daylight had come, but the sun wasn't up over the rooftops yet. Along the garden walks of the École Normale, the Germans were lying or sitting beside their weapons, which they'd laid on the ground. They were talking. Some were wearing their helmets, but others were bareheaded or just wearing their caps. One of them stood up and walked over to a plum tree, which he climbed. Père Dubois thought he wanted to see what was happening on the other side of the wall, but it soon was clear that the man was just picking plums. When his cap was full, he climbed down, brought some fruit to his friends, and went back to his machine gun, whose barrel was resting on a stump. Another soldier was sitting on the stump. Shots still rang out from time to time, but there were long moments of respite when the silence was broken only by the rumble of a few vehicles.

The two soldiers ate their plums, throwing the pits at another group of soldiers who were laughing. When his cap was empty, the man who had gone to pick the fruit put it back on his head, lay down behind the stump, and aimed his weapon. The gun barrel began spitting out little red flames, and Père Dubois instinctively dropped to the floor. There was a burst of firing. Père Dubois got up and watched the man positioned beside the gunner calmly reloading the weapon. For the second burst, Père Dubois didn't bother to move. The Germans were firing in the direction of Montciel. They ran through four belts like that; then the gunner went back to pick more plums. He did all this calmly, as if it were routine work with no danger involved at all.

"What are you doing?" shouted his wife from downstairs.

"I'm coming."

Père Dubois went downstairs.

"They were shooting from very close by," she said. "I was afraid it was at you."

"No, they don't give much of a damn about us. They're firing toward Montciel."

"Montciel?"

"Yes, and that means that they really were attacked and that the attack didn't succeed. And if you could see how they behave . . . Really, those men have gotten used to the war; it takes more than that to frighten them. People claim that they're finished, but that's not how they look to me."

Père Dubois had been deeply impressed by the soldiers' calm. Everything about them made him think that they'd be there for a long time.

When the shooting had almost stopped, Mère Dubois asked, "What are they going to do now?"

"You'd have to be pretty smart to be able to tell."

Père Dubois had scarcely finished speaking when there came

another burst of shots, very close, and, at almost the same time, shouts and a crackling sound. They listened for a moment; then the old man said, "There's a fire somewhere."

They still didn't dare open the shutters. In the darkness, they climbed upstairs. His eye glued to the hole, Père Dubois saw a thick cloud of smoke rising up in front of the sun. Another cloud was blackening the sky over toward the station. There were only a few soldiers left in the École Normale garden. He observed all this in a few seconds; then, backing up to give his place to his wife, he said, "For God's sake, they've set the whole town on fire."

"My God, all of the Rue des Écoles is in flames."

They stood there stunned for a second, then went to the landing at the top of the stairs. There daylight came in through the skylight opening onto the roof.

"If I could get up there," said the old man, "I could take a look."

"That's impossible. The ladder is in the shed."

Père Dubois gauged the distance.

"If the skylight weren't above the stairs, with a table—"

He stopped. He had just thought of the other skylight which opened into Julien's room. His wife had thought of it at the same time. They went in and pushed Julien's desk under it. He had left some notebooks and a few books on top of the desk, which Mère Dubois put on his bed. Père Dubois got up on the desk and yanked down the flowered curtain and blackout paper that covered the skylight. Standing on tiptoe, he could see the housetops facing the garden. To see the street, he'd have to open it and stick his head out.

"Hand me the chair," he said.

"You're not going to open it!"

"Hand me the chair, I tell you."

"Gaston, it's not wise."

"Nobody's going to see me!"

He had shouted. His wife lifted the chair onto the desk. Père

Dubois climbed up on it. Once up, he was a little too tall and had to lean to one side and bend his knees. Slowly, with great control, he reached for the metal hook and loosened it from the eye that held it. There was a creaking. He paused a moment, then gently raised the glass frame and put the hook in the second eye. He waited about ten seconds. The crackling of the fire was louder. The smell of smoke was already coming in through the narrow opening. When he'd counted to ten, Père Dubois carefully poked his head up until his forehead touched the glass. From there he could see a whole section of the street and the garden.

The fire wasn't in the houses across from them, but in the ones a little to the right, near the school. The flames were shooting up very high, biting and slashing at the black and gray smoke, which by now veiled a whole area of sky. A few bursts of machine-gun fire mingled with the roar of the flames.

Beyond the garden the street was deserted. The fence was intact, and the gate appeared to be still locked. The shutters on all the other houses were closed.

Nobody.

"Well?" asked Mère Dubois.

Père Dubois couldn't say a word. He looked again at the fire and then climbed down.

"Go on up," he said. "You'll see."

His wife climbed up. When she was up, he groaned, "They're capable of setting the whole town on fire."

Mère Dubois didn't say anything. Her hands gripping the iron frame were trembling. Suddenly, at the same time as he heard the sharp bark of a machine gun, Père Dubois saw his wife's hand let go of the frame and fly to her mouth.

"My God!" she cried.

"What's the matter?"

She got down so fast that her husband had to grab her to keep her from falling. Her white face was damp with sweat.

"I saw him—" she stammered. "I saw him fall—his hands clutching his belly."

She imitated his gesture and sank onto Julien's bed. Père Dubois climbed onto the desk, then onto the chair. When he got to the top, his wife added, "The baker's boy—I can't remember his name—the one who helped us with the wood. In front of the gate to the alleyway—I saw him . . ."

She repeated that phrase several times. Père Dubois looked over at the house, which he owned, too, which was located opposite the garden. A white form was huddled outside the gate, partially hidden by the trees.

"But what did he do?" he asked from his perch.

"I don't know. I saw him come out, and suddenly, there was gunfire, and he fell . . . I saw him . . . He clutched his belly with his hands, and he fell."

"He's not moving. He's gotten himself killed."

Mère Dubois stood up.

"But suppose he's not dead. Is he just going to lie there?"

"Good Lord, poor kid."

Père Dubois was still staring at the white form and the gate open onto the dark alleyway. The wind, although light, at times blew the smoke clear into the garden. The smell was getting stronger and stronger. Through the smoke, he made out another white form coming forward through the shadows in the alleyway. The form stooped down, and Père Dubois realized that the baker, without letting himself be seen, was pulling his boy back inside. Soon the alleyway gate closed.

Père Dubois got down and related what he had just seen. Then he sat down on the bed beside his wife.

Now his legs were trembling. He could feel the sweat beading his face and running down his back. His wife sat without moving, her elbows on her knees. Her eyes stared straight ahead, and from time to time she murmured, "My God . . . poor boy . . . I saw him fall . . . He clutched his belly with his hands, and he fell . . . ."

—◀{ 39 }▶—

THE morning dragged on. They spent most of the time in
Julien's room, which was the only room with daylight in it.
Mère Dubois went downstairs only to get the alcohol stove, the
bowls, and some coffee. She also brought up some bread, but
neither of them could eat a thing.

Père Dubois knew that fear had taken hold of him. The
strength that had risen in him when he'd been yanked
awake by the shooting had gone, leaving his body aching and
his head empty. His legs would barely support him. From time
to time, with great difficulty, he hauled himself up to the skylight to see if the fire was spreading. For a while, he thought
that the whole street would go up, but by the middle of the
morning he was reassured. The fire's intensity was diminish-
ing, and its focus seemed to be centered near the St.-Joseph
Orphanage. The street was deserted. One time, hearing shouts,
he had climbed up but had seen only a group of German soldiers running toward the bottom of the street. A short while
afterward there were a few volleys; then that was all. Cars and
trucks were rumbling by. Going back into the bedroom, he
was able to see that the École Normale garden was deserted.

They stayed upstairs the whole morning.

At noon, not daring to light a fire, Mère Dubois warmed a
little pot of soup over what was left of the alcohol in the
stove. When the flame went out, they slowly ate the broth with
the vegetables still stone cold in it.

Then Père Dubois stretched out on Julien's bed. He didn't
intend to go to sleep, and yet he gave in to it. When he woke

up, his wife was no longer in the room. He sat up on the bed and listened. There were voices in the kitchen.

He got up silently and went down several steps before he recognized M. Robin's voice. He entered the kitchen, saying, "What a night we've had!"

Mère Dubois had partly opened the shutters. The door was wide open and the blind lowered.

"You were able to go outside?"

"Yes, but just to come over here because there are no streets to cross. Otherwise, I wouldn't have risked it."

M. Robin explained that the Maquis forces had attacked the town. The Germans had fallen back to the center of town; then they had counterattacked, and the Maquis had fled. After their departure the Germans had set fire to several houses, killing any inhabitants who tried to escape. They'd taken about twenty hostages, whom they shot in front of the old men's home at the foot of Montciel hill.

M. Robin had learned this from a nurse from the hospital who was allowed to move about.

"It's not over yet." Père Dubois sighed.

"We're not sure, but it seems that the Germans are leaving by the Besançon road. In any case, there's not one left at the École Normale."

It was comfortable in the kitchen. They stood a moment without speaking. Then Père Dubois said, "I feel like going out to the end of the garden."

"No," said M. Robin, "don't go. It's not safe yet."

Mère Dubois gave M. Robin half the bread they had left.

"I think a lot of people will be going without bread this evening," said M. Robin.

"As though anyone felt like eating," said the old lady.

They talked again about the baker's boy who'd been killed simply because he'd tried to see what was happening in the street; then M. Robin left.

"I'll come by tomorrow morning," he promised, "and tell you if they said anything about Lyons on the radio."

When he was gone, Mère Dubois went down to the cellar to get some fruit and a bottle of alcohol for the stove. Then they carried their chairs to the door and sat down without saying a word. From there, through the blind, they could see a little of the garden and the street, where nothing was moving.

It was summer. There were birds and insects, but the wounded town lay still in the sunlight.

—◄ 40 ►—

THE town was in an uproar. With the occupation army gone, flags bloomed from every window. Père Dubois went to take a look at the Rue des Salines, where there was a flag on every floor of every house. They stayed out for a day and a half. Then, on the second day, the rumor went around that a German armored column moving north was heading straight for their town. In a matter of minutes, the flags disappeared. The streets were emptied, and the houses closed their shutters. A few FFI who happened to be around took off for the woods.

Père Dubois had come running back to take down the flag his wife had hung from the bedroom window.

Not one German ever appeared, but the city remained in a state of suspended fear until the arrival of the first American troops.

Then, all of a sudden, life changed.

Père Dubois spent hours watching the trucks roll by, tanks and vehicles of all descriptions. He would come home with his pockets stuffed with cigarettes he couldn't smoke.

"This isn't tobacco," he would say. "It's some kind of spice. But that doesn't matter; they've got one hell of an army . . . And they've got everything. It will be like in 1919. Ten years after they've gone, we'll still be selling American surplus."

Mère Dubois managed to get coffee, canned meat, and chocolate that they couldn't eat because it was so sweet.

"They're not bad fellows," Père Dubois would say. "But all the same, they do have funny habits."

M. Robin announced that the liberation of Lyons was completed. All the bridges had been blown up, but there hadn't been too many casualties. In spite of everything, Mère Dubois was still anxious and talked incessantly about Julien and Françoise.

"Maybe they'll get here in a truck," she said.

Her husband wouldn't answer, but as often as possible he would go to the corner of the Rue des Salines and the Rue des Écoles to watch the convoys go through. Sometimes civilians would get off. And others would get into the trucks. And the Americans would laugh and kiss the girls and slap the men on the back.

Several regiments of French soldiers also went through, wearing American uniforms. They were more subdued, and the public welcomed them with less enthusiasm.

Père Dubois talked with the bystanders, but he never took his eyes off the vehicles that rolled in from the road to Lyons.

On his way home, he always stopped at the area where the fire had been. Generally, no one was there. Now that the war had moved off, people sort of turned their backs on tragedy. And yet, in these houses, people had died, burned alive or shot as they tried to escape. Those who had managed to get away had lost everything.

Père Dubois sometimes stopped before the alleyway that led to the bakery where he'd worked for the best part of his life. He didn't go inside. He stared down at the sidewalk. There was a large clean spot on it. They'd washed the pavement where the baker's boy's blood had spilled onto it. Before they'd washed it, someone had sprinkled ashes over it. A few still remained in the gutter. The first rain would wash them away, it would erase the cleaner spot, and there would be nothing left of the boy but the memory of a big fellow, full of life. Always ready to lend a hand. He had left the oven only long enough to come and get himself killed out here. He had been neither a resistant nor a collaborator, that guy; he just worked, quite simply, so that people could keep on eating bread.

He must have been about the same age as Julien. And in Lyons, too, people who were just innocent bystanders must have got killed.

One evening, near the burned-out houses, Père Dubois ran into an old woman, tall and skinny, rather broken-down, who hopped along like a bird, her arms dangling in front of her. He'd often seen her in the area. She was the longtime widow of a man named Hurtin who had been killed working in the salt mines. The old woman came up to him. In a cracked voice, she said, "It's not a pretty sight, is it?"

He shook his head. The old woman was looking at the last of the burned houses. A section of wall, the roof, and the floors had collapsed. The rest was blackened, but in places the wallpaper was unharmed. A marble sink was still in position, hanging in the emptiness with a piece of pipe dangling from it. The old woman raised her hand in its direction.

"Look carefully," she said. "My teakettle is still on the sink. And I'm sure it's all right. A man with a ladder could go up and get it for me."

"It wouldn't be safe," Père Dubois observed. "The walls might collapse."

"A good teakettle," she went on. "Solid aluminum. It heated up very fast. I bought it the year before the war. You couldn't even find one like that today."

"When they come to clear away the rubble, you'll be able to get it back."

"If someone hasn't stolen it by then . . . I've already come and gotten quite a few things . . . And I'm sure there are still some left, but the roof fell in on them. And I can't possibly move the beams and all those tiles."

"You were lucky to get out alive," said Père Dubois.

The old woman gave a laugh that grated curiously.

"You call that luck—winding up at seventy-six with nothing to call your own? We lived here since 1906. The year my poor Firmin started working in the salt mines—to his eternal regret. We came here because it wasn't too far from his job, and I was able to find housework easily around here. Think of it, there are people I've been cleaning for since before the First War . . . When my poor husband died, I wanted to leave. But then, you know how it is, the years go by . . . I'm not saying that you forget, but you get used to it. And then I had so many things here the thought of moving scared me."

Her painful laugh erupted again.

"Well, the moving's all taken care of now!"

She came closer to Père Dubois, looked around; then, lowering her voice and pointing to another half-burned house, she said, "Over there, you know, there was a young couple—the Pernins. The husband was in the Maquis. His young wife was killed along with their baby. He came back, the husband. He went berserk. Then it seems that he went off, saying he was going to kill the leader of the Maquis. He said, 'If they'd waited until the Americans got here, not a shot would have been fired. The Germans would have left. And that's all.' "

She seemed a little frightened by what she'd just said. When Père Dubois didn't answer, she asked, "Are you a believer, Père Dubois?"

He gestured vaguely.

"Oh, you know, I don't know any more about that than you do."

The old woman spoke again about her kettle, and he promised her that he would come the next morning with his ladder and try to get it back. She thanked him and started explaining that she was living with some people whose housework she'd been doing for more than ten years.

"But it's not like home," she said. "It's better, and they're very kind, but it's not like home."

She came closer to him once more, lowered her voice, and asked. "Do you know why I'm not dead like the others?"

"No."

"For more than twenty years the landlord has been promising us to put plumbing in the house. He never got around to it. You have to go downstairs, cross the courtyard, and use the bathroom in the other building, the one that gives onto the Rue des Salines. Well, when the shooting started, I got so scared that I got a stomach cramp. I went over there, and the people who live there—you know the Champeaus—they made me stay with them. They live right next to the bathroom. That's all, it was very simple. And when I saw that everything would be lost, I didn't even cry. You should have seen it burn! If the other houses had been like mine, with a back exit, the people would have been able to get away . . . But no. And you should have seen it burn."

She repeated that several times, always with that same painful laugh.

She had nothing left except the few odds and ends she'd been able to pick out of the rubble. Everything else had burned, except that kettle she kept looking longingly at.

Since it was getting late, Père Dubois said, "You'd better be starting home now."

"Tomorrow morning you'll bring your ladder?"

"Yes, I'll be here."

She moved off with her hopping gait, and Père Dubois could still hear her laughing.

When she had disappeared, he slowly made his way back to his garden. There was his house, without a scratch, without a broken windowpane. The war had passed very close by, but it hadn't even trampled on the garden.

—⊰ 41 ⊱—

THE next morning Père Dubois got his ladder and headed for the burned-out houses. His wife went with him. When they got there, the old woman was inside the building, fumbling through the rubble which she prodded with a poker. She was carrying a large bag.

"You're not being very careful," said Mère Dubois. "You never know, it might collapse."

The old woman responded with a laugh and a gesture meaning that it no longer made the slightest bit of difference to her.

Père Dubois moved a few tiles and wedged down a half-charred rafter to make a flat surface. His wife helped him steady the ladder and continued to hold it while he climbed up to the sink. The kettle was neither dented nor scarred. It even still held some water. Also on the sink were a ladle and two spoons, which he brought down, too.

The old woman emptied the water out of the kettle, put the other objects into her bag, and started to laugh again.

"My kettle," she kept repeating, "not a scratch. It's a good kettle—you can't imagine how fast it heats water."

She thanked them, took the kettle in the crook of her arm as she might have held a baby, and hurried off, clutching it to her heart.

"Really," murmured Mère Dubois, "the poor woman. We can count ourselves lucky."

They went back home with the ladder; then Père Dubois said, "I think I'll take a walk into town. You never know, I might run into someone from Lyons."

"My Lord, if we only had some news!"

Père Dubois put on a clean smock, changed his cap, and set out for the center of town. He hadn't left the neighborhood at all during these last months, and he looked at everything to see what changes had taken place. Outside of the burned buildings, a few houses had been damaged in the street fighting, but not seriously.

In the Rue Lecourbe, in the square and under the Arcades, there were a lot of people. At the entrance to the Rue du Commerce, a crowd had gathered. The old man thought they must be selling food without ration coupons, and he was sorry he didn't have any money on him. He went closer anyhow, and unable to see over the people's heads, he asked, "What's going on here?"

"They're shaving the hair off all the whores who fraternized with the Germans."

Shouts and bursts of laughter rose from the crowd. Names flew from mouth to mouth, accompanied by comments on the whores' families.

"They're going to make them get up on a truck and parade them through town," one woman said.

"No, they're going to make them go on foot. And barefoot, too, it seems."

There was a great laugh, and then several voices started chanting, "Off with their clothes! . . . Off with their clothes!"

The crowd was getting excited. Now it was a question of who could make the best suggestion.

"Shave their cunts, too!"

"Tattoo swastikas on their tits!"

Everyone was pushing to get a look. Everyone was shouting. Père Dubois was still fairly far away, but without having pushed at all, he found himself in the thick of the growing crowd. All the people around him were talking at once.

"The whores are just the appetizer. Tomorrow they'll make all the collaborators parade by."

"There's a lot of them still left to throw in jail."

"Everyone who traded with the Germans and made fortunes off of us."

"And the councilors . . ."

"And the militia . . ."

"The militia . . . they all ran away."

"We'll find them even if we have to go to Berlin!"

Père Dubois suddenly thought of Paul. He felt like a prisoner of this crowd, and fear gripped him. Had his son been arrested? Had he run away? If Paul had disappeared, wouldn't they take it out on his father? Display him like some curious animal before throwing him in jail and setting fire to his house? Besides, what was he doing here? For months, he'd stayed buried in his garden, and today, foolishly, he'd landed in the middle of a hornets' nest.

It seemed to him that everyone was looking at him and trying to identify him.

Pushed from all sides, jostled, out of breath and sweating, the old man flailed out with his elbows and finally got free of the crowd. Although nobody was paying any attention to him, he took a circuitous route of alleys and back streets to get back into the Rue des Écoles, avoiding the main thoroughfares. It occurred to him to stop at Paul's house to see what had become of him, but he couldn't bring himself to do it.

He walked as fast as possible, scanning the street ahead, turning around every few seconds, sure that a hand was about to grab his collar, while a voice shouted, "It's Père Dubois. Come and look at the old bastard. He didn't lift a hand to stop his son from doing business with the Germans!"

When he got to the garden gate, he paused for a few seconds. Might they not have come to get him during his absence? He had thought that the departure of the Germans would mean the end of fear for him, of misery, of that obsession of losing everything, and here he was now with a new fear.

He went in without banging the gate. His wife wasn't in the garden. He walked slowly down the path, where the shadows of the wind-filled trees seemed to drive clouds of golden insects before him.

At the corner of the little path that led to the house, he stopped. People were talking in the kitchen. He felt that his breath was about to fail him. His legs started shaking again. He moved forward all the same, straining to listen. Finally, when he got to the bottom step, he recognized Julien's voice.

—◆{ 42 }◆—

WHEN Père Dubois got inside, Julien and his fiancée were sitting at the table. A good smell of fried pork fat filled the kitchen. Julien embraced his father; then, pushing the girl forward a little, he said, "This is Françoise . . . It's all right for you to give her a kiss, you know."

Père Dubois embraced the girl.

"You're all hot," Julien observed. "And you look exhausted."

"I'm not used to walking anymore."

The old man sat down.

"I fixed them something to eat," said his wife. "They left at five o'clock this morning, and they had to change trucks three times to get here."

Père Dubois looked at the table, where there was a little piece of butter on a plate, bread, jam, and a basket of fruit.

"Julien brought some American pork fat," said his wife. "Would you like to taste it?"

"Fix him some eggs as you did for us," Julien suggested.

His father hesitated. He looked at Françoise, then his son, then the table.

"It's not lard," Julien explained. "It's bacon."

Françoise said, "It's still lard, you know; only the name is different."

"After all," said Père Dubois, "it couldn't hurt me to try a little. And besides, it's after eleven, only slightly early for lunch."

"Do you want one egg or two?" asked his wife.

"You have as many as that?"

"I've got four left, but Julien said he'd go get some more tomorrow."

She had already put two slices of bacon in the frying pan. The odor wafted through the room. It was food, after all, and the old man felt his mouth watering.

"If you could fix two," he said, "just this once—" He stopped, looked at the table, and asked, "What about you? Aren't you eating?"

"No," said his wife. "I'll have a little jam and some fruit."

She broke the eggs. The fat sputtered. He followed her every move. He breathed in little gulps, savoring the air in the kitchen, where for months there had only been the odor of vegetable soup. Eggs and butter had gotten so scarce that his wife had taken to mixing them into their mashed potatoes.

Père Dubois ate slowly, savoring every mouthful. For a while, that was all he thought about. The eggs, the quiet kitchen. The silent young girl peeling a large pear from the garden. Julien eating jam. His wife watching them. This was tranquillity. Peace. The eggs and bacon were very good, and if he had a piece of real fresh white bread to go with them . . .

Julien was telling about how they'd managed to get there. His father listened, but absently, haunted by images of the town as he'd seen it that morning. He'd planned to describe it to his wife when he got back home. But now he didn't dare. It wasn't Julien's presence that bothered him, but that silent girl, about whom he knew nothing. When their eyes met, the girl would smile timidly. Père Dubois tried to smile back, but he felt uncomfortable.

Mère Dubois was asking for details about everything: how the girl had been able to get home and then back to Lyons, why she had made the trip, how the liberation of Lyons had gone.

It was almost always Julien who answered. She was the liaison between a Resistance group in Lyons and the Maquis in the Haut-Jura. It was dangerous. She was always carrying enough evidence to get herself shot ten times over if the Germans arrested her. Only she couldn't tell you that the first time she came.

Mère Dubois seemed to admire the girl a great deal. Yet she asked, half-angrily, "You were afraid I didn't know enough to hold my tongue?"

"No," said Julien, "but it was an absolute rule. Even I didn't know anything about what she was doing."

His mother looked incredulous. "You weren't in the Resistance?"

"No."

Françoise broke in. "He wasn't in any one group. But he still worked for us. And took as many risks as those who were doing the fighting. Perhaps—"

Julien interrupted her. "Be quiet. There's no point in talking about that."

There was a silence. Père Dubois emptied his glass. Julien offered him a cigarette, saying, "Here, these aren't American."

"By the way," said his mother, "if you want some American ones, your father brought some home, but he can't smoke them."

"No, keep them. Just give me a few packs when you want me to go get you some eggs and butter."

The silence returned. A silence which Père Dubois saw as a potential threat.

"How did you get into the Resistance?" asked Mère Dubois.

Françoise raised her eyes. She looked at the old couple one after the other; then, in a calm voice, but with a certain firmness, she said, "My older brother was in the Communist Party. So I didn't have to try very hard to get into it, too."

--◄{ 43 }►--

IT was just after noon when Père Dubois went up to take a nap. He pretended to be tired after his trip into town. It was true. The morning had taken his legs right out from under him, but not because of the distance he'd walked. And then, on top of that, there had been the blow he'd received while they were at the table.

Good God! To have worked so hard, struggled and suffered so much his whole life long, for this! A son who was turning Communist!

He lay down. He had two coughing fits and, oppressed as he hadn't been for weeks, felt utterly drained.

Communist! That word sank into him like an iron ball. Into the very pit of his stomach. Slowly crushing him.

Paul had explained Communism to him at least ten times. So he understood it clearly. As soon as the Germans were beaten, all the Communists would return. With their arms. They would be the masters. They would enter his house. They would tell him, "Père Dubois, you no longer own anything.

Here's a ticket to the old men's home. Your house belongs to us. Also your property, your garden, your tools. Everything. You'll be in the old men's home; you won't need any of it."

They would come. And among them would be Julien and that girl. That girl who looks like a little saint. A saint who makes war. Who sleeps with your son before being married to him and pushes him toward Communism after she gets her hooks into him. Although it must be said that the boy had tendencies in that direction anyhow.

But did war and politics really have to corrupt everything? You think you're out of your misery, but that's not the case. Evil enters the house. It is there, downstairs. Ready to take over everything.

No. It couldn't be possible. What had he done to be constantly pursued by a jinx? Nothing. A lifetime of work. That was all. Perhaps he'd worked too hard and not thought about himself enough. If he'd lived it up, as some people did, he'd have been dead years ago, but he'd have lived a life of pleasure and not had to go through this miserable war.

And yet his work was what he'd done with the greatest joy. So?

Père Dubois wondered about himself. He turned onto his right side, then onto his left, then plumped up his pillows and turned over onto his back. He had left the shutters open a crack. He could see a strip of bright sky. The warm air rose from the garden sleeping in the sunshine. Nothing moved. His wife must be alone, for Françoise and Julien had said they had to go and see some friends. Communists, probably.

So one war ended, and another war was beginning. It was already here. In this house. It rose among them and would set them against one another. But this time, if it came to giving up all their belongings, would his wife still support that boy and his crazy ideas? When Julien had come back from his apprenticeship with these ideas already in his head, his mother had said, "If he hadn't been exploited by a boss who treated him like a slave, he wouldn't have gotten this way."

But today he no longer had a boss to exploit him. All he had was that girl to give him big ideas. Which was perhaps worse.

And what did he plan to do? How would they live? Off painting? Off politics?

The more Père Dubois mulled over these things in his mind, the more the pain that had gripped him until he could hardly breathe changed into anger. What hurt him most cruelly was the injustice he felt himself to be a victim of. He who had never got mixed up in politics. He who had stayed out of all factions and parties. Here he was caught between two sons who didn't like each other to begin with and now would hate each other even more.

And all this was being plotted outside his control. There was a sort of enormous wheel that started turning . . . It turned, and now he was trapped, caught without being able to do a thing to save himself or anything else.

He himself had nothing. He had only his two hands, which could still feed them, his wife and himself; he had only his garden, which waited for him under the blazing sun. He hadn't done much work these last few days. The grass had grown. From the paths it had crept into the vegetable beds he would have to weed. The sun had burned the last lettuce he'd transplanted. He would have to get up, pump some water so it would have a chance to warm up a little before watering time. He would have to— He would have to find the strength and the will that he had always had. But this afternoon—perhaps because he'd hoped that Julien's return would be a sign that the war had finally ended for them—this afternoon, for the first time in his life, he had neither the strength nor the courage nor even the slightest desire to get back to work. And it was a little as if he no longer had even the desire to live.

❧ 44 ❧

WHEN Père Dubois got downstairs, there was nobody in the kitchen, with its lowered blind and closed shutters. He dissolved a piece of sugar and an aspirin tablet in a glass of water. He drank it, picked up his cloth cap, and went out into the garden.

His wife was sitting on the bench. She had a big basket of plums beside her, which she picked up one by one to pit and cut out the bad parts. She let the waste fall into a bowl held between her knees and threw the prepared fruit into a big pot at her feet. When Père Dubois came up to her, she wiped off her knife on the edge of the bowl and placed it on the bench. From the look she gave him, he understood that she had something important to tell him.

He stopped. There was a silence, broken only by the buzzing of the wasps the plums attracted. When his wife said nothing, Père Dubois asked, "You going to cook those?"

"Yes. Julien picked them before he left."

"Don't throw away the pits. Once they're good and dry, they can go into the fire."

"I know."

Silence.

Père Dubois took a few steps. His wife got up and said, "Micheline was here."

"Ah! I didn't hear her, and yet I didn't sleep at all."

"She didn't come inside. She was in a hurry. She didn't want me to disturb you."

Père Dubois felt his throat tighten. He had to make an effort to ask, "And?"

Mère Dubois hesitated, lowered her eyes, then raised them to murmur, "They've arrested Paul."

Père Dubois clenched his fists. He moved off a few steps, halted, hesitated, then came back toward his wife to ask, "Who do you mean, they?"

"There were two policemen and some men from the Maquis."

She'd paused before answering, but the words had come out all in one breath, as if she'd felt the need to get them off her chest.

"That's a fine state of affairs," said Père Dubois.

He felt helpless. Since morning, he'd been dreading this, and yet the news brought almost no reaction.

"We'll have to do something," said his wife. "After all, they can only accuse him of one thing—trading with the Germans. That's not really a crime."

She'd just finished saying what he felt like shouting. And she was the one who said it. Without anger. With a little softness in her eyes that seemed to add, "I'm sorry for you, my poor man. He's your son."

"But what can I do?"

"Nothing. Micheline knows that perfectly well. But she thought you ought to be told, just the same. She also thought that perhaps you could go and see Vaintrenier. It seems that he's at the head of the new administration."

Père Dubois sighed. He pictured Vaintrenier at City Hall. He tried to imagine the mood that must prevail in that sector. After what he'd seen in town that morning . . .

"And I," said his wife, "I thought that, perhaps, Julien— I mean, his fiancée does know people in the Resistance—"

She stopped. Père Dubois saw little black dots dancing before his eyes. He let himself sink onto the bench.

"You don't feel well?" asked his wife.

"Yes, I'll be all right."

226

"Do you want some water?"

"No, I just took an aspirin."

He sighed. Asking a Communist to put in a good word for Paul. No, he hadn't thought of that.

"Did you tell Micheline that—"

He couldn't say the word. Mère Dubois must have understood, for she said, "I only said that the child was a member of the Resistance."

"And what did she say?"

"Nothing. She was crying."

Mère Dubois sat down beside her husband. It seemed that summer had suddenly grown heavier. The wind had fallen. The tired trees drooped under the weight of the afternoon. The insects made a constant humming sound that was part of the oppressive heat of the day. Only the wasps were lively. Aggravating. Returning tirelessly to buzz around their faces. Landing on Mère Dubois' hands each time she rested them on her apron.

His gaze lost in the shadows on the path, Père Dubois saw nothing. In the emptiness that had grown inside him, there were only these words, monotonous, continuous as the buzzing of the flies: "They won't want to help. They'll do nothing for him—nothing for him."

—◄{ 45 }►—

MÈRE DUBOIS had made a tomato salad; she'd cooked string beans from the garden and opened a big jar of rabbit *pâté* she'd made herself. A neighbor had lent her some eggs to make a custard with a can of condensed milk, and there was some

American chocolate Julien had brought. Except for the bread, it was a real meal like those they used to have before the war. Père Dubois had left the garden two or three times to come and look and sniff.

"It will be a real meal," he said. "But it seems that there is always something to spoil our pleasure."

"You'll see, it will all work out," said his wife. "If the children can't do anything, you can go see Vaintrenier tomorrow morning."

Père Dubois tried to keep hold of himself, but his anxiety was getting the better of him. He watered what plants really needed watering, then went and sat down on the bench. He was still there when Françoise and Julien arrived. He stood up and forced a smile.

"Dinner must be ready. And I do believe your mother really prepared a feast. Go on up ahead of me."

Père Dubois went down into the cellar and lighted his lighter. He had a good number of old bottles left. He looked for one from the Jura that he'd bought more than ten years before the war. He raised the bottle up to eye level and ran his lighter back and forth behind it. The wine had left a little deposit on the glass, but it was clear. The cork must be very good, for the bottle was absolutely full. He carried it carefully, leaving it on its side as it had been in the rack. When he came in, Françoise said, "You shouldn't have."

"Ah, still and all," he said. "Still and all."

He slowly stood the bottle up and gently placed it on the table. He wiped its neck with the hem of his smock and went to get the corkscrew out of the little dresser drawer.

"This," he said, "this is a very good corkscrew. Because you can uncork a bottle with it without disturbing the wine. With wine like this, that would be a crime."

When he'd pulled the cork out, he sniffed it, then pressed it between his fingers to test its quality. As he raised his head, his eyes met Françoise; she was watching him and smiling. There

was a great tenderness in her look, and Père Dubois found himself comforted by it. It was a little as if a pleasant warmth had
mingled with the perfume of the wine filling the room.

"You like to take good care of your wine," said the young girl.

"Yes. And when I bottled this one, Julien wasn't any higher
than this table."

"I don't remember," said Julien. "You used to do it every
year, so— And anyway, I never understood how you find anything in your racks, since you never put labels on the bottles."

"Don't you worry, I know what I've got."

Before the young people had arrived, he'd told himself a
hundred times, "As soon as they get here, I'll talk to them about
Paul. I have to get it off my chest."

And now, as things were turning out, he couldn't even bring
it up. Yet there had been that sweet look of Françoise's. He kept
coming back to it and thinking, *She will help us. If she can, she
will help us.*

He had been afraid of the girl, but now that she was there,
sitting at the same table with him, he almost would have preferred talking with her alone. And yet she was the Communist.
She bore that frightening title that went so badly with the
gentleness in her eyes. Julien wasn't a member of that party. He
had said so. But in spite of that, it was his reaction that Père
Dubois feared the most.

They ate the tomato salad, into which Mère Dubois had
chopped two large onions and some parsley. Nobody spoke.
Père Dubois looked at them stealthily, and each time his eyes
met his wife's, he tried to make her understand that she was the
one who should speak up. She sighed. She divided the rest of
the salad between Françoise and Julien.

"You must eat," she said. "We don't know yet how long it will
take before the food situation gets back to normal."

"With the Americans," Julien said, "we stand a good chance
of being inundated with stuff."

"That doesn't make any difference." The old man sighed.

"The war isn't over yet. And then even the end of the war won't mean the end of our troubles."

He poured a little drop of wine into his glass; then, without tilting the bottle back up completely, he took a sip.

"It hasn't lost its taste. Come, hold your glasses up so I don't disturb it too much."

They drank. Mère Dubois had accepted just a finger of wine, enough to drink to Julien's and Françoise's happiness.

The taste of the wine blended perfectly with the rabbit *pâté*. It had been a long time since Père Dubois had eaten anything so good, and yet he couldn't get any real pleasure out of it. He would have liked to know what his boy would say about Paul's arrest, and at the same time, he feared that moment because he had the feeling that from then on all the tranquillity of the evening would be shattered. He no longer knew very clearly whether his glances at his wife were beseeching her to speak up or to keep quiet.

She spoke all the same. She'd taken very little *pâté*, and when she'd carefully cleaned her plate with her bread, she took a sip of wine and said, "We have a big problem, you know, Julien."

The boy looked at her. "Oh, yes?"

There was a silence. Père Dubois bowed his head. His wife went on. "Micheline came over this afternoon . . . Your brother has been arrested."

She never said "your brother"; she would say "Paul." Julien gave a sharp little laugh.

"I hate to say so," he said, "but he really asked for it."

"Don't be mean, dear. You know he never did anything wrong."

Julien sat up, put his elbows on the table, and folded his hands in front of his chin. After shaking his head and looking at his mother, then his father, he said, "Well, shit! The guy made deals with the Germans during the entire occupation, and you think he didn't do anything wrong? He buddied around with the militia. Got money from all the more or less Nazi organizations of the Vichy government, and you think he ought to get a medal!"

"Julien," cried his mother. "Be quiet."

His jaws clenched, Père Dubois contained himself with great effort.

"Be quiet," his wife repeated. "You're being cruel."

"Cruel? But what do you think he was being when he came here and talked to you about the militia and what a dirty deserter I was?"

Père Dubois was about to explode when he saw Françoise's hand move forward slowly and come to rest on Julien's arm.

"My darling," she said, "I don't know as much as you do about what your brother did. I only know what you've told me. I know that even economic collaboration is contemptible, but you shouldn't get carried away like this. Your parents are suffering—that's only natural."

"But you're not going to stand up for him!"

Julien had spoken more quietly. Almost without anger.

"I'm not standing up for him, but you seem to want to do him in."

"The truth will do him in. And if they bring him to trial, they'd better not ask me to be a witness because I'd have to tell what I overheard one night—"

For some time, Père Dubois had been clenching his fists. He banged on the table and shouted, "In God's name! I knew it— I knew it. What good does it do to talk to him about it? I knew it—"

His anger prevented him from finding the right words. As always, a fit of coughing seized him, obliging him to get up and go spit in the fire.

When he had caught his breath, he remained standing in front of the stove, uncertain about going back to his place.

"Come on, sit down," said his wife.

There was none of that gentle warmth left in the kitchen, none of those appetizing odors that accompanied the beginning of the meal. The evening was heavy, saturated with the awful heat of the day that night had chased from the garden and driven inside the house.

"You know perfectly well that I'd refuse to testify against him," said Julien. "But neither will I make the slightest effort to help him. He acted like a bastard; it's normal that he be tried and made to pay for it."

"There certainly are some people who made a mistake in good faith," said Françoise. "With those people, the juries—"

Julien interrupted her. "In good faith? You're kidding. For love of money, yes. But he'll be smart enough to come out ahead of the game, you'll see."

That was too much for Père Dubois. His wife, sitting between the table and the stove, blocked his way.

"Let me through," he muttered.

"But really, Gaston, you're not going to—"

"Let me through, I say!"

He had shouted. His wife got up and pushed her chair under the table. When he got to the foot of the stairs, Père Dubois turned around to say to Julien, "Thank you all the same. Thank you a lot."

He felt his cough coming on again. He said nothing further and went upstairs as fast as he could go.

—≼ 46 ≽—

PÈRE DUBOIS stood for a long time in front of the window open wide onto the night that flooded the garden. He needed to breathe. Needed to catch his breath, to wait until his blood flowed normally through his veins again.

He wiped his brow several times with his handkerchief.

The night was heavy, but what oppressed him most was inside him. He now knew that the departure of the Germans, the long-lost right to leave his window open, to go to bed when he wanted to, and to get up before dawn no longer mattered to him. There was another peace that he would never find again.

Stretched out on his bed, covered only by a sheet that in itself felt too heavy, he waited.

On several occasions, he heard raised voices coming from the kitchen. Was his wife trying to reason with Julien? Would she really try to defend Paul? Was it Françoise who was trying to knock some sense into that stubborn boy's head?

A waste of time. The old man knew that. He had sensed in Julien's look a firm refusal to do anything for Paul. But wasn't he, their father, a little responsible for his sons' being at each other's throats? Had he ever done a thing to bring them together?

No. He had done nothing. He had led his life as he had to lead it, always prodded, hounded by his work. And his life had never left him time to think about what really separated the two boys. What was it? A too great gap in their ages? The fact that they didn't have the same mother? The older one's indifference?

Yes, all that and also something else. Some of those things that are inside a man and have no name. Those things that escape you when you're nothing but a good artisan bound to your job. And those things were unimportant until the day when events forced men to take sides.

The real culprit was the war. Père Dubois knew it. But he didn't quite understand why. Now the war was far away. Now that men could start living their lives again, wasn't it possible to forget all that?

If tomorrow they gave him white bread and as much tobacco as he wanted, he would be able to start to live again and work, as he had before.

He kept telling himself that, but the image of that old lady and her kettle kept coming back to him, the image of the burned-out houses and the baker's boy killed in front of the gate to the alley.

What could be blamed for all these crimes and all this destruction? Who should pay for the ruins and bear the burden of the grief?

The answer was there before him, as though it had entered with the thick breath of the summer night. It was like an animal. There was no doubt about its presence, but the hand tried vainly to seize it by the halter.

Never, perhaps, had the room been as haunted as this evening. War had left town before the invasion of this new army which no longer wore the face of war. These soldiers going by, who laughed with the girls and chewed gum like sheep and smoked ladies' cigarettes—that wasn't war anymore. All that still remained of war's visit to the town had taken refuge here tonight, to inhabit this room where Père Dubois could no longer find peace. Probably because night suited war. That night into which it had plunged men for so many seasonless months.

Tonight once more it was summer.

Outside, it was summer.

A summer that breathed so heavily its breath shook all the trees in the garden and rattled the shutter.

Père Dubois got up. The floor was cool under his bare feet. He walked over to the window, opened the shutter, leaned out to hook it back, and murmured, "This wind means rain. When it comes up at this hour, we could get rain before dawn."

He stood there for a moment, taking in long gulps of the wind which had leaped over the hill to flow through town like a river risen between heaven and earth. A whole area of the sky had already lost its stars. The clouds were invisible, but they were there. They would bring the water the garden needed.

There was still talking in the kitchen, but Père Dubois no

longer felt like stealing down to try to eavesdrop on what they were saying about his son.

The close air in the room became alive with breezes and little currents. It wasn't cool yet, but it already promised to be.

—◄ 47 ►—

THEN came three interminable days.

On the first one, it rained. Père Dubois hadn't even bothered to worry about where Françoise would sleep. When he got up, he asked, "Where are they?"

"You know that we couldn't let that girl sleep here."

"And so?"

"Well, she has some friends in town who offered them a place to stay."

"That's good."

He felt hard. Closed off against everything as the house was against the rain that came to interrupt the summer.

His wife went on. "They won't be eating here at noon."

"My goodness . . ."

He went out to go down to the shed, where he spent almost the whole day puttering around. His hands went from one job to the next, from habit, but his head went its own way from one thought to the next.

And then he would look down the path. In the afternoon, he saw Françoise and Julien arrive. They went into the house, but he kept on with his work.

They stayed with Mère Dubois for a good hour. Then they came down to see him. They embraced each other, and Julien said, "We're invited out tonight. We'll come by tomorrow."

He took a step, stopped, and pulled a package of black tobacco out of his pocket.

"Here," he said, "I was able to exchange it for some American cigarettes."

"No, no," the old man began, "I don't need it—"

But Julien was already walking away.

During the second day, Père Dubois never left his garden except for lunch and a short nap. The sun was out again, but the rain had left the earth soft and easy to work.

Julien and his fiancée ate dinner with them. Almost in silence. At the end of the meal, Julien announced that they'd found a truck driver who would take them to Lyons.

"It doesn't seem as if you've been here very long." Mère Dubois sighed.

"But we'll be back," said Françoise.

They left on the morning of the third day.

Mère Dubois accompanied them as far as the garden gate, while the old man went back to the work he'd interrupted to say good-bye to them.

His son was leaving with that girl about whom he knew nothing except that she was a Communist and had very gentle eyes and a soft voice.

When his wife got back, he straightened up, folded his hands on the handle of his spading fork, and said, with a slightly forced smile, "Well, they didn't stick around very long."

Mère Dubois only answered by raising her arms, which fell back to her sides. She was crying soundlessly.

"And we still don't know very much about that girl," he went on.

His wife looked at him in silence. And he knew that she was thinking, *You don't, of course. Because you went up to bed like an oaf. But I talked to her.*

She walked off. Père Dubois let her go. Her tears had not moved him.

A moment later she was back. She was no longer crying. She

came up to him and asked, "So you really don't want to go and see Vaintrenier?"

Père Dubois took off his cap to wipe his brow. He blew his nose, slowly folded up his handkerchief, and put it back in his pocket; then he said, "No, it wouldn't do any good. They're all chips off the same block. And I'm not going to take any more insults."

He paused. When his wife said nothing but just stood rooted beside him, he raised his voice to add, "Now I'd like to be left in peace—do you understand that? People can think what they like, but I want to be left in peace. I want to work in peace, and die in peace. That's all I ask!"

She looked at him for a moment, then moved off without a word.

And Père Dubois got on with his day: work, lunch, nap, work, repeating those words over and over to himself: "Die in peace . . . die in peace . . ."

He went along like this until the end of the afternoon, when a fifteen-year-old boy Paul had hired to make deliveries appeared. The boy leaned his bicycle against the boxwood and came toward Père Dubois. His wife, who had heard the gate clang, came running.

"I've got a message from the boss," said the boy. "He said to tell you not to worry. He just got home."

The old couple looked at each other. The boy added, "Everything's all right. He'll come see you one of these days. He'll explain it to you. It was a mistake."

The boy waited a few moments. Père Dubois thought he had detected a touch of irony in that last phrase, but he said nothing.

"Is there any message?" asked the boy.

"No," said Mère Dubois. "Give them our best."

They watched the boy get back on his bicycle and ride away. Then, when he got to the gate, Père Dubois took out his tobacco box and started rolling a cigarette. He said, "You see, it was a mistake—a mistake or a dirty trick by people who were jealous of his success. Ah, that's not the end of it. There'll be more accounts to settle and little personal revenges to take!"

He stopped to light his cigarette, and his wife took the opportunity to walk away. Père Dubois didn't take his eyes off her until he saw the beaded blind in the kitchen door fall behind her.

One hand on his fork, the other holding his cigarette, he stood a long time looking out toward the street. Between the trees, he could see people he couldn't recognize passing by. A few cars went by, too. The town was starting to live at a rhythm quite different from what they'd known during the occupation. And yet, in the garden, only a somewhat sad summer evening was falling. The earth, already dry on the surface but with the humidity dug into it by his work, had a stale odor.

Julien had left. Paul was out of prison. They would find themselves alone again, he and his wife, with what little life was left before they reached the end of the road. He would be the first to go; that was only natural—he was the oldest. But he had always been the oldest. That was nothing new, and yet this was the first time that he had thought of his death with such serenity.

After him, there would be more evenings like this in the garden and in the town, but there would also be quarrels, hatreds, wars, the poisons of life.

He'd had his share of these poisons. What he had a right to hope for now was a little peace, even if he had to isolate himself further.

Here, in the depths of this garden, that should be possible. What he had to do was live for himself, without thinking of others or of what would happen to his property when he would no longer be alive.

Père Dubois shook off the drowsiness that had overtaken him. The sun had disappeared behind the hill a long time ago. He pulled his fork out of the earth and cleaned its teeth with the little scraper he kept hooked to the belt of his smock; then, slowly, he headed for the house where smoke was rising from the fire that had been lighted to heat the evening soup.

Part Four

ON THE GARDEN EARTH

─◄{ 48 }►─

AUTUMN slowly laid bare the withered garden. The hills of Montciel and Montaigu were also stripped of leaves. Day by day the earth drew closer to the night.

Père Dubois knew that winter night that wells up from the ground while the sky is still full of light and the woods of red and gold. He followed its approach day by day during the course of his labors. He studied the wind. It was mainly from the north. That was a sure sign that a bad winter was brewing up there, far away, where the war he'd hardly had time to see pass over the land was still being fought.

The papers were full of that war. They spoke also of what it had left in its wake: evil, hatred, and strife that nothing could seem to quiet.

As the season advanced and the days grew shorter, the evenings left more time in which to think about all this. Père Dubois looked at the newspaper headlines, but he had trouble reading the articles. Because, truth to tell, he wasn't really interested. So when the plates had been cleared, he would put his elbows on the table and slowly drink the linden or verbena tea his wife had prepared.

The old couple rarely spoke. When a letter from Julien would come in the afternoon mail, Mère Dubois would wait until the meal was over before reading it out loud. Sometimes she would stop, seem to be trying to make out a word, and say, "The poor boy's handwriting gets worse and worse. There are always things I can't read."

Père Dubois said nothing, but he realized that his wife didn't always read him everything the boy wrote. His letters were short; they said over and over again that life in the city wasn't easy. When she'd finished reading, Mère Dubois would go into the dining room and bring back to the kitchen table a small inkwell, a pen, and a piece of paper that still had, above the columns reserved for numbers, the letterhead of the bakery. She had saved a big package of it, which she used for all her correspondence.

Père Dubois would watch her write. She wrote slowly, stopping often to get a better grip on the pen that slipped between her fingers, increasingly deformed by rheumatism. She often remarked, "I must get a thicker pen. This one's really too thin. I can hardly feel it in my fingers."

One night, Père Dubois said, "You should wrap some string around it. That would make it thicker, and it wouldn't slip so much."

She followed his advice, and he noticed that she could write more easily.

Each time when she laid down her pen, he would ask, "Did you send them my love?"

And each time, she would answer, "Of course."

That's the way things were. Life just sort of went along. Each day passed slowly and flowed into an uneventful evening. In several letters during the month of September, Julien wrote about his marriage, explaining that it would take place in October in St.-Claude, which was Françoise's hometown. And he would say, "There will only be the two of you and Françoise's father."

Mère Dubois seemed to resign herself to this. Père Dubois sighed. "What times we live in."

That was all. The old couple waited. And then, on October 17, a letter came in the morning mail.

The sun was shining brightly. Père Dubois had been tying up the cardoons for more than an hour. In spite of the north wind that blew dead leaves across the path, he was perspiring. He straightened up now and then to mop his brow and catch his breath. He saw his wife walking slowly back from the gate, reading a letter.

She stopped before getting up to him. Père Dubois squinted at her. He couldn't make out her features because of the shadows on her bowed face, but he sensed that she hadn't stopped just to be able to read more easily. No letters ever came except those from Julien, so Père Dubois thought of him at once and had a presentiment of bad news.

He felt uneasy and shivered under his shirt. Perhaps it was the wind chilling his sweat, but perhaps also it was a fear he refused to recognize.

He hesitated. Then, as his wife began walking again, he laid down his tool and went to meet her.

They stopped a yard away from each other. His wife had let the hand holding the letter fall down against her apron. Her other hand was hanging limp, too. She slowly raised her head. Her pursed lips trembled. Tears were running down her cheeks.

Before Père Dubois could even say a word, she gave a sort of bitter smile, shook her head from left to right, and said, "No, don't worry. It's nothing serious."

Père Dubois could see her Adam's apple bobbing up and down. The skin on her neck tightened, and her wrinkles, widening, showed pale furrows in her sunburned skin. She seemed to get hold of herself. "I'm stupid—I'm so stupid to be crying like this. It's just as well this way. It's just as well . . ."

"But what is it?"

She showed him the letter.

"They're going to get married. They're going to get married

245

in Lyons. All by themselves. To save money. There. That's all."

She went on very fast, as if she were afraid of not being able to get to the end of what she had to say. "Come, I'll read you his letter."

She stepped a little to the right to avoid Père Dubois and hurried up to the house.

The old man felt nothing but relief because, for a few moments, he'd feared news of an accident. Relief also because the prospect of a trip to St.-Claude had frankly frightened him. Now that was out. Julien would be married. They would do nothing for this occasion, though he remembered that he still had, way back in the cellar, some wine that was the same age as his son that he'd been saving for his wedding. This thought caused him no emotion. It just came to him because it was natural to think of wine when you thought about a wedding. But after all, nothing was happening in a normal fashion anymore, and you had to take things as they came.

He knew that his wife was crying. He waited awhile before joining her.

He found her sitting at the table. Her eyelids were swollen. She was staring out the window. Not a muscle in her face was moving.

Père Dubois sat down opposite her and waited in silence for her to feel like reading the letter. A long moment passed. The door was wide open, and the north wind lifted the blind and rattled its wooden beads. On the stove, a pot of vegetable peelings gave off a little jet of steam that the breeze constantly molded into different patterns.

Finally, turning slowly to the table, in a weak but steady voice, Mère Dubois began: "Here is what he says: 'Dear Parents, I know that what I have to say will hurt you, but we've decided to get married here, without inviting anyone, to save the cost of the trip and cut down on expenses. Françoise's father is sick, and in any case, we couldn't get married at his house.

Besides, it's only a year since Françoise's mother died, so we couldn't have a party. We have very little money anyhow. Françoise has a job as secretary to a lawyer I know from having sold paintings to him. It's hard for her to take more than a day off. As for you, I know the trip would tire you. And we couldn't put you up here because we only have one room with one bed in it. I've applied for the papers we'll need. I hope that eventually my paintings will sell better and we'll have enough money to look for an apartment. That way you'd be able to come for the birth of your granddaughter. For I hope that it will be a girl. That will be more important than our marriage, which is nothing but a formality. Françoise is at work, but she told me to send both of you her love. I send you my love, too, with all my heart.' "

She'd read it straight through, pausing only to take a breath. She put the letter on the table.

"There . . . He also gives the date. It's the day after tomorrow."

Père Dubois sighed. His wife's calm didn't fool him at all. He knew she was struggling not to cry, and he would have liked to say something to comfort her. He searched, but he found nothing. So he sighed, raised his hand, and let it fall back onto the oilcloth; then, slowly getting to his feet, he headed for the door.

Just as he was pushing aside the blind to go out, an idea finally came to him.

"We ought to send them something," he said. "I don't know what, maybe a package. Or else, a little money. They'll surely need some money."

His wife raised her head to look at him. Her mouth was not smiling. Her face remained expressionless, but her clear eyes said thank you.

—⁘{ 49 }⁘—

THE very next day Mère Dubois sent off a big package in which she'd put some winter pears, some canned goods, a little jar of melted butter, jam, and some chocolate. That was all she'd been able to find. Père Dubois had watched her tying up the package, shaking his head. He knew that wasn't all she would send. He never took care of their money, but during the summer, they'd sold vegetables and fruit, and he was sure she hadn't taken all the profits to the savings bank.

The morning of the marriage, she said, "I have to go to the post office to send a telegram. Since we can't be there, it's only natural that they should have a little word from us."

Père Dubois had approved. All this concerned him only from a great distance. What he saw most clearly was that, after getting over her initial shock, his wife's main reaction had been to say, "For us, of course, it's no fun having them get married alone and far away. But we have to think of them. For young kids, a marriage like that isn't very festive."

Once the day was over, she began to wait for a letter telling about that poor marriage. Père Dubois felt she was strained, irritable, and he avoided talking to her. Life went on, alternating between the garden and the house. There was no apparent change, and yet he felt that something was in suspense, waiting for heaven only knew what else to happen.

The first letter arrived, briefly describing the ceremony. Mère Dubois cried a little on learning that Julien hadn't been married in church. Her husband said, "That—that doesn't make any difference. But actually, they were wrong. You should never get in bad with anybody. In this life, you might need help from everyone."

He'd almost said, "That doesn't surprise me, for a Communist!" But he'd restrained himself. The more he thought about it, the more his wife's distress touched him.

For the time being, they were really cut off from the rest of the world, and the tête-à-têtes of the evenings, like the side-by-sides of the days working, left no room for bickering. Besides, for some time now, his wife hadn't lost her temper either. Their life together almost seemed dulled by the declining season. Mère Dubois was more stooped. Her face had grown gaunter, and too often her eyes were gazing off into space.

During the whole month of November they had only one fight. It was on a Thursday. Mère Dubois had gone to market, and at eleven o'clock, when she got back, she announced, "I just ran into Madame Gresselin, the principal of the elementary school. It's been a long time since I've seen her. She's aged a lot."

Père Dubois only knew Mme. Gresselin from having met her and greeted her from a distance in the street, but his wife had seen more of her while Julien was in school.

"She must be fairly close to retirement," he said.

"She should have retired already. But with the war, she was able to stay on a few more years. What do you expect? Everyone's trying to make a little money. Life is so difficult."

She stopped talking. Père Dubois thought it had just been an idle conversation, saying something to alleviate the long silence. She put away what she'd bought, went to hang her bag up behind the laundry door, and came back, saying, "Now that there's no more work in the garden, I might try to make a little extra money outside."

She stopped. Père Dubois looked at her and frowned. When she didn't go on, he asked, "Outside? What do you mean by that?"

"Well, Madame Gresselin told me that the school was looking

for two people to work in the kitchen. To serve the children and—and clean up."

"Good Lord!" said Père Dubois. "Perhaps we're not rich, but you're not going to wash dishes as though we were in the poorhouse. No!"

He felt stung by the idea of his wife washing pots and pans, and he'd shouted at her.

"Don't get angry," she said. "It's not disgraceful. And what little I make I can send to help the children."

"Help them? But did anybody ever help us? Couldn't Julien go back to his trade or else find some other job, instead of trying to live off his paintings? What are they doing at the moment? They're living off what his wife earns! Do you think that's natural? And now you want to get into the act yourself. He'll have two women supporting him—"

"Gaston! Be quiet. You're unfair. You know very well that he might be mobilized at any moment, so no one will hire him."

She had shouted, too, and her attitude only made her husband angrier. He struck the table with the ball of his fist.

"I don't give a damn. I won't have you going out like a beggarwoman to clean up after kids and muck around in greasy dishwater . . . People would probably think that I'm making you slave to—"

As happened every time he started shouting, his voice choked on a heavy cough, rising from his ailing bronchial tubes with a flood of mucus. When he'd spat and drunk the glass of water his wife handed him, he fell back into his chair. It had been a long time since he'd had a seizure like that, and he was left exhausted, one elbow on the table, his hand on his knee, leaning forward trying to get his breath. A whole reservoir of fatigue inside him suddenly awakened. It weighed on him. It seemed to push him toward the floor, which he stared at, not finding one word to say.

The day was cold and gray. Soon winter would be there. Winter which had frightened him so for several years. Was his body really so worn-out that it couldn't stand the slightest chill? On two occasions already, in the middle of severe winters, he'd been so seriously ill with his lungs that he hadn't thought he'd live to see the spring. Would this oncoming winter be his last season? It occurred to him that it was perhaps in anticipation of his death that his wife was looking for work. Was she afraid of Paul? She'd often said, "You ought to make out your will. How much does it cost?"

He raised his head. His wife was looking at him. Her face was sad, and her eyes seemed to be saying, "My poor man, what a state you get into over such a small thing."

But she only murmured, "Still, you ought to try to see my point of view."

He felt too weary to go on with the discussion. He shook his head in a way that meant neither yes nor no. What point of view should he try to see? He was afraid to ask. He dreaded having his wife repeat that he wasn't going to live forever and that he hadn't made any provisions for her life once he would no longer be around. That perhaps wasn't what she would have answered, but he preferred to remain in doubt. And he also preferred silence. He already regretted that moment of uncontrollable anger, which had driven away the peace he'd felt himself settling into during the last few weeks, the way he settled his stiff old body into his nice soft bed.

What he finally understood that day was that the price of the peace he so desired was his own silence. He resigned himself to that. His wife didn't mention the school lunchroom until the following Monday, but he knew that she'd made up her mind.

On Monday morning, when they'd finished their breakfast, she asked, "Would you rather I gave you lunch before I leave or that I left everything ready for you to fix it at noon?"

He didn't even ask what she was talking about.

"I don't want to change my mealtimes," he grumbled. "And I'm still capable of fixing something myself."

Nor did he ask her what time she was leaving, or if she'd eat on the job, or how much she'd be earning, or what time she'd be home. He'd wondered about all these things ever since he'd become convinced that she would carry out her plan, but he'd sworn to himself that he wouldn't bring them up. Mère Dubois wanted to do things her way. She wanted to start living the way she would live once he was no longer around, and in that case, the best thing to do was to let the silence between them slowly deepen.

On the day when the final silence came, everything would be easier.

Autumn hadn't quite finished stripping all the leaves off the trees, but the rain which had moved in between the earth and the low sky for the last three days isolated the house even further from the rest of the town.

With this rain, winter was announcing itself. It would rattle the shutters from time to time and tear a leaf from the grape arbor or the pear tree. Père Dubois stared sometimes at the sky, sometimes at the glistening earth of the garden, and never before had he experienced so deeply, down to his very bones, the torpor which marks the approach of the dead season.

—◀ 50 ▶—

NOVEMBER went by. Mère Dubois would go off every morning at about ten thirty and return four hours later. She always brought back in her bag a few crusts of bread for the rabbits and a jar of soup that she would heat for the evening meal.

Père Dubois had to accept it. Living sort of like the poor. And in the last analysis, they were poor. He finally admitted it. His houses weren't worth anything. The war had absorbed the savings of all the elderly.

So his wife worked in the lunchroom. At an age when she deserved a rest, she became a servant. She went off smiling. She came home smiling, but each day her color grew sallower. Her back hunched over more, and her hips were stiff. She never complained. However, Père Dubois could see her rubbing her hands with their twisted fingers together. Her left index finger was crossed over her third finger. Her thumbs remained bent even when she opened her hands, and her wrists were swollen. "That dishwater isn't doing you any good."

She shrugged her shoulders.

"It's nothing. It's nothing. You know very well that I get like this every winter."

It wasn't true. Père Dubois had never seen her look so tired, and what's more, he'd never heard her cough as she did now.

When he timidly suggested that she rest, she would say, "Let me keep on just until Easter. When there's work to do in the garden again, I'll stop. But their baby will be born around the end of March. That's when I'll send them some money. Not before. It has to be for the baby."

Whenever she spoke about that baby, her face lighted up. Her fatigue seemed to leave her as if by magic. So her husband let her talk.

Julien had written to tell them that a friend had found him a two-room apartment outside Lyons. Only the apartment wouldn't be free until January, and it wasn't furnished. Immediately, Père Dubois had said, "They have no furniture. They'll just have to come here. What are we doing with two beds in our room? They'll take one of them. And we'll find plenty of other things. There's a table in the shed, and we have many too many chairs in the dining room."

From that day on, every now and then, one or the other of them would say, "Listen, when they come, we'll certainly be able to give them a few dishes, too, or that little dresser."

"Yes. The only problem will be the moving."

"Even if they have to rent a small truck, it will still be cheaper for them than buying the things."

At first, Père Dubois had made the suggestion because he wanted to be the first one to bring it up. But he had felt a slight tug at his heart at the thought of letting so many things go that had their place in the house. Then, without knowing quite why, he'd almost got pleasure from thinking up new things to give them.

During his wife's long absences, he would sometimes walk through the house looking for an object he'd just remembered. He also sometimes thought about the little child who was to be born. Since Paul had no children and no longer even hoped to have any, the little Dubois on the way was quite important after all.

Since the liberation, neither Paul nor his wife had been over to see them, but this wasn't the first time they'd let several months go by without appearing. After all, they had their work. Business must have picked up again. Père Dubois told himself these things so as not to have to think that events had separated his two boys forever and turned Paul away from his door. Time would heal everything.

But time also hurries the seasons along, and winter was taking great strides forward.

On December 4, when the sky barely shed enough light to announce the day, a harsh blast of wind came down from the north. There was a great rattling of naked branches. The vine shoots on the grape arbor leaned toward the window, and the house gave a long shudder of pain that deepened the grumbling of the fire. And then there was silence. Standing in front of the window, Père Dubois studied the clouds for several minutes, then said, "The north wind's going to settle in. And that could mean snow."

"I'm going to get a basket of wood," said his wife. "Then if it does start to snow, we'll have it."

She went out with the empty basket. A second blast whistled in. It didn't come as brutally as the first, which had whipped up everything before dying down. It came as a light breeze, whining as it skimmed along the gutters. Then it gathered force. It wrapped around the house and spread out everywhere, lying between the rooftops and the smoke from the town, mauling the trees and the arbor.

When Mère Dubois returned, she stood motionless for a moment, her back against the closed door, before being able to say, "That wind is made of ice . . . I thought I wouldn't be able to get my breath."

Her husband started piling the wood up beside the stove.

"You fill the basket too full. It's too heavy for you."

"No . . . But that wind caught me by surprise . . . I only had on my wool jacket and my shawl. I didn't think it was that cold."

She poured out what was left of the lunchtime *café au lait,* and holding the bowl in both hands to warm her fingers, she drank in little sips.

After Père Dubois had emptied the basket and stoked the fire, he went over to the window.

"That damn wind," he said. "It's already managed to tear three sacks off my cardoons. And I did tie the strings very tight. I'll have to go—"

His wife interrupted him.

"Don't say such silly things. You know perfectly well that if you go outside in weather like this, you'll spend the rest of the winter in bed. There's no point in asking for trouble; it always comes fast enough anyway."

She put her empty bowl down on the table and opened the door to the dining room.

"What are you doing?" asked her husband.

"I'm going to put on my coat. Then I'll go tie the sacks back down. I have plenty of time before I have to go to work."

"My God"—the old man groaned—"to think that I'm not good for anything anymore, once the cold sets in!"

Mère Dubois put on the heavy coat she'd made over from the overcoat the soldier they'd taken in during the fall of France had left behind. She had dyed it herself, and the mixture of the khaki base and the black dye had given the rough material a brownish color, slightly faded and streaked with tan. She turned up the collar, put her shawl over her head, and knotted it under her chin.

Still standing by the window, Père Dubois looked at her, then looked out at his cardoons. More sacks were tearing loose. If the wind got any stronger, it would blow them all away.

"You should take the string and a knife. I think the string I used was too weak. It's too old. With all the rain we've had, it's rotted already. There's some stronger string behind the cellar door."

Mère Dubois took a little pointed knife, adjusted her shawl again, and went out.

—◀ 51 ▶—

As soon as his wife was outside, Père Dubois went back to the window. He heard her open the cellar door. She was taking her time about finding that string! And the wind was getting on with its dirty work. It crept along the ground, lifted the mounds of earth he'd made at the base of his cardoons, tried to get in under the sacks, and there, gathering strength like a sly animal, blew itself up in little puffs. The sacks writhed. If his wife waited too long, all the strings would end up broken!

When she finally appeared around the corner of the house,

256

Père Dubois opened the window and shouted, "Start by tying the ones that are still holding. You can do the others afterward!"

She nodded her head and started into the bed. The wind caught her as she worked on the plants. Her coat was flapping. It filled at times and blew up over her skirt. On several occasions Père Dubois saw her stumble in her big wooden shoes and thought she was going to fall.

"By God, it's not possible for the wind to be this strong," he muttered.

When Mère Dubois stooped down to take the big plants in her arms and pass the string around them, it almost looked as if she were holding onto them so as not to get blown away.

Père Dubois followed her progress closely. Her fingers must have been numb, for usually she worked faster and more skillfully. She seemed to be in pain every time she straightened up. She had moments of inexplicable immobility. Leaning forward, she would hunch her back to the wind, stand there, take a tentative step, and draw back, trying to keep her balance.

In this fashion she tied up five or six plants; then, coming to the next one, instead of stooping as she had for the others, she straightened up and raised the hand that held the strings up to her chest. This hand opened, and the strings got away from her, flying off in the wind like pale little snakes in that earth-colored world.

"Good God, the strings!" Père Dubois groaned. "But what can she be doing?"

She had started to try to catch the strings, but her right hand beat the air, letting go of the knife, which fell. She stood that way for two or three seconds, like a half-uprooted scarecrow in the gale. Then her knees slowly buckled. Her right hand tried to catch hold of a cardoon stalk; her fingers slid down to the wet sack; she fell first onto her knees, hesitated a moment, then lay down slowly on her left side, her face against the little mound of earth.

"Good God," murmured Père Dubois. "What the hell's wrong with her? What's she doing?"

He felt his throat tighten. He tried to believe for a moment that she'd just lost her balance, but she kept lying there, motionless. Only the hem of her coat still fluttered, filled with icy wind.

His hand gripping the sill, Père Dubois was gasping, rooted to the spot by an immense fear.

──❦ 52 ❧──

PÈRE DUBOIS stood motionless for a time whose duration he could not have measured. A phenomenon had occurred inside him, beyond his awareness. Detached from the world and the passage of time, he was there and he was somewhere else. He saw his wife lying at the base of the cardoons and, at the same time, told himself that it wasn't true, that she was about to come into the kitchen rubbing her numbed hands together.

And then, not understanding what pushed him either, he left the window. His strength had come back, and his clarity also. He took the time to put on his heavy corduroy jacket and went outside.

On the stoop, while he was taking off his slippers to put on his wooden shoes, he felt the icy air envelop him and go down into him. He braced himself, summoning all his willpower to dominate his body, which recoiled from the cold's grip.

Then he walked down the path and went into the cardoon bed. It seemed to him that she was moving. He wanted to run, but the fear of falling held him back.

He bent over her. He barely touched her. He was beside her, and yet he didn't dare.

"What's the matter? Can you hear me? Can you hear me?"

He yelled very loud.

Nothing.

Mère Dubois didn't move.

He kneeled down and tried to put his arm under her to raise her up a little. Her breath was labored. She was gasping. Her face was purplish. Her bloodshot eyes were half-open under lids that trembled as if the wind were fluttering them.

"Good Lord. Good Lord." Père Dubois groaned.

He stood up. He felt lost. He looked around him. No one. There was only the north wind cutting off his breath and lacerating his face with a thousand blades.

He hesitated an instant. Would he, too, just fall down there and die with his old woman on that cold ground?

The idea whipped him as though it were part of the wind. A cry rose up from deep inside him. A cry that knotted his throat and was just an unintelligible howl.

Then he stooped down again. He put one knee on the ground and grabbed his wife by the wrist, remembering an old trick learned in the army for carrying the wounded. He pulled. Her breathing grew harsher. He pulled some more and succeeded in lifting her enough to wedge his back in under her inert form. With great effort, he lifted her up.

Would his trembling legs hold?

He took a step. Another step. Mère Dubois' feet were dragging on the ground. She had lost one of her wooden shoes. Her left hand was clenching three of the strings which flew in the wind.

Père Dubois reached the edge of the path. To step over the edgestone, he leaned forward more, balanced the body so it wouldn't fall, and, letting go of it with his left hand, grabbed the clothesline post.

At the foot of the steps, he had to stop. Despite the cold, he was drenched with sweat. The handrail was on his right. In order to grip it, he had to shift Mère Dubois' position on his back. He held her with his left hand by the stiff material of her coat. His right hand grabbed the frozen metal, and he went up a step.

There were ten steps. He stopped at each one. He tried to breathe, to get a little push from the wild wind that beat furiously against the house, whirled around and away again.

He could almost see these blasts of wind there, in front of him, full of a multitude of little black dots.

He knew these little black dots. He knew what they preceded, and fear seized him again. If he fell here, they both would roll down to the foot of the steps. Because of the boxwood trees, no one would be able to see them from the street or from the path. The great void that had been inside him a little while ago had been replaced by a strange lucidity. Each thought that crossed it was accompanied by its share of astonishingly precise images.

He stopped. He had to know when to stop long enough to gather his strength again. He had to impose a rhythm on his breathing. He had to avoid taking big gulps of icy air that might undo him.

He counted the steps. There were four left. He summoned all the strength he could muster and climbed those four steps without stopping.

On the landing, he staggered, and his hand fell onto the doorknob, which he squeezed very hard.

A pause. The knob turned, the door opened, and the heat of the room leaped at his face.

He pushed the door closed, and it slammed loudly against the wind.

Then he thought of the bedroom, of the bed. But there was no fire up there, and he was incapable of carrying his wife upstairs.

Perhaps she'd just had a little dizzy spell. He tried vainly to sit her up in a chair, but her body would fall to the right or the left or topple forward, drained of all force.

So, utterly exhausted, he laid her down on the linoleum.

—◄{ 53 }►—

PÈRE DUBOIS had thought that the heat would be enough to revive his wife. When she remained inert, he tried to get her to
drink a little brandy, but his hand was trembling so badly that
he didn't succeed. Tears were burning his eyes. Everything
was blurred, and when he stood up again, he had to lean on the
table to keep from falling. He looked out the window several
times, but no one was coming up the path.

He turned back to his wife. He tried to talk to her again, but
she just kept staring at him with her empty eyes, still exhaling
that rattling breath that came from the depths of her phlegm-
filled throat.

Again fear seized him.

He took a flat little pillow off a chair, slipped it under her
head, and went outside.

Where to go? Out to the street? He might have trouble finding someone. He thought of Mlle. Marthe, who lived across
from them, but she was old and hardly ever went out anymore.
He ran down to the bottom of the garden, around the shed, and
into the courtyard of the house where M. Robin lived.

He looked at the kitchen window, and through the fog of
tears and cold that clouded his vision, he thought he saw a
pale form. He ran faster, and raising his arms, he started to
shout, "Hey! Hey! Hey!"

His voice choked and his cough shook him, obliging him to
stop. The window opened and Mme. Robin asked, "What's
the matter?"

Père Dubois made an effort to speak, but his cough was strangling him. He could only gesticulate and barely heard, "We'll be right down!"

The window closed. Père Dubois tried to get hold of himself. He tried to spit, but the wind plastered his spittle against his jacket, and he got angry, looking for his handkerchief to clean it off.

When M. Robin and his wife appeared, he'd stopped coughing, but he still couldn't speak. He dragged them with him, and only when they'd reached the garden was he able to stammer, "Go quickly . . . my wife . . . my wife . . . I can't make it."

Mme. Robin went running off toward the house, and Père Dubois felt M. Robin take him by the arm to hold him up. For a moment, it seemed to him that a great pit was opening in front of him. He stopped, held his breath for a few seconds; then, slowly, he began to walk again.

When they got inside, Mme. Robin was kneeling beside Mère Dubois and holding her head in her arms. Mère Dubois' face was very red. Her shallow breath came with great difficulty through her violet lips.

"She's very congested," said Mme. Robin. "We'll have to call a doctor right away—and we ought to carry her up to bed."

"My lord. My lord." Père Dubois groaned.

M. Robin helped him sit down. He seemed very calm.

"I'll run home," he said. "I'll send our cleaning woman over here, and I'll telephone your son right away. He'll bring a doctor . . . Have you got his number?"

Père Dubois shook his head, and M. Robin raced off.

For the time being, Père Dubois felt relieved of a great weight. He was no longer alone. He was no longer the one who had to decide. He watched the little woman in the blue coat coming and going, her loose brown hair falling in waves over her shoulders.

She was talking. He listened without really hearing her.

"I'm going to heat up some water," she was saying. "The

doctor might need some . . . Is the fire lighted, up in your room?"

"No . . . My Lord."

"I'll go upstairs and light it . . . Is there any wood up there?"

"Yes. There must be some."

"And paper?"

"There's some here."

Père Dubois held a piece of newspaper out to her and fumbled in his pocket for his lighter.

"I'm going up with you."

"No, no, stay there . . . You can hardly stand up. When our cleaning woman gets here, we'll put Mère Dubois in bed."

Mme. Robin went upstairs, and Père Dubois heard her bustling about in the bedroom. From his seat, because of the table where his elbow was resting, all he could see of his wife was her head. She was still lying on the floor. She seemed a little less red in the face, but her eyelids were still half-closed, and her expression was lifeless.

Beyond all emotion, Père Dubois sat there, leaning forward, one elbow on the table, the other on his knee, and he stared at his wife's face, repeating, "It's not possible . . . It's not possible."

--⥼ 54 ⥽--

WHEN M. Robin got back, Mme. Robin and the cleaning woman had already put Mère Dubois to bed.

The cleaning woman was a big Italian woman of forty, stronger than many men. She had picked up Mère Dubois under her arms, and Mme. Robin had only had to support her legs to keep her feet from bumping against the stairs. Père Dubois had followed them. The fire was crackling in the bedroom when M. Robin joined them.

"I tried to call two doctors," he said. "They both were out. So I called your daughter-in-law. She's going to come with Dr. Letty, who lives next door to them."

"In the meantime," observed Mme. Robin, "we'll make her a mustard plaster . . . The trouble is surely in her chest. It will loosen her up and bring down her fever."

Père Dubois had sat down in the armchair at the foot of the bed. The gray day that entered the room cast only a pale cold light on Mère Dubois, so that he could hardly distinguish her features.

"She seems to be having less trouble breathing," observed Père Dubois.

"That's true, but I don't think her fever's going down."

M. Robin was holding Mère Dubois' wrist. He added, "Her pulse is regular, but very fast."

The two women had gone downstairs to make the mustard plaster. M. Robin sat down facing the old man on the little low chair where Mère Dubois laid her clothes at night before going to bed.

Now her clothes were on the foot of the bed alongside the one she was lying in. Père Dubois made an aimless gesture and said, "She made that coat out of a soldier's overcoat . . . You know, that that boy from Villefranche left us—Guillemin, if I remember rightly . . . He helped me make the bread during the retreat . . . A fine boy . . . I don't know what ever became of him."

M. Robin shook his head.

Père Dubois fell silent. He didn't know why he'd said all that, but the act of talking had done him good.

M. Robin asked, "She was in the garden?"

"Yes. She wanted to go out and tie down the sacks around the cardoons—I'm not much use anymore . . . But I shouldn't have let her do it. Only, you know how she is, you can't keep her away from her work! Like at that lunchroom. I've told her time and again she'll lose her health for a few pennies."

M. Robin got up and went to the window. "Her wooden shoe is still out in the garden," he said. "When I go downstairs, I'll get it."

"Of course," said Père Dubois. "I wasn't thinking about it. I never even thought I'd be able to get her this far—"

M. Robin interrupted him.

"I think that's the doctor."

The old man stood up and started for the door.

"Don't bother to come down," said M. Robin. "The women will bring him up."

Père Dubois stood undecided for a few moments, listening. He could only hear a very distant murmur of voices. Finally, there were steps on the stairs, and the bedroom door opened.

The doctor was tall and thin. He wore thick glasses. He said hello and asked for some light.

"We don't have electricity," said Père Dubois.

The doctor seemed astonished.

"Then this will be all right. I've got a flashlight."

He rummaged in his bag, and Père Dubois saw him bend over the bed. The examination was very brief. When the doctor turned away, he said, "There's no doubt about it. Pneumonia. She must have been incubating it for several days, and the cold this morning did the rest."

Only at that moment did Père Dubois become aware of the presence of his daughter-in-law Micheline, standing near the door.

"And what should we do?" asked Micheline.

"She ought to have an injection for her heart right away. I don't have the necessary things with me, but the sisters are right nearby. We'll go downstairs for the rest. I'm going to give you a prescription."

"I made a mustard plaster," said Mme. Robin.

"By all means, apply it. It can only relieve her."

He hesitated an instant, looked at Micheline, and added, "I trust a sister will be able to get here fairly soon. Otherwise, I could stop at my office and—"

"No, no," said Micheline. "I'll take care of everything. I'll go get the sister. I'll bring her back here."

She opened the door and started down the hall, saying, "Come on, we'd better let her rest."

Père Dubois stayed behind. Before leaving, he looked once more at his wife and murmured, "My Lord, what's to become of us?"

—◄{ 55 }►—

Père Dubois looked at the five people filling all the space in the tiny kitchen. He kept to the foot of the stairs, leaning against the dining-room door. He said, "We should get some chairs from the next room."

But no one paid any attention to him. On one corner of the table, the doctor was writing out a prescription and giving directions to Micheline. Across from him, Mme. Robin and her cleaning woman were preparing the mustard plaster.

Everybody was talking. But Père Dubois was in no condition to follow what they were saying. He understood only that M. Robin was offering to go to the sisters' and the pharmacy, and Micheline was answering, "Let me, let me. I'll take care of it."

The doctor and Micheline left together. The two women went back upstairs with the mustard plaster. Père Dubois sat down.

M. Robin sat down beside him. "Don't worry too much," he said. "Pneumonia responds very well to treatment, you know . . . Do you want me to go get you some wood? You'll need quite a lot for her bedroom."

Père Dubois shrugged his shoulders in despair.

"What's to become of us?" he repeated.

"We'll help you," M. Robin promised. "My wife will come. And then you have your daughter-in-law, who'll be coming back. You'll see, it will be nothing."

He said that a little as if he were talking to a child. Père Dubois was aware of it, and it seemed to him that if this man spoke to him like that, it was a sure sign that Mère Dubois was lost. He wanted to question him but recoiled before the words. He had the feeling that if he mentioned death at that moment, he might attract it. He merely said, "I'd like to smoke a cigarette, but I doubt if I'd be able to roll one."

M. Robin pulled a pack out of his pocket, and Père Dubois took one. His hands were still trembling, and even the cigarette trembled between his lips as he lighted it from M. Robin's lighter.

"I'll leave you the pack."

"Thank you. Thank you very much."

"You must take care of yourself. You should drink something hot."

M. Robin went over to the stove. But the pot on it contained only water.

"When the women get back downstairs," said Père Dubois, "I'll go up and change. My undershirt is soaking wet. If I got sick now, it would be the end of everything."

The two women came down, and Mme. Robin said, "Leave the mustard plaster on her for a while. I'm going home, and I'll bring you back something to eat."

"As if I had the heart to eat."

"You must force yourself. You need to get your strength back. It will make you feel a little better."

"I think a bowl of soup will be enough for me."

"We'll leave you for now," said Mme. Robin. "But don't you worry. I'll be back. And if necessary, I'll send Louisa this afternoon."

The Italian woman agreed, and all three departed. Père Dubois could only repeat, "What troubles, what troubles . . . What will become of us?"

As soon as he was alone again, his anguish returned. He waited a long time before deciding to go up to the bedroom. However, he felt the cold getting the better of him, and the need to change his shirt pushed him more than a desire to see his wife. He was a little afraid of being alone with her.

He climbed the stairs slowly. He stood a moment before daring to open the door, paralyzed by the idea that he might find her dead. But as soon as he'd opened it, her heavy, rattling breath reassured him.

He went over to her, touched the burning hand resting on the sheet, and asked, "Don't you hear me? Can you see me?"

Her empty look pained him. It seemed impossible to him that she could have changed so much in less than an hour. He saw her again at the moment when she had left the kitchen to go out into the garden, and he stood a long time trying to remember the words she had spoken as she went out the door. Had she said something about the cold? Or the string? Or else the knife? That's right, the knife must have been left in the garden with her wooden shoe. The wooden shoe—M. Robin had promised to bring it back. He had forgotten. That's the way people were—always making promises. And his wife had promised to come back. The mustard plaster—it shouldn't be left on too long.

He went to the window. The wooden shoe was still in the garden, where it made a yellow spot on the black earth. But the knife was invisible. It had a black wooden handle. If the blade were stuck into the ground, it probably couldn't be seen from

here. It was a good little knife, the kind they hadn't made anymore since the war.

Père Dubois shrugged his shoulders and went back to the
bed. He was still trying to remember the words his wife had
said as she went out the door. It wasn't important, but this gap
in his memory bothered him.

He looked for a clean undershirt in the closet with the squeaky
door. When he'd found one, he unfolded it and held it over the
stove for a moment. A nice smell of herbs rose from it. That was
her mania—Mère Dubois'—putting dried flowers and herbs in
the linen.

Père Dubois was still in the bedroom when Mme. Robin returned. She removed the mustard plaster and then asked, "Did
you put some more wood on the fire?"

The old man reloaded the stove.

"Come on downstairs," said Mme. Robin. "I brought you
something to eat."

They went downstairs. There was a little aluminum container and a red and white enamel pot on the stove.

"You must eat," said Mme. Robin. "It will do you good. She's
resting. She doesn't need you now, and the sister will be here
any moment. I'm going back home now because my husband
has to leave very early to get to Poligny before two. But I'll be
back as soon as he's left . . . There's some vegetable soup in
that container. And some peas and a slice of meat in the pot."

"But I'm not hungry. I'm not hungry."

The woman left after insisting once more that Père Dubois
must force himself to eat.

He took a plate and a spoon out of the cupboard. It was true
that he didn't feel at all like eating. But he knew that a little
soup would make him feel better. The soup was good, with all
the vegetables mashed up in it and an aftertaste of smoked
sausage. He ate everything in the container. Then he waited a
moment before deciding to get a fork and taste the peas. He

tasted them first right out of the pot. They were good and melted in his mouth. He took three spoonfuls of them and cut off half the meat. He told himself that it wasn't very fitting to eat like this while his wife was sick; then he told himself that he must, at all costs, try to regain his strength. If he found himself saddled with all the work, and on top of that having to climb the stairs twenty times a day! He thought about that winter when he, too, had had pneumonia. He'd spent more than a month up there. And his wife had taken care of him. Only she wasn't seventy-one years old. And yet she had often said that those stairs were killing her legs. Besides, she was a woman and knew how to nurse people. No, he wasn't the type to nurse a sick person all by himself and take care of the house and do the shopping . . .

He felt overwhelmed by everything that lay in store for him. Up until then he'd been too shocked by the suddenness of the accident to be able to think clearly. But as the food began to bring his strength back, he imagined what his wife's illness could mean to him if it dragged on. He pictured himself alone. Would the neighbors help him? Would Micheline come often? And that Italian woman of Mme. Robin's—she was as strong as an ox, but if she came regularly, he would have to pay her.

He had finished eating. He poured himself a half glass of wine. There was no coffee made, and he put two lumps of sugar in his wine and added some water. They were right—he had to get his strength back.

He drank his wine, lighted a cigarette from the pack M. Robin had given him, then looked at the clock. It was half past twelve, and the sister wasn't there yet. That was quite a long time for a thing the doctor said ought to be done as quickly as possible.

He hurriedly cleared the table, put out his cigarette and stored it in his tobacco box, and went up to the bedroom.

Mère Dubois' face had been transformed. From very red it had become very pale. Her sallow cheeks had sunk, and her lower lip was hanging. Her eyelids were closed, and nothing but a feeble little moan came from her half-open mouth.

Père Dubois slowly reached out his hand until it touched her shoulder.

"Not feeling so good? What's the matter?"

He leaned over a little, and raising his voice, he repeated, "What's the matter?"

Mère Dubois' eyelids fluttered slightly but did not open.

Père Dubois waited for a few more seconds; then, seized anew by fear, he left the room, fled down the stairs, and ran outside without even putting on his jacket or his wooden shoes.

⫷ 56 ⫸

IN his slippers, Père Dubois hurried over the frozen ground to the bottom of the garden. When he got into his neighbor's courtyard, he saw the Robins' boy's face at the window. The child disappeared, and at once M. Robin came and opened the window.

"Come quick," cried the old man. "It doesn't look too good!"

"My wife's coming down!"

Père Dubois turned and went back toward his house. He was hardly halfway there when Mme. Robin caught up with him.

"What is it?" she asked.

"I think my poor wife is nearing the end." He choked up on the last word.

"Has the sister come yet?"

"No . . . No . . . Nobody came. They'll leave us to die all alone."

Mme. Robin broke into a run again. Père Dubois couldn't

keep up with her. When he first came out, he hadn't felt the cold, but now the north wind hitting him full on interfered with his breathing. He felt its needles on his face and through his wool sweater. The cold from the ground had penetrated the soles of his slippers and was freezing his feet.

In the kitchen he had to stop a moment, one hand on his chest, the other flat on the end of the table.

He heard Mme. Robin's footsteps overhead; then the door opened, and the young woman called, "Monsieur Dubois! Come upstairs."

He slowly climbed the stairs. He wasn't thinking about anything. He no longer even felt fear or the pain the cold had awakened in him.

The bedroom door was wide open. Mme. Robin, who was standing motionless beside the bed, turned to the old man and took two steps toward him. When he stopped, she said slowly, "Monsieur Dubois— Your wife has gone."

Père Dubois looked at the bed. His wife was still in the same position. Only her mouth was wide open. Her eyes were closed, and her face paler still than when he'd left her.

"My Lord," he murmured. "My Lord . . . going away like that . . ."

Mme. Robin was weeping silently.

They stood there for a long time without saying a word, without moving, as though paralyzed by Mère Dubois' presence. She had died. All alone. While Père Dubois was running through the garden. And now it was all over. There was nothing more to do. He waited. And he didn't even know what he was waiting for.

The cold was coming in through the wide open door. Finally, Mme. Robin started for the door and murmured, "We must go downstairs. I'll go telephone your daughter-in-law."

She went downstairs, and Père Dubois followed her. They'd scarcely reached the bottom when a footstep grated on the front doorstep. Mme. Robin went to open the door.

A nun in a brown robe and a white coif came in. She was

carrying a little leather bag, which she put down at once on the table, saying, "We just received a call to—"

Mme. Robin interrupted her. "It's too late, Sister. Our poor Madame Dubois is dead."

The sister didn't seem surprised. She folded her hands under the rosary that hung from her neck and asked, "For very long?"

"No, just for a few minutes, I think."

There was a silence. The sister's lips were moving. Père Dubois thought she must be praying.

After a long pause, Mme. Robin asked in a shaky voice, "I don't understand why you didn't come sooner. It's not very far away."

"Sooner? But we just got the telephone call less than ten minutes ago."

The sister, who was short and rather plump, had a big, chubby, red face. Her brown eyes glistened in the shadow of her coif. Her lively look darted back and forth between Père Dubois and Mme. Robin.

After another pause, Mme. Robin went on. "Maybe nobody was there at the convent during the latter part of the morning."

"Nobody? But there's always someone there, always. You know that."

Père Dubois' eyes met Mme. Robin's.

The little woman wasn't crying anymore. Her face had hardened. Père Dubois felt that his legs were about to give way, and he sank into a chair, murmuring, "I don't understand . . . It's not possible . . . dying like that . . . dying like that . . ."

"Will you be needing our services?" asked the sister.

The old man made a vague gesture and looked at Mme. Robin, who said in a rather cold tone of voice, "I believe the sisters are familiar with handling these things."

"Of course," said Père Dubois, "it would be the best thing."

Mme. Robin, who was still staring at him, asked, "Should I telephone your daughter-in-law?"

"If you would."

The little woman was starting for the door when the sister asked, "Would you also be kind enough to call our superior? Tell her what the problem is. She'll send one of our sisters to help me. Then I won't be obliged to go back there, and Monsieur Dubois won't be left alone."

She gave Mme. Robin the telephone number. Then Mme. Robin went out without a backward glance.

—◀ { 57 }▶—

PÈRE DUBOIS had explained to the two nuns that they would find whatever they needed in the bedroom closet. He no longer felt strong enough to climb the stairs. People came and went. Mme. Robin. The Italian woman. Then there was the arrival of Paul and Micheline, who was weeping.

Père Dubois gathered that she was talking about a nurse who lived on the Rue de Valière and who hadn't been at home that day. She was talking fast and loud. She stopped to weep and to answer questions from the sister. At a certain moment, Paul went up to his father and said, "We can't leave her up there. With all the people who'll be coming, it wouldn't be practical. We ought to put her in the dining room."

"But there's no bed there," Père Dubois remarked.

"There's a single bed in Julien's room, isn't there?"

"Yes."

"Well, we'll bring it downstairs."

"But how are you going to do that?"

"Don't worry. I'll take care of everything."

Père Dubois understood that there was nothing more for him to say. His wife had been dead for less than an hour, and everything was already in a shambles. He felt the world slipping out from under his feet. All around him, there was nothing but noise, talk, commotion. As though death had occasioned a mad whirl, a sort of horrifying dance which he alone did not enter into.

He saw Paul and the Italian woman carry the table out of the dining room, and the rug with the red flowers. They lowered the two window shades.

"You're not going to leave that table outside?" he said timidly.

"Of course not," said Paul. "Don't you worry about the table. We'll put it in the cellar."

They went out as Père Dubois muttered, "Oh, I'm not worried about it. What use have I got for a table now?"

All this upheaval, with the doors wide open, which nobody closed, brought the winter cold into the kitchen. Père Dubois coughed several times. It was no use putting wood on the fire and standing next to the stove; he was still shivering.

Mme. Robin came down from the bedroom and offered to take him to her house.

"You can come back when everything's been arranged," she said.

"No, I want to stay here."

When he saw the Italian woman and the younger of the nuns carry down his wife, already dressed in black and seated in a chair, his throat knotted. He stood up, automatically removed his cap, and was shaken by a great sob that finally released his tears.

"My Lord . . . my wife . . . my poor old lady . . . She shouldn't have been the first to go."

Paul came up to him.

"Come on, don't cry. You'll make yourself cough. It doesn't do any good to cry. We all have to go sooner or later."

"Still, I was older than she was."

He said that in between sobs that wrenched his throat.

When everything was ready, they let him go into the dining room. The bed was in the middle of the room, instead of the table. Mère Dubois was laid out on it, in her black dress on the clean white sheet. She was as pale as the napkin they'd knotted around her face to hold up her chin. She no longer had any lips, and her mouth was nothing but a straight black line. They'd put a tablecloth on the little nightstand. A candle was burning, lighting one side of her face. In front of the brass candlestick was a saucer in which the nuns had placed a branch of boxwood.

The older of the nuns came up to Père Dubois. He recognized her from often having seen her in the street. She also used to come to the garden to get fruit or flowers, which Mère Dubois gave to the orphans.

"She didn't receive the sacraments," said the sister, "but we will pray for the repose of her soul. We all knew her. She was a woman of great generosity. She didn't have much, and yet she could always find someone poorer than herself to give to . . . The good Lord will know His servant."

She was silent. Père Dubois raised his eyes to her. She was a person of about fifty. With a rather square face whose already hardened features were accentuated by the linen coif binding her temples and chin. She was praying under her breath, and her dark eyes left the dead woman every now and then to rest on the faces of Paul and Micheline, who were standing next to each other on the other side of the bed. Père Dubois could see only three-quarters of her face, but it nevertheless seemed to him that her gaze, full of compassion when it rested on Mère Dubois, was charged with reproach when she looked at his son or his daughter-in-law. Those two never raised their eyes.

They stood like this for a long time; then, when someone knocked on the kitchen door, Micheline left the room, saying, "Don't move. I'll see who it is."

She came back right away with Mlle. Marthe on the arm of another neighbor. Mlle. Marthe was weeping. She made the sign of the cross with the holy water and turned back to Père

Dubois, murmuring, "Sweet Jesus, how little we count for in this world . . . I saw her go by just last Saturday, on her way to work . . . She didn't look sick . . . And today, she's not here anymore . . . How little we count for!"

She stopped. There was a long silence; then the older of the sisters crossed herself and went out.

Père Dubois stared at his wife's hands. Her large hands with their prominent joints and deformed fingers were folded over the lower part of her chest. Her fingers seemed to be joined by a rosary of purple beads. The flickering candle flame made a little spark dance on the small white metal crucifix at the end of the rosary.

Père Dubois felt someone take him by the arm.

"Come," said the sister. "We'll have to open the window. Come, don't take a chance of catching cold."

⸺❦ 58 ❧⸺

PÈRE DUBOIS sat in his chair until nightfall, looking alternately at the patch of ground where his wife had fallen and the grill on the stove. The Italian woman had gone out to get Mère Dubois' wooden shoe, and she had also found the knife. The north wind was still tearing at the cardoons. More strings had broken, and the sacks were flying away, rolling or dragging over the beds toward the pump. The straw was scattering. One of winter's great rages had fallen on the garden.

In the kitchen, people came and went. Père Dubois wasn't even aware of them.

Paul had asked him for the family records for the formalities and for Julien's address so a telegram could be sent to him.

Père Dubois had said, "It's in the drawer of the buffet in the dining room. There must be letters from him in there, with his address on the envelopes. Just bring the drawer in here; it'll be easier to look."

Paul had gone into the dining room with his wife. They had stayed there a few minutes. They had found the family record book and an envelope from Julien, and Paul had left.

Père Dubois stood up only when the priest arrived. He took off his cap and began to cry again.

The priest's visit was brief. Night was falling. Micheline, who had accompanied him out onto the front step, came back inside and announced, "Now it's starting to snow."

Père Dubois said, "That's all we needed."

And he got up to light the oil lamp and close the shutters. The north wind was full of little white flakes that raced past the window.

Paul returned a little before seven. His eyes were bright, and he smelled of wine. He said that everything had been taken care of.

"Did you go by the house?" asked Micheline.

"Of course. The maid will bring us something to eat. Father will eat, and then he'll go to bed. We'll both wait up."

"There are also some neighbors who've promised to come," said his father.

"They shouldn't bother," said Paul. "There's no point in disturbing people by asking them to come out in the middle of the night in weather like this. It doesn't bring back the dead."

Several more people came, and then the delivery boy brought a basket. Micheline heated the meal, and the three of them ate. Before leaving, the Italian woman had relighted the fire in the bedroom and made up the bed for Père Dubois. Micheline went upstairs twice with the night-light to put more wood on. Each time she said, "How quaint, not having electricity!"

Père Dubois didn't answer. On several occasions he'd felt like asking Micheline why she hadn't called the sister when she left, as she'd promised to do, but he hadn't dared. He remembered that upon her return she'd said something about a nurse. He hadn't understood very well, but he was afraid of making his daughter-in-law angry by asking that question. And yet each time their eyes met, Père Dubois felt uneasy.

They'd been finished eating for almost a quarter of an hour when M. Robin arrived with two other neighbors. They went and administered the holy water; then Micheline and Paul brought some chairs from the dining room.

"You'll stay and have a drink," said Micheline.

Paul looked at his father and asked, "You have some bottles, don't you? I'll go down and get one."

The men protested. They didn't want to drink wine at that hour.

"I have some coffee," said Micheline.

"There we are," said M. Robin. "For a wake, coffee's the best thing."

"But you're not going to wait up," said Paul. "Not at all. Just have a little something with us, and then everyone will go to bed. My father, too. My wife and I will stay here, but we'll sleep on the sofa. It doesn't make any sense, staying up all night. Those customs are going out of style."

The neighbors looked at each other, then looked at Père Dubois, who saw a question in their eyes.

"Paul's right," he said. "If he and his wife are willing to stay . . . You know, with this cold, it's not a good time to be out at night."

There was an embarrassed pause. Micheline served coffee to some and tea to others. Someone mentioned the war. And for a moment, the conversation picked up. They talked about the liberation of Strasbourg and the French First Army operations in the Sundgau. This name came up several times, but Père Dubois didn't know it. He believed it might have something to do with Alsace, but he didn't dare ask for an explanation. He listened. They talked about the war and the winter which might slow down the Allied advance, and yet the war had moved far away from him. It was true that winter had come. One might say that it had actually come that very morning. Père Dubois had scarcely had time to feel its presence before it had taken his wife from him. And why? For a few cardoons that would end up frozen anyway.

Père Dubois soon stopped trying to follow the conversation between his neighbors and his son. He relived the day, starting from the time he got up that morning. He reconstructed everything that happened in perfect detail. Every gesture of his wife's. Each of her words. When he got to the moment when she'd put on her heavy coat to go outside, the words that she'd said then came back to him spontaneously, without his even having to search for them.

Then, winding up his pursuit of the thread of the morning, he focused his attention once more on the evening at hand. The others were discussing the question of nationalization of the coal mines in the north. Père Dubois only listened for a few seconds; then, raising his hand, he said, "Do you know what she said to me?"

The others stopped talking and looked at him; more quietly and slowly, he went on. "Do you know what she said to me, just before she went outside?"

He paused for a moment, not expecting an answer.

"Well, she said to me, 'I'm going to put on my coat. Then I'll go and tie the sacks back down. I have plenty of time before I have to go to work.' "

He'd produced no effect at all. The neighbors looked at one another and shook their heads. And Paul said, "Well, what about it? You already told us that she'd gone out to tie down the cardoons."

Père Dubois raised his voice. "I'm not talking about that. But I couldn't remember the last words she said to me. And I just remembered them. She said, 'before I have to go to work.' "

Paul shrugged his shoulders.

"You ought to go up to bed," he said. "You're tired."

"Yes, I'm tired . . . Work . . . That was the last word she said to me, you see . . . The last."

Père Dubois stood up. The neighbors did likewise, saying that since they wouldn't be needed, they wouldn't stay any longer.

As soon as they had gone, Père Dubois went into the dining room and closed the door behind him. Since his wife had died, this was the first time he had been alone with her. It was very cold in the room, but in spite of the open window, the smell of death was already strong. He went over to the bed. The candle had burned way down, and its flame flickered constantly because of the draft coming in through the cracks in the shutters. He murmured, "My poor little wife . . . There you are in winter already . . . And before you left, you spoke about work . . . And then it was over."

He no longer knew how to pray, so he simply added, "Dear God, if there is a heaven, her place must be there. If she never went to church, it was always because of work."

He repeated that word several times. Then, as he felt the cold getting to him, he sprinkled her with a little holy water and went out quietly.

—◅{ 59 }▻—

IN the bedroom, the bed in which Mère Dubois had died had been torn apart. All that remained of it was the mattress and the quilt folded over the iron footrail. The other bed had been made up for Père Dubois with clean sheets and one lone pillow in the middle of it.

He put the night-light down on the walnut cover of the old

flour bin that separated the two beds, then went back to the stove. He opened it, poked the embers a little, and threw on a big log. The north wind had died down somewhat, and the old man thought that the snow was sure to fall more heavily now. By tomorrow there might be quite a lot of it, and his wife wouldn't be there to sweep off the steps and scatter ashes. Nor would she be there to go get wood from the shed and water from the fountain. She wouldn't be there for anything. Not the cooking or the shopping or anything at all. Of course, as long as she hadn't been buried yet, there would be people around to do everything, but once she had left the house, there would be a great emptiness. There had been too much going on today for him to have found time to think about that. Only now that he was alone in the bedroom, everything crowded into his head. Each part of his life he thought about made a great stretch of emptiness appear. With his wife gone, his life became impossible. She had died so quickly! And just like that, full of vigor and hard at work. And the last word that she had spoken had even been the word "work." Work had taken up so much time in their life together that it was only natural, after all, for her to have gone in this fashion. But it was too soon. She had been young enough to see him through to the end of his life. Left alone, she would have known how to cope with life better than he could.

She had left him, and he didn't even know if he had any money. She was the one who always took care of everything. There were several deeds at the bank and an account in the savings bank. In the drawer of the buffet in the dining room, there must be the money from the summer crops, plus what she'd earned at that lunchroom. The burial would surely cost a lot.

Père Dubois had undressed slowly. When he got into bed, his legs were gripped by the damp cold of the sheets. That was something else she used to do: bring up the bed warmer and come up to move it three or four times before he went to bed.

That night no one had warmed the bed, and despite the fire, it took Père Dubois a long time to get warm again.

Usually he put out the night-light before even getting into bed. But tonight, he couldn't bring himself to do it. He stared at the ceiling where the glow from the uncertain little flame danced.

And he repeated to himself that Mère Dubois was dead.

She'd left him alone with many worries on his mind. Her troubles were all over. She was still in the house, but downstairs, in that freezing room where they ordinarily never went, except to get something out of one of the drawers.

They'd taken the table out and put Mère Dubois in the middle of the room on Julien's bed. She was already stiff and cold.

Père Dubois turned over a little onto his side and pulled up his legs. It had disturbed him to find himself lying in the position of the dead. He felt fatigue overwhelm him and sleep slowly coming on. He raised himself up onto his elbow to blow out the lamp; then he lay back down on his side.

He thought about his wife, and he also thought about that old dried-up skeleton Julien had brought one night, which was still out in the loft above the shed.

Mère Dubois still had the face of a woman, but in reality, she was now nothing more than that skeleton.

She was downstairs, and Père Dubois thought that that was probably where they would lay him out, too, someday or other, when his troubles were over.

--≼ 60 ≽--

THE next morning, when Père Dubois got up, Micheline was alone in the kitchen. She had heated some *café au lait.*

"Paul left," she said. "You understand, there's his work. He has to check the truckloads. We have two drivers who go out on the road this morning and another who should have gotten in from Bresse last night."

"Of course. I know that life doesn't stop just because my poor wife passed away."

There must have been daylight outside, but the shutters were still closed and the oil lamp was lighted.

"I'll open the shutters," said the old man.

"There's lots of snow. And it's still coming down."

He opened the shutters. The garden was white, and the cardoons looked like big, carelessly built snowmen. The north wind had plastered snow against the stalks and leaves, as well as onto the sacks it hadn't been strong enough to tear away. It had stopped blowing. The sky was very low, and the scattered flakes that still fell flew about in every direction. It was a light snow that only severe cold brings.

"I'm going to leave, too, to wash and change my clothes," said Micheline. "But I'll send the boy over to clean off the steps and the path; otherwise, the kitchen will be flooded when the people start coming by."

She spoke quickly, and her voice betrayed irritation.

"I'm causing you a lot of trouble," observed Père Dubois.

His daughter-in-law looked surprised. She hesitated a moment before answering, "The ones who go have no worries at all. It's the ones who are left behind who have all the problems."

Père Dubois sat down, and Micheline served him his *café au lait*. He started breaking his bread into his bowl; then, as his daughter-in-law was putting on her coat, he said, "We'll have to pay the doctor. Yesterday, I wasn't really thinking, and it didn't occur to me."

"We'll take care of that later. Paul paid him yesterday afternoon, when he went to ask him for the death certificate. Don't worry about it."

She started for the door and added, "Do you at least have

284

some money? You won't need it, but you still should have some here."

"There's sure to be some in her wallet. And there must also be some in the dining room. I'll look."

She opened the door and said, "When the boy comes, tell him to get you some wood."

She went out, and Père Dubois began to eat. The *café au lait* didn't have the same taste as his wife's used to have. He ate his dunked bread slowly but had trouble drinking what was left in the bowl. As soon as he finished, he rolled a cigarette; then, just as he was about to light it, he stopped. Laying it on the edge of the table, he went into the dining room. An almost-new candle was burning. Mère Dubois' face had sunk in further, and her forehead was glistening, as though covered with frost.

"My poor little woman," he murmured. "It's not very warm in here . . . It's a bad time of year to die."

He stayed only a few seconds. The cold and the odor were insupportable. He pulled the top drawer of the buffet all the way out. He put it on the kitchen table and closed the door again.

When that was done, he lighted his cigarette and contemplated the drawerful of papers, all in disarray. He knew nothing about paper work and hesitated to touch it. Probably Paul had mixed everything up, looking for the family record book and Julien's address. However, he had to find out how much money his wife had because the burial would cost a lot.

Père Dubois took out of the drawer old post office calendars, a recipe book, several notebooks with blue covers in which his wife had noted, over the years, what she had sold: rabbits, vegetables, fruit. Another notebook containing addresses which he had trouble reading. He put this notebook to one side, thinking that it would come in handy when they had to send the announcements. That's true, there was still the problem of announcements, but Paul must be taking care of that. That was arranged along with the burial. He found a thick bundle of letters, almost all from Julien. The wallet was in the very back of the drawer. A large yellow leather wallet, rather stiff, with a big brown tab that snapped loudly when you closed it. The tab wasn't closed. Père Dubois had often seen his wife putting money into this wallet or taking money out of it, when they had to pay for wood, for example, or for a barrel of wine.

He opened it and took out three ten-franc bills and two fives. He thought for a moment. It was impossible that his wife wouldn't have kept more money than that in the house. He knew that she hadn't been to the bank for several months. Had she given it all to Julien? But she was always saying that she wanted to wait for the birth of the baby. Had she hidden the money somewhere else? Père Dubois took out the few papers that were still in the drawer. They were insurance policies and postage stamps of the Seine River. He examined everything that he'd laid out on the table and opened a little cardboard box covered with yellow and white material, very worn, with tiny red and blue flowers on it. The box contained a few old coins that were certainly no longer in currency. He also found his old lottery medal in it. It was a round enameled medal, black on the back and white on the front. All around it was a double stripe of blue and red. In the middle, an inscription: "Military Conscripts. Class of 1893." In larger characters, the number 156. There still was a faded piece of tricolor ribbon attached to the medal, with an enormous safety pin stuck in it. Père Dubois turned the medal over and over in his hand. He could still see that day in 1893. It was springtime. With bright sunshine and lots of young men laughing. Others were complaining about having drawn a bad number, which meant they would have to serve three or four years far away from France. Père Dubois began to tell himself the story of his military service, but he didn't get very far. It wasn't the right moment. He had to look elsewhere for the money. He put back into the box a red velvet sacred heart on yellow satin, enclosed under a dome of glass held in an oval brass frame. A piece of a fountain pen. A tiny purse of fine mesh containing a bronze penny and two medals of the Virgin. An old lighter with no wick and another little purse made out of shells. An inscription too small for him to decipher was embroidered on it, and he remembered that it said "Cette." He'd been there one day for a sports meet, and he'd brought it back as a souvenir for his first wife, whom he was then just engaged to.

It wasn't exactly yesterday, but he remembered perfectly the beach where he'd gone to swim after the meet. He could see the girls lifting up their skirts to run barefoot, gathering up shells when the waves retreated. It seemed to him for a moment that the sunshine of that day was coming into the kitchen and that he was about to hear the shrieks of those girls as they ran back onto the dry sand when the waves came in.

He breathed deeply, lowered his eyelids, and sat there a few seconds with his eyes closed. When he opened them again, everything in the kitchen was blurred, and he felt tears running down the sides of his nose.

He wiped his eyes, blew his nose, and put the drawer back in place. He kept out only the wallet, which he had some difficulty fitting into his pants pocket. He preferred to keep that money on him. With all those people coming and going, you never knew. Then he looked for Mère Dubois' own wallet in the dresser drawer in the kitchen. It was an old wallet made out of black oilcloth that she'd sewn up countless times, held together by a shoelace. It contained only a five-franc note and a few coins. In another pocket there were their ration cards and a picture of Julien with a four-leaf clover taped to it.

Père Dubois thought that she might have hidden some money in the bedroom closet. He hesitated. If he went upstairs, he couldn't lock the front door, and anyone could get in without his even hearing them. Ordinarily he wasn't so suspicious, but suddenly the feeling had come over him that someone might want to steal what little he had.

He stood undecided at the foot of the stairs; then he made up his mind. Looking through the closet would take a lot of time, but he could just lock it and keep the key on him.

He had trouble with the lock, which hadn't worked for years. He was hot. He felt a little like a thief hurrying for fear of getting caught. It was stupid. He knew it and kept telling himself that he was in his own home and free to act as he saw fit. But nevertheless, as soon as he'd succeeded in locking the door, he went back downstairs as fast as he could go.

No one had come. He rolled a cigarette, which he lighted while poking the fire; then, sitting back down in his place, his feet in front of the stove, he started to wait.

—◅ 61 ▻—

THAT day was exhausting. The morning dragged on with waiting until eleven o'clock. Then the boy came, bringing a pot of stew, a container of soup, and some applesauce. He swept off the steps, and Père Dubois had to go out twice to tell him not to knock the broom against the iron balustrade. He was a fresh kid, and the old man had his doubts about entrusting him with the key to the shed so that he could go get two baskets of wood.

After the boy had left, Père Dubois had a visit from M. Robin, who had come to see if he needed anything. No, he didn't need anything, and if he did, his children would help him. He had thought a great deal about Mme. Robin's reaction to that business about the nurse and the sister, and he felt ill at ease. M. Robin wanted to administer some holy water, and Père Dubois accompanied him. He said again that it was unfair for his wife to have died before him. He repeated that to every visitor.

Julien arrived shortly before noon. He had taken the only

morning train. He embraced his father, saying, "Where is she?"

Père Dubois indicated the dining-room door with his chin and went in behind his son.

Julien leaned over and kissed his mother on the forehead; then, kneeling beside the bed, he began to cry, his head against the sheet.

Père Dubois watched him a moment, and tears came to his eyes.

When they went back into the kitchen, Julien asked, "But what happened? What was it? An accident?"

Père Dubois told the whole story in detail. The north wind. The cardoons. Mère Dubois insisting on going outside. The trouble he had carrying her back. His going to the neighbors. The help he'd got. The doctor's visit. And there he stopped.

"And what did this doctor say?"

Père Dubois gestured with his hands.

"What do you think? She was very sick. He said some injections—I don't really know what. The sister finally did come, but it was too late. She must have been walking around with pneumonia for several days. And you know she was never one to complain. She never talked about herself. For her, as for me, work was the only thing that mattered. We had to be that way. We had to live. And the war didn't make things any too easy. Work, that was the last word she said to me."

And Père Dubois repeated his wife's last words. Then he explained that she had been going to that lunchroom every day to make some money for Julien and Françoise and the baby that was coming.

Then he stopped again. Julien was listening to him, sitting on the second step of the stairs, his back hunched and his head bowed.

"And the worst thing about it," said the old man, "is that I don't even know what she did with the money."

He took out the wallet and showed him its contents.

"There. That's all. But she must have more hidden away somewhere."

Julien didn't even raise his head to look at the bills. He simply said, "If you knew how much I don't care about that money . . . It's not possible . . . Not possible . . . When I think that we left her in perfect health . . . But after all—"

He fell silent. He wiped his eyes and raised his head. Then only, did Père Dubois notice that he had shaved his beard off and that his hair was much shorter. His cheeks were hollow, and there were dark circles under his eyes.

"You don't look very well."

The boy shrugged his shoulders.

"We'll eat," his father went on. "Micheline brought me something. And there are still some leftovers from last night. There's plenty for both of us."

"You go ahead and eat. I'm not hungry."

"Me either, but we have to keep our strength up. And there's no point in waiting until all the people come to pay their respects."

They sat down at the table, and while they were eating, Père Dubois talked about the little errand boy he didn't like.

"When you've finished eating," he said, "you can go down to the shed. Make sure he locked the door properly. And you might even go inside and see if he tried to go through the tool cupboard. And I had two billhooks in there near the woodpiles. See if they're still there. They're good billhooks. You'd have to pay a lot for them today. And besides, with the war, I don't know if you could even find any that good. The smallest one, you know, that's almost straight near the top, with the split handle. I've been meaning to repair it for years. But I never had time. When the weather's good, the garden takes up all my time, and when it's bad, I can't go and work in that unheated shed. I always said that I wanted to close it in a little better, but that's not a job for someone my age . . . Yes, now what was I saying? . . . Ah, yes, that billhook, you know the one I mean.

Well, I bought it at Raginot's sale. You must have been about three or four years old. Don't you remember? Raginot, he used to live behind the hill in Mancy. A good fellow. That billhook, he must have used it himself for at least thirty years. I met him when I got back from the war . . ."

Julien didn't budge. From time to time he nodded his head, and Père Dubois went on through an interminable account of which the billhook remained the central theme, but from which innumerable stories branched out, running into one another, cutting back and forth, following one another to meet up finally with some trail that always led back to the story of that old billhook.

Père Dubois went on and on, rolling his yarn down the bumpy road of his memories, and as he went along, it seemed to him that his grief diminished a little.

It returned, however, with the first visitors. Each time he would have to tell the story of his wife's death over again. He would start off with the same words, the same rhythm, and it would go along fine until he got to the doctor's visit. There he had great difficulty, departing from the truth to plunge into a sort of vague jumble of words. He would say that she was very sick, that it was too late anyway, but he knew perfectly well that something was missing from his account. He didn't really have the feeling he was lying, but only the conviction that he was passing over certain details that wouldn't interest anybody. Only, to do it, at a certain definite point he had to leave a path clearly marked with facts to take one whose words no longer represented anything he could see or touch. For him, who had several hundred long stories stashed away in his head, it was a new experience, and he had trouble getting used to it. Up until the time of the doctor's visit, he would use the same words, the same rhythm, sighing in almost the same places. From then on, he could feel his account wandering off, and soon he was seized by the fear that Julien would notice it and ask him some direct questions.

He felt a certain relief around four o'clock, when Julien announced, "I have to go out for a moment."

"Be sure to be back by five, above all, when we put her in her coffin."

"I won't be gone long. I'm only going to see Monsieur Robin."

"But—but—"

His anguish, which had been relieved for an instant, returned tenfold. And yet he could say nothing. There was a great turmoil inside him, increased by the presence of a few old friends he hadn't seen in ages who were staying on. For each newcomer, he would start his story again, and those who had already heard it would follow along with nods of their heads and shrugs of helplessness. Wouldn't one of them suddenly point out that there was one passage where he didn't seem to be absolute master of what he was telling?

Gradually, he was exhausting himself. At several points he was wracked by fits of coughing that forced him to keep silent for a while.

Julien was gone for only a half hour. When he returned, Père Dubois searched his face, and it seemed to him that it had hardened. His expression boded no good. He hesitated a long time before asking, "Well, did you see them?"

"Madam Robin was alone."

"And what did she have to say?"

The boy shrugged his shoulders.

"What did you expect her to say? What people always say under the circumstances. She liked Mama very much, and I think she was really moved."

Père Dubois sighed. Had little Mme. Robin really refrained from mentioning the sister's delay in coming? Did Julien want to wait to bring it up until everyone had gone? Until Paul arrived? Until Mère Dubois was buried? Or was he, Père Dubois, exaggerating? After all, what had happened? A sister was supposed to come; she hadn't come right away. There'd also been some talk about a nurse. And his wife had died. If the doctor hadn't done anything, it was because there had been nothing to do. That's the way life was, with death at the end of the road. And death came the day your strength gave out. That's all. They'd both used up all their strength, but perhaps Mère Dubois had had less than he to start with. Age didn't really count. She'd never been willing to take care of herself. She didn't want to give her pennies to some doctor. She'd even made a bandage herself, out of an old corset, for the hernias that bothered her so much. All that, just to save a few pennies.

And Père Dubois told himself all this in bits and pieces, between the comings and goings of people he didn't always recognize, who obliged him to start the story of his wife's death over and over again.

At five o'clock the undertakers arrived with the coffin. The kitchen wasn't very warm anymore, but the door had to stay open a long time, and winter finally invaded the house completely. The cold, the snow people tracked in on their boots, the falling night that dimmed the lamp, all winter really, came in to seek out Mère Dubois.

There was a great commotion of furniture and ladders in the dining room because of the black drapes the undertakers hung up all around.

And then came the moment to put Mère Dubois into her coffin. Until then she had still been with them. No longer the same, but present anyhow. Each time Père Dubois had found himself alone in the dining room with her, he had talked to her as if she were still alive. Now she was really leaving. She was no longer at home in this transformed room, and they removed her even further by putting that lid on top of her, which the men in black screwed down very quickly. Père Dubois was crying, but he was also noticing that these men had good tools and were very skilled in their work. He felt someone take his arm. It was Julien, who was crying beside him.

They stood there until the wooden coffin was put in place on the trestles and covered with a black cloth embroidered with a large cross of silver thread. Next, the men lighted two candles on either side, and the people who were there administered holy water with a big sprinkler standing in a metal pail.

And then, as everyone withdrew, Père Dubois went back to his place in the kitchen.

–◄ 62 ►–

PAUL DUBOIS had come to be there when they placed his step-mother in her coffin. Père Dubois had seen him talking to Julien without being able to hear what he was saying. He'd left immediately afterward. Micheline had gone a little later, but visitors had come one after the other until eight o'clock at night.

The last visitor was M. Vaintrenier, who said, "Please forgive me for not having come sooner, but City Hall gives me a lot of trouble."

He had been head of the City Council since the Liberation.

"Of course, you're forgiven," Père Dubois said. "Just because one of us dies, life doesn't stop for the others."

It was a formula he'd repeated many times during the course of the day. And invariably he would add more quietly, "And that's too bad because, believe me, there's nothing left for me now on this earth."

People would protest, try to find comforting words, but Père Dubois would stop them, saying, "I comfort myself, you know . . . I comfort myself by thinking that it won't be too long before I follow her."

As she left, Micheline had said, "If you don't mind, we won't be over tonight, since we already spent last night here."

When they were alone, Julien said to his father, "Why didn't anyone offer to come to the wake? It's astonishing."

Père Dubois felt his embarrassment return. He stammered, "What do you expect? It's done less and less now . . . And then, Paul and his wife stayed last night. Tonight, as long as you're here— Anyhow, you don't have to wait up. Especially now that she's in her coffin. If you want to go to bed, we'll make up the bed—"

Julien interrupted him. "It's not worth the trouble. If I want to rest, I'll use the sofa."

Père Dubois didn't insist. He started heating the leftovers, and they both ate, almost in silence. Mère Dubois' chair was empty. The old man looked at it frequently. He also looked at this son, who never took his eyes off the back of that chair where she had sat for so many years.

When they finished eating, Père Dubois got out his tobacco box and rolled a cigarette. He lighted it and then took the pack his neighbor had left him the night before out of his pocket.

"Here. If you want one of these—Monsieur Robin gave them to me. Yesterday my hands were shaking so much that I couldn't have rolled one."

When Julien didn't react, he pushed the pack a little ways across the oilcloth, adding, "Go ahead, help yourself."

"No, thanks, I stopped smoking."

"Really?"

"I sell my cigarettes. Or trade them in for sugar."

"Ah . . . Well, smoking is my only pleasure."

He wanted to ask Julien what kind of work he was doing and how they were getting along in Lyons, but he didn't care. He simply asked, "Well, then, your wife will be arriving at about eleven tomorrow?"

"Yes. She couldn't ask for two days off."

Julien sat motionless before his empty plate, his elbows on the table, his head resting on his right hand. Père Dubois felt silence settle between them. The silence pained him, but at the same time he was afraid Julien might speak. It was a vague apprehension, but it had been with him since the boy's arrival. He finally said, "I'm going to do the dishes. And then I'll make some tea. Would you like some?"

"No. But don't get up. I'll make it for you. And as for the dishes, I've got all night to do them."

As soon as he'd drunk his verbena tea, Père Dubois sighed and stood up. "I'm going in to say good night to her. And then I'm going upstairs to bed."

Julien accompanied him into the dining room. They stood there a few moments in silence. As they were going out, the old man said, "This is the last night she'll spend in this house. Good Lord, how little we count for in this world! Well, I'm going upstairs. I can hardly stand up."

—≪{ 63 }≫—

THAT night Père Dubois didn't sleep very well. He was even tempted to get up several times. It seemed to him that it wasn't quite fitting to leave his son downstairs alone with his mother. And then he would tell himself that perhaps it was better that way. They'd always enjoyed their little secrets anyhow. He had never really shared their special intimacy. No doubt Julien preferred to spend this night alone with her. Père Dubois didn't hear a sound, but he imagined his son opening the door from time to time and going to sit beside the coffin for a few minutes. He tried to remember the death of his own mother, but that was more than forty years back, and he'd forgotten most of the details. He could remember less important things that had happened before that very clearly, however, probably because they were associated with life.

What had also kept him awake was the idea of his solitude. When everything was over, he would be left alone. And if he found himself really alone, there would be nothing left for him to do but let himself die also. Although he'd never thought about it before, he now had the feeling that his wife had always protected him from sickness and death. Probably Paul and Micheline would suggest that he come and live with them, but he already knew that he would refuse. He wanted to die here in his own house, in the midst of his garden. The year he'd been ill, he'd refused to go to the hospital precisely because he was afraid of dying. It had been that, plus the certainty that no one would be able to take care of him the way his wife could. At the time he hadn't really thought about it, but tonight he realized that had been one of the reasons for his determination to stay at home.

In the morning, when he got up, his head felt heavy, and he had to take an aspirin. He could see nothing ahead of him but a twilight through which he would have to make his way alone, with no guideposts and no one to help him along the difficult road.

At ten o'clock Julien left to go into town and order a funeral wreath. He had said he would stop by the station and meet his wife, but he must have been delayed because Françoise arrived alone. She stood a long time weeping silently beside Mère Dubois' coffin. As soon as she left the room, Père Dubois said to her, "I'm very happy, in a sense, that you got here before Julien . . . I wanted to tell you . . . Well, it's just that— You know my wife loved you very much."

The young woman looked at him. Despite her tears, she still had that gentleness in her eyes that Père Dubois appreciated. When she had arrived, she had embraced him more tenderly than Julien had.

Pushed by the fear of his son's return, he finally found the words he was looking for.

"You know," he said, "if I had been the first to go, I'm quite sure my wife would have asked you to come live with her. So, you see—"

Françoise made a little gesture and nodded her head. Believing she was about to speak, Père Dubois was silent. Perhaps a minute went by. Then, when she said nothing, he went on. "Life isn't always easy in the big city . . . And here, when you have your baby, there's always the garden."

Françoise finally said, "It's not up to me to make any decisions. But anyhow, I have a job in Lyons. And I don't know what Julien would think about living here . . . You'll have to ask him."

Père Dubois said nothing. There were footsteps outside the front door. It was a young girl bringing flowers. When she left, he said,

"Shouldn't we have given her something?"

Françoise called the girl back and gave her a little money.

"I'll pay you back," said Père Dubois, digging into his pocket.

"No. Please don't."

She sat down at the end of the table in the same chair she'd occupied when she had eaten there.

"Sit over near the fire, why don't you?" suggested Père Dubois.

"No, I'm not cold."

She sat stiffly in her chair. Her pregnancy was barely visible under her full black dress. As Julien had done the night before, she stared at the back of the chair that had always been Mère Dubois' place. That was where Père Dubois had asked her to sit so that she would be nearer the fire. In spite of himself, he imagined her there, replacing his wife and taking care of the house.

As though she'd read his thoughts, she stood up and said, "Perhaps I should fix something to eat."

"Don't bother. Paul's little errand boy is supposed to bring something over. There'll surely be enough for the three of us.

Since yesterday, you know, no matter how I force myself to eat, I just don't have any appetite."

He sighed. Looked again at Françoise's clear eyes. They were bluish gray, a little like Mère Dubois'.

He would have liked to talk to her further about his plan, but he couldn't find the words. To tell the truth, he wasn't really looking very hard. He'd already understood that she couldn't decide anything. In relation to Julien, she must be a little the way his wife had always been: willing to accept everything, to approve and support him in anything he undertook, also willing to sacrifice herself and stand in admiration of him. That was undoubtedly why Mère Dubois had liked her right away. After they had left, she had said, "I really feel much better knowing that he's with that girl." There you had it. Mère Dubois had been the one to see it clearly. And Père Dubois realized that for her, Julien must be what mattered most. So he, Père Dubois, really meant nothing to this girl. She was kind and generous— her eyes showed it—but as he had with his wife, Julien filled her heart. At the moment there was no room for anyone else.

So more than ever, Père Dubois felt himself alone. In a scarcely audible voice, he said, "Death is over quickly for those who die, but for those who are left behind, it's a different story."

⊰ 64 ⊱

MÈRE DUBOIS' burial took place at three o'clock in the afternoon. Despite the snow and the cold, a lot of people came, and the house had stayed open to the icy wind for an interminable length of time. Père Dubois, who no longer had the strength to stand on his feet, sat in his chair, where people came to shake his hand, tracking in snow all the way to the stove.

Père Dubois rose to his feet only when they carried the body out. He took off his cap and murmured, "My poor old lady . . . my poor old lady . . ."

And a great sob that had been burning his chest for a time devoured the rest of the sentence.

Of course, he wasn't able to follow the procession in the cold, and so far, to the other side of town. So Mlle. Marthe, who wasn't able to go either, stayed with him. First she mopped the floor, then she sat down in Mère Dubois' place, and they built up the fire a little to try to get the house warm again.

Then they talked about Mère Dubois. About old times before the war and evenings spent chatting on the bench in the garden. They relived all that, each contributing his own special set of memories. And it all fitted together, overlapping into a monotone recital for two voices, which could have gone on forever. They also talked about the war. Not at all about what it was like at the moment. What was happening so far away no longer concerned them. They talked about the First World War, then about the one which for them had ended the day the Germans left town. Could they ever have believed that? They had been born right after 1870. During their youth, there had been much talk about the Prussians occupying the town.

There they sat, talking like that, without grief and without joy, about a whole world of memories where Mère Dubois had had her little place. And from time to time, Père Dubois would stop to say, "Well, she has no more worries now . . . She never saw her little grandson. And I won't see him either."

The old spinster, who was about as old as Père Dubois, didn't react like all the others. She didn't protest. Each time she said, "What do you expect? We can't live two lives on this earth."

And when the others got back, Mlle. Marthe went home, with Françoise to accompany her.

Next, Père Dubois explained to Julien what he should get from the cellar. Julien brought up an old bottle of white wine, which Père Dubois uncorked with great care, and it filled the room with the strong smell of the wine cellar.

And there they sat, silent before their glasses. Père Dubois was in his chair near the window, whose shutters he had closed. Françoise was sitting in front of the cupboard in Julien's old place. Paul, at the end of the table, was turned sideways so as not to have his back to Julien, who was sitting on the stairs. Micheline was the one who sat in Mère Dubois' old chair.

Paul said, "It was a good thing you didn't come. It was cold as hell. And standing at the door shaking hands with people who didn't really give a damn—that's never much fun."

"That's true," said Micheline. "I just can't seem to warm up my feet again."

"You should take off your shoes for a while," said Père Dubois.

"No. I have to go home. I have things to do."

"Go on ahead," said Paul. "I'd like to talk with my father a minute while Julien's here."

Micheline emptied her glass, then got up. She brushed Père Dubois' cheek with her lips, bumping her hat against the brim of his cap and knocking it askew on his head. Before going out, she looked at Françoise, then at Julien, and suggested, "You know you can come sleep at the house if you like."

"No," said Julien. "We have to get back. There's a train at seven thirty; we have plenty of time to make it."

Paul smiled contemptuously and asked, "You have to get back to your work, I suppose?"

"Exactly!"

Julien's tone of voice alarmed Père Dubois, who hastened to say, "If they have to get back, there's no point in their spending the night here. There's no point in it."

Micheline was near the door. Julien got up and went forward. Françoise got up, too. Micheline held out her hand to her, saying, "Good-bye, my dear."

"Good-bye, madame," said Françoise.

There was a pause. Père Dubois looked at Micheline. Their eyes searched each other for a minute. Micheline turned to Julien and held out her hand, saying, "Good-bye."

"Good-bye."

She went out very fast.

Silence.

Micheline's heels tapped down the steps, then nothing more.

Françoise gave a little cough and said, "Perhaps I should go on ahead. If you have things to talk about—"

"We don't mind talking in front of you," said Paul.

"But of course," said the old man. "There's nothing to hide. Micheline left because she had things to do, but—"

Julien, who was still standing, broke in. "Françoise is right. She can go over to Madame Robin's. I have to stop by there and say good-bye. She can wait for me there."

Père Dubois tried to say something but only began a sentence which he didn't finish. "But after all, why impose on other people—"

He had seen that Françoise was looking questioningly at Julien. She got up. It was just as he had thought. She was like his wife: Even a look was enough to convince her. Père Dubois felt lost. He felt stupid. He no longer knew why he had hoped for something from this girl, and he no longer knew just what it was that he had hoped for.

As she came over to embrace him, he stood up and removed his cap. His voice trembled when he said, "Good-bye, my dear, good-bye . . . You know, my wife was very fond of you . . . She—well, think about me from time to time . . . Lyons isn't so very far away for the young—"

He felt that he was about to cry, and he stopped. He saw that Paul was observing him with a half-smile, and he coughed to cover his confusion.

Françoise kissed him as she had done that morning. She whispered into his ear, "Good-bye, Papa. Good-bye. And take care of yourself."

She put on her coat, picked up her purse, and slung its strap over her shoulder; then she shook Paul's hand as he rose slightly from his chair.

Before closing the door, she gave Père Dubois one last look. A very soft look, from eyes that glistened much brighter than usual.

As soon as she went out the door, Julien sat down at the chair she'd just left and folded his arms on the table.

"Well," he said to his half brother, "what do you have to say?"

"Since you're in such a hurry to leave, we really must discuss certain things that should have waited at least a day or two."

"That's true," said Père Dubois, "but it would be nice if you could come back anyway."

"Certainly not right away," said Julien.

There was a brief silence. Père Dubois stared at his two sons, and the fear grew in him that they were about to leap at each other's throats.

"What I have to say is very simple," Paul began. "Father can't live alone. So he'll have to come and live with us, and we'll make an arrangement—"

Père Dubois sat up in his chair. His hand, which had moved out onto the table, gestured: no, no.

"There is no question of my leaving this house," he said firmly. "And if no one wants to help me, then I don't need anyone!"

He had almost shouted that last sentence. He felt that his strength wouldn't last long at this rate, so he hastened to add, "If there are things to be settled about my wife's inheritance, the notary can take care of them. I don't know anything about accounting, but I trust that I'll have enough to live on without asking anyone for anything . . . And if I live through the winter, I still have my hands to work the garden."

His hand came down heavily on the table, and the glasses rocked.

"Don't shout," said Julien. "You'll make yourself cough."

Père Dubois looked at him, surprised. That was a phrase of his mother's, and he pronounced it exactly as she had.

Paul emptied his glass, crushed out his cigarette in the copper ashtray, and stood up, saying, "If that's the way things are, then we have nothing to discuss. And yet there will surely be things that have to be settled."

"If it's the burial you're talking about," said Julien, "don't worry, I'll pay my share."

Paul answered only by shrugging his shoulders, and Père Dubois quickly said, "That's my responsibility. I'm not completely poverty-striken."

"No," said Julien, "and I also think that if you do need money, you could perfectly well sell the house with the bakery and get someone in here to take care of you."

Père Dubois was about to say that for nothing in the world would he sell his property when Paul spoke ahead of him. Starting with a nasty laugh, he said, "I was just waiting for that. Sell everything to keep on eating. That's a real bohemian or Communist idea."

Julien jumped up and shouted, "Fuck you, bohemian! Piss on that Communist shit!"

"Julien!" cried his father.

But Julien wasn't listening. As Paul groped for an answer, he shouted at him, "I'd rather be dead broke than squatting over those piles of money you got from dealing with the Germans."

Père Dubois saw Paul's face disintegrate. He saw him clench his fists. There was a silence that seemed to him like an eternity; then, in a very soft voice, which could hardly be heard because the kitchen was still echoing with his outburst, Julien added, "I'm ashamed to be shouting like this in this house where Mama just died, but I won't stand for your snickering. What I'm doing is none of your business."

Paul was still extremely pale. The look he gave his father was full of hatred. With a violent shove, he pushed in his chair, and its back struck the edge of the table. Then, he headed for the door, opened it, and went out, saying, "Good night, Father."

"Paul!" cried Père Dubois.

But the door slammed, and Paul ran down the steps.

Père Dubois waited. He hoped that Paul would come back or that Julien would go open the door to call him back. But Julien sat down slowly and placed his trembling hands on the table.

"I beg your pardon, Papa . . . But . . . but—"

He fell silent. Père Dubois let a minute go by. Then, when the night remained silent and Julien speechless, he slowly said, "Now I know what's left for me to do. Die . . . Die all alone . . . And as fast as possible, and when that's finally over, since you two won't ever haved tried to get along, you can sell off everything and divide the pennies between you . . . And we will have worked all our lives, your mother and I, for it all to be frittered away, eaten up in a couple of months . . . There . . . That's how it will end . . . And don't worry, it won't take long."

He was silent. Julien looked at him. And Père Dubois saw that his eyes were brimming with tears, and then, just when he thought he was strong and able to dominate the boy, he burst into tears himself. Julien stammered, "My poor Papa . . . my poor Papa . . ."

Père Dubois blew his nose and coughed.

"Do you want me to stay tonight?" asked Julien.

The old man felt like crying out to him, "Yes. You and your wife stay. And not only tonight. I'll give you everything if you'll only stay. Everything. But I don't want to be alone."

He felt like shouting that, but he knew that if he did, he would start crying again. So, summoning up all the strength he had left in him, steeling himself, he said in a firm but not angry voice, "No. Your wife is waiting for you. You must go to her . . . And try to work for that child your poor mother would have so loved to see. I don't need anybody anymore . . . to get where I'm going."

Part Five

THE LONELY ROAD

65

THAT winter was like a long sleep, filled with dreams, into which Père Dubois fell after the death of his wife.

The day after the burial Micheline came with a cleaning woman and the little errand boy. She asked Père Dubois to come live with them, but since he refused to leave the house, she didn't insist. The house was cleaned and put back in order. Since the old man was worried about his wood supply and complained about having to walk upstairs to heat his bedroom, they decided to set up his bed in the dining room. That way, by forcing the fire a little and keeping the connecting door open, he was able to sleep in a warm bed just a step away from the kitchen, where he spent his days. In the morning, at eleven, the boy would bring his meal, carry in more wood, and get him whatever he needed. Almost every day, too, Paul or Micheline would come to see him, concerned about his slightest desires and making sure that he was comfortable.

He got into the habit of being pampered like this very quickly, and his wife's absence was bearable.

Time went by quietly. He had no worries about money or about food. On the contrary, the meals they brought were much too big for his appetite. He would often say, "You're trying to spoil me. I can't eat as much as that."

And Paul would answer, "You've worked hard enough in your life. And been through enough. It's only natural for us to

take the best care of you we can. You know very well that we
want you to have everything you need."

Whenever Paul or a neighbor came to see him and spoke
about his past life, Père Dubois would enjoy lingering over it.
He loved to talk about it, and when he was alone again, he
would continue telling about the happiest moments in his life
or the most difficult. Even in his solitude he would talk as if
someone were listening to him: "Listen, I can remember, before 1914, when I was making deliveries on horseback . . . I'm
not talking about yesterday . . . We didn't have the roads that
we have today. And the winters were harder. Winters like we're
having this year, three out of four of them would be like this.
And the roads weren't always cleared. Or else they'd been
cleared by horses going through. The snow would just be
packed down, and it would be like ice . . . But I had a good
horse. And I always kept her well shod. With spikes in winter
and all that. Well now, I remember one night when I was in
Messia; I was coming out of La Toinon Vignet, which was a
restaurant. And what do you think I saw? A kid about eight
years old hollering right near my wagon. Luckily I had a horse
that didn't get excited. And beside the kid, there were two
drunks who were laughing. 'What's going on?' I asked. 'This
dumb kid,' they said to me, 'we were showing him the iron rim
on your wheel, and we told him to lick it to see what happened.
He put his tongue on it. And look, he left a piece of skin stuck
to it.' They were a couple of quarrymen. With the cold, they
weren't working, of course. They'd spent the day drinking. And
they told me that perfectly calmly. Well, I got mad all right.
'You're the dumb ones,' I said, 'not that kid.' One thing led to
another, and they started threatening me. So I took hold of the
small end of my whip. Those days it didn't take me long. Strong
as oxen, those quarrymen, but they didn't know the meaning of
fast. One of them got away with his nose pissing red all over his
jacket, and the other, half-unconscious, was trying to get away,
too. 'Not so fast,' I told him. And I brought him back into La

Toinon to find out his name so the kid's parents would know who to get after. Well, believe it or not, the parents never even thanked me."

So went his lot of memories, weaving together throughout the length of the days, one leading into another, or with some tenuous thread tying them to an actual event that someone had just told him about.

When the German offensive at Ardennes began, it seemed as if the war were about to take on an aspect in some ways similar to the campaigns of 1914–18. So that whole period came back to him in bits and pieces. It was far away and yet much closer than what was currently happening in Bastogne.

Paul often brought the newspapers over, but Père Dubois' eyesight had weakened so that he confined himself to reading the headlines. Anyhow, these newspapers interested him less than the ones from his own time, from before the First World War. He'd found two thick bound volumes of *L'Illustration* up in the bedroom. One from the year 1890, the other from 1897. Not an afternoon went by that he didn't take those two volumes and open them up on the table. There was a whole series of pictures in them that he'd marked with pages from the almanac. The first showed military maneuvers at the frontier, August 16, 1890. In it you saw the Alpine troops assaulting Mount St.-Agnes, near Menton. The officers with their sabers drawn, the soldiers with bayonets fixed, the buglers. When he looked at them, it was another regiment that he saw, the Forty-fourth, that regiment from Sambre-et-Meuse whose marching song would start to ring inside him. In the November 1 issue, there was a page he looked at often. It showed a picture of the installation of the crematory oven and colombarium at Père-Lachaise. Père Dubois would shiver an instant, then pull himself together and think about the plot of ground where he would sleep one day. In the year 1897, his twenty-fourth year, there were several pages in color on the life of the young soldiers. The barrack room, the soldiers in red pants jumping over a

wall, a drill in the courtyard, a foot check by a medical officer—
all that was real, as though present, dated only yesterday. The
great maneuvers of September also held his attention. A double
page showed a regiment charging across a wheat field. That, he
had lived through. And at twenty years old, because he already
had respect for the bread that had taken up his nights for the
past seven years, it had made him suffer. Today it still made
him suffer. But inexplicably, it was a pain he liked to revive.

Some careless person had slipped a page torn from an issue
of *Petit Journal* into this volume of *L'Illustration*. It was a front
page, in color, where you saw the terrace of a café in Paris during the summer of the great heat wave. All the customers, as
well as the waiters dressed in black and white, were very hot.
The page had been torn, and the date was missing. That was
something that bothered him. He ransacked his memory for
the year of that terrible drought, and just when he thought he'd
found it, a detail would come back to him and throw the whole
thing into question again.

"But no, it couldn't have been in '91. That was the year we
bought Ripan, the big gray horse we only kept three months
because he bit. And I remember it was raining all the time
. . . In '92? Perhaps . . . And yet '92, that was the year my
father planted the boxwood near the pump . . . So that
couldn't be it . . ."

So the long hours went by, which finally turned into days and
then weeks.

Mère Dubois was not absent from all this. She had, however,
very quickly become a silent witness, without substance and
without age, who knew when to efface herself and return at the
slightest summons. The fact that one cold day in December
they had carried her remains to the other side of town had not
driven her from the house. It was like that because it had to be
like that, and without actually admitting it, Père Dubois felt
strongly that she had only gone first down a road that he was
already traveling. After keeping in perfect step with him for a

long time, she had suddenly quickened her pace and reached the end before him. But all that was of no great importance, since it was only a question of time. And from then on, time didn't matter. Everything showed him how unimportant the passage of years really was. He could live as easily in his fifteenth year near the lighted dome of the oven where his father taught him how to line up the large round loaves as he could live in the present, sunk into a twilight of silence and calm.

Julien's letters, always short and more and more infrequent, were the only mail he still received. He had a great deal of trouble reading them, and it would have been impossible for him to answer them.

After all, the boy knew where to find him if he wanted to see him, and Lyons wasn't so far away. Julien had behaved badly toward Paul, and nowadays it was Paul who took care of him. And yet Mère Dubois had always felt that Paul and his wife were a couple of egotists. If she could see them today from up there, she would certainly have to admit her error. Naturally, it had been her presence and Julien's that had kept Paul and his wife away from the house for so long. Julien was living his life as he saw fit. He kept his distance. He had, he wrote, found a job that took up all his time. If it was a real job, one could only rejoice about it. His absence was not a burden. For Père Dubois, no absence was hard to bear. Or rather, there were no absences. There was only room for the people with whom he carried on his interminable dialogue. He no longer even wondered whether these people were already dead or still living in this world.

66

Julien was really an odd sort of boy. When the notary had written him to settle his mother's inheritance, he had answered that he would leave everything up to his father and sign any documents that were forwarded to him. The notary therefore came one afternoon, accompanied by Paul. He read a complicated text out loud, and Père Dubois had to struggle to stay awake during it. Once this reading was over, Père Dubois signed the papers; then he asked, "As I understand it, everything is settled?"

The notary explained to him that, in accordance with his expressed will, after his death his two houses would go to his son Paul, subject to the payment of a certain sum by Paul to Julien. This sum wasn't very large, but Paul agreed to undertake the care of Père Dubois, who would continue to enjoy his holdings.

"This way," Paul added, "you can rest assured that your houses won't be sold to strangers. And as for Julien, he needs money much more than he needs property."

They drank a glass of old wine, and Père Dubois talked about the times he used to harvest grapes in Vernantois.

A few more weeks went by; then, one afternoon, Paul came to announce that the notary in Lyons in charge of witnessing Julien's signature had returned the papers. So now everything was in order. And Paul explained, "You see, I took care of everything. It saved you a lot of trouble, and this way you have nothing to worry about. You won't even have to work in your garden, since you're assured of having whatever you want."

"I'll still keep up the garden. I got rid of the rabbits, but don't get the idea that I'm going to let the garden run to weeds."

"Without letting it run to weeds, there's a way for you to stop slaving the way you do."

"I'll slave right up to the end. If I didn't, I'd get bored."

"You're bored because you're living alone, but if you weren't so stubborn, you'd come and live with us, and you'd be much better off."

"No. I've said no once and for all. I don't want to leave my house."

Paul didn't insist, but Père Dubois had the feeling that he was really angered by his flat refusal.

From that day on, Micheline and Paul's visits became rarer and rarer, and sometimes the old man had to wait for his meals until one in the afternoon. When he remarked about it to the little errand boy, he answered in such a way that Père Dubois, white with rage, got up, went around the table, and slapped him, shouting, "You snotty little kid, I'll teach you to—"

He couldn't say anything more. A fit of coughing seized him, forcing him back into his chair, exhausted. Once he'd got rid of the phlegm that was choking him, he sat for a long time without moving. His hands were shaking with tremors he couldn't seem to control. The boy had left, slamming the door. It took Père Dubois more than an hour to recover, and that day he wasn't able to eat at all. He kept repeating to himself, "Snotty little kid . . . He dawdles along the streets. And my dinner gets here stone cold . . . And at all hours . . . I'll have to speak to my son about it."

He repeated this more than twenty times, trying to find a way to get hold of his son, who hadn't been to see him in more than two weeks. It was the beginning of February and still too cold for him to go outside to his house. He watched the path, waiting for M. Robin to go by so that he could ask him to telephone Paul.

The afternoon wore on. He couldn't bring himself to close the shutters until it was completely dark outside and absolutely impossible to see anyone coming down the path.

At six o'clock, his stomach growling, he put the cauliflower in white sauce and the container of soup that wretch had brought on the stove. His anger had cooled, but it was still there inside him. Tomorrow the kid would be back, with his sneaky look and that nasty smile he always wore that seemed to say, "You can talk all you want, you old fart. It's no skin off my ass!"

That's what Père Dubois had often read in the kid's snotty expression, and the mere prospect of seeing him come in was enough to make his hands shake.

His meal was almost heated through when Paul arrived. His face was red, and his eyes were glittering. Without even greeting his father, he said, "Well, what's gotten into you now? Now you're slapping my boy around!"

For the moment, Père Dubois' breath was taken away. Was Paul joking? Had he come to find out what had happened or to lay into his father?

There was a silence, during which Paul sat down at the end of the table, pushed his hat back on his head, and lighted a cigarette. As Père Dubois remained speechless, his son went on, "Well, what is it? Now you're not content to be served at home like a prince! One might think you'd always lived in a palace. Maybe when you were running that bakery, you used to get your boys to work by giving them a kick in the ass, but you ought to realize that times have changed quite a lot. You can't treat the help the way you used to in the old days . . . Here's a kid fifteen. You slap him, and an hour later his mother's over to see me! She's talking about getting the union and the work inspector down on my neck. And some position I'm in—if I don't want to wind up in court with the worst kind of problems, I have to see to it that they keep their mouths shut. And do you know what that means? Do you know how much that's going to cost me?"

By this time Père Dubois didn't understand a word that he was saying. The boy had been disrespectful to him, he'd barely touched him, and now he was being accused of—of . . . He no longer knew where he stood. Since his son was looking at him, seemingly waiting for an answer, he could only stammer, "But after all . . . that snotty little kid . . ."

Paul interrupted him. Lifting his arms to the heavens and letting his hands fall back onto the table, he began to shout, "Ah, for Christ's sake! If someone comes to see you about this incident, don't use words like that. You'll be sued for libel. And I'm still the one who'll have to pay. You don't know what they're like. The father was shot by the Germans. The mother's a member of the Communist Party. They're the masters these days. They have all the rights. Even at your age, they could throw you in prison just like that!"

Père Dubois had started to shake again. He no longer thought about all the things he'd planned to say to his son. He could only repeat, "But after all . . . If that little kid . . . after all . . . well, I don't understand."

"Obviously. How could you understand? You insist on living in another world. I can't be constantly on your back. Admit that if you agreed to come live with us, it would make things a lot simpler."

Père Dubois no longer had the strength to get angry. He merely shook his head, and Paul looked grim.

"You're determined," he said, "to worry me to death as thanks for my having done everything I could to make you comfortable . . . Well, how are we going to work things out now? I ask you. You don't seem to question that we have our work to do. The boy refuses to come anymore. He said so. And I can't force him to. It's not his job. He wasn't hired to do that. So I'll have to send your food over with the maid. Only, since she can't be everywhere at once, she won't get here until the afternoon. She'll bring the meals for that night and the next day. You'll have to heat them up. I don't see any alternative."

Père Dubois remained speechless. He looked at his hands resting on the oilcloth, which trembled the minute he lifted them. He felt crushed. As if they'd thrown his anger into the bottom of a hole and him on top of it and then covered the hole back over. He didn't even dare look at his son.

He could picture him sitting across the table, clinging to the idea of taking him off to live in his apartment, and as for him, he clung just as firmly to the idea of staying in his own house. Winter would soon be over, and there would be sunny days that would call him into his garden. He knew his son's apartment. Dark rooms, either looking out onto the street or onto a narrow courtyard. The big kitchen where the maid was always bustling around, always playing the radio. He could imagine the confusion. Meals never served at the same hour. The noise from the street and the noise from the neighbors. No, he'd taken it into his head to stay at home, and that's what he would do. After all, if they brought his meals in the afternoon, he could at least eat them when it suited him. And he would never have to lay eyes on that snotty kid again.

As Paul stood up, Père Dubois asked, "And the wood? Will your maid be able to bring that in, too?"

Paul gave another great groan of despair. "Ah, shit! That's right, there's still that damned wood. You really must admit that you're making life pretty hard for us."

"Apparently"—Père Dubois sighed—"I guess your life will be a lot easier after I'm gone."

Paul gave him a hard look and shrugged his shoulders.

"Don't say stupid things . . . About the wood, I hope the maid won't think it's too heavy. But really, when I think how comfortable you'd be with us!"

–◆{ 67 }◆–

THAT visit of Paul's and his anger stirred up an uneasiness that Père Dubois felt for several weeks. He tried to suppress the idea that his son had waited until the estate was settled before making it clear what a burden he was. Not a day went by that this idea didn't come to plague him several times. He pushed it away by saying, "It's not possible. They have their life . . . we're not of the same generation, and they think that I'd be able to adapt to their way of doing things . . . Of course, for them, it would be easier."

Right after Mère Dubois' death, since the errand boy didn't work on Sundays, it was Micheline who would bring him his meals. Now the maid brought a little more on Saturday, and he got along as best he could over the weekend. Sometimes she would be in a hurry. She would say, "You still have some wood left. I'll bring you more tomorrow."

And the next day, as though on purpose, she would be late. Night would be falling. She would arrive all out of breath, put down the basket, and leave immediately, saying, "I've got to run. There's company, and I haven't made dinner yet."

The next morning Père Dubois would get dressed in warm clothes, put a heavy wool scarf over his mouth to avoid breathing the cold damp air that activated his asthma, and set off for the shed to restock his wood supply. He would take the opportunity to open the cupboards in his workshop and make sure that his tools weren't rusting too much. On each visit he was frightened to see the woodpiles getting lower. The question of heating always worried him. His wife was no longer there to write to the woodcutter and order more wood. Neither Paul nor Micheline came anymore, and he finally had to ask M. Robin to write the letter.

"I'll have to cut the wood and have it finished before the cold weather sets in, so, to do a good job, you must ask him to deliver it in the spring."

Then he added, "I don't know if I'll be able to make it through another winter, but in any case, I don't want to be without heat."

M. Robin wrote the letter. He often did Père Dubois little favors. He asked for news of Julien, but he never mentioned Paul. Père Dubois didn't speak about him either. It was like a little ditch between them that they both measured with their eyes without either one of them daring to cross it. Out of some sort of pride he had trouble defining, Père Dubois also didn't dare ask M. Robin to write to Julien begging him to come see him as soon as he had a chance. It was that he dreaded such a visit as much as he desired it. Paul was neglecting him. He wasn't even suitably fulfilling the obligation he'd taken on in accepting the terms of the estate, but he dreaded Julien's finding that out. He clung to the hope he placed in the coming of spring. There would be the garden, the wood to cut as soon as it had been delivered, and that would be enough to fill his days. The nights would be shorter, it would be warm, and he would be able to get out of the house, go out to the street, and chat a little with the neighbors.

The big pollard oak that grew beside the pump at the very bottom of the garden hadn't been pruned for five or six years. All its branches had grown, which made for quite a lot of wood, and he'd promised himself to get after it as soon as the weather permitted.

In the beginning of March there were a few days of sunshine. He started by pruning several trees that grew along the path, carefully picking up the branches and tying them into little bundles. He tired easily, but it was that way after every winter, and he knew that working would bring his strength back very quickly. After four days, because the good weather was holding and the ground had dried out enough for him to put a ladder up without its sinking in, he started pruning his oak. He had carefully sharpened his compass saw, and the work was going along well. The branches fell one by one, and as he worked, he thought about his father, the little Savoyard chimney sweep who had come there around the year 1840 and had planted this tree so that the pump would always be in the shade.

By the middle of the morning more than half the branches were on the ground, and Père Dubois was getting ready to come down and move his ladder when he saw his son entering the garden. Paul was not alone. He had two men with him who stopped by the first bed, while he headed straight for his father.

As soon as he was within earshot, he shouted, "Are you crazy? At your age, doing work like that. You might fall and break your hip or even kill yourself."

"Now don't bawl me out," said Père Dubois.

Paul gave a smile.

"Of course not, but you scared me."

"What do you expect? It's more than a month since I ordered some wood, and they haven't delivered it. What little I get done will still be done."

"Don't worry about your wood. You know perfectly well that we won't let you freeze."

Père Dubois stood on the ground before his son. He tried to see, through the still-bare trees, the two men who were waiting by the gate.

"Who've you got with you?"

"You know him, it's Valentini the builder. He's with an architect."

"Ah!"

"Yes, I brought them over to take a look around the property. You know we'll have to conform to the building line, so we have to see where we can plan to build."

Père Dubois hesitated. He lifted his cap to mop his brow; then, almost timidly, he asked, "Build? But build what?"

"Well, for the time being, I'll put up some garages for my trucks; then, later on, I'll go up a story or two."

Père Dubois laid down his saw at the foot of the ladder, scratched his chin, and thought a few moments before asking, "Do you mean to tell me that you intend to build during my lifetime?"

Paul looked embarrassed. "After all," he said, "I haven't had the plans drawn yet, but . . . I've got problems with my warehouses. You know one of them is very old. Full of rats . . . And then I have to pay a very high rent. So the sooner I can get the work started, the better it will be."

Père Dubois controlled himself. He felt everything start to churn around and words occur to him that he had trouble holding back.

"As for your tree," Paul said, "just leave it. I'll send one of my men around to finish it."

Perhaps it was this unfortunate blunder that made Père Dubois' anger explode.

"Shut up!" he shouted. "I don't give a damn about that. But what is this story about building? You want to ruin my garden? Wreck everything when I would never even touch it, not even to bring in water and electricity? For Christ's sake, you want me to die before my time!"

Paul looked around them. The sunshine had brought people out into the neighboring gardens.

"Don't shout like that. You're going to get the whole neighborhood stirred up."

But Père Dubois could no longer control himself. He'd suddenly seen an aspect of his son that he'd always refused to acknowledge.

"I'll shout if I want to! I'm still on my own place, God damn it! And you'll do me the favor of getting the hell out of here along with your two stooges, or else I'll take a pitchfork to you!"

Paul made a few feeble protestations, but Père Dubois didn't even hear them.

"Get the hell out of here!" he roared. "Or the whole neighborhood will know that you're letting me starve to death and that you only come to see me to try to get me to die faster!"

He'd got carried away, but he still had enough lucidity to realize that a coughing fit was coming on. He stopped, breathed deeply; then, picking up a branch a yard long and thick as his arm, he headed for the two men. Paul ran ahead of him and quickly dragged the architect and the builder out of the garden. Père Dubois didn't stop. Speeding up, he went all the way to the gate, which he double-locked. The trio had started up the Rue des Écoles. Brandishing the key in one hand and his club in the other, he yelled, "You come back, and I'll get the police after you."

But the three men kept walking without looking back.

Out of breath, Père Dubois stood for a long time with his back against the gate. Then, when a window opened in the house across the way, without even looking to see if it was Mlle. Marthe or some other busybody, he went slowly back to the house.

—◀{ 68 }▶—

ANGER, as usual, had tired Père Dubois much more than a day of the hardest work, and yet it also seemed to have freed him from a great weight.

When he got back to the house, he sat down for a moment,

then poked the fire, where a few coals remained from the logs he'd burned to heat his morning coffee. It was after eleven, and he felt hungry. He looked with disgust at the contents of the two pots the maid had brought the night before; then he went and put them outside on the steps, muttering, "Some food! It doesn't even keep overnight . . . Garbage . . . Too bad I don't have my rabbits anymore."

He kept on going down to the cellar, where he got a few potatoes and two big onions. After he'd peeled them all, he put two spoonfuls of fat in the iron pot and cut up the potatoes and onions very finely into it. The simple fact of preparing all that, breathing the odor of hot fat and hearing it sizzle, sharpened his appetite even more.

"Too bad I don't have a piece of salt pork to add to it."

Since the death of his wife he hadn't eaten any potatoes fried slowly in a pot like that. He added a big clove of garlic, two bay leaves, and a little thyme.

While the fire hissed under his meal, he fixed himself a glass of wine with lots of sugar in it.

"By God," he muttered, "he'd like to see me dead. Well, we'll see about that . . . Wreck my garden? We'll really see about that! When I've worked all my life manuring the soil, planting trees, just to have it all dug up with a bulldozer! God damn it! Just because I didn't move all winter, perhaps he figured I went to sleep. Hell, no!"

He carried on like this, drinking a sip of wine, stirring his potatoes, breathing in the intoxicating odor of bay leaves and onions.

"Been quite awhile since the house smelled this good."

He talked without stopping, as if he hoped the words would keep alive the old fire that had been rekindled inside him. Just the threat of his big stick had been enough to drive away those three men, the oldest of whom was thirty years younger than he, and the memory of their flight made the blood run quick and hot through his muscles, filling him with energy.

324

"By tonight I'll have finished pruning that tree, and there's a good chance I'll have tied most of the branches into bundles . . . And anyone who thinks I'm ready for the scrap heap can just come take a billhook, and we'll see who gets the most work done . . . What can they do with their money and their brief-cases? Do they call that work?"

He talked like this throughout the entire length of his meal, sometimes raising his voice as though he were addressing a large audience.

Once he'd drunk his coffee, he poured himself a good shot of marc.

"It's not a Sunday or a holiday, but I feel that I need it . . . I'll do the dishes tonight . . . I'm going out now and knock off a little more work while the sun's still shining."

He'd finished the pruning and started hauling the branches to the shed when his daughter-in-law arrived. Since the gate was still locked, she'd taken the path that ran the length of the garden, and he hadn't noticed her until she was a few feet away. The sight of her irritated him. He put down the branch he was holding and stood there, one hand in his pocket, and the other holding the butt he had just unstuck from between his lips. Micheline came closer, looking very disturbed. After a few seconds' hesitation, she kissed him on both cheeks. She was heavily perfumed, and Père Dubois noted that her hair was a lighter shade of blond than usual.

"My God," she sniveled. "My God, my poor Papa, what is happening to us?"

"You must have a pretty clear idea, since you're here. Be-cause I can't say that your visits have exactly been tiring me out for some time!"

He'd spoken without shouting, but in a very cold tone of voice. Micheline looked at him in silence, batted her eyelids, and burst into tears.

"I deserve your reproaches," she said. "Oh, how I do de-serve them! And how I blame myself for not having neglected my work a little and given you more of my time. One always tries to do too much, and then where does it get one? I ask you."

Père Dubois, annoyed by this too-sudden flood of tears, interrupted her. "I don't think Paul sent you over to ask me that." She feigned great surprise and fear.

"But he didn't know I was coming," she said. "Poor Paul, if you could see the state he's in."

"I don't care. And don't bother putting on a performance for me either."

"Don't shout, my poor Papa. It's not good for you. I'll explain everything. But we can't stay here."

Père Dubois' heart was growing harder and harder. His anger was a solid block to which he clung. Micheline's forced behavior strengthened him. She'd burst into tears too easily. She sighed too much, and he found something almost comical in her chest heaving at every sob, stretching the material of her blouse to the bursting point. He waved his hand toward Mancy, where the sky was clouding up a little.

"It might rain tomorrow. And I've got to get my wood in before it gets muddy. I don't have time to listen to your sob story."

"My God, I would never have believed you would be so unfair and mean to me. And to poor Paul, who wasn't able to eat a bite for lunch—"

"Well, I was able to eat very well. I made myself some home fried potatoes . . . Your pots from yesterday are on the steps. You can go pick them up. And don't bother to bring my meals anymore. I'll manage by myself. And by the way, the gate's going to stay locked."

He turned on his heel without a thought for Micheline, who stood rooted in front of the shed door, her handkerchief in her hand.

"Go ahead and cry," muttered Père Dubois. "You'll piss less. But it won't make you any thinner, God knows."

He nurtured his anger. He hugged it around him like a tough

cloth, impervious to the tears and sobs of this fat woman who got on his nerves.

Each trip he made, Micheline would start in afresh. "Poor Paul. If you knew what he was going through. 'My poor father's going to curse me,' he was saying. 'And I wanted so much to make his old age easy for him.' "

Père Dubois made four more trips. It was no longer anger seething inside him, but a sort of impatience that made him feel like picking up a good springy switch and whipping his daughter-in-law's fat buttocks with it.

On the fifth trip, unable to control himself any longer, he planted himself in front of her, and forcing himself not to shout to avert the cough that would have kept him from finishing, he said, "I've had enough of this for today. You'll kindly do me the favor of getting the hell out of here. And don't set foot back here until I'm dead and gone. At that time, you can do what you want with my land, but as long as I'm alive, you're not going to start any dirty business around here!"

Micheline backed off; then, before turning away, she sobbed. "But my poor Paul will be sick about this!"

"Then tell him not to drink so much, and he'll feel just fine . . . But he'd better not come around and bother me with his big ideas and those stooges with briefcases!"

--◄{ 69 }►--

THERE was a little cool spell with some rain and a few showers, but sustained by the strength his anger fostered in him, Père Dubois didn't stop working. He divided his time between the shed, where he sawed and split the wood from his pruning, and the garden, where he began his spring cleanup. As soon as the ground had lost its excess moisture, he would start spading.

A little before the middle of March, he received a letter from Julien announcing the birth of a son. The boy was named Charles Gaston Dubois. On that day, the old man worked even better than usual. And when M. Robin went by on the path, he asked him into the kitchen. He showed him Julien's letter, and after M. Robin had congratulated him, Père Dubois, with tears in his eyes, asked, "Would you write a short letter for me?"

"Of course. Shall we do it right away?"

"Please. If you could mail it for me as soon as possible, and also, if it's not too much trouble, I'd like to send them a little money. You understand, I'm not able to buy them a present. So I'd rather send them a little money. I have the money from the bakery rent and, for the moment, no great expenses."

M. Robin wrote the letter, and Père Dubois signed it at the bottom with a trembling hand.

"Ah, what a shame," he said. "How happy my wife would have been about this! . . . Tomorrow, if the weather looks all right, I'll go to the cemetery. I haven't been there yet. I haven't felt up to it. But now—"

"Do you want me to ask my wife to go with you?"

"No, no. I already give her enough trouble with my errands."

Since Père Dubois had locked the gate and decided to refuse the meals his son owed him, it had been Mme. Robin who took care of buying him his bread, meat, and milk. From time to time, she would bring him a portion of dessert. She did it nicely and always said, "You'll be doing me a favor. I made too much, and my husband would be cross if he saw me throwing it away."

The next morning, as soon as he was up, Père Dubois looked at the sky. The dawn foretold a sunny day. A fresh little wind blew out of the east, clearing the sky of its nighttime mists. He put two shirts, two undershirts, and a few handkerchiefs he had to wash to soak in the tub; then, having put on a clean shirt and his corduroy jacket, he took his iron-tipped cane and went out.

To avoid the center of town, he crossed through the fair grounds, went down the Rue Regard, then the Quai de Solvan. He walked at a steady pace, happy that there were only a few people in the streets. He was going to the cemetery, to visit his wife who'd been buried at the beginning of the winter, but he wasn't sad. He was just going to say hello to her and bring her a piece of good news.

After three-quarters of an hour's walking, he got to the road to the cemetery. At the same time, but coming out of the Rue du Puits-Salé, appeared an old woman he thought had been dead for years. She was an old customer from the days when he was running the bakery. She didn't seem surprised to see him and started walking beside him, talking exactly as though they'd just seen each other the day before.

"Well, so you're going to see your wife?"

"Yes," said Père Dubois, "it's been a long winter. And when it's cold, there's no point in my trying to go outside."

"Me either. I never go to the cemetery when the weather's bad. But still, since I live nearby, whenever I see a ray of sunshine, I come . . . Of course I don't stay long. Just a little hello, and then I'm on my way . . . But the dead understand . . . They know me. They know that as soon as the weather's fine, I'll stay for a while."

"You come to see your husband?"

The old woman stopped, put one hand with its fingers spread wide on the small of her back, and straightened up a little to look at Père Dubois.

"My husband? Heavens, no! He's been dead for forty-two years. And he was buried in Bourg where he was hospitalized . . . I didn't have enough money to buy a plot, so he must have been dug up for a long time. No, no, I have nobody here. But still, I do have quite a group of friends."

They'd reached the entrance to the cemetery, and the old woman waved her hand to include all the graves.

"You," she said, "you're up there on the left?"

"Yes, above the little steps, beyond the big trees."

They took the path to the left, and walking more slowly because of the slope, the old woman spoke again. "It's a good spot.
Not damp at all. And in the sun more or less all day long.
They're better off up there than they would be near the entrance. It's healthier, and there are fewer disturbances."

She stopped long enough to pick up a vase that the wind
had blown over on a little grave covered with white pebbles.

"That's Pauline Richard," she explained. "The one who
used to run La Civette in the old days. Did you know her?"

"Good Lord, did I know her!"

"She was a good simple woman. But she doesn't feel at home
here. There are a lot of big shots in this area."

She jerked her chin toward enormous tombs of blue and
black marble, vaults surmounted with columns and sculptures,
others surrounded by iron railings. She stopped before a mau-
soleum that tilted to the right where the earth had settled under
it.

"You see," she remarked, "that's no better than a simple
stone. All these fancy things fall to pieces sooner or later. And I
wonder if the dead are really any better off underneath them."

Taken aback at first, Père Dubois now listened as though
she were talking about living persons. She sometimes gave a
little laugh that didn't even seem out of place in this locality,
inhabited much more by life than by death.

For the sun, already hot, had brought the cemetery to life.
Gray lizards scuttled away across the stones and slid into the
cracks, gnats danced in the sunlight, and the first tender green
buds already showed on the lilac bushes planted along the enclosure wall.

When they got under the trees, the old woman took a paper
bag full of bread crusts out of her shopping bag. She crumbled
them between two graves, saying, "I give the birds a little something. They come to keep the dead company."

Père Dubois started up the narrow graystone steps, and the

old woman followed him. As soon as they came out onto the upper path, he walked over to a mound covered with faded flowers.

"They haven't set the stone in yet," he remarked. "With the freeze, the ground didn't settle very fast."

"Now, unless there's a lot of rain, it will settle quickly."

He sat down on the edge of the neighboring grave, and with both hands on his cane, he said, "I'm going to rest a little, and then I'll clear all that trash away."

The old woman stood beside him for a few minutes. She had folded her hands in front of her, and her black bag hung down to her knees. Only her lips moved, without a sound coming from them.

"Well," she finally said, "I'll be off and leave you two alone. I'll go have a little visit with the others."

She moved off slowly, and Père Dubois saw her stopping before the graves, standing motionless, righting a vase, pulling up a weed, or replacing a crucifix. When she had disappeared, he looked at the yellow earth under which Mère Dubois rested and said, "It's true that this is a pleasant spot. And now the worst of the cold weather is over."

He paused for a fairly long time. "And you know that Julien has a boy . . . Ah, yes, some of us go and others arrive. That's the way the world is."

He put down his cane, stood up, and started cleaning off the flowers that winter had flattened against the earth. He left only the two pearl wreaths. Julien's and his own.

"My poor woman," he said, "I've had my share of troubles since you've been gone. And I wonder if it's worth it to set the stone in . . . When I see how peaceful you are here . . ."

He didn't feel sad. It even seemed to him that he felt as comfortable here as he did at home. It was a garden where no one came to say cruel things to you. Either people didn't come at all, or else they came as friends, like that old lady wandering off to have her little chats with the dead.

When he'd cleaned off the grave, he'd gone to wash his hands at the faucet up a little ways, then come back for his cane. He continued: "I've just seen that Félix Ramillon and his wife are right next door. And farther up, there's the Cretot girl. They're all people you knew well."

With the end of his cane, he destroyed a dandelion that was peeping up between two clumps of dirt; then, starting down a cross-path, he murmured, "I'll take the other path back. That way I can see a few more people. As it stands, I have more friends here than I do in town."

—◁ 70 ▷—

AFTER his visit to the cemetery, Père Dubois got back to work again. He felt calmer, as though he were really sure now of being on the right road. He no longer needed anger to lash him; he felt strong enough to go on alone to the end. He had kept his work well in hand, and work had held his life together in return. They could move forward like this, he and his work, the one supporting the other, without bothering to count the days.

Two weeks flew by, with fine weather that pushed the sap to the tips of the branches and pulled the grass up from the ground. The grass always grew too fast, but the good thing about it was that it inspired him to sow and plant. Père Dubois began by spading up the beds behind the house, sheltered from the north and ideal for early seedlings. He cleaned out one section and spread manure on it.

By the beginning of the third week he'd got his second wind; the fatigue always brought on by the first labors of spring diminished. He'd got into the swing of it, and although he worked alone, he wasn't behind schedule. One morning he had the pleasure of seeing young Picaud, the woodcutter, arrive.

"Luckily, I know the house," Picaud said. "I tried to open the gate, but it was locked."

"That's right, I don't unlock it anymore. Anybody who really wants to see me knows the way."

"Are you afraid of robbers?"

Père Dubois hesitated. He blew his nose to give himself time for reflection; then he said, "No. But the lock squeaks, and I haven't had time to fix it."

The woodcutter spoke about Mère Dubois' death and apologized for not having come to the funeral. The old man shrugged to show that that was of no importance, then inquired about his order of wood.

"I can bring it over next week, but I thought that if you wanted to make some more bundles, I'd bring them down at the same time."

"Of course, but it's not kindling that I need so much. It's big wood, and not sap-pissing green either."

The woodcutter gave a big laugh. "I can only deliver what I've got. And it's this year's wood."

They argued the matter for a moment, but the woodcutter had no seasoned wood in stock, and Père Dubois couldn't get anything better. Picaud, who had already started to leave, suddenly stopped and retraced his steps.

"I just remembered," he said. "There is one thing. Five or six years ago we cut down two big lindens that were blocking our clearing. We trimmed them, but I couldn't sell the trunks, which were worm-eaten. Obviously, they're not top-grade firewood, but if you want to split them, they're already sawed into lengths, and you'd only need a sledgehammer and wedge. Linden splits like anything. We'd stick them on the truck, and you could make do with them while the others age a little."

Père Dubois thought about the long distance he'd have to walk to reach the forest. As he hesitated, Picaud said, "Of

course, soft as that linden is, I know that sledgehammering is
no work for a man your age."

Père Dubois straightened up, hurt to the quick. "What do you
mean? Do you think I'm completely done for? Ever since my
poor wife passed on, I've been doing all the work by myself.
And you can see that nothing's going to the dogs."

He gestured at the garden all around them.

"Well," said Picaud, "it's up to you."

"It's decided. You'll just have to explain to me where it is."

"It's not far from the clearing where you made the bundles
of stovewood. It's right above Perrigny on the slope of the hill
that faces due south, at the beginning of the valley."

With one knee on the ground, he drew a map of the route on
the dirt path.

"Yes, yes," said Père Dubois, "I know. I've gone that way
many times to pick mushrooms . . . In your father's day, and
I even think your grandfather was still alive . . . I'm not talking about yesterday . . ."

He made a long story of it, and that led into another that he
kept on with until Picaud interrupted to say, "I've got to go. I
have deliveries to make. Just bring an ax for your first cuts and
your sledgehammer. You can make wooden wedges up there."

"Don't worry, I've made more wedges than you'll ever make,
even though you are a woodcutter."

He watched the big fellow move away, slouching along, swinging his arms. He'd learn a thing or two, that one, about whether
he was too old to work with a sledgehammer or not!

"These young people get used to machines; their strength is
gone before they're even forty . . . When his grandfather was
alive, the boss used to cut trees down just like everyone else.
He would even set the pace. Nowadays they only give orders
and sit in their trucks. And when you speak about the old days,
they don't even listen respectfully."

After he'd taken up his work once more, Père Dubois went
on talking to himself like that for a long time. He spoke without

anger, and even with a sort of newfound joy, which gradually acquired a form and fullness within him.

From time to time, he would straighten up, study the sky, and sniff the wind. It was coming out of the northeast, and since it had held steady for more than three days, he was sure that the week would run its course without a drop of rain.

The rest of the day passed very quickly. The old man kept picturing the road, rummaging in his memories for every little path through the forest where he'd been so often. And this journey into the past warmed his blood, sending a current of strength through his veins that made him forget the present.

Before nightfall he got his sledgehammer ready, filed his ax, and sharpened his billhook on the whetstone. Then, back in the kitchen, he greased his hobnailed boots and some old leggings that would protect him from the dew. He ate and made coffee so he'd only have to heat it up in the morning.

And that night he went to bed without having to light the lamp.

ᐧᐧᐧ{ 71 }ᐧᐧᐧ

THE sky was just lightening when Père Dubois left his house. He'd tied his ax and sledgehammer together and carried them over his left shoulder. In his musette bag he had his billhook and something to eat and drink. In his right hand, he carried his cane, making its iron tip ring out on the pavement.

The air was still, but he knew that the wind would come up with the sun, and he wanted to be at the clearing as early as possible. It's never easy to walk with the wind in your face and the sun in your eyes. And also, he wanted to get through town before people left their houses. He met only a few workers from the cheese factory. Farther on, several cyclists passed him on their way to the optical works.

Once over the railroad bridge, he slowed down. The road was starting to climb, and he wanted to save his breath. He felt steady on his legs, and he still had a good reserve of strength, but he wanted to avoid a spell of coughing that always left him half-exhausted. So, every now and then, he'd rest a minute, giving himself a chance to contemplate the town that lay behind him, gray and blue in the early morning cool. His gaze lingered on the cemetery.

"My poor old lady," he murmured, "you must think I'm crazy, at my age, to take on this job. But what do you expect? You know we can't burn that green wood they bring us. If people weren't so unscrupulous—but this filthy war has killed their honesty. The old people are just left to die by themselves. When I used to tell you that, you wouldn't believe me. And yet it's the truth."

At each stop he switched his cane and the musette bag from hand to hand and shifted his tools from one shoulder to the other. In his mind, he followed the map drawn in the dirt by the woodcutter's big finger.

When he reached the old Roman road, he bore left into the shortcut that climbed straight up to the edge of the woods and led into another road, well before St.-Étienne-de-Coldre. Halfway up the hill, he had to stop. The slope was steeper. He turned around and looked out over the village of Perrigny. The road leading to Haute-Roche went off to the left and dipped behind the tree line. That was just as Picaud had described it. Père Dubois started off again. When he'd got to the upper road, he turned right and counted three hundred steps before beginning to look for the path.

Brambles had overgrown the embankment, but he spotted the beginning of the old path to the clearing by the worn look of the ground.

"I certainly was right to bring my billhook . . . And I also was right to wear my leggings."

He started by cutting a long ash pole, which he stripped of branches, leaving only one bottom stub to form a hook. Then, pushing aside the brambles, he cut them with his billhook as close to the ground as possible. Then, snaring them with the hooked pole, he slid them in bunches onto the other side of the road at the foot of the embankment.

With the opening cleared, he was able to see that only ferns had overgrown the path to the clearing. He would only have to trample them down a little to make a path over which he could easily carry his wood. He took off his jacket and his musette bag, which he hung from a maple tree near the road; then he sought out the cut-up tree trunks which were half-hidden by the ferns. The woodcutter had said that the trunks were less than a hundred yards from the main road, and he hadn't been too far off. He counted eight large pieces, three yards in length, and figured that four of them, when split, would make him a good load of wood.

Before making his wedges, Père Dubois wanted to see if this wood was worth splitting. He trampled down the ferns all around the first log, cut away a few brambles, and sank his ax into its thickest part. Two slanting chops, and a chip as wide as his hand flew away, leaving a white, healthy cut.

"It looks pretty good on the surface."

He chopped deeper. The heartwood was softer, beginning to rot, but the rest was sound.

"You shouldn't look a gift horse in the mouth," he reminded himself.

The rising sun topped the ridge of the hill; its first rays spilled like a spring flood through the tree trunks, licking the earth and the dark-green ferns where the dew sparkled. In the early light the woods were reddish, as on a brilliant autumn day. Only a few green shoots protruded here and there. The wind had risen, but it passed high overhead, sighing through the bare treetops.

Père Dubois spotted and cut an acacia tree for his wedges, which he quickly fashioned. He prepared to test his strength, to see if he could still handle a sledgehammer at his age.

Energetically, he attacked the first trunk. It wasn't easy. The dry, close-grained wood had aged in the seasoning sun and rain.

"It's done to a turn," Père Dubois kept repeating. "I might have known it . . . It splits hard, but then, it makes nice firewood."

The hardest part was the first blow at the end of the log. If it split the end completely, he could then, with wedges and the hammer, easily split the log in two from end to end. If the first split was shallow and short, only a small crack, he would put a holding wedge in the crack, remove the ax, and extend the split by making his next ax stroke hit on a line with the first, just where the crack petered out. As he feared, the split did not go very deep. Père Dubois gave a little laugh. The wood was resisting. If it wanted a fight, well then, they would fight.

"By God, we'll see who gets the upper hand!"

A sort of friendly furor drove him on. He spoke to the wood as to an old companion. And yet he struck hard with his sledgehammer, giving out grunts that came from the depths of his chest. The sledgehammer blows splayed the broad ends of the wedges, which, nevertheless, sank deeper with each blow. The log protested, making tearing sounds as it split. Père Dubois started a second split on the opposite side from the first. Then he came back to his first point of attack, took up his ax, and swinging it almost parallel to the ground, sank the blade into the base of the log on a line connecting the two cracks in the log. The head of the ax buried itself, sticking fast. The old man left the ax in place to use as a wedge. Then he took the sledgehammer and climbed onto the trunk in order to swing more easily from directly above. The hammer landed squarely on the steel ax head, which rang out clear to the other side of the valley. The log split from end to end. Père Dubois gave a laugh and grunted triumphantly, "There!"

He stepped down and, leaning all his weight on the ax handle, levered the split pieces apart, breaking all the fibrous splinters still bridging the split.

The first slab detached from the trunk lay there at his feet. The open face of the trunk was still alive with broken fibrous bands, which slowly fell back into place.

"There's your answer!"

He picked up one end of the slab and moved down the length of it until he held it balanced in his hands. Then, flexing his knees slightly, he swung it up onto his shoulder and carried it with short steps to the edge of the main road.

The hardest part was over. He knew that now the conquered tree would give in easily. The wood had understood that all resistance was useless. He, the old man doubted by the wood-cutter, the old man they wanted to bury before his time by taking away his land on the pretext that he no longer had the strength to work the ground and make it pay, he had got the better of this linden tree and all its knotty toughness.

He was sweating. He got his jacket and put it back on. Now that he'd gauged the work and measured his strength, he was no longer in such a hurry. The walk and that first log had made him hungry; he was entitled to take a little something from his noonday meal. He unhooked his musette bag and, to get out of the chilliness in the woods, moved to the road, looking for a sunny spot on the embankment to sit and eat.

—✦{ 72 }✦—

WHEN Père Dubois finished his snack, the sun was already high and hot. He was glad to get back into the woods, where, even without leaves, the branches filtered the sunlight. He hung up his coat and began to work, moving at his own pace, sure now that he would finish the job to his satisfaction. For a change and to give his hands a rest, he carried the wood to the road as soon as he split it.

When he finished the second log, he went over to his jacket and looked at his watch. It was barely eleven; he had time to split one more log before lunch. He drank a half glass of the diluted wine he'd brought along, then got back to his logs.

As he was tramping the ferns down with his boots, he noticed a movement of something under or near the log. He froze.

A rat or some other filthy thing, he thought, dismissing it.

After taking the first bite with his ax, he examined the chip. This log was even more worm-eaten than the others. Not only was the heart rotten, but it was hollow. All in all, that was not a bad thing because it would split easily.

Père Dubois sighted a place where a crack had already started and, with a master stroke, sank his ax into it. There was a splintering noise, then a peculiar spitting sound such as wet wood makes when thrown on hot coals.

"Good Lord! It's weeping before it even gets near the fire."

Leaving the ax embedded in the log, he took up his sledge and came down hard on the steel axhead. This time the splitting noise became a prolonged hissing, and Père Dubois was alarmed.

"Good God, it wouldn't surprise me if there were a viper's nest in there."

Retreating a step, he regretted having driven his ax in so deep. It would have made a handier weapon than his sledgehammer. But at the same time he thought that it would be better to pick off the beast as it came out of its hole in the log than to let it escape under the ferns. With his sledgehammer firmly in hand, he waited a few seconds. He was about to pound on the log when a triangular head appeared and flowed like red glue from the opening he had made with his ax.

"Christ! A red one!"

The sledgehammer fell, crushing its head. The body spurted blood and writhed in the ferns. Père Dubois was already stepping forward to finish it off when another viper came out, faster than the first. As he raised his sledgehammer, the beast was already gliding away over the grass.

The heavy hammer landed on the middle of its back, stopping it in its tracks.

Lord, thought Père Dubois, *they're breeding in there!*

He'd scarcely moved back into place when a third snake appeared, then another close behind. Still others emerged from the ferns behind the log.

"Good God, it's not true. It can't be true."

Retreating instinctively, Père Dubois felt himself step on another snake. He'd planted his left heel right on the midde of an enormous viper whose head struck at his leather legging while its tail lashed his boot. He kept his foot on it.

"Bastard!"

The hissing was coming from all over. Père Dubois was drenched in sweat. He swung his hammer at the nearest snake, almost cutting it in two; then he looked at the big one still writhing under his heel. No matter how hard he bore down on it, he could feel its body just sink deeper into the soft layer of moss and ferns. If he raised his heel, it might strike above his protective legging. Trying to stomp its head with his right foot, he lost his balance. Using his hammer as a cane, he kept himself from falling. Freed, the snake coiled itself. Père Dubois saw its bright little eyes glittering. He would have to be faster than this red coil with death in its mouth. Barely lifting his hammer, he stabbed out with its heavy head.

Saved, Père Dubois took one more look at the log, whose dark mouth continued to vomit vipers.

Fear suddenly overwhelmed him. He felt as if he were living a nightmare. He fled to the road. Safe there, he stopped. He thought then of his jacket, his ax, of everything he'd brought into the forest. Wiping the sweat from his eyes with his shirt sleeve, he stared at the underbrush near the logs. Even from where he stood, he could still see some of the snakes moving.

"Filthy sons of bitches!"

A terrible anguish knotted his throat. His head rang as the hollow log, where the vipers were sleeping, must have rung when he struck it.

Could he make it safely back to his jacket? The thought of his billhook came to him. His best weapon would still be a strong, flexible stick. With his billhook, he could cut one.

Not making a sound, watching where he put his feet, still holding his sledgehammer slightly raised, he went back to his jacket. Unhooking it and taking the musette bag and his cane at the same time, he returned to the road. He was dripping, and his legs shook. Only the thought of his good ax still sunk in the tree trunk kept him there. He forced himself to breathe slowly and gathered his thoughts. Then, getting ready to beat a hasty retreat, he put on his jacket and slung the musette bag over his shoulder.

Because his hands were trembling so, he had trouble untying the laces of the musette bag. He'd tied them in bows, but pulling on the wrong end, he only tightened the knots. His big fingernails couldn't loosen them, so finally, he took out his knife and cut the laces.

He stood in the middle of the road, and while he was doing all this, he kept an eye on the ground around him. He took his billhook from the bag and stuck it in his belt. He picked up the stick he'd used earlier to push aside the brambles. Holding it with both hands, he beat the grass along the ditch making a path to a hazelnut bush that he wanted to cut for a whiplike weapon. Since nothing moved, he went in carefully, sliced off the slender hazelnut trunk with two strokes of his billhook and took it out into the road. Choosing two good branches, he cut them and stripped off their twigs. He put his billhook back in his musette bag and tried out the two switches, making them whistle through the air. He then whipped the embankment, where the grasses flattened under his lashes. Carefully adjusting his cap and slinging his musette bag onto his back, he slowly entered the path into the clearing.

Eyes peeled, he moved ahead soundlessly, his right hand holding a switch raised before him, ready to strike. From time to time, he gauged the distance still separating him from his ax. Sunk deep into the log, the ax would take him awhile to free. A good while, and he would need both his hands. He would have to lay down his sticks and stand within a yard of that black maw that could spit out vipers at the height of his knees.

"Good Lord, what a mess!" he kept muttering.

When he was halfway there, he saw a shiny red streak slithering through the grass. The beast came from behind him and passed him. He took two rapid strides, and his stick fell. But the stiff ferns softened the blow, and the viper got away. He looked back. If he'd passed that one without seeing it, others might have moved out toward the road, too.

He stood glued to the ground for a moment, turning to look all around. The silence of the forest frightened him. Even the wind seemed to have stopped. There were no birds. Nothing. A great emptiness.

The idea that all this was unnatural occurred to him. He pushed the thought away. After all, this wasn't the first time that he'd killed a few vipers! Yes, but he had never seen so many at once. He'd heard tell of old stumps where they sometimes came in great numbers to hibernate, but rarely . . . Wasn't there something queer about it? And about this silence? He was convinced that millions of little eyes were staring at him. That all of a sudden an army of reptiles would attack him. He looked up to make sure there weren't any in the trees.

He felt ridiculous, and yet he couldn't throw off his fear.

His eyes went back to his ax. He couldn't just abandon it there. It was a wonderful ax, of good metal and sturdy. An ax that he'd had since right after the First War.

He wasn't going to leave his ax to the snakes, Lord no!

He took a few more steps. Changing tactics, he stomped the ground at each step, preferring to see the vipers move at his approach rather than to pass them without even suspecting their presence. In this fashion, he got to within a few yards of the log, to the place where his wood wedges lay.

Couldn't the vipers, alarmed, all have left their nest and scattered in the forest?

To see, Père Dubois took both sticks in his left hand, and picking up one of the wedges, he aimed at the log and threw it with all his strength. It hit the tree just below the hole. There was a hollow thud, and immediately two triangular heads appeared at the hole, while, raising itself halfway, another viper, coiled at the foot of the stump, flicked out its forked tongue. Père Dubois was too far away to hear it hiss, and yet it seemed to him that the woods were hissing all around him. Frantically, his eyes darted from one place to another. Were the woods really swarming with them? Or was this all happening inside his head? Had he lost control of his reason, started imagining vipers everywhere? He hesitated again. Shuddered. One invisible force pulled his body toward the ax, while another pushed him toward the road.

"Shit!" he cried in a choked voice.

Then, running, stopping when he thought he saw something move, running again, he rushed back to the road.

Still holding his sticks, he picked up his sledgehammer and his iron-tipped cane. He looked back one last time at the woods, where he thought he saw several snakes moving toward him. Then, panicked by a fear he could no longer control, instinctively avoiding the shortcut, he fled from the woods, carefully keeping to the middle of the road.

—◄ 73 ►—

ALL night long Père Dubois vainly tried to get to sleep. The
vipers were there, more real than in the forest. They came up
to him, cold, silent, elusive. As soon as he would start to fall
asleep, they would come closer. He tried to escape, but the red
beasts were all around him. He struck. He killed hundreds and
hundreds, but they still kept coming. He would wake up with
a start, covered with sweat, and if he succeeded in banishing
their image from his nightmare, other images would come which
he couldn't completely chase away. He would think about his
ax. The woodcutters would find it when they went to get his
wood; they would see the vipers and figure that he'd run away
like a child in a panic. And he would also think about his
musette bag which he'd left in the kitchen. Without realizing
it, couldn't he have brought back two or three snakes inside it,
which would come and attack him during his sleep? It was an
absurd idea. He knew it. And yet it kept coming back to him.

At times he doubted himself. He doubted his own sanity,
wondering if he hadn't been the victim of his own fatigue, if he
hadn't fled from the forest after having seen only one viper.

It occurred to him to go back there and get his ax, but as soon
as he got up, he realized that that was no longer possible. The
struggle and the flight had so shaken his body that he felt weak.
He was barely able to drink a few swallows of his *café au lait*.
A deep disgust remained inside him, and his mouth had such
a bitter taste in it that even tobacco smoke seemed sickening to
him.

In the garden, he worked as usual, pushed by the instinct

that had always inhabited him, forbidding him to remain in-
active as long as the weather permitted any kind of work to be
done. But his heart wasn't in it. Nothing moved ahead. The day
weighed on him and around him exactly as if an immense fatigue were crushing the earth. For him the sky, flooded with a
light that brought back life to plants, to birds, to insects, was
bleaker than the sullen, icy sky of winter. His legs carried him;
his arms and hands accomplished tasks repeated thousands and
thousands of times over the years, but everything happened outside of him.

That day his lunch consisted of nothing but bread and cheese.
That evening, very early, he drank a big bowl of tea and went to
bed. His accumulated fatigue brought him a sleep that lasted
almost dreamlessly till dawn. But his strength didn't return,
and the following days seemed interminable to him. His work
wasn't moving ahead. For the first time in his life, he found himself in the grip of the notion that the work itself was devoid of
meaning. He hoed, he planted, he sowed—to do what with his
harvest? Would he even live to see his harvest? And if he did
succeed in prolonging his aimless existence until then, would
he have the strength to do the harvesting? Would he even need
his harvest? Hadn't he signed papers that assured him of being
taken care of until all this misery was finally over?

On several occasions, he had to make a great effort of will not
to go find his son and say to him, "Do what you want with the
garden, but I don't want to have to worry about my food, my
heat, and my dishes."

The past still came back to visit him, but only in visions that
he was astonished to find were still so clear. They rose from the
depths of his memory. As a child, he'd known an old assistant
baker who'd been in his father's service for a long time and
whom they'd sheltered and fed until his death. The old man
lived in a corner of the flour storeroom, behind the stable, on a
pile of empty sacks that reeked of his sweat. Each of his wrinkles
was a black crack full of dirt. The old man must have sensed

that he was an object of disgust to others, for he refused to sit with them at the table and ate his soup all alone. In summer he sat in the sun in a corner of the courtyard; in winter he sat with his back to the warm wall that separated the flour room from the ovens. The cockroaches and crickets were his only companions. When anyone spoke to him about the old men's home, he would fly into a furious rage, start to tremble and weep and wail.

"I'm going. You'll be rid of me. I'll go off and die under a bridge!"

The bakers said that that was just a form of blackmail, but they always gave in and let the old man stay. His only friend was the horse, which he fed and groomed until the end. Père Dubois didn't remember the old man's death except from having often heard the story that they'd found him one morning huddled on his sacks, in the same position he slept in every night. It was winter. There had been a frost, and the night before, on the way home from making the rounds, the horse had broken a leg. Upon learning that they'd had to shoot the horse, the old man had lain down without eating, never to get up again.

That story wasn't one of the ones Père Dubois used to tell very often, but now it came back to him all the time. He would begin at its beginning, trying to remember forgotten details. The old man's face was still with him. And his poverty, too. Even the odor that rose from the pile of sacks where he slept.

Is that the way he would end up? Would he insist on living alone, on turning away everyone who tried to get near him?

The week ended with two days of rain. Two long days which he spent in the corner by his fire, looking at the wind blowing over his garden. And his gaze often fell on the piece of ground where Mère Dubois had fallen. A few frozen cardoons were still there, blackened by the first rays of sunshine. Out of some feeling of respect which he couldn't master, he'd decided not to touch that bed. From the bottom of the garden all the way up to the house, everything else had been spaded, but that narrow band of earth made a rise that ran from the flagstones bordering the path to the fence along the road.

He looked at it, sighed, then murmured, "My poor old lady . . . What's to become of me?"

Even during the long solitude of that last winter, he'd never experienced his wife's absence so painfully. That was because up until now he'd never had to think about making a decision. The only time he himself had ever caused an upheaval in his life, by throwing his oldest son out, had been in a fit of rage.

He didn't really regret that rage, for it had allowed him to get his strength back a little, but it seemed to him that that strength, now vanished, had left him like a twig at the mercy of the floodwaters of a storm.

So, watching the rain run down the windowpanes, he just sat in his chair, all slumped over in his heavy woolen jacket, sunk into his waiting, hoping and fearing he knew not what from the days that lay ahead.

−◄{ 74 }►−

ONE morning the following week the woodcutter came to deliver the wood. As soon as Père Dubois saw the big truck loaded with logs stop outside the garden, he felt his fear of being ridiculous spring up again. It occurred to him to lock himself inside the house and let the men unload the wood outside the gate, but he realized that if he didn't pay the woodcutter that same day, he'd still have to face his visit sooner or later. Anyhow, Picaud was already walking up the path.

"I'm coming!" he shouted.

He got the key and went to the gate. From a distance, he'd recognized his linden logs on top of the load, longer than the cut wood and paler with their freshly opened flesh.

The woodcutter's helper was already up on the truck, ready to get the wood down.

"Do we put it in the street?" he yelled.

"Wait a minute," said Picaud.

Père Dubois opened the gate and shook Picaud's hand. Picaud said, "You see, we brought what you cut, too. I wouldn't have believed you'd get so much done."

"Goodness knows," sighed Père Dubois, "I'm not so young anymore."

They talked for a moment about the quality of the wood; then the woodcutter said, "Didn't you forget your ax?"

Père Dubois felt hope and despair at the same time.

"Yes. And I only remembered it when I'd gotten to the bridge at Perrigny. But I was too tired to go back up. I was pretty sure you'd find it."

Picaud got the ax out of the cab of his truck. The metal had rusted. It bore a lighter mark on the part that had stayed buried in the trunk.

The old man thanked him. But he didn't dare look at Picaud. He went and rested his ax against a stone in the path, and as he was returning, Picaud asked, "Well, shall we put it in the street? Are you going to get it in today?"

Père Dubois shook his head. Would he ever be able to lug all that wood down to the shed in one day? He thought very fast and said, "Wait a minute. That first bed hasn't been spaded yet; if you could back your truck up against the fence, you could throw the wood over there. That way, even if I can't get it all in before night, it will be safer than in the street."

"That's very easy."

Picaud climbed back into the cab, revved the motor, pulled forward, and backed up. Then he rejoined his helper, and together they began throwing the logs into the garden as close as possible to the path. While they were unloading, Père Dubois carried his ax back and returned with the cart. When all the wood was on the ground, he brought the two men into the house and poured them a glass of wine. He watched them covertly, wondering if they were going to mention the vipers or if, on the contrary, they were keeping quiet to make a fool of him and tell the whole town that Père Dubois had left his ax to the snakes.

When the men were about to leave, unable to stand it any longer, Père Dubois asked them, "Did you see anything else in the clearing?" They looked at each other.

"No."

"Because I killed two vipers. I left them near the trunk."

"Well," said Picaud, "you're not likely to find them a week later. We kill quite a few of them ourselves in the clearings. But the minute we've turned our backs, the hawks and buzzards come and get them."

Père Dubois suddenly felt relieved. Going out with the two men, he asked, "They were two red ones. Big fellows. Are there a lot of them around there?"

"I'll say. Plenty. A slope facing due south, that's what they like. Especially in spring."

"Right now," said the helper, "you have to watch out for them. They're mating. That's when they're most dangerous."

The men told a few stories about vipers; then, climbing back into his truck, Picaud said, "That's not all, but we still have some deliveries to make. And we've got quite a ways to go."

Père Dubois thanked them again, then watched the truck pull off and disappear around a bend in the road.

He went back, closed the gate, but just as he was about to turn the key in the lock, he paused, shrugged his shoulders, and simply pulled out the key and put it in his pocket.

He'd watched the two men unloading the logs, and now it was up to him to pile them onto the cart and haul them down there, way to the end of the garden, to the shed where he'd have to saw and split them before winter. And because of the steep slope at the end of the path, he'd only be able to carry a dozen pieces on each trip.

He started the job, but something told him that he would never finish it.

On the third trip he was so tired that he could no longer climb the slope and had to carry half the load, log by log, into the shed. He was about to start pulling the cart again when Mme. Robin appeared.

"But you'll never manage," she said. "That's no job for you anymore."

All the pity in her voice and in her eyes came through to Père Dubois. He was old. He was at the end of his rope. It must be written on his face, if someone talked to him like that.

Up until then he'd gone along sustained by a vague remnant of hope that kept him from giving in. And now, because of the strength he'd seen in the two woodcutters, because of those few words spoken gently by a woman who took pity on him, perhaps because of thousands upon thousands of accumulated little details, now he suddenly felt drained. He held on for a few more seconds; then, letting go of the cart handle, he raised a hand to his forehead and murmured, "Yes . . . It's too much for me . . . Too much for me."

His voice, which had risen in tone, broke. He made a desperate effort to choke back the sob that burst like a bitter bubble from his lips. "I'm done for . . . done for. For good . . ."

And without shame, without thinking about anything except his strength which he would never find again, he began to cry.

—⊸{ 75 }⊶—

PÈRE DUBOIS let himself be led into the house.

After the long period during which he'd steeled himself against anything that might come from the outside, after the seclusion into which he'd shut himself, imposing a rhythm of work on himself that no longer corresponded to what his body could do, he let himself go. He listened to the words of friendship unprotestingly. And when Mme. Robin told him that he was wrong to lock himself up like this, in solitude, when his oldest son was ready to help him, he nodded his head. "They can do whatever they please . . . Whatever they please . . . I really am at the end of my rope."

That was his way of saying that he felt his life ebbing away; it was a way of avoiding a word he was a little afraid of.

Alerted by Mme. Robin, Micheline and Paul came to see him that same night. They arrived just as Père Dubois had lighted his fire. Micheline placed a large basket covered with a napkin on the table; then, embracing the old man, she began to sob, saying, "My Lord, my poor Papa, how cold you've been to us . . . Every day we waited, hoping for a sign from you."

His elbows on the table, his head lowered, Père Dubois simply repeated, "I'm done for . . . Done for . . . You can do what you like."

They talked to him for a long while. He didn't really listen to what they were saying. It was like a soft, monotonous song that made him a little sleepy. He stared at the basket and the white mound of the napkin. And yet when Paul asked him if he'd decided to move in with them, he straightened up and found a remnant of vigor.

"No. Don't keep bringing that up . . . I'm only going to leave this house feetfirst."

"You really have a hard head," grumbled his son.

But Micheline, leaning toward Père Dubois, said gently, "Come now, Paul, if the poor man absolutely wants to stay in his house, you mustn't contradict him. When you're his age, you'll feel just the way he does. You get attached to things. We're all the same. I understand it very well."

She uncovered the basket and took out a container, which she put on the stove.

"It's some vegetable soup. Nice and thick the way you like it, with the vegetables all mashed up. And there are some peas with salt pork in the casserole. I also brought you some cold chicken. Some figs. Some jam and cheese."

"But I don't need all that."

"You have to eat . . . You'll see, you'll get your strength back . . . You'll see how well we're going to take care of you."

"My strength—that won't ever come back . . . And yet I'll need at least enough to get my wood in and get it cut. And then, I've got the garden started—"

Paul interrupted him. "I'll send a man over to get your wood in tomorrow. And someone to come cut it for you, too. As for your garden, since you've already started part of it, we'll help you with that, too. You'll just have to give the orders. But as for the rest of it, if only you'd listen to me."

Père Dubois heaved a long sigh. There was a silence. He looked at Paul, then Micheline, then the basket and everything that was laid out on the table. He turned to the window. A little daylight still came in, no longer enough to see their faces by.

"You really should light the lamp and close the shutters for me," he said to his son.

Micheline pulled down the lamp and awkwardly lifted the glass, which knocked against the shade. She lighted the wick, which Père Dubois had to trim for her. In watching his daughter-in-law, he thought about his wife, about her cleverness with everything. About the tranquillity he'd known when he'd been able to rest all his burdens on her.

Paul had closed the shutters. He went back to his chair and lighted a cigarette from the butt he then crushed out in the ashtray. He offered one to his father, who refused.

"No, I just smoked one . . . You know, even tobacco doesn't give me much pleasure anymore."

There was another painful silence. The idea of the garden where Paul wanted to start building lay between them, almost tangible. Père Dubois felt it. Paul exhaled his smoke, which fanned out over the table; then, looking at his father, he asked, "What would be the point of a garden you couldn't work anymore?"

Père Dubois shrugged his shoulders.

"I know. The land goes to seed very fast when you don't give it your time."

"Well, do you think that's a good thing? Weeds growing everywhere and blowing over into what you still can grow to keep yourself busy?"

"Of course not."

He wasn't able to go on, to ask Paul exactly what it was he was planning to do.

"You talk about the earth," he added, "but there are also the trees. They don't take much work, and yet the fruit brings in quite a bit."

"If that's all it is, you know I'm not going to cheat you out of what you can make from the fruit. And then what have you got out in the front plots? The big plum tree. It's old; it's—"

His father broke in. "It's old, but it still bears well. Good healthy fruit."

He was attached to that old tree he'd planted and tended for so many years.

"And then," he went on, "there are some peach trees that are at their peak."

"Listen. I'm not arguing. It's up to you to figure out what they'd bring you each year, and I'll pay you whatever you want."

Père Dubois envisioned his garden. He remembered its summer crops. The work he'd put into that ground. He also imagined what he'd feel seeing his beds invaded by weeds. He knew he couldn't bear to look at the weeds without trying to do something about them. It would be a struggle in which he would use up his health. A struggle he might not win.

"You know that I don't need money," he finally said. "But all the same, seeing the whole thing torn up—"

"Don't exaggerate. You know perfectly well we'd only take a little piece."

When Père Dubois didn't answer, Micheline, who was folding the napkin to put it back in the empty basket, asked, "Do you want to give me your laundry tonight, or would you rather have the maid come get it tomorrow?"

"I washed a few things last week, but pumping that water breaks my back."

"You see," observed Paul, "that's another detail you're not taking into account. But if I started building, the first thing I'd do is bring in water. Even if you don't want it brought all the way up here, you could still have a faucet down at the end of the garden."

"Of course, I don't want a ditch dug all the way up here!"

Père Dubois had almost shouted. Paul hastened to say, "No, no, of course not. We'll do whatever you like. The only thing I ask of you is to let me start building my garages, that's all."

Père Dubois got up to put another log in the stove. He did it slowly. It wasn't that he wanted to give himself time to think. He'd already made up his mind. He was simply granting himself a slight delay. As long as he hadn't given his answer, the garden belonged to him alone. He knew that the words he was about to speak would be definitive. They were inside him, ready to come out, but he lacked the strength to pronounce them.

After he'd shut the stove door, he leaned over to poke the

coals and make the ashes fall through. Then he hung the poker on the brass rail and watched it swing back and forth. He felt his son's and daughter-in-law's eyes boring into his back. The poker still swayed imperceptibly. When it had come to rest, Père Dubois turned slowly to his son, gave a little cough, and in an uncertain voice finally said, "All right . . . Since you're really determined, go ahead . . . For the little time I have left, I'll try to make the best of it."

ONCE again Père Dubois had overestimated his strength. Once again he'd been thinking like an old man, way behind the times. He'd pictured a few workmen arriving one morning to take out his fence, whose pickets he'd be able to save. He'd keep the best ones, and the others would make good firewood. During the four weeks that had passed before the work began, he'd spent most of his time in the front plots of the garden. Little by little, he'd got used to the idea of the building site. He'd cleared a place behind the house where he planned to have the workmen bring the topsoil when they started digging the foundations. It all had been planned out in his head.

And then, one Monday morning, he was shaken from sleep by the roaring of a motor which made the whole house shake. He lay for a moment paralyzed in bed, trying to think where this noise night be coming from. Daylight was there, showing through the cracks in the shutters. The noise was coming from the street. Père Dubois leaned out the window. His hands gripped the windowsill, and he could only gasp, "Good God! Good God, it's not possible!"

He was incapable of moving. Incapable of uttering another word.

The fence had already disappeared. A truck had parked in the street, and an enormous machine whose name Père Dubois didn't even know was gouging up the dirt from his garden. A long, jointed arm bent, straightened out, brandishing a tool whose jaws bit into his good black dirt, raised it by the barrowful and poured it into the dump truck.

"Good God, it's not possible!"

He went downstairs and, without even bothering to put on his jacket, went out into the garden.

From the window, he'd been able to see only part of the site, but as soon as he was in the path, he realized that the whole left part of the garden had already been dug up for a distance of more than thirty yards. He saw only two men, not counting the one who was in the cab of the monster with the long arm. The iron gate, ripped off and twisted, lay in the road beside the garden. The path itself had been dug up, and Père Dubois had to go around the hole to get to the street. As soon as he was within earshot of the two men who were leaning against the truck, he shouted, "What are you doing? You must be crazy!"

The workmen looked at him. One of them took a few steps to meet him. He was a skinny little man, with black hair and a mustache, about forty. Because of the noise, he hadn't been able to understand what Père Dubois shouted. When he got up to him, he asked, "What did you say?"

He had a strong Italian accent.

"I said you must be crazy. What are you doing? You're wrecking everything!"

The man seemed taken aback. He turned toward his companion, who hadn't moved. Père Dubois pointed to the truck, half-filled with dirt, with pickets and wires sticking up out of it. "What are you going to do with that?"

"Take it to the dump."

"To the dump! Topsoil like that? And why are you taking it away? You were just supposed to dig up enough for the foundations. Stop it, it's not possible."

The man walked over to the machine, jumped onto the running board of the cab, and started to talk, gesticulating. The long arm rested its enormous jaws on the ground, the motor slowed to an idle, and the Italian returned with the driver.

The driver was French. Barely taller than his companion, he was broad and heavyset. A blue undershirt bared his bulky, muscled shoulders. His hands and forearms were black with grease.

"What's going on?" he asked.

Père Dubois explained once more that he didn't understand, that this wasn't what had been planned.

"I'm just following orders," the man said. "We're supposed to dig down four and a half feet before starting the foundations. That's what was on the plans."

"Four and a half feet," stammered Père Dubois. "But—but the topsoil . . . I've got a place ready, over there, behind the house."

The men looked at each other; then the foreman said, "But how do you expect the trucks to get over there?"

"I thought . . . After all . . . But it's not possible . . . Not possible."

He hadn't even dared mention a wheelbarrow. He stared at the big machine, whose engine coughed, shaking the sheet metal that covered it. He looked at the dump truck with its double wheels almost as tall as he was. Never had he felt so helpless, so small, so poor as at this moment.

"And my fence," he muttered.

"We put the gate in the road. If you like, we'll carry it to the house."

Père Dubois raised his hands and let them fall back to his sides. He was crushed. Having come there to chase away those men and their big machines, now he felt stricken by an overwhelming weakness. When he stood there, silent and benumbed, the foreman went back to his cab. As soon as he was settled in the seat, the engine roared, the little chimney that rose up behind the cab emitted a puff of blue smoke, and the caterpillar tracks ground in as the arm rose, opening its jaws with their long, shiny teeth.

For years, Père Dubois had dug into that dirt every spring with his spading fork. The machine's teeth were of the same steel; they gleamed, too, but they bit into the earth with a thousand times more force. With a kind of evil rage. Each wound hurt Père Dubois as if he himself had been struck by the steel.

The Italian driver still stood beside him. They watched for a moment; then the old man asked, "The trees—if you can, please leave them in the road for me. I'll saw them up."

"Sure. That's easy."

They looked at each other, and Père Dubois thought he saw a glimmer of pity in the small man's black eyes when he asked, "Would you like us to bring you the gate?"

"My Lord, we can't leave it there."

The driver called his buddy, and together they carried the gate in one run to the shed. The old man knew that he couldn't have even lifted it. And yet he remembered the day when he'd hung it. When he had been running the bakery. He'd done it one evening with his helper. And they hadn't had any more trouble than the two drivers.

When the men had stood the gate against one of the shed posts, he asked them, "Would you like a glass of wine?"

The two men followed him up to the house, where he got out glasses and a bottle of wine, saying, "You ought to call your friend."

"No," said the Italian. "We can't just stop like that. Machines get rented by the hour."

Père Dubois raised his glass. "To your health."

"To yours," said the Italian.

The other man also raised his glass, saying a few words Père Dubois couldn't understand.

"He's not French?"

"No, and he doesn't speak it . . . He's a prisoner. But he's not German. It seems that he's a Pole who got drafted into the German army by force. He only understands one thing."

The Italian turned to his companion and said to him, laughing, "War *kaput*. War over."

The other started to laugh and raised his hand, repeating, "War *kaput*. War over."

It was true—the war had been over for more than a week. On May 8 the German surrender had been signed. Père Dubois had read about it in the newspapers M. Robin had bought him, but for him, this event had changed nothing.

Since 1939 the war had passed through town twice. Each time the garden and the house had been spared. Today the war was over, but he felt something else was ending. And then something else was beginning. Another time was coming that he could not understand. A time that didn't even take into account the old man he had become through years of waiting for he knew not what.

Mère Dubois was gone. The garden was going, and he? He was standing in the kitchen, drinking a glass of wine with an Italian and another man whose native country they didn't even know.

Decidedly, the world was no longer the same.

"We've got to go," said the Italian.

They emptied their glasses and went out. Père Dubois followed them. The dump truck was full, and the man who didn't speak French climbed into the cab. The engine rumbled, and the truck rolled down the street. The Italian had moved off, and when Père Dubois turned around, he saw him getting into another truck just like the first, which he hadn't noticed because it had been parked a ways up the street, in the entrance to the École Normale. The empty truck came to replace the one which had just carried away his fence and the first load of that good black dirt that he had fertilized with so much manure and so often wet with his sweat. He looked again for a moment at the heavy jaws coming and going; then, exhausted, he slowly went back to his house.

--- 77 ---

THAT summer was longer and more depressing than any winter. Père Dubois retreated into his house and went out only to draw water or to go to the shed, where for an hour or two every day he cut wood. Sometimes he got a few tools out of the cupboard and oiled them before putting them back in place. He knew perfectly well that he would never use all these planes, shears, chisels, and bits again, but he continued to take care of them as he had always done, out of habit. Each one of them had its own history, which he recited to himself. Then a moment from the past would come back to him and liven his solitude with happy faces.

He'd stopped working in his garden, and the part that had been spared by the building was gradually getting overgrown, invaded by the weeds he'd battled for so long. Paul had indeed sent over one of his workmen two or three times to help the old man, but these visits had stopped, and he hadn't protested. He'd even given up complaining.

When he looked out toward the street, the cement walls that rose the length of the garden filled him with a sort of disgust. When it wasn't too hot, he would go sit near the pump, behind the boxwood which hid him from the site. His hands folded over his cane, his body shrunk, and his neck sunk into his shoulders; his eyes half-closed beneath the visor of his cap, he sat for hours and thought back over his life. And it was always to the days of his youth that he returned most eagerly, pondering names, faces, places, and dates, which sometimes got a little bit confused.

He was there one afternoon in August, dozing, when Françoise arrived. He heard her calling up by the house, "Anybody home? Anybody home?"

He recognized her voice at once, and his heart tightened so that he had trouble shouting back, "I'm here!"

He stood up and walked down the path, which now was nothing but a narrow trail through the weeds, where, here and there, some hardy flowers peeped out. Françoise came to meet him. When they got up to each other, Père Dubois took off his cap, embraced the young woman, and murmured, "My God . . . My God."

There was a lump in his throat. He struggled to keep back his tears. They returned to the house where Françoise had parked a black baby carriage with its oilcloth hood folded back. A fat baby with blond curls was lying in it, bare-legged, roly-poly, looking up at the sky with big blue eyes.

Père Dubois leaned over. He wanted to speak, but a great sob suddenly burst forth as he was saying, in a small, trembling voice which rose into nothing but a broken cry, "It's not possible . . . It's not possible . . . My poor old lady . . . If she were only here . . ."

Françoise picked up the baby and held him out to Père Dubois. The old man felt awkward. He dropped his cane and reached out his trembling hand to touch the child's bare arm.

"You see," said Françoise, "he looks like Julien."

Père Dubois took off his cap again to kiss the baby, who laughed and waved his hands.

They stood there for a few minutes, embarrassed, not knowing what to say. Père Dubois was smiling, but the tears continued to run down his white-stubbled cheeks. He wiped his eyes, blew his nose several times, and muttered, "We must go inside . . . We can't just stand here."

Françoise followed him, carrying the baby. They sat down in the kitchen, whose shutters were closed.

"It's cool in here," said Père Dubois. "Won't the baby be cold?"

"No. He's just fine."

"He's very lively."

He looked at the child, and it was Julien he saw. In the same place, on Mère Dubois' lap.

"And Julien?"

"He wasn't able to come. They don't give him much time off from his job."

Pere Dubois bowed his head. He wanted to speak, but what he had to say wasn't easy. He was just about to open his mouth when Françoise asked, "And you, Papa, how are you?"

"Me? Oh, me . . ."

After a long silence, during which his hand gripped the edge of the table, without really having decided to say anything, Père Dubois finally blurted out, "Me, I'm done for. In any event, I know there wasn't much left for me to do . . . But still and all . . . Still and all. They're trying to make me die before my time. Die. You've seen what they're doing out front. They've ruined everything. Everything. And they're walling me in behind that cement. When the north wind blows, it makes a draft in here that's unbearable. This winter I won't even be able to keep warm . . . It's terrifying. They didn't have any right to do this to me . . . They could easily have waited until I was gone . . . I won't be around for that long."

He stopped. He'd spoken loudly, and the baby was staring at him, intrigued.

"My God," he said, "I'm frightening him."

"No, no, he's listening to you."

"Perhaps we ought to give him something."

"No, he's had his bottle. Anyhow, I'm going to put him back in his carriage. He'll go to sleep."

She went out and came back inside very quickly. Père Dubois hadn't moved. He had more to say, and he felt that he must speak. He listened to the young woman explaining to him that she'd been to St.-Claude and had only stopped in Lons-le-Saunier for a few hours to see him and introduce him to his grandson. She still had that soft voice and those very gentle eyes. When she'd finished, Père Dubois tried to speak. He murmured, "You must tell Julien—"

But he stopped. The words were choking him but refused to cross his lips.

"He has to come see me," he went on. "He has to . . . It's important . . . I can't explain it to you, but he has to come . . . I shouldn't have done what I've done . . . It's important for him, too . . . For him and for you."

One by one, he got out the words that were torturing him. "Do you understand?" he asked.

"Julien will come. He'll come as soon as they have less work."

"But on Sunday—he could surely come some Sunday?"

Françoise lowered her eyes. She seemed to hesitate. When she looked up, her eyes were more brilliant. Speaking quickly, she explained, "You understand—with the baby, I had to quit my job. Julien feels the same way I do. We don't want strangers taking care of him. So, since we don't have very much to live on, on Sundays, Julien goes to work for a pastry chef."

"That's nothing to be ashamed of. It might make him think about taking up his old trade again. Perhaps it's better paid than his painting work . . . And then, you could always hope to set up your own business."

Françoise only made an evasive gesture, and Père Dubois understood that that still probably wasn't what his son had in mind. Yet he couldn't help adding, "If only you'd come back here—"

He broke off.

It was calm and cool in the shadowy kitchen. Nothing had changed since Mère Dubois' death, and yet the old man was alone. He knew it. The thought was with him every second. Françoise had come, but she would leave, carrying off the baby he would never see again.

Nothing had changed inside the little house, but as soon as you opened the door and stepped outside, the building site appeared. The cement walls, with the iron rods of the armature sticking up out of them like spears, were there. The cement had devoured the garden and killed the trees.

"You can't imagine what they're putting me through."

Père Dubois had spoken without even realizing it. Probably because that was a phrase he repeated to himself all day long when he was alone.

He got up, went into the laundry, and returned with a pot whose cover he removed.

"Here, take a whiff of that."

"But you should throw that away. It's gone bad."

"Of course, I'll throw it away. But that's what they brought me to eat yesterday. And sometimes they don't come for three days."

"But they were supposed to—"

Père Dubois raised his hand to quiet her.

"I have nothing to say. Nothing!"

He returned to the laundry with the pot and came back and sat down. A moment passed. They looked at each other without saying a word, and because he hated giving in to his troubles again, Père Dubois stiffened. In a firmer voice, he went on. "I have nothing to say. I brought it on myself. It's up to me to live with it . . . Luckily, I have good neighbors . . . But you can go and ask Madame Robin, she'll tell you . . . She'll give you the whole story of what they put me through . . ."

He turned his head and stared at the cold stove. Again tears came to his eyes. In a voice that had begun to tremble again, he said, "You must tell Julien . . . You must tell Julien that—"

He fell silent. Outside, the baby had started to cry, and Françoise went running to him. Père Dubois waited a moment, then went out and joined her. She'd picked up the little one in her arms and was wiping away two big tears that had rolled down his chubby cheeks. He'd stopped crying already.

"What was the matter?" asked Père Dubois.

"Nothing. He must have felt lonely. Or else, perhaps it was his teeth. But you know, he doesn't cry very often."

Upon seeing Père Dubois, the baby smiled and waved his hands.

"My God, how happy he'd be here in the garden . . . It's still quiet way down at the end, and the air's much better than in the city."

He watched the child a moment without speaking; then, in a more serious tone, he added, "Poor little thing. Who knows what he'll have to go through? Will the world ever be the same again? The other day Monsieur Robin told me about that bomb they dropped on Japan. Of course, that's the end of the war . . . But what does it mean? Me, I'm at the end of my road. But when I see all the madness in the world, I don't feel so bad about going."

"We really have to hope that this war will be the last one. Otherwise, it wasn't worth the trouble."

"My poor little girl"—the old man sighed—"that's just what they were saying in 1918. And you see . . ."

Françoise sat the baby down in his carriage.

"We could go down to the end of the garden," Père Dubois suggested. "That's where I always sit . . . At least, it's quiet."

The young woman pushed the carriage down the path, but the weeds got in the way. She had to stop and lift the front end and turn it around. It was easier pulling it.

"If my poor wife could see her garden in this condition, my Lord, she wouldn't believe her eyes . . . Would you like to take some flowers with you? They're about all that's left from when she was alive."

"I don't want to take them; they'd be all faded when we got there, and with the baby, I already have enough to carry. But I'll pick some just the same. And when I leave, I'll stop by the cemetery . . . I think it would be nice to bring her some flowers from her own garden."

"I'm sure that would make her happy . . . sure . . . I can't get there anymore myself. I don't have the strength."

They'd reached the spot where Père Dubois had left his chair.

"I'll go get you a seat," he said.

"No, don't bother. You stay here with the baby. I'll go cut some flowers, and by then it will be time to leave."

"You'll find a basket and some shears behind the cellar door."

Françoise moved off. Left alone with the baby, Père Dubois moved his chair close to the carriage and sat down. The child was watching him. There was a rattle at the foot of the carriage, and the old man picked it up and waved it in front of the little one, who began to laugh.

"Ah, you little rascal," Père Dubois said. "You're a real little Dubois . . . Hey! You see how happy you'd be in the garden? And if you had your grandma . . . If you had your grandma . . ."

He tried to master himself once more, but he didn't have the strength. So, still playing with the baby whose chubby hands were clutching the rattle, in silence the old man began to cry.

⋯⊰ 78 ⊱⋯

AFTER Françoise's visit, Père Dubois lived with the image of the baby smiling at him. It was a more recent memory than all the

others which endlessly came back to him, but hazier. Blurred
with tears. Now he no longer cried. He lived like a sick plant
whose sap gradually dries up as the season advances.

Letters from Julien and Françoise came more frequently.
Now that there was no more garden gate, the mailman brought
them to the house. Père Dubois watched for him. He was a big
man of about fifty, with a red face and a black mustache. He
loved having a little nip. Père Dubois would offer him a glass
of wine and ask him to read the letter. The man read slowly,
sometimes fumbling for a word. When he'd finished, he would
invariably say, "There, that's all."

And invariably Père Dubois would ask, "He doesn't say when
he'll be coming?"

"No, he doesn't mention it."

When the first frosts came, Père Dubois was confined to his
kitchen. Each morning, starting at ten o'clock, he would stand
in front of the window, with the visor of his cap touching the
glass, and watch the path out to the street. By eleven he knew
that the mailman had gone by without bringing him a letter,
and he would sit back down in his chair.

The days passed like this, and Père Dubois went out only for
water and wood. He didn't go up to the bedroom anymore, but
one morning there was a big noise up there that made him
jump. He got up and climbed the stairs. It was raining, and the
heavy sky let only a little sad gray light into the room, leaving
the corners in shadow. At first, he couldn't see anything out of
place. He looked especially at the ceiling, fearing that a tile
might have come loose. Finally, as he was moving toward the
bed, he noticed a too-white area on the faded blue-gray wallpaper. The paper had been torn off, and a piece of plaster was
missing.

"It's the photograph . . . The photograph."

He went over between the bed and the wall. A big gilt frame
was standing on the floor, its glass broken. Père Dubois had
framed that photograph of his parents himself. It had been

taken on the garden path, one summer morning whose every detail he could remember perfectly.

He passed his hand over the damp wall, then picked up the frame and carried it to the window. He just kept repeating, "The photograph . . . The photograph."

He stood looking at it for a long time. Then, as he felt the damp cold penetrating him, he went back down to the kitchen.

All that day, he lived with his parents, remembering their gestures, their words, their way of life, and, above all, the work in the bakery which they had taught him. Because of that perhaps, because of this house and garden where he'd come to live after them, it seemed to him that they'd never really been dead. They had continued to live in his memory, in these places where nothing had changed. And then, this morning, because the rain had soaked the wall and rotted the plaster in that room he never opened anymore, the big photograph had fallen. Was it really a sign that everything would soon be over? That everything was already over?

Until evening, Père Dubois was haunted by this idea. He grumbled about winter coming before fall was even over, he grumbled about the weather, about the house, and he cursed the building that Paul was having put up, which he blamed for funneling the cold wind into every part of the garden.

That night he went to bed very early.

In spite of the bed warmer he'd put between the sheets, he had a great deal of trouble fighting off the cold that kept him from getting to sleep.

The next morning he woke up drenched with sweat and short of breath. It wasn't daylight yet. He got up anyhow, lighted the fire, made himself some tea, and changed the damp sheets on his bed.

A great fear goaded him into doing everything very fast. He had several coughing fits, which brought up a lot of mucus.

"This is all I needed . . . All I needed . . . And being all alone."

Before going back to bed, he'd opened the shutters. Leaning back on his two pillows, he waited for daybreak. The rain had changed into a very fine mist that he'd felt on his hands and face when he leaned out the window. All he could hear now was the water running from the gutter into the big zinc trough.

"If I can't go outside, that trough will overflow, and the water will get into the cellar."

Night was plastered against the windowpanes, a glaucous night, pierced only by the distant light from the factory, which could be glimpsed beyond the wall of the École Normale.

Imperceptibly, the sky grew paler.

It wasn't even a presage of day, but a slow metamorphosis of night. It was the previously invisible mist which, little by little, finally showed behind the windowpanes.

When Père Dubois got up to reload the fire, the school rooftops were gleaming, paler than the sky. But the garden remained in the dark. Night refused to lift its siege. It clung to the earth all around the house, which nothing linked to the rest of the world. Only a few yards of garden separated it from the road, but they were enough to make Père Dubois feel completely alone with the fever consuming him. A great fire raged throughout his chest, and yet shivers ran endlessly up and down his back. He stood against the stove for a moment, his hands gripping the brass rail, the small of his back turned to the heat, his thighs close to the grill before the hissing wood. Because of the heavy sky, the chimney drew poorly, and the wood burned slowly.

"Good Lord, being this alone . . . I could easily die . . . Die of misery."

He said this without anger, mostly because he needed to talk to keep the silence of the night at bay. He said this because no other words came to him.

And these words made Julien's face rise out of the shadows, and especially Françoise's gentle smile.

All he had on were his long underdrawers and his woolen jacket over his nightshirt.

"I really ought to get dressed. You never know."

He went back to his bed, put on his pants and his socks, then returned to the kitchen. He wasn't hungry and made do with another bowl of tea. He rolled a cigarette, lighted it, but the first puff made him cough. He let the cigarette go out by itself between his fingers, knocked the ash off, and put the butt in his tobacco box.

"If I can't even smoke anymore, what have I got left?"

He didn't want to go back to bed. It seemed to him that the act of staying in bed would attract the illness. He went and got a blanket to wrap around himself and came back and sat down by the fire. He stared at the path which slowly emerged from the shadows. To tell the truth, he didn't expect to see a soul on it. Only M. Robin might be passing by, but he never went out that early.

From staring at the same spot, his eyes began to hurt. His lids grew heavy, fluttered a little, then closed. From time to time, his cough would seize him. When he got up to spit in the fire or throw on another log, he could feel his legs buckle under him. Black dots danced before his eyes.

At the end of the morning, when Mme. Robin came to see him, Père Dubois had fallen asleep in his chair. When he heard her knocking, he woke with a start. Since the door was still locked, he got up to go and open it and had to lean on the table for support. The effort provoked another coughing fit, more violent than the others. When it was over, with his eyes full of tears, his ears ringing, he heard the young woman telling him, "We have to notify your son. He'll send for the doctor. You can't stay here like this."

Père Dubois had already wiped his eyes, but his vision remained blurred.

"Oh, no . . . No, no, it's nothing . . . If you'd just fix me a mustard plaster."

"But that won't be enough. You have to see a doctor."

He summoned up a little strength.

"No. They'll send me to the hospital . . . I don't want to go. I don't want to."

"But you must get into bed."

"No. I'm better off beside my fire."

Mme. Robin fixed the mustard plaster, went and got a basket of wood, then spoke again of calling a doctor. Père Dubois stuck to his guns. As she was going out the door, he shouted, "Don't call anyone . . . Nobody . . . I don't want you to."

The fear of his illness tortured him, but the fear of leaving his house was stronger still.

Mme. Robin came back several times and sat with him a good part of the afternoon. He forced himself to talk, to appear strong, to control his cough.

"You see," he said at the end of the afternoon, "I'm feeling better . . . Much better. I knew that you shouldn't call anyone."

The young woman left, and as soon as she was out the door, Père Dubois got back into bed without undressing and pulled two blankets and a big feather quilt up over himself.

--◃{ 79 }▹--

In the night that followed, his fever rose. Père Dubois could feel the work that it accomplished in him. He'd left the night-light burning at the head of his bed, but around four in the morning, as the flame was dying, he decided to get up to get a candle. He sat up slowly on the edge of the bed, put on his slippers, and waited a few moments. The fire must have gone out, for it was cold in the room. He conjured up the motions he would have to go through to relight it, and the task seemed overwhelming to him. When he tried to stand up, he felt dizzy. The whole house rocked, the floor gave way under his feet, and he had to sit back down.

"Done for," he muttered. "Done for."

He tried two more times. Then, paralyzed by a fear of falling, he grabbed onto the back of the chair where he'd laid his heavy corduroy jacket and managed to urinate into the chamber pot.

Then he got back into bed. The sweat was pouring down his face and body. His cotton nightcap was cold and clammy, but he didn't dare take it off.

When his fatigue had quieted a little, he started thinking, almost with serenity, that he was going to die right there, like that, without anyone to help him. He would go out like the lamp running out of oil, whose tiny flame wavered, no longer lighting more than the marble night table and the corner of the buffet next to it. He dwelled on this idea until the moment when the flame leaped up in one last burst and then went out, leaving a red glow no larger than a cigarette end. When the red glow had disappeared, Père Dubois raised himself on his pillows and began to yell, "Bastards . . . Bastards . . . They're letting me die . . . They're letting me die like a dog . . . Bastards . . . Bastards!"

Exhausted, he let himself fall back. His head sank into the hollow of his pillows, and his eyes stopped searching the night.

When he awoke, Mme. Robin was beside him. The night before, Père Dubois had given her a key, and that was the first thought that came to him.

"You were right to take that key," he mumbled. "I'm not doing so well, you know . . . I don't think I could have gotten up to let you in."

He felt almost comfortable in his bed, and her presence in the house reassured him.

"Could you light my fire for me?" he asked.

"It's already done, Monsieur Dubois. And I brought you some coffee."

He drank a good hot bowl of *café au lait* and thought that he'd been very frightened of an illness that was already on the wane.

"Perhaps I'll be able to get up."

Mme. Robin made him stay in bed.

"I'm going to get my cleaning woman, and we'll change your sheets. But in the meantime, don't move."

She left and returned with the Italian woman, who helped Père Dubois over to sit down by the fire.

"You shouldn't have gotten into bed with all your clothes on."

"I was cold. And then, when I tried to get up—"

He stopped. He fought against his cough for a few seconds but had to give in. The seizure rekindled the fire in his chest, and he began to sweat again. The women made him get undressed and helped him back into bed. His breath was short. Once in bed, he heard the two of them talking in the kitchen without being able to understand what they were saying. He also heard the sound of the door opening and closing, and called out, "Are you still there?"

The Italian woman came in to him.

"Madame has left, but she'll be back."

Père Dubois felt like asking if she'd gone to call a doctor, but he kept still. The woman stood beside his bed, her arms dangling, looking embarrassed. He closed his eyes and waited.

When he came to again, he realized that he had slept a long time. The sound of voices in the kitchen had awakened him.

"What's going on?" he cried.

Micheline came in and said at once, "Don't worry, Papa. We're here. And the doctor is coming . . . It's nothing. A touch of flu. With this weather, it's to be expected, you know."

His eyes half-closed, Père Dubois looked at her. She seemed

very far away to him, and her voice echoed strangely. When she'd mentioned the doctor, he'd felt a flash of his old anger but had said nothing. He no longer had the strength to shout, and he dreaded the cough that reawakened the pains in his chest.

However, his strength returned after the doctor's visit, when Paul told him, "You're coming home with us. The car is waiting. We'll carry you—"

"No. I don't want to . . . I don't want to . . ."

He hadn't shouted very loud, but enough to set off his cough. When he'd coughed and spat, he felt so weak that he didn't even try to argue. He merely told them what to put in a bag and bring along. His razor, his shaving brush, his leather strop, the wallet containing his money, his few papers.

"I'll come back for whatever you need," said Paul.

"You really could take care of me here," he murmured. "You must tell Julien to come . . . his wife . . ."

Paul's voice rose, harsh and hissing. "Be quiet. You're in no condition to make decisions. We don't have anyone to stay with you, and you'll be warmer over there."

"Don't shout," Père Dubois begged him. "Don't shout."

He felt as weak as a baby, and the sensation increased when he'd been wrapped up in a blanket and was being carried away. One of his son's drivers, a big fellow of thirty who'd come a few times to bring in wood for him, took him in his arms and picked him up, saying, "Don't be afraid, Grandpa, you're perfectly safe. We'll soon be in the car."

His mouth and nose hidden by the blanket, Père Dubois could feel only the damp cold smarting his eyes. Tears came to them at once, and he saw the house and what was left of the garden through a luminous yellow mist.

"The sun's shining."

"The sun," said the driver with a big laugh. "Oh, no, we haven't had any sun for ten days."

They went around the new building which was now two

stories high. Père Dubois saw an enormous gray mass with shadowy black holes swim before his eyes.

When they got to the car, the driver began to laugh again and said, "I could have carried you like that all the way to Montciel and even farther."

The man got in next to Père Dubois, and Micheline sat in front beside Paul, who was driving.

"Did you remember to close the shutters?"

"Yes," Paul shouted. "Don't worry."

"And the door—did you lock it?"

"Of course," said Micheline, "there's nothing to worry about."

Each jolt of the car reverberated inside him. He tried to look at the street, but his tears blurred everything. In a scarcely audible voice, he murmured, almost without stopping, "Good Lord, going away like this . . . Leaving my house . . . Going away like this . . . Abandoning everything . . ."

At his son's house they carried him up to a room that was too big, with a too-high ceiling, dimly lighted by a pair of windows that looked out onto a narrow courtyard. There was a large, square cast-iron stove in it, and Père Dubois spotted the bucket of coal immediately. As soon as he'd been put in a very low bed, he said, his breath coming short, "Open the window a little . . . I can't breathe . . . That coal—it's not healthy in a bedroom."

"No, no," Paul snapped. "It's not that. It's because you've just been breathing the cold air. You'll get used to it."

"Don't shout like that . . . I'm not deaf . . . And it hurts my ears."

Paul shrugged his shoulders and went out, followed by the driver.

"Don't you worry about a thing," said Micheline. "The maid will bring you some tea. And at four o'clock the nurse is coming to give you your injection."

"Do I need injections?"

He couldn't hear his daughter-in-law's answer. She spoke with her back turned, rummaging in a closet. To himself, he added, "Do I need injections to get where I'm going?"

⟶⟨ 80 ⟩⟵

By the next morning Père Dubois had lost all track of time. When he was conscious, whatever the hour of day or night, all he could see was a vague colorless glow that feebly lighted the wall and the bed. When he moved his hands, he saw them as very far away, vaporous and transparent. His chest hurt. Not with the burning he'd dreaded so much, but with a pressure, like a corset that now and then squeezed him so tightly he couldn't breathe.

When the pain subsided, he tried to lie still to keep it from starting again.

Between him and what he could see of this room, between him and the people who came in from time to time, he saw a constant flow of images. Sometimes extremely sharp, sometimes fuzzy, sometimes blended together, the images followed one another unevenly; slowly or quickly, they jerked in and out of his vision.

The most detailed, the most persistent, were scenes from his childhood, his youth, and his daily work. The dough in the kneading trough. The glowing oven, its mouth spitting tongues of flame. The loading paddle with its long handle scraping across the red-hot bricks. The armfuls of wood. The hot fresh-baked bread whose odor came back to him, filling the room. Sometimes the dough he was kneading would turn gray, then brown, then almost black. His motions would change, too, the

377

teeth of his spading fork replacing his hands. It was no longer dough being kneaded, but dirt from the garden turned over a thousand times, raked, hoed, spaded, fertilized with manure and compost. The good smell of seasoned wood burning clean in the oven firebox changed into the odor of dead plants and leaves smoldering in huge piles on foggy fall mornings. From the fire and smoke, the cries of children sometimes rose; their laughs and calls answered Mère Dubois' voice. Julien ran through the smoke on his way to school. Was it really he? Wasn't it maybe his grandson growing up at home, where they all were living together again?

These visions died like autumn fires under the heavy mist that falls with evening. And then a break would open in the mist; a watery sun would appear; the wind of dawn would revive the fires, from which more memories would rise. Their pace would quicken. The dead mingled with the living. The dead killed by war or by work. Laughter was always softer than sighs; joys were less vivid than sorrows. Now and then, very faintly from a distance, snatches of song would come back, recalling a harvest festival where they'd sung about the golden wheat, the poplar trees, and cherry-blossom time. But those were never more than very faint echoes, soon drowned out by laments of men kneading dough or turning over the soil.

And then, strongest of all, images of vipers crawling everywhere, slithering away at his feet, sliding under the door to come and coil around his icy legs, which then twitched convulsively. The snakes were evoked with images of logs in the clearing, the stovewood, work he'd done alone, and with Mère Dubois.

For Mère Dubois, discreet but vigilant, was always there, a motionless figure whose tired features were undimmed by the parade of other images.

She was there for all the work Père Dubois had done, over and over again without relief. She was there for the soil, for the bread, for the wood, for the deep snow on the back steps and in the garden. She was a part of every season, of every effort, of every trial.

Her silence was a part of that life he endlessly relived. She was there even when Père Dubois saw nothing but her soldier's coat lying near the cardoons on the frozen earth of the garden.

Soon there was nothing left but the fog of an interminable twilight, where the only live things were Mère Dubois' clear eyes and faintly sad smile.

Her smile froze. The darkness lightened. It finally vanished at the moment when Père Dubois became lucid enough to remember that his wife had died before him.

Then another smile emerged from the mists.

Françoise's.

Wasn't Julien going to come with her? Weren't they going to come take him home where he could get well? Back to his house and his garden?

Had they called Julien? And Françoise, whose voice was as gentle as Mère Dubois' voice?

There are faces, eyes, gestures, and voices which have the power to heal. There are people whose mere presence ameliorates suffering and banishes pain. But these people are not always there when you need them!

If he could only find the strength to cry out! To call a name.

To think that he'd been so strong in the old days, and now he couldn't even make a sound.

As the light dimmed, sound also diminished. However, when he woke up after several hours, Père Dubois would sometimes be alert enough to hear cautious footsteps on the bedroom floor. He would understand what was being said around him and try to respond. But he could no longer speak; the slightest effort left him breathless.

He was in his son's house, in a room so big and so high that he could see neither the ceiling nor the walls. His bed was in the middle of an immense void where voices had a strange resonance, where each sound was distorted, amplified, multiplied into echos which passed through the walls and lost themselves in the night that went on endlessly in search of dawn.

The night went on, but it led only to other nights, equally dark.

And he went on, too, in the heart of this continuing night, carried on a wave that sometimes rocked the bed, which was too large and soft for him.

How many days' journey was he from his own house? Where was his garden? Had they locked his door securely? Had the fire gone out when he left the kitchen? And what about the shed? And his tools? Would the oil protect them from the dampness until spring?

His billhook was in the musette bag. Tomorrow he would leave with Mère Dubois for the mountain. They would find their cart in the forest . . . Bundles . . . They would cut bundles of stovewood . . . And have a fine load on their four-wheeled cart. And people would say, "That Père Dubois, that old man, he still knows how to make good bundles . . . And stack a fine load on his cart."

In the forest where he was walking, the ground gave way beneath his feet, as loose as the dirt in his garden, as supple as the dough rising in the kneading trough. The ground gave way, warm as the dough and cold as the snakes.

He lay there. He. Père Dubois. All alone in that starless night. In that night where no wind blew. Where the earth itself had stopped driving the sap up into the hearts of plants.

He lay there. He. Père Dubois. All alone on this road leading nowhere.

The night paled. The night deepened.

It was warm inside him, but all around there was an icy winter that kept eating into him.

It was warm inside him, but gradually the warmth ebbed, evaporated, absorbed by the cold that dripped from the heavy sky and oozed up from the dark soil.

The falling drizzle penetrated him; the water rising from the ground froze his legs.

He was there, all alone, and no one came to help him find his way.

Would they all abandon him?

Would they leave him prey to this icy universe where life no longer existed?

Inside him, there were curses, shouts, cries.

Did another world exist outside the boundaries of this world in which he'd labored so?

The priest had come. Père Dubois could recognize his black vestments, and mostly he knew the man was a priest because, since Mère Dubois' death, no one else had come so close to him; no one had spoken to him with such gentleness. He couldn't understand the words the priest spoke, nor was he able to speak. It seemed to him that this face stayed very close to his for a long time; then the silence and the cold enveloped him again.

Time stopped. Nothing moved. Nothing lived around him anymore.

Hours and hours went by like this without his attempting anything beyond the immense effort required for every breath. His breathing now was but a series of shorter and shorter sighs, closer and closer together, less and less painful, too.

His mouth was open and dry, his throat irritated. His chest barely moved. All the flour dust inhaled during his life as a baker took its toll.

The heat from the oven and the hot sun beating on the garden built a fire in his chest that consumed what little air his throat let through at each desperate gasp.

All was dark, and then, suddenly, an invisible hand tore a piece out of the blackness. The silence broke open. Footsteps approached. A face came close, closer. Something cool touched his forehead. A voice murmured in his ear, "Papa, Papa, I ask your forgiveness."

These words sank into him, and the same words rose from his heart like an echo. But his tightened throat blocked them.

The face moved away. Another face leaned down a little, and a heavy hand shook Père Dubois' shoulder. Like a thunderclap, Paul's voice boomed out painfully, "Oh, Father. It's Julien! Julien. Don't you recognize him?"

More quietly, the voice added as the face moved away, "You see. It's over. He can't even see anymore."

Père Dubois wanted to speak. His strength seemed suddenly about to return. He raised himself a few inches, he filled his chest with one last breath, but all that passed his throat was a rattle.

A long sigh rushed from the depths of his chest. A sigh like those he used to heave each night, when he had completed the final act of an endless day's work.